AS
IF
DEATH
SUMMONED

A NOVEL OF THE AIDS EPIDEMIC

ALAN E. ROSE

AMBLE
PRESS
ANN ARBOR
2020

Amble Press

Print ISBN: 978-1-61294-185-1
Amble Press First Edition: December 2020

Printed in the United States of America on acid-free paper.
Cover designer: Ann McMan, TreeHouse Studio

Amble Press
An Imprint of Bywater Books
PO Box 3671
Ann Arbor MI 48106-3671
www.bywaterbooks.com

The poems excerpted in this novel are either in the public domain or referenced as permitted under Fair Use practices and are as follows: "Auguries of Innocence" by William Blake, "The Loss of Love" by Countee Cullen, "Because I could not stop for death" by Emily Dickinson, "Everything mortal has moments immortal" by Amy Lowell, "Dirge Without Music" by Edna St. Vincent Millay, "Paradise Lost" by John Milton, "A Dream Within A Dream," by Edgar Allan Poe, "At the Bomb Testing Site," by William E. Stafford, "And death shall have no dominion" by Dylan Thomas, and "Leaves of Grass" by Walt Whitman.

To the many unknown and unsung heroes of the AIDS epidemic, the brave men and women who accompanied the unknown and unsung hundreds of thousands on their final journeys making those journeys a little more bearable and a little less lonely.

Though they go mad they shall be sane,
Though they sink through the sea they shall rise again;
Though lovers be lost love shall not;
And death shall have no dominion.

—Dylan Thomas

AUTHOR'S NOTE
On writing about the AIDS epidemic
in a time of Covid-19.

This is a work of fiction. Still, works of fiction carry their own truth, truth that transcends "facts" and "dates" and "names" and can speak beyond a specific time or a particular people. And in this current moment, we are in need of all the truth we can get.

I find a peculiar symmetry that, just as I am bringing one defining epidemic of my life to a close with this book, another epidemic begins. There are similarities between them beyond both being caused by viruses—a retrovirus earlier, a coronavirus now. Once again, we have a president slow on the uptake, realizing too late that he has a national health crisis on his watch and displaying an almost callous lack of concern and leadership. In both epidemics, it has been doctors and public health officials who have had to provide that missing leadership, often requiring them to delicately skirt political obstacles, egos, and ignorance—though in the earlier epidemic they were aided (some would say, terrorized) by AIDS activists fighting for their lives. And once again there is no vaccine, no cure to help stop the spread of contagion. (Contrary to some uninformed sources, the CDC has not found hydroxychloroquine to be effective against the coronavirus. They also strongly advise against ingesting bleach.) It took thirteen years before protease inhibitors transformed AIDS from being a death sentence to a manageable chronic condition, thirty years before the approval of a pre-exposure prophylaxis (PrEP) that can help reduce the risk of becoming infected. We expect the timeline to find a vaccine for Covid-19 will be much shorter.

But there are also significant differences between the two epidemics: This time it is not happening to "Those People," but to all of us. This time our government swung into quick(er) action, its delay measured in months, not years.

Another big difference: This time people care. Resources and funding for research were readily made available. The media provides daily updates on numbers infected and numbers of those who died. Mayors, governors, the White House itself have given daily briefings. Also a major difference, this time we know what we are dealing with and began to marshal a nationwide response, however clumsy and uncoordinated, to combat it. For much of the first two years of the AIDS epidemic, it was a mystery why gay men were getting sick and dying.

Many of the emotions amid this current epidemic are familiar: anxiety, fear, grief at the loss of loved ones, "anticipatory grief" of yet more losses to come. But there is no shame, no stigma in getting Covid-19—unless you were among those who loudly decried it as a political hoax. That could be a bit embarrassing.

Today, once again it is the poor and communities of color who are disproportionately affected by this epidemic due to limited, little or no health coverage, and an ongoing legacy of racial inequality. As in earlier epidemics, there are always "those people" who are not us. Until they are.

There were benefits and lessons learned from the AIDS epidemic, gained at a terrible cost: medical advances, advances in public health policy and strategies for tracking and combating an epidemic. Also, societal advances in the decriminalizing and de-perverting of gay people in the public's mind. What gay activists had been asking their queer brothers and sisters to do for decades—coming out to families and friends, to coworkers and fellow church members—was finally accomplished, often by a terrible necessity. ("Mom, Dad, I'm gay . . . I'm also dying.") The AIDS epidemic became the occasion for young gay men in San Francisco, in Los Angeles and New York City, to "come out" to their families back in Iowa, in Vermont, in Louisiana and Wyoming. As a friend once said, "It's a helluva way to come out of the closet." People across the country began to discover that "those people" were their own sons, and brothers, and nephews and uncles, that "They" were us. "They" always had been.

What will we gain this time? I wonder. What benefits and lessons will we learn? It's too early to yet grasp the full impact of this epidemic on our lives, but we already suspect it will be profound, wide-reaching, deep and lasting. Many of us realize we will never be returning to "Normal." And maybe that's okay. We can do better.

At the very most, we can hope that our global community—humanity—will emerge from this viral crucible stronger, wiser, more compassionate, guided by the better angels of our nature. History tells us that some will; and it tells us some won't, not until a vaccine is finally developed and deployed against our human ignorance, our bigotry and prejudices. And even then, there will always be the anti-vaxxers.

At the very least, we may come out of this current pandemic with a better understanding of who we are as a people, and as individual persons, so that when we, too, are finally "summoned," we may depart with more wisdom, greater self-awareness, and perhaps not so much strangers to ourselves.

Alan Rose
Lewis River Valley
Washington State
June 2020

AS
IF
DEATH
SUMMONED

There once was a Chinese philosopher who dreamt he was a butterfly.
The dream was so real that he wondered whether it had been a dream.
Or was he a butterfly, now dreaming he was a Chinese philosopher?

Prologue

In the Victorian Alps, some 150 miles north of Melbourne, there lies a vast plateau at six thousand feet called the Bogong High Plains. Part of the Great Dividing Range of Australia, it stands isolated and austere, composed of rock and heath and grasslands. The region was once sacred to the Yiatmathong people. They would climb its higher elevations to escape the antipodean summers' heat and there listen to their ancestors' songs carried on the winds. The Europeans who followed were more accustomed to the sacred being enclosed within a building, and with their arrival the aboriginal people were soon decimated, their ancestors' songs lost, and the land, once sacred, became grazing ranges for the White Fellas' sheep and cattle.

In 1936, three men—Mick Hull, Howard Michell and Cleve Cole—attempted the first winter crossing of the high plains. Overtaken by a blizzard, they became lost and wandered for five days in sub-freezing temperatures. Hull and Michell survived the ordeal, but Cole died from exposure. Two years later, a hut was constructed in his memory as shelter for others caught in the area's changeable weather. In the decades since, there have been reports of a lone figure seen wandering over the heathlands. When approached, he vanishes and no trace of him can be found.

I am haunted by dreams of the Bogong High Plains.

Chapter One

Déjà Vu, All Over Again

[10:00 p.m., Friday, February 24, 1995,
Providence Hospital, Portland, Oregon]

I've been here before: Walking down the corridor of some hospital, bracing myself for what I know is coming, pacing myself for what I know will be required. At the nurses' station, they direct me to the second-floor waiting room where I find Sandy, arms crossed as if holding herself together. She stares out the window at the city's night lights, sees my reflection in the glass, and turns, her face tight with anxiety.

"How is he?" I ask.

Eyes red, she shakes her head—"Not good"—then puts a hand to her face, and her shoulders begin shaking. I reach out and we fold into an embrace. She sobs once. *Be strong. Be strong,* I want to tell her. *I need you to be strong.*

We hold each other like that until she pulls away, removing a handkerchief from her jeans. "Let's sit down," I say. It's almost ten, and we're by ourselves. I'm grateful for this at least. I don't feel like sharing a room with other grief-shattered people this night.

"How was the conference?" she asks, wiping her eyes.

3

"Fine. It was fine. Thanks for getting word to me. I was able to catch an early flight out of Dulles. How long have you been here?"

She looks exhausted as she checks her watch. "Since four. I came in with him."

"What do the doctors say?"

"Not much. They've managed to stabilize him . . . they think. They say now it's wait and see. Probably won't know until morning. And even if he does . . ." Her voice trails off.

"Right. So, what happened?"

She fills me in; talking seems to relieve her, so I listen, thinking of the one in the ICU with drips and tubes sprawling from him like some high-tech marionette. It all came as a surprise, but then, not really.

When she finishes, I say, "You look beat. Why don't you go home. I'll stay."

"I don't know. I should be here in case . . ."

"I'll call if there's any change. I promise. There's nothing you can do now. And I'm sure Fernando must be worried about you. You know how caring and considerate cats are."

She looks up and I'm grateful to see her cracked smile. "Like you care about Fernando."

"But I do. I do." Fernando and I had taken an immediate and mutual dislike to each other upon our first meeting, and our relationship only deteriorated from there. "Go home," I urge. "You need to get out of here." I'm glad she doesn't resist.

"Call me if—"

"I'll call. I promise."

And soon I have the room to myself. Just me and a few dozen ghosts. Sliding into a chair, I swear under my breath, *"Damn, damn, damn . . ."* I had promised myself when I returned from Australia I wouldn't go through this ever again: Never again keep a midnight vigil in some hospital, awaiting the inevitable. There had been too many. I had promised myself. Never again.

And here I was.

By my own diagnosis, I'm borderline burnt out. And I should

4

know. I'm a mental health professional. Fortunately, one's own mental health is not a prerequisite for the job. It's been a year since I returned to the States, exhausted and drained of life. Aside from brief visits, I had been away for twelve years, first living in Japan, then Australia. Mom was happy to have me home, the Prodigal Son returned. That first night back I would have preferred just going to bed and sleeping for the next month, but she had killed the fatted calf and made a huge dinner of it, invited Sis and her homophobic husband, and chattered happily, managing to forget the circumstances that had brought me back.

We sat around the dining room table, I with no appetite, force-feeding myself to be polite, catching up on all the news. Family news. News of people I went to school with. News of people at church. Mom was a fount of unwanted information. Silently I listened as she went on and on.

"Oh, and did I write that Carol's been diagnosed with breast cancer?"

Carol was my age. We had dated during high school, back in those early, preconscious days.

"No," I said. "I don't think so." More information I didn't need right then.

"Yes," she sighed, adjusting her bubbly mood to the weight of the news. "It's serious I'm afraid. But that's a part of life. Eventually, you reach that age where your friends start getting sick and dying."

My sister and her husband were stunned at Mom's comment. Even Dad caught it.

I said, "Mom, my friends have been getting sick and dying for the last ten years."

Thirty-one by last count, as my plane lifted off from Melbourne. It was the thirty-first death that was bringing me home. She started to speak, then, realizing what she'd said, nodded and resumed eating.

And yet, in spite of my exhaustion, in spite of my burnout, in spite of my resolutions on that long flight back to the US, within a month I was sitting in a ventricle of the heart of the epidemic, volunteering for more action.

Dad expressed concern about this. We'd been outside in the yard on a late winter's day, pruning his trees and preparing his garden for spring's return. Some people are easy to be with when grieving, people you can be comfortably silent with. Dad is one of them. Clipping dead branches, he asked, "Are you sure about this?" He meant volunteering. Hadn't I had enough of this AIDS? Maybe it was time for me to get on with my life. To realize there was more to life than death.

I turned the soil for his garden bed. "No. I'm not sure. But I'm not sure I have a choice." To his bemused look, I said, "I remember you telling me how the day after Pearl Harbor, you and your brothers went down to the Army office and signed up."

After serving his three years, he had the chance to return to being a civilian again, to marry and get on with *his* life. And he signed up for yet another tour of duty. Why? I once asked. He'd hated the military, hated the regimentation, the fighting, the food. But there was a war on, you see, and the war dominated those years, shaping his generation, infusing every aspect of their lives, and overriding any personal plans. He could not *not* be part of it.

"That's kind of the way it is with me now," I told him. "This epidemic is *my* war." He nodded, saying nothing further, and we returned to our work.

War was the right analogy, and I knew I was suffering battle fatigue even when I showed up to volunteer at Columbia AIDS Project, or "CAP" for short. Originally, for a brief time, it had been called Columbia *River* AIDS Project, until someone noted the regrettable acronym. Fortunately, those were the early days, before they could afford letterhead.

There are people you instinctively know do not appreciate humor. I knew this instinctively about Charles Philpott, CAP's volunteer coordinator. We were about serious matters here. About life and death, where there is no room for humor. Levity is to be discouraged lest people misunderstand how terribly serious we are here.

Charles was prim, proper, somewhat prissy, and very, very neat.

His cubicle screamed Obsessive-Compulsive. Papers stacked neatly. Books and binders arranged neatly by size. Everything neatly in order, not one renegade paper clip out of place. I sat in his cubicle, hesitant to move for fear of disturbing the artificial order of things. He was polite, with that air of social politeness usually reserved for church, as if his tone had been selected like his tie that morning. One could almost see his mental checklist:

Establish rapport with prospective volunteer (Check).

Express appreciation for candidate's willingness to volunteer (Check).

Evince—I'm sure the word for Charles would be "evince"—*a personal interest in said candidate* (Check).

That done, he opened a desk drawer labeled New Applications, removed a file, and handed me a number of forms. "You'll need to complete and return these to me as the first step in becoming a volunteer."

He walked me through the forms I should take away, "study," sign and return. There was the basic four-page volunteer application, a two-page medical history, a twelve-page personality profile, confidentiality statement, list of all the volunteer positions available at the agency, release form requesting a police background check—it hadn't been this difficult to gain Australian citizenship.

I shuffled through the papers as he kept talking.

"Then there will be several trainings our volunteers take prior to working with our clients." *Our* volunteers. *Our* clients. It all sounded terribly possessive. There would be a three-hour orientation to the agency, its mission, its services, policies and procedures; a required two-hour diversity training workshop; and then program-specific trainings on blood-borne pathogens, HIV 101, home care, self-care, homophobia . . .

"I just hope I get to volunteer before the epidemic's over," I joked, forgetting my earlier judgment that levity here would not be appreciated.

He offered a polite smile. "I'm sure you will."

"I did bring along my résumé," I said, pulling it out of my daypack.

7

"Oh good. That will be helpful," said Charles, receiving it from me—a slight frown at the dog-eared corner. *Tsk. Tsk.* "I will still need you to complete the application, even if the information is already included in your résumé." Charles knew that little boxes on forms were not created without a purpose. Bureaucracy, taking its cue from nature, abhors a vacuum. As he said this, he skimmed the résumé, his eyes stopping on something of interest: Australia. Victorian AIDS Council. Founding member. Developed and coordinated care teams. Designed HIV prevention campaign. Master's degree and background in mental health.

"I see you already have experience," he said, continuing to read. "Australia. You lived there for ten years?"

"Yes."

"I've always wanted to travel there. Did you like it?"

"Yes." Was this part of the interview?

"How did you come to live in Australia?" His interest was piqued, almost in spite of himself. I wondered if he was concerned about professional boundaries.

I paused. "It's a long story." Translation: I don't want to talk about it. But Charles kept looking at me, so I added, "I fell in love with an Australian." He seemed, what, surprised? I shrugged. "It happens."

"Ah. So, what brought you back?"

"He died."

"Of?"

"Yes."

"Oh, I am sorry."

I looked away. "Me, too."

He now studied me in a new light. I knew what he thought he saw, and he offered delicately, "Perhaps you'd like to sign up for our client services. I mean, while you're here and all."

I turned back to him. "Thanks, but I don't have AIDS." *I just look like shit.* It seemed I was having to explain this to everyone since I'd returned. To Mom and Dad. To Sis and homophobic hubby. To old friends. To volunteer coordinators. Not that I cared what people thought. I had gotten over that long ago with Gray. Everyone just assumed I, too, was positive. Let them think what they will. I'm not dying. I'm already dead.

"We happen to have a position open for a mental health specialist."

"Thanks, but I'm not looking for a job here. I just came to volunteer some hours."

"You already have a job?"

"No."

"You've got the right credentials and experience. We've been trying to fill this position for over three months."

"I really don't think I'm—"

"Let me call our client services manager." He was so insistent I wondered if he was getting a commission. "Would you be willing at least to meet her?"

Now, sitting in this hospital waiting room a year later, I realize I should have said, *No. No, thank you. Really, no.* But then, I would never have met Sandy. Or Steve, or Cal, or Lukas, or . . .

I was directed to the client services manager's office where I found a hefty woman with short hair, dressed in jeans, banded-collar shirt, and vest, holding a thick file. As a program manager, she had moved up the food chain from a cubicle. Her office was a shambles, resembling a paper-recycling center. Folders strewn about. File drawers gaping open. Stacks of papers everywhere, all suggesting creative chaos—or maybe just chaos. An autographed poster of k.d. lang was tacked on one wall, on another a poster of planet Earth ("We all live downstream"). After Charles's cubicle, this immediately put me at ease.

As I came to her door, she shouted, "Three weeks!" I looked behind me to see who she was shouting at, and found that it was me. "*Three weeks* I worked to find this guy a place to stay. I pulled strings. I bribed the housing authority. I nearly prostituted myself with the HUD case manager to get this guy off the streets. And now I learn he's taken off to LA!" She threw the file on the desk, placing her fists on her hips, shaking her head. "I just want to kill him before AIDS does."

Then she held out her hand, smiling. "Hi. I'm Sandy. Don't mind me. I'm just venting. It's Monday." She had a strong, masculine grip, making me glad I wasn't her client, wherever he was. I introduced myself and handed her the photocopy Charles had made of my résumé so he could keep the original, which I was certain he had by now filed away. We sat down and she quickly ran through it. "Charles says you just came back from Australia. You look like shit. Rough flight?"

"I've been back a month now."

"Oh." I knew what I looked like: dark circles under my eyes, pale skin, gaunt and skinny. No wonder Charles thought I was a client.

"How come Australia?"

"My partner . . . *was* Australian."

She nodded once—"Sorry"—and returned to studying my résumé. I'd found this lack of sentimentality before among those working on the front lines of the epidemic. Perhaps it was a shield, a carapace over our hearts, protecting us from feeling too much, too deeply. I suspect it's the same during wartime: There are casualties. It's a given. So, quickly bury the dead and move on to the next battle. Keep moving. Don't think too much about what you've lost. We'll grieve when it's over. We promise to grieve when it's over.

"We could really use you," she said. "You have both the mental health background and the HIV experience we need."

I smiled through my fatigue. "I'm not exactly a poster boy for mental health right now."

She shrugged. "Who is? Especially in this work."

It was then I met Steve. He poked his head in the door. Charles must have told him about me. "Hi!" He was a handsome man in his mid-thirties, about my age, with the outgoing, bright-eyed manner of an Eagle Scout. Sandy introduced him as the HIV prevention program manager. He was friendly, immediately likable, and, as I would find in months to come, habitually excited. Right now, he was excited about the mental health specialist position.

"This is the third time we've advertised for it. None of the people we've interviewed had what we're looking for."

"You should consider it," said Sandy. "It's easier to become an employee here than a volunteer. Fewer forms to fill out."

"We're working with Charles on that," said Steve. "We lose people all the time."

Then they talked about how they needed someone with my background and experience for both their programs.

"I could use your help with the care teams," said Sandy. "Father Paul is in charge of them. A wonderful human being, a prince of a guy, our own in-house saint, but not the most organized person in the world. He needs help coordinating the program and training the volunteers."

"And I need someone who can help my team design prevention programs," said Steve. "Someone who understands human behavior and behavior change."

Do I understand human behavior? I once thought I did. Now humanity seems increasingly alien, or perhaps it's my own humanity that's become so alien. Steve continued speaking excitedly about the position. *Clean, wholesome, decent* were words that came to mind as I studied him. And *enthusiastic*. He exuded enthusiasm. One of those guys you know was on the cheerleading team in high school. This was "a wonderful opportunity," he said. I would be playing "a really significant role" in this epidemic. It was *critical* they have a mental health specialist at the agency.

"Really," agreed Sandy. "You should see all the dysfunctional people and personality disorders we have to deal with on a day-to-day basis—and then, of course, some of the clients are pretty strange, too." Both of them laughed, and I found myself smiling. They were easy to be around.

"I assume you're talking about FY," said Steve.

Sandy explained, "That's our finance director. Franklin Youngson III. He signs all his memos FY, which could be for his initials. Steve thinks it stands for Fiscal Year. I think it's short for Fuck You, which reflects Franklin's attitude toward the staff. The ED keeps him on because he's good with numbers and has saved the agency several times. Still, we're weighing the cost."

11

"I don't know." I was wavering, feeling my resolution sinking out from under me. "I don't think I'm in the right mental space to give you what you need."

"Maybe this is what *you* need," said Steve. "You know, something to take your mind off . . . whatever you need to take your mind off of." I suspect Charles had also told him why I returned to the States. Then he glanced at his watch. "I've got to get back to my meeting." He stood and we shook hands. "Please, think about it. We really do need you."

Once he left, I said to Sandy, "His enthusiasm is infectious."

She eyed me. "Yeah, well, be careful. That's not all that's infectious about him."

"Oh." I felt an immediate sinking in my stomach. *Why am I still surprised?*

"By the way, that's not breaching confidentiality. Steve's very open about his status. About half the guys who work here are positive, though only a few have symptoms yet. And then, too, Steve already has a partner."

"Oh, I'm not interested in a relationship," I said. "And besides, he's really not my type—you know, good-looking, charming, intelligent." And I realized that's exactly how I'd describe Gray. No, I wasn't interested in a relationship. Not then. Perhaps not ever again.

Sandy looked at her watch. "It's almost noon. Hungry?"

"Not really."

"Good. You'll be a cheap lunch date. It's my treat."

"Thanks, but—"

"No, really, I want to talk to you some more. I'm going to wine 'n dine you until I convince you why you need to join us."

Out of courtesy I agreed to lunch, and in a manner befitting a nonprofit agency, Sandy wined and dined me at the nearby Subway sandwich shop.

Chapter Two

The Bogong High Plains

[Northern Victoria, Australia, March 1991]

The Bogong High Plains held some mystical affinity for Gray. They evoked in him a deep sense of the holy he found nowhere else. It was on these plains he felt his own spiritual connection to the earth. It was here he entered the Dreamtime.

The two of us sat next to the campfire, he staring into the flames as I read my book. He'd always enjoyed campfires. The flickering, dancing, waving lights beckoned him, producing mild trance states where his imagination and memories wandered hand in hand. Although he'd become a barrister like his father and grandfather, at heart, Gray was a romantic.

"To the aboriginal peoples, these plains were sacred."

The statement came out of nowhere, apropos of nothing but his flame-lit reveries.

I looked up from my book. "To the aboriginal peoples, the *entire earth* was sacred," I reminded him. "They dwelled in a sacred universe."

"Yes, I know but . . . some places are special," he insisted.

"What, like they're sacred-*er*?"

"Some places remind us that *everything* is sacred."

This affinity related to an experience he'd had as a young boy. Each summer he and his brothers accompanied their father camping on this vast plateau in northern Victoria. His father said it was how he got away, "far from the madding crowd."

"Your mother didn't go along?" I'd asked.

"Mother *was* the madding crowd. Besides, she detested camping. Considered anything beyond Melbourne's city limits the Outback and not fit for human habitation."

Gray and I would go up there several times a year, staying at a favorite secluded camping spot from which we hiked and back-packed in spring and early summer, and skied cross-country in winter. I didn't share his attraction to the high plains. To me, they were bleak, barren and unwelcoming, a vast empty landscape. Fifty percent heath and scrub brush, twenty-five percent grasslands, scraggly trees here and there, the rest rocky outcroppings, I found them scruffy and desolate. I've always preferred mountains—admittedly, not abundant in Australia—and put our difference in landscape preferences down to my growing up in the Pacific Northwest with the Cascade peaks always in view. Gray thought it had more to do with our sun signs.

"You're Capricorn," he'd say. "Earth sign. The goat. So, yeah, you're drawn to mountains. I'm Aquarius."

"What's Aquarius drawn to? Scrub brush?"

"Air sign"—and he'd raise his hands and eyes overhead—"Sky. Infinitude. The eternal."

He'd been brought up in the Anglican Church, so he was not particularly religious. The high church tradition offered pomp and pageantry and exquisite liturgical music, but as to the human hunger for mystery and the mystical, Gray turned to what he called his "aboriginal roots," the land.

He was staring again into the fire. "Maybe the indigenous people didn't express it conceptually like we do, but they sensed it. *I* sense it."

"Sense what?"

"These plains are haunted."

By then, I'd heard the folklore that Cleve Cole's restless spirit wandered this land. "You mean haunted as in ghosts?" I asked.

"I mean haunted as in holy."

Every people, in every place, in every period of human history, have believed that certain locations—mountains and volcanoes, deserts, forests, springs and watering holes—were repositories of special energies, holding special powers. I remain a skeptic on the subject, intrigued, intellectually curious, but skeptical. Gray, however, was a believer. Though questioning, even cynical about so much else—politics, the law, his mother's artificially youthful appearance—he was a believer in the sacredness of these plains.

"This is where I want my ashes spread," he said on that occasion. "This is where I belong."

He'd just been diagnosed that week with AIDS, and hearing his words unnerved me.

"We've got plenty of time to talk about that," I said, and without commenting further, I returned to my book and he returned to his fire reveries. It turned out we had less time than we thought.

It was several weeks after arriving home that I began to have recurring dreams of the Bogong High Plains.

————— ————— —————

"I was hoping I might just sit with him. I realize he's unconscious."

The nurse is kind. "I'm afraid it's not possible. He's still in critical condition and being actively monitored. I'm sorry."

She seems genuinely sorry, so I offer a smile. "Well, no harm in asking."

She gives a warm smile in return. "No harm at all."

I start to leave for the waiting room, then turn back. "It's just that . . ." I'm struggling for words. "If he regains consciousness, even momentarily, it's very important I speak with him. *Very* important, if only for a couple of minutes." *We have some unfinished business,* I want to tell her. *Business that needs to be finished before he . . .*

"It's really not my decision," she says, "but I'll see what I can do once he comes out of the recovery unit."

"I would be ever so grateful." It sounds strangely formal in a Jane Austen kind of way, but a simple *Thank you* doesn't seem adequate for what I'm feeling.

I return to the empty waiting room, settling into one of the chairs, groggy and thick-headed, and glad Sandy went home to care for herself and Fernando. I would make miserable company tonight. By now, I've gone more than twenty hours without sleep and am badly in need of caffeine. Unfortunately, the hospital cafeteria is closed. There is vending machine coffee, but I'm not yet that desperate. My preferred sources of caffeine are Pepsi and Coke, I don't care which—I always failed their taste tests—but the soda machine is out of order.

There was a time, back in Melbourne, when these vigils were happening with such regular frequency that I kept a daypack in my car with essential items. You never knew when you'd get the call. ("He went into the hospital, we think for the last time. Come if you can.") By then, I had it down to a science: No-Doz tablets, thermos to fill and refill with strong black coffee, two novels (in case one was a dud), notebook and pen, change of shirt, toothbrush, toothpaste, razor (some vigils went on for days), energy bars, a couple of apples, extra tissues—not for me but for the others who would come by to sit a while and who needed to talk and maybe to cry—and finally the list of phone numbers when it came time to make "The Call," notifying family and friends the vigil was over.

But this time I was caught unprepared. Rushing in from the airport, I don't even have a book and am now left with nothing to read but old issues of *Bon Appetit!* on the waiting room table. Apparently, the selection of magazines depends on whatever the staff brings from home. So, I scrunch deeper into the chair, feeling bereft without my life support system and with only my memories to occupy myself.

I already know this vigil is going to be different. But then, they're all different. Unlike the memorial services, which over the years begin to blend and blur together, merging into one montage of loss, the vigils remain distinct in my mind—*this* specific time, *this* specific place with its own emotional atmosphere, contoured to fit *this* individual now dying. Memorial services are communal events; vigils are deeply personal. Often, I've been left by myself, after family and friends depart, choosing to remain to keep what the writer Paul Monette called "the last watch of the night."

No need for you to stay, a kindly nurse or hospice staff person will say. *He doesn't even know you're here.*

But I stay anyway. There's this sense that much more than a life is ending. An entire world is coming to an end, a multitude of experiences, millions of moments and memories, hopes and goals and desires and dreams, all reduced to this: a biological organism slowly releasing its hold on life, a vast network of physiological processes gradually shutting down. Seems like someone should be here to witness it. You sense the presence that was this person has already departed, a presence no longer present, and not for the first time wonder *who* or *what* is actually dying.

With each vigil, a part of my soul died with that person. I seem to have less and less soul left. This vigil will be no different. I close my eyes and pray, *Don't let him die before we make peace*, forgetting that I stopped praying years ago.

Chapter Three

On the Art of Dying
(Instructions included)

[Portland, Oregon, February 1994]

I can pinpoint precisely when this epidemic started for me.

There's talk of a gay cancer back home.

A gay cancer? You mean, like we have our own?

Yeah, seems only queers are getting it. In New York City and San Francisco.

It's September 1981, in a restaurant in the Shibuya district of Tokyo, talking with Peter who has just returned from visiting family and friends in the States. A gay cancer? We both think it sounds suspicious. We joke that the Moral Majority is probably behind it, coating Barbra Streisand records with carcinogens, and we move on to other, more relevant topics—like the beating the dollar is taking against the yen, or Reagan's deep compassion for the wealthy, or Peter's latest infatuation. I won't give his comment another thought for many months. There's nothing about a gay cancer in the English-language *Tokyo Times* or *Mainichi Daily*. Indeed, I'll learn there's no mention of it in most newspapers back home either, so how serious can it be?

It will be almost a year—well into 1982—before I begin hearing of friends in Portland becoming ill, and no one knows why; and besides other queers, it seems no one cares.

Fast-forward to February 1994. I return home where over a half million Americans have been infected with HIV; more than 300,000 have already died, most of them gay men, though not, it turns out, from Barbra Streisand records.

I had been with Columbia AIDS Project two weeks before I met its executive director, Caleb Stern. He missed a lot of time, Sandy told me. Cal Stern had end-stage AIDS. We were in the conference room as people gathered for the monthly staff meeting. He sat next to Steve at the head of the large table, a waxy sheen to his skin as if he were the latest addition to Madame Tussaud's museum, representing the AIDS epidemic of the late twentieth century for some future generation to stare at. Emaciated, with sunken eyes appearing too big for his face, he had the look of one not long for this earth.

"What's he doing here?" I whispered to Sandy. "Shouldn't he be home in bed?"

"He should be dead," she whispered back. I was always struck by her bluntness. Sandy said what others only thought. "Besides, there's nothing for him at home. His partner died three years ago. His family's back in Oklahoma."

It was like having death sitting in our midst. And yet, as if to dispel that image, when he looked at me, his eyes had a luminous quality I'd seen in the faces of others who had come to this point. Maybe it was their steadiness. Rather than darting about, looking here, looking there, as most of us do, his eyes seemed to linger on whatever they were seeing at that moment, taking it in, as if this might be the last time they would ever see this slant of light, or that person laugh, or this group of friends. When our eyes met, he smiled, nodded, his gaze slowly moving on.

I was drawn back to the other people in the conference room.

With few exceptions, they were all young, most in their twenties, a rambunctious, boisterous group filling the space with much laughter and joking. This was the first time I had seen the full staff together. It was divided about half and half, men and women, with quite a few lesbians. God bless the lesbians. They were there from the beginning, in those early days in New York City and San Francisco and Los Angeles and Melbourne, when the hospitals were refusing to take gay men for fear of the uncertain contagion. These brave women, our sisters, joined our care teams, stayed with our friends in their homes, wiped up their vomit and diarrhea, held their hands as they died. I have often wondered, if it had been reversed, say, if there had been some strange little virus targeting lesbians, would we gay men have been there for them as they have been for us? Would I? In shame, I doubt it.

The meeting began with various introductions and updates. Next to Steve and Cal Stern sat Franklin Youngson III, the finance director, a tall, thin man in his thirties, blond and not unattractive, but with pinched, narrow features suggesting less a physical disease than some spiritual malaise too deep for any drugs to cure. He held his head aloft, his thin, pointed beak of a nose turning here, turning there, like a hawk condescending to be among all these lowly sparrows. He and Charles, the volunteer coordinator, were the only ones wearing ties.

Steve chaired the meeting. Although it was only February, they were already planning this year's staff and volunteer picnic in June and the AIDS Walk in September. A heated discussion was under-way about the picnic. Most of the gay men wanted to organize an afternoon of Earth Games, noncompetitive group activities requiring cooperation where everyone wins and there are no losers, while the lesbians pressed for a down and dirty softball game, wanting to kick some serious butt. As problematic as stereotypes are, they usually contain an embarrassing kernel of truth.

It looked like it was coming down to a vote. Lionel raised his hand, and all faces turned toward him. A big, Black brawny bruiser of a man with smooth shaved head, he easily stood six foot two, with biceps larger than my thighs. He was on the HIV prevention team, coordinating the bar outreach program. "I vote for a softball game," he announced in his deep baritone voice.

"Wait a minute," said Chad, also on the prevention team. "Before the meeting, you agreed to vote for Earth Games."

"Yeah, but Annie said she'd buy me a beer if I voted for softball."

There was laughter. Annie sat next to him, petite, maybe one hundred pounds at most, very cute with elfin features as she blushed and whispered, "You weren't supposed to tell them that."

Chad was clearly exasperated. "Where are your principles?"

"Hey, I've got principles," said Lionel. "But I also have priorities."

The exchanges became more and more raucous, the lesbians gleefully casting aspersions on the gay men's masculinity, and the gay men likewise casting aspersions on the lesbians' masculinity. Above it all, sitting there with his gray, ravaged eminence, Cal Stern watched the proceedings with a gentle smile not unlike, I thought, the detached, compassionate smile one sees on statues of the Buddha, as if he had already taken leave of this world. There is a lame-duck quality to the dying. You could almost see the thoughts on his face: *I won't be here for the AIDS Walk this year. I'll never see that. I wonder if I'll make it to June.* He looked at peace. One more thing he wouldn't have to worry about, thank God. Or maybe he was just relieved he wouldn't have to participate in the softball game. He knew lesbians played for blood.

The room hooted and howled, everyone laughing except Franklin who looked upon the proceedings with a kind of disdain, like an older child watching the antics of his rowdy younger siblings wrestling in the dirt. He caught my eye, shaking his head in a kind of assumed camaraderie of the superior. I smiled back and shrugged. Cal, too, was laughing, his frail body rocking with laughter, his eyes alight, and I thought, *This is why he comes to work. Here there is life and energy. Here there is connection. No, he needs this. To be part of the still living.*

"He really should resign," said Sandy. She, Steve and I were leaving to get lunch. "For the sake of the agency as much as for himself. It's a burden on us managers, trying to do his job as well as our own."

"Yes, but he's kind of an icon here in Portland," Steve explained to me as we went down the back stairwell.

"That may be," said Sandy, "but we need an executive director more than we need an icon right now."

"I know. Many things get dropped," Steve admitted, "but I can't think of anyone better to head this organization. He still goes out and talks to groups when he can, raising money for our programs. And he's a living lesson in how to die with grace and dignity. It amazes me how he still does it. The pain, the continual nausea, the lack of energy, yet he plugs along. I just hope I can muster half the dignity and courage when my time comes."

There was an abrupt shift in our mood, and Sandy said, "You've got nothing to worry about. They'll find a cure long before you get to that point. So, face it: You're going to grow old, fat, and ugly with the rest of us."

Neither Steve nor I said anything as we descended the steps and went out onto the street. There used to be a lot of that kind of talk, in the early years, when we thought we could stop this epidemic. The rallying cry was "Be here for the cure." For those uninfected, stay that way. Use condoms. Play safe. Remain healthy. For those infected, hang in there, take care of yourself, eat right, exercise, *remain positive* (a bit of gallows humor), it's only a matter of time before they find a cure or an antidote. Many of our friends had lived with that hope. Many had died, abandoned by hope. And too many simply ran out of time. Over the years, it became more and more difficult to sustain that optimism, until now one rarely hears people say it anymore. I think we no longer believe.

It was later that day Cal invited me to his office. He was standing behind his desk as I came to the door. He must have once been six feet. Now he looked shrunken, bent, and fragile, his body appearing two sizes too small for his clothes; they hung on him as he moved slowly, like an old man. Yet he welcomed me with a surprisingly firm handshake.

"I know of the Victorian AIDS Council," he said. "The Australians have done some very innovative prevention work down there. I want us to do some here as well."

"I hope my experience can be useful."

He motioned me to a chair and sat down at his desk. "My staff is excited to have you here. They speak highly of you."

"They speak highly of you, too. This organization is a testament to your work."

He shrugged. "It's always been a cooperative effort."

I noticed his uncapped fountain pen, lying atop several blank sheets of paper. "Is this a convenient time? I could come back later."

"No, no, this is fine. I was having a mental block anyway." He looked down at the pen and paper. "Another eulogy. I'm to deliver it on Saturday." He turned back to me. "After so many, you'd think it would get easier."

"I can't imagine it getting easier."

His eyes fell away. "No, it doesn't." He capped the pen, laying it aside. "After I attended my one-hundredth funeral, I vowed I'd never attend another. Except my own, and I wasn't even sure I wanted to be present for that one. No one should have to go to that many funerals, except maybe ministers and undertakers. Each one seemed to siphon off a part of my soul. So I promised myself: no more funerals, no more memorial services, no more wakes. I'd had enough for one lifetime."

"I understand. On the flight back from Australia, I made the same vow. After a while, they all blur together. It's not the way I'd like to honor a friend's passing."

He seemed interested. "Oh? And how would you like to honor a friend's passing?"

I thought for a moment. "I think I'd rather go off by myself and climb some mountain. I'd sit up there alone, remembering this friend and recalling the times we shared together. I'd eat an orange in his honor, whisper his name to the wind, and say good-bye."

He nodded. "That would be a fitting tribute to any friend." Then he turned back to the task before him. "Of course, given my position, my resolution wasn't realistic. There were board members, founders of this organization, wealthy donors—as well as good and dear friends—whose funerals required I be present." He looked down again at the paper on his desk. "This will be number one hundred and forty-two."

"I probably won't be able to keep my vow either."

"No." He gave a great sigh. "At times, life calls us beyond our vows."

Remembering Sandy's comment, I said, "It must be hard carrying the weight of this agency, all that needs to be done."

"No, that's not so hard. I've got good managers. They bear the greatest share of the responsibility now, they and the board. Oh, they whine and moan about having to do my work for me, but it's good for them." He smiled. "It's character-building." Then he looked out the window at the Portland skyline. "And someday, someday soon, they'll need to know how to run this agency. They'll need to teach the new executive director what to do." He turned back to me. "You see, there's method to my madness."

He reached for the glass of water on his desk and drank. I noticed his hand shaking.

"No, what's hard now is trying to find the time for my own dying. The daily dying." He looked at me with those sunken eyes. "You know how we workaholics get so caught up in our work we lose track of living?"

I nodded. I knew. Gray was forever reminding me.

"The same is true of our dying. At times I forget, and that's not good. To live each day to the fullest now, I need to remember that I'm dying."

It was one of the benefits I'd found from this epidemic: the lack of bullshit. We have no time for it. *No time*, that was a recurring theme. People cut to the chase.

Cal offered, "Samuel Johnson once observed that 'when a man knows he is to be hanged in a fortnight—'"

"'It concentrates his mind wonderfully.'"

He laughed. "It's true. I think there's an art to dying, just as there's an art to living. What's surprised me is to find they're pretty much the same: Stay focused on the present, on the here and now, not the past or the future. Live each day as if it were your last. Be with each person as if this were the last time you would ever see him or her. Pretty basic stuff. I had expected something more profound. But that sums it up, I think. And I've found that if I'm living this moment fully, I don't mind that it might be my last."

"I've heard several staff say you are a model to them on how to live, and how to die."

"Yes, I try to discourage that. People around here expect me to be some kind of saint. You know, to die by the book. Nobly, with dignity, grace and wisdom, at peace with God and the world. You're familiar with Kübler-Ross's stages of dying? People see me at the acceptance stage. All the other stages—the sadness and the anger, the depression and the denial—I go through alone each night by myself."

He took another drink.

"My parents back in Oklahoma want me to come home. I tell them I have my work to finish. They say, come back just for a visit. But I fear if I went back, I'd never return." He had a slight Midwest accent. "I left Tulsa over twenty years ago. To return now would seem a kind of failure, going home to die. And, believe me, the Bible Belt is a terrible place for a gay man to die."

"There aren't that many good places."

He chuckled. "True. But the Midwest is rather thick with that brand of Christian who's fond of saying they hate the sin, not the sinner. Though from my experience, it's too fine a distinction for most of them to make. Father Paul reminds me we shouldn't judge Jesus and Christianity by his groupies." He smiled as if just remembering. "My father wrote me a letter last week. 'Have you made your peace with God?' he wanted to know. I wrote back, 'We've never quarreled.'" He chuckled again to himself. I could detect no bitterness in him, no sadness, no self-pity, which given the circumstances, could have been forgiven.

"You appear to be at peace," I said. I was feeling a kind of envy.

"I have my moments. This is one of them," he said. "You have family around here?"

"Yes . . . We have our issues, too." Then I added, "My partner died three months ago. I'm familiar with the routine: the nausea, the diarrhea, the medications. I know the drill. So, if I can be of help . . ."

"Thanks, but I have wonderful brothers and sisters here who are caring for me. Like many of us, I had to find a new family who would love and accept me for who I am. I feel very fortunate to have their support. Why would I want to go back to Tulsa? No," he shook his head heavily, "they can have my ashes."

I paused before speaking again. "I'm not sure I can be what people here need right now."

"I know you have your issues to work through. Sandy told me. You should know there are no secrets among this staff." He smiled. "Father Paul is always saying that we, each of us, is here for some reason. For some purpose. Do you believe in God?"

" . . . I'm no longer sure."

"I do. Now. I didn't for much of my life. Being born in the Bible Belt, I naturally developed an early aversion to Christianity. But through this epidemic, through my work, I've rediscovered my faith. And, too, dying puts a different spin on things. Wait and see."

I nodded. *Sure, maybe I'll wait and see.*

Then he said something that surprised me. "We're very fortunate, you know. To be here, to be part of this."

I murmured noncommittally. *Fortunate* wasn't exactly the word I would use to describe these past ten years.

"There are few jobs, I think, that take one into the very heart of life, that allow us to accompany people through their dying and put us in touch with our own spiritual depths."

His eyes shone once again with that strange luminosity, as if already catching the light of some supernal realm they were about to enter.

"This epidemic has done wonderful things for our souls. I've had more and deeper experiences in the past thirteen years than most people would have in a lifetime. I've seen the best in a man rise up, surprising even himself. I've witnessed such bravery and courage, such acts of self-sacrifice and compassion that are usually only found on a battlefield. I've seen the soul pass out of a man with his last breath. I swear I did; it was a small puff of vapor and light. It sounds strange, I know, and I don't always feel like this, but I wouldn't have missed it for the world." He looked down at his shaking hand. "When all is considered, the body is a small price to pay, don't you think?"

I smiled with some embarrassment. "Careful. You're almost sounding like a saint."

He sighed. "Yes, I've got to watch that."

I could tell he was fatigued. His voice was hoarse, his breathing labored. I made movements to leave. "I should probably be going."

"I've enjoyed our talk. I hope we'll have more opportunities. Some people center me simply by being in their presence. You're one of them. Father Paul is another."

"I was thinking the same of you. Well, I'll let you get back to writing your eulogy."

As I stood to leave, he said, "A favor?"

"Name it."

"When my time comes—or rather, when my time is up—I expect there'll be many people attending my memorial service."

"I expect there will."

"I'd like you not to be there."

I blinked.

"On that day, go off by yourself. Climb some mountain. Eat an orange in my honor and recall the times we'll have shared together. Whisper my name to the wind, and say good-bye."

Tears were welling up, and I said softly, "I promise," then turned and left.

In the few months Cal had remaining, we spoke often, when he was in the office and feeling up to it. And when he no longer could make it into the office, I would visit him at home, and then in the hospital, and then in hospice. We shared a common philosophical bent and had great conversations, about life and death and the possibility of a human soul, about some kind of afterlife, or a cycle of incarnations, cycling, cycling, forever cycling toward perfection. Perhaps what made these discussions so special was that we knew one of us was very close to the end of his life, and that both of us were facing unknown futures.

Almost in spite of himself, Cal remained a saint to the end, playing his role on how to die fully conscious and with dignity. He had been right. His memorial service, held in the downtown Unitarian Church, had standing room only. Attending were his staff, his board of directors, the mayor and members of the city council; the governor had come up from Salem; hundreds of clients and volunteers and friends were there to say good-bye. He was forty-five years old.

On that day in early May, I climbed Table Mountain out in the Columbia Gorge. The day was especially clear, the wildflowers spreading across the hillsides like confetti following one's going-away party. I reached the summit in the afternoon, grateful to have it to myself, and sat there, shirt off, feeling the sun on my back, the breeze murmuring in my ears like the faint whispers of distant ancestors. I peeled my orange, eating it slowly as I recalled Cal and this brief time our paths had come together—while remembering another farewell, not that long ago, staring up into a star-filled sky arcing over the Bogong High Plains. A different sky, a different hemisphere, the same grief. Immensity, whether a starry tapestry overhead or sitting atop some mountain, is a good antidote to sorrow and death.

I withdrew from my daypack an old battered collection of the sonnets of Edna St. Vincent Millay. The cracked binding fell open to the page, as if the volume knew what the moment required. To me, the words had become an anthem for this modern plague.

Down, down, down into the darkness of the grave
Gently they go, the beautiful, the tender, the kind;
Quietly they go, the intelligent, the witty, the brave.
I know. But I do not approve. And I am not resigned.

I sat there, watching the sun cross the sky, watching the great river flow, metaphorically like time, down to the sea of eternity, until day's end nudged me with a chilling touch. I closed the book, replacing it in the pack, slipped on my shirt, and stood looking over the Gorge as the sun, like some fellow traveler, began taking its leave into the west. I whispered Cal's name. *Here we go our separate ways, my friend. Godspeed on yours.* Then set off down the mountain to continue my own journey, alone.

His ashes were sent back to Oklahoma.

⁓⁓⁓ ⁓⁓⁓ ⁓⁓⁓

Friday, February 24, 1995
10:58 p.m.

Providence Hospital, Portland, Oregon

Sometimes I'm wandering in a blizzard, knee-deep in snow, unable to see six feet in front of me. Sometimes it's spring, the brush and heath decked out in their dusty-drab, Down Under version of green. Sometimes it's autumn. Yet always the same dream: I'm lost. I'm alone. And I'm looking for someone.

"For your partner, Gray?" O'Shaughnessy asks.

"No. Even in the dream I know he's dead. Someone else. I'm looking for someone else."

Opening my eyes, I squint against the fluorescent light, grounding myself once more in this second-floor waiting room as the dreamscape fades. Must have dozed off. The room remains empty, hospital sounds murmur and hum and *ping* in a low-level audio blur. Otherwise it's quiet. Less trauma and drama than the first-floor waiting room next to ER. This is for the long-term emergencies. Like me.

I pull myself up in the chair, checking the clock on the wall. Approaching eleven. But I'm operating on East Coast time; as far as my body is concerned, it's 2:00 a.m. Too bad I've never been able to sleep on planes, buses, trains, in cars—anything that's not my bed—so unlike Gray, who could sleep on a roller coaster. A flicker on the television screen draws my attention. Eleven o'clock news. I find the remote and listlessly aim it at the TV, taking it off mute.

"Tonight, a major setback in the Department of Justice's investigation into allegations of corruption by members of the Portland Police Bureau..."

I'm immediately, fully awake. The story has been dominating local news, and, like most of the city, I've been watching since it broke in early January.

"The primary witness in the Department of Justice's investigation was shot this afternoon by an unknown assailant and is at this hour reported to

31

be in critical condition. The witness, whose identity has not been released, presented evidence alleging extortion and civil rights abuses by members of the police bureau . . ."

The anchor goes to a reporter on scene at the hospital, this hospital, who is downstairs and outside in the chilly temperatures. She has little to add, so she notes the heavy police presence, that the witness remains in critical condition and is under round-the-clock guard. She reminds viewers there is still a second witness, a police officer named Blake O'Connor, who recently came forward to testify. He looks young in the official department photograph shown on the screen. Third-generation police officer, I'd read. His face and name have been in the news during the past week. Originally, his identity was suppressed, but once leaked by the grunge press, he was identified by the mainstream media as well. By testifying against his fellow officers, O'Connor was breaking the police's unwritten Code of Silence—the same code, it was pointed out, as the criminal underworld's. A recent editorial in *The Oregonian* commended the young officer for his courage and integrity, hailing him as a true representative of the men and women who loyally serve Portland on the police force. The mayor praised him. The police chief praised him. He was toast.

At the end of the newscast, I switch off the television and feel a new heaviness descend over me. I know more about this investigation than I should, more even than the police or the FBI. I know way too much . . .

Chapter Four

The Mount Bogong Tragedy

[Northern Victoria, Australia, October 1984]

On August 5, 1936, three men set off from Hotham Heights on a skiing expedition to Mount Bogong. All were experienced skiers. Cleve Cole, thirty-seven years old, was a leader of the Lone Scout organization in Melbourne and co-author of a book on scouting; Howard Michell, twenty-three, was the scion of a wealthy textile family in South Australia; Percy E. "Mick" Hull from Hawthorn, Victoria, also twenty-three, was well familiar with the highlands. They were in good spirits when they departed. They would be the first men to cross the high plains in winter. Their plan was to ski up the summit of Mount Bogong, then on to the Staircase Hut, where they'd left a cache of provisions for their return trip. They never made it to the hut.

I learned of the famous disaster on my first trip into the Bogong High Plains. It was 1984. I was new to Australia, and Gray was so excited to show me the region. We stopped in Glen Valley, a jumping-off point to the numerous bushwalking trails and campsites. I was still adjusting to Aussie terms: While he pumped the *petrol* (gasoline), I went inside the *milk bar* (convenience shop) to use the *loo* (toilet) and buy some *biscuits* (cookies) for our *tea* (dinner). In there, I found a wall display filled with flashy, touristy brochures of the Victorian Alps: Mount Hotham, Mount Beauty, Mount Bogong, and the high plains that lie amid them. To a person from the Pacific Northwest, calling them "mountains" and "alps" seemed a misrepresentation. These terms must be understood in the context of the largely horizontal topography of Australia, the flattest of the seven continents. Mount Bogong, the highest "peak" in Victoria, rises to only about 6,500 feet and appears more like a rounded hilltop. Among the brochures, I also found an older sun-bleached, flyspecked pamphlet, mimeographed on cheap paper. The title in faded ink read, *THE MT. BOGONG TRAGEDY.* I took one, along with the chocolate biscuits, and read it as we got back on the road.

On August 6, the three skiers had been overtaken by a sudden blizzard. They dug a snow cave where they waited three days for the storm to end. But on August 9, running low on food, they decided to make a break for the Staircase Hut. They soon became lost in the white-out conditions and for the next five days wandered with little food, exposed to sub-freezing temperatures and severe winds. On Friday, August 14, they finally descended Mount Bogong into the rugged and largely un-surveyed Big River Valley country. By then, suffering from exhaustion, hunger and hypothermia, too weak even to continue carrying their sleeping bags and gear, they dumped them and tried to find their way through the thickly timbered wilderness with its steep ravines. They had matches to start a fire, and now wood, but their fingers were too badly frostbitten to use them. Cole's feet were blistered, making it impossible for him to walk any farther, so they decided Michell would go for help. The remaining two men took shelter in a hollow log. According to Hull's later account, after three days Cleve Cole lost hope that Michell had made it through, and at that point he seemed to lose his will to live. Hull woke later that night to find his companion missing and went out looking for him. Discovering him unconscious and partially covered in snow, Hull managed to drag him back to their log.

34

By that time, he, too, doubted they would be found alive.

But the night before, on Sunday, August 16, Michell had reached Glen Valley, stumbling into the township so debilitated that he could give only the sketchiest details of where he'd left his companions. He was driven to the Omeo District Hospital where he would eventually recover, though needing two toes amputated. The alarm was sounded, and search parties set out early the next morning. Every able-bodied man in the vicinity joined in the effort. Skiers came up from Melbourne. Both the Maude and Yellow Girl mines suspended operations so their workers could join the search. More than 120 men set out into the rugged country with no clear idea where to find the missing skiers. They started on horses, but soon had to leave the animals behind as they climbed into the difficult terrain. Meanwhile, back in Glen Valley, the women prepared food to send out by packhorse to the parties over the coming days.

On Tuesday, August 18, at around eight-thirty in the morning, one of the search parties climbed a high ridge overlooking a valley. A member shouted across the expanse, "HALLOOOOO!" and was surprised to hear a faint whistle. Below them, they saw Hull emerge from thick brush. The seven men made their way down the slope to find him in a gravely weakened state. Cole was in even worse shape, lying unconscious inside the log. For the next two hours, they administered first aid to the badly frostbitten men and fed them hot liquids. Too weak to walk, the skiers were carried on stretchers improvised from saplings and oilskin coats. In rain and hail, against a strong north wind, it was slow going out of the steep gullies and ravines. The team took turns carrying Cole and Hull on the makeshift frames. Holding them shoulder high, they crossed the rushing Mitta Mitta River, wading waist deep into its freezing waters. In six hours, the party had covered only three miles. Exhausted, they made camp at four in the afternoon, continuing to care for the two men as best they could.

Early on the morning of Wednesday, August 19, they set out again. A member of the party was sent ahead to get help. Incredibly, by early afternoon the young man had covered fifteen miles and was close to Glen Valley when he came upon another rescue party led by Harold Hull, Mick's older brother. Word was sent to the township the two men had been found, and the second search party went out to help bring them in. A Sister Watson of the Bush Nursing Association drove a motor car up the river as far as the road would go to meet them, returning to Glen Valley with Cole late in the afternoon. Suffering severe hypothermia, he was too fragile, his condition too critical, to move him to the district hospital. A doctor from Omeo attended to the unconscious man. Cleve Cole died shortly after nine that night, having never regained consciousness.

By all accounts, it was a disaster with a tragic ending. But it also became a stirring piece of Australian lore and a source of national pride, how the townships had rallied to save two of their own. *The Sydney Morning Herald* hailed the effort as "a magnificent example of the working of the bush code." *The Western Mail* in Perth called it "one of the most thrilling alpine dramas enacted in Australia." The following years saw the construction of a series of huts on the Bogong High Plains to provide shelter to future skiers. The first to be constructed was the Cleve Cole Hut.

Certainly, it was a moving and inspiring tale, but as I would later learn, there was more to the story that never made it into the newspapers or the Glen Valley pamphlet.

Chapter Five

Into the West Hills

[Portland, Oregon, April 1994]

I admired the large house as I walked up the extended driveway. Over-looking Portland, its two wings arched from the three-story center peak, suggesting a glass pterodactyl. A Saturday afternoon in April. One of our major donors, a Jerald somebody-or-other, was hosting a fund-raiser at his home in the West Hills. By then Cal was in the hospital, so the board president had asked the management team—Steve, Sandy, and Franklin—to accompany him in Cal's place. They, in turn, asked Father Paul and me to come along. "You make good impressions," Sandy said. "You're both educated and cultured, you speak well, and you don't drool down your front." Father Paul looked like a priest from central casting: mid-fifties, he was the oldest person on staff, some-what portly, with gentle gray eyes, a thatch of iron-gray hair, and a perennial smile. No one had ever seen him riled. They gave me an address, telling me to show up between three and four.

A number of BMWs, Lexuses, and Aston Martins, as well as one aloof Lamborghini were parked in the circular driveway and down along the road. My sensible little Subaru looked as if it was crashing the party. On this pleasantly warm day, I dressed in a sport coat and slacks. The front door stood open, and I entered a large room where many people mingled, each carrying the requisite glass of alcohol. I was relieved to spot Sandy. She came up to me, looking very stylish in a summer dress with a woven wrap about her shoulders. "Oh, good," she said. "We're all here now. You, me, Steve, Father Paul, and FY."

"You look great," I exclaimed. I hadn't seen her dressed in anything other than jeans and vests, basic butch wear, since I joined the organization. "Very elegant."

"Thanks. I can clean up when I need to."

I was also relieved to find the party a relaxed affair compared to the black-tie functions Gray had dragged me to in Toorak. A string quartet from the Oregon Symphony played something Dvorak-ish in the corner. People stood around chatting meaningfully on meaningful topics, laughing lightly, sipping their martinis and glasses of champagne. There were gay couples, straight couples, plus a number of singles aspiring to couple. At that moment Franklin entered the room, appearing absolutely effervescent. "Franklin looks happy," I said. Indeed, I had never seen him so happy.

"Yes, he's in his element," said Sandy. "Franklin aspires to be one of the A-Gays. He has the right attitude and he speaks their language—Snob-ese—but unfortunately lacks the money to be a member of this club. Oh, look, he's coming this way. Watch him pretend he doesn't know us."

Franklin greeted me jovially like we were old friends, pretending not to notice Sandy. "So glad you could make it," he said, a hand on my shoulder. He burbled on about what a beautiful spring day it was—"Portland at its finest"—and that there were some "absolutely wonderful people here." Then he moved on, our finance director the social butterfly, fluttering over to another small group.

Sandy tossed back her drink. "Well, I was 50 percent right."

"He probably just didn't see you standing there."

I also met Steve's partner, Mark. They made an attractive couple, both HIV-positive, though neither yet showing symptoms. As we went

38

to the open bar and got our drinks—a very fine Chardonnay for Sandy, a truly exquisite soda water with lemon for me—we could overhear a nearby group remonstrating against Clinton's economic policies, clear signs of the coming apocalypse.

Sandy turned to me. "You've got the background in psychology. Explain this to me: How can a gay man be a Republican? I mean, isn't that a little like Jews campaigning for the Nazis?"

"That might be a bit too strong," I said. "But, yes, it does demonstrate the human mind's capacity to compartmentalize. The party that condemns you as a pervert is also the party you believe is best for your business interests. They call themselves Log Cabin Republicans."

"Is that because the sixteenth and arguably our greatest president was rumored to be homosexual?"

"Except Lincoln wasn't. All the heterosexual historians agree he wasn't."

"But I read that as a young man he shared a bed with his best friend for four years."

I assumed a professorial air. "Yes, but, you see, it was customary in the nineteenth century for males to share beds in frontier towns—even though Springfield was no longer a frontier town, and even though Lincoln and his friend Joshua Speed later had other sleeping options."

"Plus, I read that he wrote very passionate letters to this Joshua Speed."

"Yes, but it was not uncommon in the nineteenth century for males to write other males with flowery and effusive terms of endearment, though neither Lincoln nor Speed appear to have written such flowery and effusive letters to their wives, or any women we're aware of."

She leaned closer. "What else?"

"Well, there's also the niggling rumors that a handsome young captain slept in Lincoln's bedroom whenever Mary and the children were away. Of course, this is all just gossip—"

"Which I admittedly love."

"And which was backed up by a number of witnesses. When Carl

39

Sandburg was researching his biography on Lincoln, he found, as he delicately put it, a 'streak of lavender' running through the president's story."

Father Paul was speaking to a couple and waved for us to join them. He wore his clerical collar, though he was no longer affiliated with any church or denomination. He'd left the church, I'd been told, or the church left him. To a number of staff and clients who'd been burned by the church's intolerance, judgment and rejection, he was an antidote, a reminder that Christianity had another face and another heart. We began walking toward him and the two men he was with. They were not just a couple; they could have qualified as twins: both blond, both tanned and gym fit, both dressed in identical royal blue blazers and white slacks, handling their champagne flutes in their right hands while balancing cigarettes in their left.

"Oh, look," said Sandy. "How adorable. I wonder who dressed them?"

"Now, now, behave yourself," I whispered.

Father Paul introduced us to Brandon Chittock, the older "twin," and—I forget his blond, blue-blazered partner's name since Brandon did most of the talking.

"We were just discussing the prevention work you're doing with Steve's team," said Father Paul.

"Yes," said Brandon. "I was telling Father Paul here that I believe the solution to preventing the spread of HIV is in establishing loving and committed relationships." He turned to his clone and they pecked each other on the lips. "Gay men need to grow up and stop all this juvenile screwing around and one-night stands. That would do it. Then it would only be the IV drug users getting infected, and, in truth, we're all much better off without that lot anyway." He looked as smug as his words, confident in his place in the universe and clearly in control of it. I felt myself bristle, but remained quiet, swallowing a gulp of the soda water along with what I wanted to say.

"I'm sure the Prevention Team values committed, monogamous relationships as one way to stop the spread of the virus," said Father

Paul. I didn't look at him or respond to his peace-making comment. I was too busy staring daggers at Brandon, who continued giving us the benefit of his wisdom.

"Oh, I realize our opinions," speaking for both of them, "may be terribly un-PC."

"PC?" asked Sandy. "Personally Courteous?"

He stared at her. "Politically Correct. Not the opinions straitjacketed into the approved views of the day. No, I'm afraid we're far too independent-minded to allow ourselves to be so straitjacketed. Liberals fight for the freedom of expression of views, so long as they are their own politically correct views."

"I respect your views, as your views," said Father Paul sincerely. "People become infected for a complex variety of reasons. Which is why an effective prevention program must be equally complex and varied in its approaches."

"I'm sorry, Father, but after thirteen years, there's no excuse any more to get infected. It's been over ten years since it was determined to be a virus and understood how it was transmitted. Gay men have known how to protect themselves for the past decade, and they haven't. As far as I'm concerned, they've got no one to blame but themselves." He drew on his cigarette, making a big effort of blowing out the smoke as if it required immense thought and concentration.

"It's not like they haven't been warned," agreed Brandon II.

So much for brotherhood. They stopped just short of saying "those people" deserved it, whereby I would have ripped out their cancerous lungs.

"Eventually, one has to grow up and take responsibility for one's actions," Brandon opined from his view on top of Olympus, "and that means accepting the consequences of those actions. In a way, it could be said they deserved what they got."

Perhaps sensing my lung-ripping-out intentions, Father Paul quickly responded. "As I said, the reasons people become infected are many, varied, and complex. Our role is to support those who are infected and to prevent others from becoming infected, without judgment." I stood fuming next to him and sensed that Sandy, by her uncharacteristic silence, was also busy fuming.

"Well, you're a better man than I, Father," Chittock offered. (*Fuck yeah!*) "And out of respect to you, and our dear friend Jerald, I shall make a personal donation to your organization. We only came to support Jerald during his time of penance."

The Brandons exchanged droll smiles, as if saying, *Oh the tales we could tell.* Then he took his partner his champagne flute, placed his cigarette in an ashtray, and took out a leather checkbook and gold-plated pen from his blazer. He wrote the check, blowing on the ink, tore it out, and handed it to Father Paul. I so wanted to say something to these two offensive, un-PC pricks when I became aware of Sandy holding my arm as Father Paul graciously and gratefully accepted the donation "on behalf of those who shall benefit from your generosity."

Brandon II nodded in the direction of the open door.

"Ah, yes," said Chittock. "If you'll excuse us. We're leaving Tuesday for Cancun with another couple, and they just arrived. We still need to coordinate our departures."

"Thank you again for your donation," said Father Paul.

Once they left, I spewed out the breath I'd been holding in. "Insolent, insufferable, insensitive pricks!" I hissed. I hadn't hissed in a long time. Sandy was still holding on to my arm like we were a couple, though her grip was in danger of stopping my blood flow. Perhaps she feared I was going to hurl the bowl of caviar after them. "Now, now," she said, "I can forgive an awful lot of insensitivity if one is willing to contribute to our cause. How much is it?"

Father Paul held up the check. One hundred dollars.

"Why that insufferable prick!" hissed Sandy. "I hope he gets sunburn in Cancun."

I was even more incensed. "That's pocket change to him. It's an insult. I think we should tear it up in front of his face. Show him we don't need his measly charity."

"But we do," said Father Paul, folding the check and slipping it into his pocket. "We do need his measly charity. The people we care about need it. And it is one hundred dollars more than we had before."

"How can you excuse such behavior?"

"It's not my place to excuse or accuse. I try to accept people for where they are, without judging them."

Sandy released my arm. "Honestly, Paul, you should try judging people sometime. It can make you feel really, really good."

He smiled at her. "I'm too great a sinner myself to sit in judgment of others. And I know that people are continually changing. As for Brandon, it's not yet his time."

"His time?"

"To empathize. To understand and feel compassion for others. It's not his time."

"If they ever give Nobel Prizes for niceness, you're a shoo-in," said Sandy.

"I'd still like to tell him what he could do with his 'donation,'" I said.

Perhaps concerned I might say something we would all regret—though giving me immense, if momentary, pleasure—Father Paul remarked, "The balcony has a wonderful view of the city. Why don't you check it out?" Translation: *Cool off before you do or say something harmful to our efforts here.* I saw Sandy nod in agreement, so I set down my glass and walked onto the large balcony, gripping its railing and taking several deep breaths. It *was* a sweeping view of Portland, with Mount Hood shining white and conical in the distance. I tried to focus on the mountain to calm myself.

In a way, it could be said they deserved what they got.

I'd heard that same supercilious, self-righteous attitude before. We were leaving the memorial service in Toorak where we'd sat divided, with Gray's many friends and his many family on separate sides of the aisle, like at a couple's wedding. I was coming down the steps of the Anglican church when I saw his mother standing with two of his older brothers. The oldest was saying in his phlegmy, throaty barrister way, "Grayson knew better. He was raised better than this. He made his bed. Now he must lie in it." I became enraged: *Your brother is dead,*

43

you plump partridge! and felt Rod gripping my arm, holding me back. His mother placed a hand on the partridge's sleeve. "Please, Geoffrey, don't. Not now." Then she turned and saw me. The Gorgon Mother, Gray had called her, dressed all in stylish black, her unnaturally blond hair, her plastic face-lift now covered by large black sunglasses. She had pretended not to know of my existence for all these years (when Gray died, she saw to it that he was still listed in the society pages as one of Melbourne's most eligible bachelors), but now she appeared crushed and my heart went out to her. She left her sons and walked toward me. I offered her a smile, of compassion, of shared sorrow, and was ready to embrace her. Perhaps we could become friends, finally united by the death of the man we both loved.

"You'll never get a dime of Gray's money," she said.

Stunned by her venom, I composed myself. "You look good in black, Samantha. It suits you."

"Great view, isn't it?"

I swung around. An old man was sitting by himself on the balcony in a patio chair, his thin legs crossed, a metal walker next to him.

"Oh hello," I said. "Yes, it's a wonderful view." He wore a strange smile, his narrow face etched with a neatly trimmed beard that failed to hide his sunken cheeks. Although it was a warm day, he was bundled in a heavy sweater with a Christian Dior muffler around his neck and wrapped in a beautifully woven blanket of South American design. I went to him, extending my hand, and introduced myself.

He took my hand. "Oh, I know who you are. We went to high school together. I'm Jerald Sherwood, though you knew me as Jerry."

Jerry Sherwood? It was one of those stutter-moments when you can't think of anything to say. Clearly, I hadn't covered my surprise very well.

"Yes, yes, I know," he said. "I haven't changed a bit."

Overcoming my shock, I sat in the chair next to him. "Sorry I didn't recognize you. You didn't have a beard back in high school."

"No. Nor AIDS."

"No," I mumbled. "Nor AIDS."

"Now *you* I would recognize anywhere. And I just did."

"Well, I don't have a beard." Like me, he was in his late thirties, yet he looked to be in his late sixties. Very late. "I grew the beard to cover the lesions. Typical queen, vain to the very end," he said and gave a dry, hacking laugh. It was a stretch, but I could still see the handsome, popular boy from our high school days. He'd been one of the in-crowd. Went on to an East Coast university, fraternity, finance, MBA, marrying into money. "Welcome to my humble abode."

"It's a beautiful abode," I said, genuinely impressed. "Looks like you did all right for yourself."

"Yes, it's amazing how easy it is to make money when that's all you care about. By the way, I'm a substantial donor to CAP." He raised his eyebrows. "*Substantial.* So be nice to me."

I smiled. "Okay."

He asked me about my life, and I gave a quick rundown on the years since high school: university, graduate school, training in psychotherapy, teaching in Japan, living in Australia for the past ten years. And the reason for my return.

"*You* had a partner?"

"You act surprised."

"Well, I guess. I remember you as the Eternal Loner. Goodness, now that *is* gossip for our twentieth high school reunion." I must have looked alarmed. "Oh, I'm just joking. I won't be alive for it next summer, so don't worry. I'm carrying your secret with me to the grave."

"Oh, here you are." We both looked up to see Steve coming toward us.

Jerald smiled at him. "Hello, Steve. We were just reminiscing about our high school days."

Steve looked at me with surprise. "You knew each other in high school?"

"Yes," I said, "though we ran in different circles."

Jerald turned to me. "I don't remember you having a circle."

I turned to Steve. "It was a very small circle."

"Our graduating class voted him 'Most Likely to Be Marooned on a Desert Island—by Choice.'"

"Though strangely, there's no mention of that in our yearbook," I said.

"You believe me, Steve, don't you? And remember, I'm a substantial donor to your organization."

Steve grinned. "Your sister sent me to find you. She says it's time to call everybody together."

Jerald sighed. "Right then. Let's go welcome them, thank them for their money, and send them home so I can go back to bed."

Steve and I each took an arm so Jerald didn't need his walker and moved slowly toward the door. "It's been a long time since I've had a handsome gentleman on each arm," he remarked. As we entered the house, he turned to me and said, "Let's do lunch this week to catch up on the past twenty years, shall we? I really don't plan anything further out than a week since I'm not sure I'll be here."

"Fine. Where and when?"

"I'll call your office once I've checked my social calendar. I can still command the best tables at the best restaurants in Portland, although these days my lunch consists basically of a half-glass of Ensure."

Chapter Six

Strangers to Ourselves

[Portland, Oregon, April 1994]

On Tuesday, I met Jerald in a small private dining room at the down-town Heathman Hotel. "I thought this would be more intimate," he said. "And so people don't stare." He was dressed fashionably, but the clothes hung loosely, as though he were a human clothes hanger. The servers were all, *Yes, Mr. Sherwood. Of course, Mr. Sherwood. Whatever you need, Mr. Sherwood.* As they scurried to get our drink order, Jerald said, "I admire obsequiousness in people, don't you? Everyone knows me here. Everyone knows me *everywhere.*" Then he added, "I tip big."

I picked up the menu, but he told me not to bother. "I've ordered for you."

"Oh. What did you order?"

"All my favorite dishes."

"*All?*"

"Yes, everything I love here. I can no longer eat them, so I'll enjoy them vicariously through you. That's how I enjoy most things these days."

"I tend to be a light lunch eater."

"Do it for me. Please? I sense this is going to be a long lunch."

And it was. Three hours. I now remember that marathon meal and our discussion (or really, Jerald's monologue) by the courses I was served. Jerald took an occasional sip of broth and nibbled on half a roll. Over my Caesar salad and warm, fresh-baked sourdough bread, he summed up his life, like some opening symphonic overture, setting the tone for what was to come.

"If there were to be an epitaph on my grave, it would read 'He was a jerk'—only because no self-respecting cemetery would allow 'asshole' on its tombstones."

Buttering the bread, I said, "I don't recall you being a jerk in high school."

"I was a jerk-in-training back then."

I put down the butter knife. "I do remember hearing rumors that you got Betsy Morton pregnant."

"Now *that's* not true. It was *she* who got me pregnant. Try to set the record straight at the class reunion, will you?"

"Jerald, you know I don't go to class reunions."

"Just as well. It would probably be too much of a shock to their middle-aged systems to see you."

"I doubt they'd even remember me."

"There you are wrong," he said. I looked up from my salad. "I think they held you in a kind of awe. I know I did. You were one of those unapproachable people made for pedestals. So serious. Always so serious. And so self-contained. You didn't join any club, didn't belong to any group. It was like you didn't *want* to belong, like you didn't need anybody. How strange was that to the rest of us for whom belonging was all that mattered? I mean, what's the point of being part of the in-crowd if the important kids don't want in?"

"I don't think I was an important kid," I mumbled.

"You were one of the leaders at school, though more like the independent congressman with immense credibility and standing and no party affiliation. You seemed to rise above the politics of adolescence."

"I remember high school . . . differently."

"I always thought you were destined to be alone."

I stopped eating. "Looks like you were right."

"How on earth did you ever allow yourself a partner?"

"There was enough space in my relationship with Gray for me to be a loner when I needed to be." I resumed eating. "Anyway, I'm more interested in hearing about your life."

"Ah yes. So where was I?"

"You were a jerk."

"That's right. I was a real jerk. I married after college and cheated on my first wife with other women and blamed her. Then I married again, but it seemed my second wife had the same problem as my first. It took me three marriages, looking for the perfect woman, to realize it wasn't a woman I really wanted."

"How could you not know?"

"Believe me, if we could only harness the power of denial, we'd have a new and perpetual energy source. All those years I thought I was a heterosexual guy who occasionally got it off with men. Sure, I cheated on my wives with men. But I cheated on them with other women, too. Like I said, a real jerk."

Some things don't change. I remembered "Jerry" in high school as a charming, funny raconteur, always quick with some witty commentary: on Mr. Skylar's hairpiece ("I've seen healthier looking road kills"), or which cheerleaders should not be wearing the school colors with their complexions. So, I suppose the signs had been there from the beginning. He was still the entertaining raconteur, though his observations had become less frivolous, his commentary more piercing and trenchant. The tone, too, had changed, from the lighthearted take of a youth with his life stretching before him like an endless horizon to the tired old man sitting across from me now hurtling toward that horizon. Over soup he told me about his coming-out years.

"That's when I found God—the god Eros, I mean. It was quite exhilarating. *This* is what I had been missing! I became a real party boy, and my parties were legendary in the West Hills, my life one continuous round of sex, booze, and drugs. No kidding, if it weren't for AIDS, I'd be dead by now." He laughed, which turned into a coughing spasm.

"Some water?"

He waved his hand as he recovered. "My goal in life was to sleep with every handsome male in Portland, regardless of race, age, or sexual orientation. I would have made it, too, if my time hadn't run out." He leaned back in his chair. "I know, looking at me now, it's hard to believe I was once handsome and desirable." It wasn't. I had envied Betsy Morton in high school. "But you should see the magnificent painting of Dorian Gray I have hanging in my attic. He's still young and beautiful." He reached for his glass of water. "Fuck him."

I had only made it through the soup and salad, and I was already full.

"You'll love the first entrée," said Jerald as a waiter removed my bowl and another refilled my water glass.

"The *first* entrée?"

"Be sure to save room for dessert. It's *delish!*"

Over the first entrée, his party life abruptly came to an end. "AIDS was my wake-up call. I don't know how long I'd been infected. With all the screwing around I was doing it never occurred to me that I could get HIV. I knew, of course, the virus was out there, but like most of us, I guess I just thought it didn't apply to me. I didn't get tested until I was in the hospital with my first opportunistic infection. That's when they told me." He stopped to take a sip of his broth, his third so far. "And that's when I met Cal. By the way, how's he doing?"

"In Providence. Next stop, hospice." With others, I would have tacked on *unfortunately* or *sadly* or something like that. But with another veteran, we tended to dispense with such sentimentalities. Likewise, Jerald didn't engage in the socially appropriate *How sad* or *I'm sorry to hear that.* It was all understood.

"I met Cal at the first AIDS fundraiser I ever attended. I could still hide my status then and pretend I was spurred from some altruistic motive, which, to say the least, would have been out of character for me. Cal was the first person I told. It was he who got me involved with CAP, saying I could still make a positive difference in my time remaining. That was five years ago." He said wistfully as if to himself, "I hope I have."

A waiter removed the remnants of the broiled salmon as another placed a roasted pheasant with sautéed vegetables before me. I stared at it.

"You know, you don't need to eat all of it. I meant for you only to have a taste of my favorites."

That was nice, but as a member of the Clean Plate Club since childhood, I had fully imbibed that peculiar mother logic that if I didn't eat everything on my dish, poor children in China would somehow starve. Over the pheasant, Jerald told me about his life change.

"So, I set about cleaning up my life. Gave up the sex. Gave up the drugs. Gave up the booze. Remained a jerk. I needed to hold onto something of my previous life."

There is this need to tell one's story. I have seen it many times before as one senses the end approaching. I expect it accounts for the plethora of memoirs we see in this self-centered, self-publishing age. It's as if in the telling, people are trying to understand what it was all about, this life they lived. I realized I was the excuse for Jerald to express his thoughts for himself to hear and ponder.

"My diagnosis and meeting Cal shifted something in me. My life was no longer about just pleasure and getting high. I wanted it to *matter* before it was over. Maybe I could do something good with my money and my time. So, I became a volunteer, still pretending my motives were wholly altruistic. I raised big bucks. Even served on a care team and saw firsthand what awaited me.

"And you know, what was most surprising was I didn't miss my former life. It was more like, *What a waste of my time!* Now it all seems like so much fuss and bother. I've come to the conclusion that the best people are those dying. Or maybe it's that people are at their best when dying, although that's not altogether true either. I've known some real assholes who were determined to remain assholes to the very end."

Over the third and fourth entrees, he told me of his experiences on the front lines of the epidemic, and how they changed him.

51

Eventually, as the lesions had started to appear a couple of years ago and he began spending time in the hospital, he could no longer pretend. Over dessert, an extremely creamy crème brûlée, he brought us up to the present.

"My volunteering days are almost over." He paused. "My *days* are almost over."

In earlier years, when someone said that, I would demur, "Oh, no, you've got plenty of time left," or "I hear they're coming out with a new drug. The trials sound very promising," or whatever I could think to say. I had stopped some time ago after I'd found the person was almost invariably right. My words had been to comfort me rather than him.

He paused. "AIDS made me slow down and think about how I was living. I know it sounds trite, but AIDS has given my life meaning."

"From my experience, there's nothing trite about AIDS."

"I'm now working on humility. That's a tough one. But Cal inspired me."

"Cal has inspired many."

"Yes. Unfortunately, we can't all be saints. You need to have some of us sinners to balance the human equation. Actually, a lot of us sinners. I would say 100,000 sinners for every saint. Those are the odds."

He looked fatigued as a waiter cleared the table and I drank my cup of tea.

"I'm ready," he said. "I think Kübler-Ross needs to add another to her stages of dying. After Acceptance, add Fatigue. One gets to the point of just wanting it all to end. No more goals. No more desires. No more struggles. I have no illusions of a heaven or afterlife. The 'peace of the inanimate' sounds pretty good to me these days."

I put down my cup and folded my napkin.

He was nodding in his thoughts. "Strange where life brings us, isn't it? Sort of makes you wonder what it's all been about."

I have often thought back to that distant lunch. We spend this short time on earth—for some, even shorter—and hardly have time to think about our lives as we're living them. And then, seemingly suddenly, seventy years, or eighty years, or thirty-seven years, and it's over before we know it, and we depart like Jerald, wondering what it was all about. He was just more witty and entertaining than most, and perhaps more self-insightful. But then maybe not. I suspect most of us die strangers to ourselves.

Steve had been impressed that Jerald and I were friends in high school. That was Jerald's recollection; I would have said we had a few classes together. He was eager to hear how our lunch went after I waddled back to the office, slumping into my desk chair and renouncing food forever.

"He really is one of our largest donors," said Steve.

"I know. He told me. Several times."

"And he's not as much of a jerk as he likes to pretend. He not only makes large donations to the organization, but he's also personally paid for others' meds when they couldn't afford them. Cal knows that if there's someone in need of help, he can call on Jerald. Are you going to get together again?"

"Probably. But not to eat, I hope."

And we did get together every few weeks as I checked in on how he was doing. One of the last times was in Providence Hospital a couple of months later. I was with Janet, his sister, at his bedside. Jerald had been largely unconscious for the past two days. It was growing late and, at my urging, she'd finally left to go back to her family. "I'll call if anything happens," I promised her. By then I had kept a number of these solo vigils and made a number of calls when something had finally "happened."

I sat in his room, reading, remembering, reflecting on this old, withered man who was my age as I listened to his raspy breathing, and I could still recognize the handsome boy from high school. It seemed like only yesterday. Then around 4:00 a.m., I was dozing when I heard a stirring and jerked awake, opening my eyes just as Jerald was opening his, both of us groggy. He looked around the dimly lit room, appearing confused. Seeing me, he asked, "Am I in heaven?"

"No. Providence Hospital."

"Thank God. I would have been seriously disappointed if this were heaven."

"Would you like some water?"

He nodded. I held the cup as he sucked from a straw, then smacked his lips. "Well, since I'm not in heaven, I might as well eat. I'm hungry for once. See what they have on the menu, will you?"

"Jerald, this is a hospital, not a hotel."

"At what they're charging me, I can order whatever I want whenever I want it."

"I think you have a little more work to do on the humility bit."

"Oh, fuck humility. What good did it ever do me anyway? By the way, what are you doing here? You're not family or any of my many fawning beneficiaries."

"I just happened to be in the neighborhood."

"You just happened to be in the neighborhood. I find that hard to believe."

"And I had nothing better to do on a Saturday night."

"Now *that* I would believe."

"Screw you. So maybe I just wanted to see an old friend off."

He suddenly teared up, his bottom lip quivering, and he whispered, "Now that I would believe, too. Thank you."

Feeling our combined embarrassment at his emotion, I rose from my chair. "I'll go see what they can rustle up around here at four in the morning."

"Yes, do," he said as he dabbed his eyes with the top of his sheet. "Use my name. Tell them I tip big."

He died a week later at home, between one caregiver's leaving and the next caregiver's arrival, several weeks after Cal. Saint and sinner. In the end, they die the same.

There's a coda to this memory. It was a number of months later, in early September, that I was at the front desk helping our receptionist Connie prepare files for an upcoming county audit, when we heard the familiar *ping!* of the elevator and Brandon Chittock stepped out from its doors. I would have bristled had he not appeared as he did—dark circles around his eyes, obviously hadn't shaved in a couple of days, disheveled, dressed in wrinkled shirt and slacks looking like he'd slept in them. He was shattered. He came to the front desk and asked for "the priest who works here. I've forgotten his name." He didn't meet my eyes. Either he didn't remember me, or was too ashamed to remember me.

"Father Paul," said Connie.

"Yes, Father Paul."

"I'll see if he's available."

Father Paul came out from Client Services and greeted him warmly as an old friend, and they went into a counseling room. Connie and I had just finished the files an hour later when they emerged. Clearly Chittock had been crying; his eyes were puffy and red, but he was now calm, his posture once again erect; he was back in control of his emotions, if no longer in control of the universe. Father Paul walked him to the elevator where they exchanged final words and shook hands. Once the elevator doors closed, Father Paul turned and saw me staring. He walked over and said, "Yes."

All my rage and detestation for the man had drained away. I whispered, "He's become infected?"

"No. Not Brandon. His partner."

He handed me an envelope. "You might be interested in this. Then perhaps you'd give it to Franklin."

I opened the envelope and peered inside. It contained a personal check for $100,000. I looked back up at Father Paul.

He said softly, "It's his time."

Chapter Seven

Premonitions of the Past

[Bogong High Plains, April 1986]

"I was lost out here once."

I looked up from my book. "Oh?"

Gray was staring into the fire. "About this time of day. Sun going down. I was maybe ten or eleven."

It was April, early autumn in the antipodes, bringing an early chill to the night. We each had a mug of hot milk tea as dusk settled around us. He said nothing further, so I went back to reading a history of Australia's European beginnings, as the dumping ground for England's convicts and political undesirables. *"Between 1787 and 1868, the Crown sent 825 shiploads of prisoners, with an average of two hundred per ship, to this penal continent, approximately 165,000 convicts within eighty years—"*

"I was collecting wood for that night's fire."

I glanced up again. He was still gazing into the flames, the mug in his hand apparently forgotten. I realized he was in a distant memory and put down my book. "You were collecting firewood," I prompted.

He started, as if just remembering I was there. "The area had been picked pretty clean, so I kept wandering farther and farther away from our camp, finding a dead branch here, another there, until I finally had an armload. The light was fading fast, like now, and I needed to get back. But when I turned around, I couldn't see our camper or tent, or recognize any landmark. I'd wandered so far, in so many directions, that I didn't know where I was."

The night was moving quickly upon us, shouldering the pale daylight aside. The fire glowed brighter against the encroaching darkness, as if rising in our defense.

"I called out for my father and brothers. But the plains were so vast, so endless, they seemed to swallow my shouts." He paused. "They seemed to have swallowed *me*." He again fell silent, lost in the memory.

"What happened then?"

"I just kept wandering, in one direction, then another, carrying my load of wood and calling for somebody. Anybody. But no sounds came back. I was wearing only walking shorts and sweatshirt, and it was getting cold. I knew I'd be without light soon. And out here by myself."

I studied his sharp, flame-lit profile as he gazed into the fire.

"Just as I was starting to panic, I saw a figure in the dusk. A man walking over the plains. Thank God! I'd never been so glad to see anyone in all my life. I dropped the wood and began running after him, yelling as I went. But he didn't seem to hear and kept walking. I tripped over some roots and fell. Got back on my feet, and he was farther away. I was running as fast as I could—and screaming by then—and still he didn't stop, didn't even turn around. So, I kept running and yelling. As I drew closer, I saw he was dressed oddly for this time of year. Autumn, but he was wearing winter clothing, a heavy coat, cap and mask with eye goggles, snow leggings—"

I closed my book. He had my full attention.

"I kept yelling, 'Stop! Stop!,' but he didn't. I was almost out of breath when I tripped again. Just lay there in the dust, panting. And when I got to my feet . . . he was gone. I scanned the horizon in every direction, but there was no sign of him. It was as if he'd vanished into the dusk."

There was a chill, but no longer from the oncoming night. I had an idea where this story was heading.

"I was just about to start some serious crying when, in the direction he'd been heading, I saw it: the top of our camper poking above the heath."

A smile came over his face. "At that point I almost began crying from joy, and I quickly hurried through the brush to our camp, back to my father and brothers." Still smiling, he shook his head. "At the time, it seemed just my dumb luck that, in following that man, I'd found our camp. I figured he must be camping somewhere nearby."

The crackle of the fire became magnified in the silence; the cold evening hunkered down between us, brushing my face. I remained quiet. I sensed the story wasn't finished. It wasn't.

"Several years later—I was at Geelong Grammar, so probably thirteen or fourteen by then—reading for my Australian history class, I came across the 1936 skiing disaster on Mount Bogong. At the end of the account there was this toss-off sentence. I memorized it: 'Over the years, there have been reports of seeing a man, dressed in winter garb, wandering alone on the high plains. Local lore says that it's Cleve Cole's spirit.' I remember going cold reading those words."

I went cold listening to them.

After another silence, I said, "That's . . . well, that's some story. How have people reacted when you've told them?"

He turned to me. "I never told anyone . . . until tonight."

I nodded. "I can understand why."

"I know it sounds far-fetched. But I swear, that time I was lost out here I'd never heard of Cleve Cole. I just saw an oddly dressed man walking over the plains and knew he was my only hope. But now I'm sure."

"Of what?"

He turned back to the fire. "That, like some guardian angel, he was *leading* me, showing me the way back to my camp."

"Interesting," I said, and I returned to my book on Australia's European beginnings with the transportation of convicts. But I was unnerved by Gray's story, as if it held some special meaning or significance I couldn't yet grasp.

And I was right. It would not be the last time Gray saw the ghost of Cleve Cole.

Chapter Eight

Oregon Pioneers

[Portland, Oregon, March 1994]

It was bold. It was daring. It had never been done before.

At the beginning of my second month with CAP, Steve spelled out the challenge at a prevention team meeting: Gay men in Portland were not showing up to test for HIV at the public health sites. "The county wants us to get more guys to test," he said. Since the county's grant paid a big chunk of the agency's prevention budget, we understood this "request" was to be taken seriously.

"It's not going to happen," said Chad. "We're not going to convince guys to go into the health department and get tested."

"Chad's right," Lionel said. "They don't trust the health department. It's government."

"But, my God," exclaimed Steve, "half the nurses there are gay men!"

"Doesn't matter," Chad said. "It's an image problem."

Steve tossed the memo into the center of the table. "Well, they're building it into our contract, so we better find a way to deliver. The feds are pressuring the state, the state's pressuring the county, and the county's pressuring us."

"Great, so what do we do?" said Chad. "Go home and yell at our dog?"

"I didn't know you had a dog," said Lionel.

"Shut up, will you? It's like a metaphor or something."

"No, this is important," Steve said. "We need to know how the epidemic is playing out here in Oregon. We've only got anecdotal information and the numbers of those who've already advanced to full-blown AIDS. And guys need to know their status so they don't infect their brothers." Brothers. That was Steve-talk. Coming from anyone else, it might sound corny or phony, but in Steve's world we were all brothers. Personally, I didn't believe the fractious political groups making up the so-called gay so-called community were brothers, but I appreciated that he did.

There were five of us on the prevention team. Each member had specific responsibilities. Chad, a psychology major at Portland State University, coordinated the men's discussion groups. Puppy dog cute, he was one of those people who exudes sexuality. He had introduced himself to me as the "Prevention Team slut." Like Steve, he was HIV-positive but, unlike Steve, had begun to show symptoms and was now taking eighty-plus pills a day. Nonetheless, he didn't let that slow him down from being the poster boy for safer sex ("I give lots of demonstrations"), emphasizing that one can be HIV-positive and still have a fulfilling sex life. "*Very* fulfilling," Lionel always added. African American, six foot two, of which 98 percent was muscle, Lionel coordinated the bar outreach program. Andie was the program assistant ("the token woman," she called herself). Super organized, she kept the team on task and timelines. Still in her early twenties and pretty, she was forever falling in and out of love. "I'm in love with Chad," she confided to me when we first met.

"Chad? Isn't he—"

"Yeah. All the men I fall in love with are gay."

"Have you considered maybe expanding your social circle?"

And then there was Leo. Like me, he was new to the team. Twenty years old, he was an extremely handsome—*beautiful* some would say—Mexican American developing an outreach program to the street kids, having been one himself not long ago. He had straightened out his life over the past two years and was now attending Portland Community College. I'd been told he had some connection to Sandy.

"Okay," said Steve, "let's brainstorm ideas on to how to get guys to test. Remember, this is brainstorming. Say the first thing that comes to your mind. No idea is too dumb or too outrageous." Andie went to the whiteboard to write down the ideas.

Lionel raised his hand. "We could offer a free blow job with each test."

Steve stared at him. "Now *that's* a dumb idea. Any serious ideas?"

Lionel mumbled, "It was the first thing that came to my mind."

Without their hearts in it, the team began tossing out ideas.

"We could pass out coupons so guys can test for free," Leo offered.

"They've tried that," said Steve. "It's not a money issue. It's a trust issue."

Lionel tried again. "How about with every test, you get a free pass to the baths."

"Isn't that kind of like handing out matches and gasoline to prevent fires?" said Chad.

"Is that another metaphor?"

"So what's your idea?" Steve asked Chad.

He thought. "Maybe you get a coupon for a free drink at Silverado with each test. The owner there supports our work."

"Oh, sure," said Andie. "Ply them with alcohol and further dull their powers of judgment."

"Okay, okay," said Steve. "More ideas."

"Steve, face it," said Chad. "It's not going to work. No one wants to go to the health department where they have to admit they're gay or may have had unsafe sex."

Lionel agreed. "Being tested by the health department is like getting a physical exam from your mom."

The team was collectively squirming at the thought when it

suddenly came to me.

"So, we'll do it."

The others looked at me.

"Do what?"

"*We'll* test gay men."

"What do you mean?" asked Steve.

"We develop and train a team of volunteers, all gay men, and offer HIV counseling and testing here once a week in the evening. We'll devise some ID system so guys can test anonymously. We'll keep their names, and the health department gets the test results."

"Neat idea," said Chad, "but the county'll never allow nonprofessionals to do the testing."

"If they want test results badly enough, they might. Especially if they can oversee the testing."

Steve was intrigued. "You might have something. Do you know any precedent for this? Anywhere testing is being done by volunteers? Bureaucrats love precedents."

"I could do a lit search when I'm at school tomorrow," offered Chad.

"Or maybe we pitch it differently," I said. "*We* will be the precedent."

"Yeah, like a pilot," said Leo.

Andie jumped in. "We'd be pioneers. This is Oregon. Pioneers are part of our history."

"What 'our' history?" said Lionel. "You're from Ohio."

The team became excited. It was an innovative concept—even daring for its time—to train and equip the target population to test their own people. We would provide a safe space for gay men where the counseling and testing would be done by their own "brothers." Steve immediately left to call and propose the idea to the county's HIV Program manager.

He came back to us the following day. I was right: bureaucrats are by nature timid. They don't like to take risks. But they were also desperate to produce the results the feds wanted. And with his natural enthusiasm and Boy Scout wholesomeness, Steve was the perfect person to pitch the idea. If he believed in something, he could convince anyone. And he believed in this idea.

"They want to try it. They'll build it into our contract and provide extra funding. We've got one year to show results. They've assigned their head epidemiologist to work with us. Arthur's a gay man himself, and he supports the idea. He'll handle the technical aspects of the training and the phlebotomy—"

"The what?" asked Lionel.

"Blood draws. They'll assign a phlebotomist to us who will also be a gay man. Our job is to recruit, screen and train a team of volunteers to handle the counseling part. They want this program up and running by Pride Weekend."

Chad whistled. "That's only three months from now."

Steve turned to me. "I want you to coordinate this program. It was your idea."

"I'll get started immediately."

But where to start? All I knew about HIV testing was from the wrong end of a needle. The next day I met with the epidemiologist to piece together how such a program could work. Arthur reminded me of a Swiss watchmaker: slightly stooped, pleasantly plump with a pink complexion, a walrus moustache, and gentle sleepy eyes. Though only in his mid-forties, he was already bald with a curly fringe of blond-white hair. Next, I placed an announcement in the newspaper, describing the project and calling for volunteers. Within two days forty men had applied, and we set up interviews for the following week. I decided we'd select twelve candidates so that, allowing for dropouts, we would end up with a team of ten. Those not selected could be held in reserve for the next training and a second team. I'd design the counseling curriculum and, along with Arthur, oversee the ten-week training.

Steve pulled me aside. "This is big. It's not just the county. The state and feds are watching how it goes, too. Andie's right: We're going to be pioneers!"

Arthur and Steve joined me for the interviews the next week. Because of the tight timeline, we would conduct group interviews, roughly eight candidates each night. It would also give us an idea how they'd work in a team as they interacted with the other candidates and answered a series of questions: Why do you want to volunteer for this program? What experience have you had with HIV? Have *you* been tested?

Not surprising, a large number of helping professions were represented: gay men who were teachers, nurses, social workers, counselors. We could have staffed the team with only nurses, which Arthur favored. But Steve and I wanted the program to reflect the diversity of the gay community, with counselors who were African American, Latino and Asian, as well as the different "types" of gay men. "I want counselors guys can identify with," Steve was saying as we watched the first group of candidates gather in the lobby, "from the super butch to the flaming queen."

It was at that moment the elevator doors opened and Lukas flamed in. "Bonjour, everyone!" he announced with outspread arms. All heads turned. "I have arrived!" He was one of those people who doesn't enter a room so much as invades it, bringing his own band, fanfare and spotlight with him. Mid-twenties, slender to the point of being skinny, dressed in slacks and a neon pink satin shirt, he was already going around greeting men there, half of whom he seemed to know.

I turned back to Steve. "I think we just filled the Flaming Queen slot."

We began the interviews. I asked each applicant to introduce himself. Lukas immediately launched forth. He was a walking stereotype, worked in a fashionable hair salon on Broadway and performed as a drag queen at Darcelle's on the weekends. ("Many of you know me as

Lady Bianca.") Reviewing Lukas's application, Arthur asked, "You list 'medical' under interests. Do you have medical experience?"

"Well, I just *adore ER*. I've seen every episode twice!" The group chuckled.

"So, you're interested in medicine?"

"No, I'm interested in the hunky doctors." Arthur stared at him as the others guffawed.

Steve said, "A number of gay men are deaf, and we need to do a better job of reaching out to them. Lukas, I see on your application that you sign."

"Some. Enough for basic communication."

"How basic?"

"Well, I know," *flurry of fingers*, "Do you come here often?" and, *flurry of fingers*, "Take me home with you.'" Steve stared at him, much like Arthur had. "I also know the alphabet."

"Well, it's a start," said Steve.

One hundred eighty degrees from Lukas was John, a retired Air Force colonel in his late fifties. Sitting ramrod straight in his chair, he introduced himself by declaring that he wasn't gay. So why was he here? He wanted to volunteer, wanted to offer what he could, because he had a gay son living in Los Angeles. It was his way of supporting his son. He looked uncomfortable as he spoke. How would guys coming in to test feel with him? I listened politely as he responded to our questions, but had already scratched him off the list.

Many of the candidates had lost friends or lovers to AIDS; all wanted to make a difference, to do something; perhaps they could keep others from becoming infected.

At the end of the evening, after the candidates left, the three of us discussed them and what each might bring to the program. Arthur had reservations about Lukas. "I'm not sure he has the right professional attitude for this."

"I understand what you're saying," I said, "but it may help to have a social butterfly on the team."

"Social butterfly? He's an entire *swarm*."

"And we may need some comic relief," said Steve. Arthur reluctantly assented. In the months ahead, Lukas would be the glue holding our team together, the court jester willing to play the fool, bringing wit and humor to work that would have its grim moments.

I had two concerns among that first evening's candidates. Tyler was a sophomore at Portland State University, a sweet-faced kid, eager as a pup, and it couldn't have been more obvious if he wore a sign around his neck: VIRGIN. "He's only nineteen. I think he's too young for this."

"Leo's only twenty," said Steve.

"Steve, there's no comparison. Leo was living on the streets when he was fifteen. Tyler comes from Lake Oswego, for god sake. And just look at him. He's going to get hit on by every guy who comes in here."

Steve was philosophical. "The kid's going to have to grow up sooner or later. And it's better he learns to say *no* here than in the bars. Besides, if we want to draw young guys to test, we should have young guys on the team." Arthur agreed.

My second concern was John. "I'm not sure about our retired colonel. I wonder whether he can remain neutral and nonjudgmental."

Arthur shared my concern, but Steve said, "I'd like to give him a chance."

"Are you sure? I think guys won't feel comfortable with him. And him with them. I advise against bringing him on."

"It's your program and your team, but I'd ask you to give him a try. You'll have ten weeks of training to see if he's appropriate or not. And he may wash out anyway."

"Why do you want him?"

"I think it would be good to have an older man on the team. And he kind of reminds me of my dad. I know how hard it would be for my father to do something like this. I'd like to think someone would give my dad a chance."

Arthur gave me a nod-shrug. It was against my better judgment, but like the rest of the prevention team, if Steve asked me to march into Hell with him, I'd only want to know what I should pack. "Okay.

We'll see how he does."

He flashed his boyish grin. "Thanks. I owe you one."

By the end of the week, we had interviewed all the candidates and selected nine to start the training—joined by Chad, Leo, and Lionel from the prevention staff, who Steve wanted to be involved—so we had our twelve. Now the work to shape them into a team would begin.

Chapter Nine

"We few, we happy few, we band of brothers"

[Portland, Oregon, April 1994]

In the first session of the training program, Steve welcomed the group with his usual cheerleader enthusiasm. "You will be making a real difference," he told them. "You'll be saving the lives of your brothers. We can stop this epidemic in Oregon because of volunteers like you." I noticed the change in the room's atmosphere as he spoke, people sitting up straighter, a certain swelling with pride. Steve always had this effect upon people. He ended by thanking them for being part of this effort that had never been tried before. "You are going to be pioneers!"

We began with self-introductions. The colonel led off. "Hi, my name's John. I'm not gay." *Hoo boy. Great start.* My eyes slid over to Steve, who smiled and shrugged his shoulders as if to say, *We've got ten weeks.* It was very important to John that everyone know he was not queer. "But I have a gay son, and I'm here because of him." The group welcomed him.

Next to John was a handsome, dark-eyed fellow. "Hi. My name's Marco." (Lukas whispered to Chad, "Love to see his Polo.") Marco shared that he was HIV-positive and in a monogamous relationship with his partner, Terry, who was negative.

Lukas's self-introduction was animated and entertaining. He began by sharing that he came from a small town "forty miles and fifty years north of Portland." After he'd been speaking for eight minutes and only gotten to his coming out in first grade, I feared we were going to get his complete and unabridged life story. I interrupted him. "Excuse me, Lukas. We need to move on."

"But I'm not finished."

"I know. But in the interest of time, this is only a ten-week training."

After the others introduced themselves, I gave an overview to the program: Arthur would handle the technical information and procedural part; I would handle the counseling and team building. They were each provided a thick binder on HIV and AIDS and standard counseling procedures, and later would be divided into practice teams. I emphasized that everything shared here was confidential, as it would be in the counseling rooms, with the exceptions that we were required to report any instances of sex with minors or a person who by his words was threatening to harm himself or another.

"It's not our role to judge. We're here to help." I was speaking to John. "And to do that we have to build trust with each person who comes in. That means being nonjudgmental of sexual behaviors that might be foreign to us."

"I can't imagine any that'd be foreign to me," said Lukas.

Each session would be divided into one hour of technical training on HIV/AIDS, and one hour on basic counseling techniques and team building, during which they could ask other members of the group any personal question they wished. The one being asked could choose not to answer.

In their second session, Marco asked the colonel, "How long were you in the military?"

"Thirty-five years."

"Oh, I love men in uniforms, too!" burbled Lukas.

The others laughed but John just bristled. I suspected he'd be doing a lot more bristling over these coming weeks. "I'm not gay," he said, in case anyone had forgotten.

Reggie, a young Black computer programmer, asked Lukas if that was his real name.

"No. I chose it. I wanted to call myself Tom Cruise, but that name was already taken. I loved the 'cruisey' part."

It came John's turn. He was clearly uncomfortable as he addressed Lukas. "Have you always been like this?" The "this" was understood.

"Yes!" Lukas squealed. "*Always!* Isn't it wonderful?!"

The others chuckled and laughed, but John just stared at him. It wasn't so much a look of disapproval as of distaste, so I decided to put them on the same practice team.

In the third session, we began counseling techniques appropriate for HIV testing. The twelve participants would be divided into their practice teams. Before that evening's session, Arthur and I met with Chad, Leo and Lionel, who would each be assigned to a different group.

"The role-playing the volunteers will be doing can be emotionally intense," said Arthur. "It's important that we staff maintain professional boundaries."

"Professional boundaries?" asked Lionel.

"I mean that we not become emotionally or sexually involved with the volunteers."

Chad meekly raised his hand. "Uh, too late."

Arthur looked at him. "Oh. Well, we'll put you and the other fellow in different practice groups. Who is it?"

He looked sheepish. "Darren." After Leo, probably the handsomest guy in the group.

"You dog, you!" said Lionel, punching him on the shoulder.

"Okay," said Arthur, "so we'll put Darren—"

"And Frank."

" . . . Okay. So, we'll put Darren and Frank—"

"And Reggie."

Arthur stared at him.

"And Lukas."

Exasperated, Arthur said, "Are there any of the volunteers you *haven't* bedded?"

Chad thought. "Um, John, the straight guy."

"Thank God," breathed Arthur.

We began the first hour with team building. By this time, they were becoming more daring with their personal questions, and when it came John's turn, he asked, "I'm just interested: Have any of you ever had sex with a woman?"

All shook their heads. Except Lukas, who shot his hand into the air like an excited kid with the answer to the algebra problem. "I have! I have!" he shouted. "Four, maybe five times. It was great!" Then he looked at the others staring at him. "Okay, so I admit I occasionally get off on kinky sex."

The team members laughed, but John was appalled. "*Maybe* four or five times. You don't know?"

"I might have been a little inebriated on those occasions."

"All right," I said. "Your turn, Lukas."

He turned to John. "Have you ever had sex with a man?"

John immediately shifted into bristle-mode, arms crossed, insulted even to be asked. "No. Never."

Lukas studied him for a moment. "Let me amend the question. Have you ever had sex *with another boy?*"

We saw the colonel redden, a flush rising to his face, his brain stalling. He cleared his throat. "Once."

"Bingo!" Lukas cried. "So, we're both experienced in the ways of the other."

The group was laughing. Still red, John explained, "We were two thirteen-year-olds fooling around."

"Oh, I just *adore* fooling around!" said Lukas.

Later, as we wrapped up that hour, John confessed, "I've never told anyone—not my wife, not my gay son—about . . . about that time." There seemed to be a melting going on in the group, a warmth and acceptance being shown toward him.

I said, "Thank you, John. For your honesty. And for trusting this group with that information. I remind everyone that what we share here remains confidential." The others nodded soberly. Lukas made a zipping motion across his mouth.

Following the break, Arthur began training them in how to ask the required questions in a direct and nonjudgmental way. He demonstrated the technique, and they began practicing in pairs, using the pretest questionnaire. I kept my eye on John as I floated around the room, listening and observing.

"In the last thirty days have you engaged in oral sex?" "In the last thirty days have you engaged in anal sex?" "In the last thirty days . . ."

But he was good. He stayed with the script, kept his tone professional and neutral, didn't stutter or gag at behaviors that must have been exotic to him. I was impressed. It turned out the greater challenge was keeping certain of the other volunteers to a professional and neutral manner.

"My God! Five guys in one night?" shouted Lukas. "That even beats my record!"

"Uh, Lukas . . . " Arthur began gently. "Try not to editorialize."

"Oh, sorry." He sat up straight, held his questionnaire in front of him, and resumed. After ten minutes, they switched partners for the next set of questions.

"Oh, honey, I love your shirt. Where did you get it?"

"Lukas, stay focused on why you're there with the client," said Arthur.

"But I'm establishing rapport!"

"Yes, well, keep your rapport-establishing to a minimum, please."

On some things, it was Arthur who had to adapt. Lukas was asking his "client" in the role play, "Within the last thirty days have you engaged in . . . oral-anal sex—What is that, anyway?"

"Rimming," said Arthur.

"Then why don't we just say rimming?"

"It's advised that in these settings we use clinical terms rather than the street terms."

"But we all know what the street terms mean."

The others agreed. If the point was to make gay men feel comfortable with us as other gay men (excepting John), we should use our own language, they argued. I nodded to Arthur, supporting the team, and he acquiesced on this point. It would be acceptable—here only—to use street terms.

The training proceeded. After switching partners again, Lukas asked Frank, "In the past thirty days have you engaged in sex with other men in public venues?"

"Yes. Up in Washington Park."

"The Fruit Loops? Which part?"

"Behind the tennis courts in the woods."

"Oh, is that any good? I haven't tried it there—"

"Ah, Lukas. Focus, please?" said Arthur.

Lukas took a big breath, sat up straight in his chair, then winked at Frank, whispering, "We'll talk later."

Next, John and Lukas were paired up, John looking distinctly uncomfortable. "Well, let's get to it."

Lukas gave a brisk salute. "*Oui, mon Colonel!*"

I was waiting for John to request a different partner, or a different practice team—any team without Lukas—but he didn't. He got right into the questionnaire. "Do you know your blood type?"

"Um, red?"

Before John left that night, I checked in with him as he was putting on his coat. "How's it going?"

He smiled, shaking his head. "It's an education, all right. I'm beginning to understand the meaning of vanilla sex."

"You're going to learn more about gay sex than you might want to know."

"No, no, it's fine. As the Roman poet Terence said, 'Nothing human is strange to me.'" He glanced over at Lukas. "At least, not anymore."

"Yeah, well, I doubt Terence ever spent a night on the Fruit Loops."

By the fourth session, I noted a certain warming up to each other. John, too, was becoming more relaxed, and I could see all of them beginning to cohere into a team. They were avid to learn about HIV/AIDS and proper counseling techniques. Arthur was still having misgivings about Lukas.

"Lukas, don't flirt with the clients."

"I wasn't flirting. I was bonding."

"Then don't *bond* with the clients. You don't have time."

And increasingly, as I predicted, Lukas became the glue holding the team together with his wit and whimsy and willingness to be outrageous.

Arthur began, "Tonight we're going to be discussing issues facing sero-discordant couples."

Lukas looked up from his notepad. "Sero-discordant?"

"Where one person is positive and the other negative, like Marco and his partner, Terry."

Lukas shook his head. "Do you lie awake at night thinking up these terms?"

For the team building in the second hour, I divided them into two groups and had them talk about their families.

"My mother's been wonderful," said Lukas. "She admits she dresses much better now because of me. Our family, you see, has been fashion-challenged for generations."

"And what about your father?" asked Chad, who was facilitating that group.

"Oh, my father's ashamed of me. Has been all my life. I'm a great embarrassment to him. But then, he is to me as well. Absolutely no sense of taste!" His group, with the exception of John, laughed.

"So, your father doesn't accept you as gay?" said Chad.

"My father doesn't accept me as *anything*. You'd think he'd have gotten over it by now. Like, maybe I'll still turn butch someday?" He added in a sing-song voice, "I don't think so."

"Same with my dad," said Reggie. "Supposedly because the Bible says it's an abomination."

"Oh, my dad tried that on me, too," said Lukas, "but, really, he doesn't know the New Testament from the Old. He couldn't tell Luke from Leviticus."

John cleared his throat. "Maybe if . . ." All heads turned to him. "Maybe if you tried to act a little more . . . well . . ."

Lukas sat back in his chair, theatrically crossing his arms and legs, which, given his string-bean frame, made one think of how pretzels must be made. "Yesssssssss?"

"Maybe more . . . you know."

"Mas-cu-line?"

"Yes."

He immediately unwound himself. "Oh, I tried that. Honestly, I did. When I was younger, I tried to walk like other boys, tried to control my hands from flying around. I went out for all the sports at school until the coaches begged me not to. Tried to show interest in "guy" things. Dad would be telling our neighbor the Portland Trail Blazers won their game last night, and I'd say, 'Fabulous! How many touchdowns did they score?'"

Then, for the first time in these four weeks together, we saw Lukas's flippant and flamboyant manner fade. "I wanted him so much to love me. I would have done anything for his approval. But by the time I was fifteen, I stopped trying. I knew it was hopeless. I was this way, for whatever reasons, and knew I couldn't be any different." He took a deep breath and set his shoulders. "So, I decided then and there that my father would just have to learn to accept me as I am." A sadness washed over his features. "But he never did."

"Your father's still not able to accept you?" asked Chad, who I could tell was practicing Active Listening from his psychology course.

"When I go home to visit Mom now, he walks out of the room. I don't think we've said more than ten words to each other in as many years."

"Thanks for sharing," said Chad.

I watched John watching Lukas and thought I saw genuine commiseration on his face—for Lukas's father. Was he thinking, *Thank God, at least my son is a man?*

Steve usually dropped in each night before he left for home, sometimes observing part of the sessions. I could tell he was pleased with how the team was developing. He stayed the entire evening on the fifth night when we conducted a midway evaluation. The feedback was very positive: Every member was enjoying the training, felt he was learning new and important skills and knowledge, with John adding that the program had spiced up his and his wife's sex life. "We've tried out a number of, uh, behaviors I'd never thought of before. Now, when I come home from training, Maggie often has candles burning, my dinner on the table, dressed in her negligee, greeting me at the door with a glass of wine. She's fully supportive of my volunteering." To which the group clapped, hooted and cheered, and John broke out into a wide smile. He was becoming one of the boys.

Later, in the team-building portion, I divided them into two groups, where John once again mentioned "my gay son."

"You always refer to him that way. Like, that's his only quality?" asked Chad.

"No. No, he has many fine qualities."

"For example?"

"He's probably the brightest of my sons, certainly the most sensitive, sensitive to other people's feelings. Has been since he was a child. I feared for him back then, that he'd be hurt by people not as sensitive as he was. But I needn't have worried. He also has a strong inner core."

"Sounds like you love him."

John looked surprised at the statement. "Of course I love him. I love all my sons."

"I believe you. Have you told him or any of your sons that?"

John admitted he'd not told any of his sons he loved them since they were children. "It would embarrass them and me. And besides, they know it."

"Oh, how do they know?" asked Chad.

"It's understood. Always has been." He crossed his arms, signaling Chad not to take this any further.

Chad shifted focus to the group, asking, "How many of your fathers have told you they love you since you were twelve? Raise your hands."

Not one of them raised his hand. Chad turned back to the colonel. "At least you're not alone, John. It's a father-son thing. I'm sure it's understood."

Floating between the two groups, listening in, I realized that I would have been the only one who could have raised his hand. Dad in the emergency room, his eyes glassy, face red, looking so incredibly distraught as he stared at his eighteen-year-old son lying there, coming out of the intentional drug overdose. He'd said the words, but I hardly heard them, drugged up on the drugs they'd given me to counteract the drugs I'd given myself. And feeling shitty because I'd failed in the attempt to end this life he and Mom had given me. Dad said the words but I shifted my head away, just wanting to sleep and be left alone. I've thought back to that moment many times over the years. It was a lost opportunity. He never said it again.

I turned away from the group, closing my eyes. *Father, forgive me.*

――― ――― ―――

Providence Hospital, Portland, Oregon

Her fingers caress the rosary beads, lips moving silently in prayer. I'm surprised to find an older woman sitting across from me, facing me. I didn't see her come in. Weathered, worn face, salt-and-pepper hair draping over her shoulders, she wears a shapeless dark dress and shawl. Latina, my guess.

And she's staring at me.

I sit up, jerking into a smile of greeting. But nothing comes back. No social acknowledgment, no awkward, embarrassed turning aside. Nothing. She just stares at me, and my eyes dart away, as if *I* had been the one caught looking. I sneak a peek back.

Still staring.

It creeps me out. I notice the room's gone cold, like someone left a window open, except these hospital windows don't open. I squirm under her blank, unblinking gaze. She seems not to be looking at me so much as *through* me. As if I were a ghost, someone physically here once but no longer. I wonder if I've slipped between dimensions again.

Her gaze is becoming uncomfortable. I want to get up and leave the room. And find I can't. I'm frozen in my chair! I shudder at the realization: *She's a witch.* She's put a hex on me, like those animals in *The Chronicles of Narnia,* turned into statues by the evil witch. What was her name? (You'd think at a time like this I'd remember something as important as the name of the evil witch of Narnia!) I also realize I'm getting a little dopey from lack of sleep.

And she's still staring at me!

It's then I notice the woven bag in the chair next to her. Protruding from it is a folded white cane.

She's blind?

Oh, for crying out loud!

My whole mental landscape shifts. Instead of panic, I'm feeling like a fool, which is not really much of an improvement. Okay, so she's not a witch. She's just an old blind woman saying her rosary in the waiting room of a city hospital. I must be losing it. I feel I should apologize. *Sorry I thought you were a witch. Nothing personal. You just look like one.* I realize this is one of those times it's probably better I keep my mouth shut. Her unblinking gaze is still unsettling, even if she can't see me.

Turns out she's not only not a witch, but she's not all that old either, not as old as I first thought. Maybe only a few years older than me, but life has not been kind to her. I can see she was once beautiful; the traces are still there. My eyes fall to the rosary in her hands. A slow, steady, unhurried grace to her movements, a rhythm, a tempo I find calming. My breathing slows as I watch the fingers pray, holding a bead for a moment. Then moving on to the next. And then the next. And another, and I ease into the relaxed rhythm. The crucifix dangles from her palm, Christ suspended in space and time, arcing back and forth like a metronome, as her fingers touch, caress, fondle, bless each bead.

Movement in the room.

My eyes flutter open. A young police officer carrying a cup of vending machine coffee nods to me, then takes a seat against the wall. I nod in response and turn back to—

The old woman is gone.

Her chair, empty. I must have dozed off and she left. I hope her prayers were answered. I check my watch—more than twenty-five hours since I last really slept—and rub my face, glancing over at the officer. He's staring at the floor, unmindful of my presence. I recognize him from the eleven o'clock newscast: *"The primary witness in the FBI's investigation was shot this afternoon by an unknown assailant and is at this hour reported to be in critical condition . . ."* Officer Blake O'Connor. I suspect I know why he's here. He sits, lost in thought. Thinking he could have been the one now lying in the ICU? Or maybe that he could be next? Nice-looking fellow. Looks younger than his photo on TV. Probably mid-twenties at most. The newspaper says he's the son and grandson of police officers. And now a witness in the Department of Justice's investigation into police corruption in Portland. Praised by the mayor and police chief for his courage and integrity, he's become a pariah within the force for breaking their code of silence. Given the option of administrative leave with pay, he chose to remain on the job. Rumors say he now rides solo in his patrol car, that no one will ride with him. I hope the rumors are untrue. But here he is, in uniform, and alone. I suspect his career in law enforcement is over.

The radio on his belt squawks, sounding grotesquely loud in the quiet space. He quickly turns down the volume. "Sorry," he says.

"You don't need to listen to it?"

"I'm on break. Just stopped in to check on someone."

"Is he still in critical condition?" I ask, signaling I know who he is and who the "someone" is he's checking on.

He nods. "Yeah. And you?"

"I'm waiting to see if a friend makes it through the night."

"Sounds serious."

"Yes . . . he's in critical condition, too."

"Sorry." He takes a drink of coffee.

After a pause, I say, "I admire what you did. This can't be easy for you."

He gazes at the floor again. "I can't talk about it."

"Of course."

Then he looks up. "You're not a reporter, are you? I hope to God you're not another reporter."

I smile. "No. I'm a counselor. And I hear a lot that's confidential—and that remains confidential with me." *And I know all about the investigation. I was there at the beginning. I was there before there was an investigation.*

Not meeting my eyes, he speaks softly even though we're the only ones in the room. "It's not just me. There were others going to testify, too. Several of us were coming forward to tell what we knew to the investigators. But the others changed their minds." He stares into his cup. "I don't blame them. They've got families." I notice he wears no wedding band. "And there is some risk."

"So, why didn't you? Change your mind?"

Even though he's no doubt "lawyered up" not to speak, he seems relieved to be talking.

"I knew what was going on. We all did. This investigation gave us the chance to tell what we knew. And I couldn't let the citizens of Portland think that all cops are bad apples." He meets my eyes. "Most of the officers I work with are good and decent, brave, dedicated men and women. The best."

I hold his gaze. "I don't doubt that for a minute."

His face flushes as he turns away.

"I hope your father and grandfather are proud of you."

"My grandfather is. And my father . . . he understands. He's just worried."

He suddenly looks embarrassed and straightens up in his chair. "I've said more than I should." He checks his watch. "I need to get back on duty."

As he stands, I say, "On behalf of the citizens of Portland . . . thank you."

Again, not meeting my eyes, he nods. "I hope your friend comes through this."

"Thanks."

As he leaves the waiting room, I whisper, "I hope you do, too."

Chapter Ten

Underworld Tours

[Portland, Oregon, April 1994]

Long before Hell, there was Hades.

That was my thought as we walked down West Burnside on a late Sunday night in April. For the ancients, the underworld was a place peopled by the shades of the once living, a gray realm of gray non-beings. Hell was a later invention, introduced in the time of the Romans as a realm of torment and perpetual punishment and was quickly embraced by the early Christians. It sounded like their kind of place . . . for others. Burnside on a Sunday night is more Hades than Hell, and Leo was my guide into this shadowy underworld of the not-dead and the no-longer-living.

We had just started the counseling and testing training when Leo invited me to "walk the streets" with him. He had been hired to develop an outreach program to street youth, to prevent them from becoming infected and the next victims of the epidemic. "Sure," I'd said. "Be glad to."

The drizzle, a fine spray, kept everything damp and chilled, insinuating itself under my jacket, creeping down my collar even as I shoulder-hunched against the night. I wore a baseball cap for some protection. Leo had only a sweatshirt with a hood, but seemed indifferent to the cold and the wet. He walked silently next to me, shoulders back, hands in his pockets, with a graceful, fluid movement. A handsome, slender Mexican American from eastern Oregon, he had the face of an angel—but an angel who'd been to Hell. Often. I'd been impressed with him from the first meeting of the prevention team, by his quiet dignity, by the way he spoke, softly, thoughtfully amid the loud and boisterous staff, and with a vocabulary one wouldn't expect from someone of his street background. Like most of us at CAP, this wasn't a job to him; it was a personal crusade. The street kids were his cause. He had been one of them.

He and Steve regularly knocked heads about what the program should be accomplishing. Steve would probably have fired him if not for Leo's connection with Sandy. At the beginning of my third month at the agency Steve asked me to work with Leo: *"Maybe he'll listen to you."* Fortunately, Leo had already invited me to go out and walk the streets with him. "Steve's a good man," he told me. "He means well, but he doesn't understand." (*"Leo's a good kid, but he doesn't get it."*) I'd listened to Leo vent his frustration. "These street kids are nothing like the Boy Scouts and cheerleaders Steve grew up with. They don't need a caseworker; they need a friend." (*"Leo's unable to separate himself from the kids. He's supposed to be an outreach worker, not their pal."*) "The problem is white, middle-class types thinking like white, middle-class types," said Leo. "They have their neat little ideas of right and wrong, black and white, and how the world should be. And the streets don't fit into that world." (*"Leo's enabling them. They're not going to change unless they have the incentive to change."*) I was in the unenviable position of seeing the validity of both their arguments. "I don't blame Steve," Leo said. "He wants strategies based on what he knows, on what would work *for him*. But this is a whole different culture, and it doesn't fit into the county's categories of what can be 'measured.'" (*"I can't just tell the county we're 'talking' to the kids or 'building trust.' I need to show them something. What are they getting for the taxpayers' dollars?"*)

As we walked along, I hoped I looked suitably grungy. I certainly felt it. Leo had encouraged me to "dress down" for the tour, so I hadn't shaved the past three days, had found ripped jeans and a ragged jacket to wear. Not having a shirt sufficiently shabby, I scrounged one from the bag of clean rags in my father's garage. It wasn't until putting it on later that I realized it smelled strongly of turpentine.

Few people were out this late. A group of twenty-somethings emerged from a club, laughing, chattering, passing a sixty-something pushing a grocery cart stuffed with her pathetic belongings. The street lamps seemed less for illumination than for creating atmosphere—a heavy, brooding mood—where sounds were both heightened and dulled by the darkness and the cold. Drippy, glaring lights reflected off the glistening streets as if they'd been run over.

A police car was approaching, slowly moving down the street, when a bright light suddenly hit us in the face. I shielded my eyes with my arm, but Leo just stared at the car, his gaze direct and, I thought, defiant. After a moment, the light went off as quickly as it had come on, and the car, never stopping, glided past like a shark. Inside, two officers stared at Leo. He met their stare with his own. Once they were gone, he resumed walking without comment.

We passed inhabitants of this nocturnal underworld. Panhandlers wearing trash bags for protection against the rain, hands out, needle tracks visible on their arms. People stumbled along, dizzy on cheap booze or cheap drugs, some with the shrunken heads from extended meth use, cheekbones protruding like ghoulish Halloween masks. I fought the temptation to look away from the broken lives. A group of young men were heading toward us. In the street lamps' shadows, I couldn't tell whether Black or Latino or whatever. I hoped I looked poor, wished I didn't look quite so white, and tensed as they drew closer. Where was the patrol car now when we needed it?

Leo called out, "*Órale vatos!*," which I gathered translates into something like "Yo, dudes!," and they came up to us, speaking a street slang with Leo as if I weren't there, which was fine with me. After a brief exchange, they bumped knuckles and moved on. In Chinatown, Leo introduced me to various young people we met. "He works with me," he said. "He's cool." I tried to look cool. They talked with him, ignoring me, except one girl who asked for a cigarette. "Sorry, I don't smoke." She immediately lost interest, returning to Leo and her friends, and I returned to my ignored status. The conversations were usually brief and to the point.

"Where's Noodles?" asked Leo. "Haven't seen him for several weeks."

"He'n Skater're up in Seattle."

"Why? What's up there?"

The kid shrugged. "Seattle. They'll be back."

"So, when you see him, tell Noodles I have a dentist who'll work on that tooth's been bothering him."

As we walked on, Leo explained the mobility of the street kids, hitching rides up and down I-5, between Seattle, Portland, and San Francisco. I wanted to know how they ended up on the streets.

"Most are runaways; some were kicked out. I'd say 60 to 70 percent of the boys are queer. Probably 90 percent of the girls were sexually abused by their dads or older brothers or mothers' boyfriends. Say 'home' and most people get all warm and gooey. Home to these kids was just a place they escaped from, family just some weird fucked-up affair." He shook his head. "Do-gooders like Steve want to save them from the streets. They don't understand that the streets saved these kids. You should hear some of their stories."

"I'd like to hear your story."

So, as we walked, Leo told me of growing up on a farm outside Madras, Oregon, where his father and older brothers worked.

"One day Dad found me and a friend together. He couldn't stand the thought of his son being a *maricón* and threatened to shoot me if it happened again. And if he wouldn't, I knew my brothers would. When it happened again, he went to get his gun, and I decided it was time to see the world. I hitched a ride to Portland, arriving here with the clothes on my back and two dollars in my pocket. I dropped Emilio and became Leo. I was fifteen."

"Your mother?"

"Left when I was a toddler. Can't say I blame her. Don't know whatever happened to her."

Leo quickly learned how to survive living on the streets. He had two assets. The first was his looks. "Men, wealthy men, wanted to keep me as their 'boy,' their very own Ganymede." I could believe it. He was handsome as a young man of twenty; he must have been a beautiful boy at fifteen. The other asset was a love of reading. "I liked school and was good at it. I'd skipped a grade and was a junior in high school when I took off. Missed it." Even living on the streets, he regularly got books from the Multnomah County library.

"How did a homeless kid get a library card?"

He shrugged. "It was just easier to steal the books," then he added, "But I returned them. Or most, anyway." It also explained how a street kid had his vocabulary. He had received his GED within a year after leaving the streets and being taken in by Sandy.

But it was more than just his vocabulary. Leo carried and conducted himself unlike any street kid I met that night, possessing a stately dignity, a centered calm. "I wasn't living on the streets all the time," he explained when I commented on this. "There were stretches during those three years when I was 'adopted' by several sugar daddies."

"Here?"

"Here. San Francisco. I rarely stayed with any of them for more than a few months. I needed my freedom. Just long enough to get my sugar fix. And some of them had lots of sugar."

"Who were they?"

"A lawyer, a major realtor in town, a city commissioner. Most were in the closet. Some liked to show me off to their friends as a trophy boy, so they bought me clothes and taught me how to dress in their world, how to conduct myself at the table, how to speak. I liked to spend time in that world, but I didn't want to live in it permanently, or be owned by anyone. I'm still friends with some of them."

The police car we'd seen earlier returned—or was it a different patrol car?—creeping slowly along the street, like some predator. In the past, I would find a police car reassuring, a symbol of my safety; but tonight, dressed like this, I began to see the cops through the eyes of the street people, a threatening surveillance. The police were here to protect the good citizenry against the likes of me. While I tried to avoid eye contact, Leo stopped and stared at them, and they at him, as if daring the other to blink first.

We resumed walking in the light rain, continued to meet groups of young people, and I made mental notes, trying to come up with "measurable outcomes" Steve could report to the health department that wouldn't compromise Leo's relationship with these kids.

"How does one gain their trust?" I asked as we left another group.

"One doesn't. They have a basic code of survival: Trust no one."

"That's too bad," I murmured.

"Not really. Distrust is a survival mechanism on the streets. It's like taming a wild animal. When I was a boy, there was this young mule deer that would come onto the farm where we lived. Over several weeks, by offering it slices of apple each day and patiently waiting, I tamed it. I was probably ten at the time and proud of myself. But in taming it, I made it vulnerable. My dad saw me with the deer one day, ran into our cabin, got his rifle and shot it, even as I was feeding it." Sadness flashed over Leo's face. "He only saw venison. And maybe he already suspected I wasn't like my brothers and other boys. Real men don't feed and tame deer; they kill them." He shook off the sadness. "Try to build trust with these kids and you might make them vulnerable, and on the streets they can't afford to be, not for a second. And they practice survival ethics."

"Meaning?"

"They do what they need to, to survive. They scrounge, they steal, they sell, whatever it takes. They have their own code of conduct, and it little resembles Steve's middle-class morality. They stick together, look out for each other, share their last hit or dollar with another kid, but they'll also steal from each other if they need to. They've become masters at survival. Steve wouldn't last a week on these streets."

I was thinking: Neither would I.

It was past midnight when a young teenage boy approached us. Leo called out, "Hey, Danny." The boy called back, "Hey." They locked fists in a greeting-grip. Probably five foot two, maybe weighing ninety pounds at most, he was a skinny kid with a splattering of freckles on his cheeks and dirty strawberry blond hair creeping over his ears, poking out from under his cap. He wore a ragged pair of sneakers, no socks, dirty jeans and a torn sweatshirt over a flannel shirt so washed out I couldn't tell what the original color had been.

"'Sup?" asked Leo.

"Lookin' for Elliot."

Leo introduced us, but the boy never met my eyes or said a word to me. Yet I felt he was watching me in his peripheral vision the entire time they talked. His eyes had the wary look of the wild animal, just waiting for me to make a sudden move to bolt. I sensed they would've had more of a conversation without me standing there. The boy looked uncomfortable; he wanted to move on.

"Okay, see you later," said Leo. Danny quickly turned and left. I watched him go.

"How old is Danny?" I couldn't think of him as a "young man." He was a kid. A child.

"Eighteen."

I arched a skeptical eyebrow.

"On the street, age is relative," explained Leo.

"So, what's his relative age?"

"Depends how old they want him. If they want legal, he's eighteen. If they like them young, he's twelve."

"My guess, he's fourteen or fifteen."

"Fourteen, going on forty."

"And he lives on the street? Where does he stay?"

"Wherever he can crash."

"What's his story?"

"Let's just say that compared to Danny's dad, mine could get the Father of the Year award." We resumed walking. "Originally he's from southern Oregon. Was in a couple of foster homes before splitting and coming up to Portland and's been living on the streets for the last year."

I turned to Leo. "My god, since he was thirteen?" I felt momentarily sick, that a kid that young was out here by himself.

"He's a survivor," said Leo.

"So where do most of these kids stay? The shelters?"

"Some. But they get the Bible read to them and have to pretend to pray. Most would rather give blowjobs and earn some money. Plus, adult shelters can be dangerous. We need a youth shelter in this city."

Another mental note: *Find funding for youth shelter.*

At an intersection, we saw two girls get into a silver Lexus. I doubted their relative ages were eighteen. Noticing them, Leo commented, "It's safer to go in pairs. And most of their customers don't mind two for the price of one."

I realized all the kids we'd met that night traveled in numbers for safety and companionship. All except Danny.

We were heading down a dark side street when a tall hulk of a man came lurching toward us. A bruiser, he was obviously drunk, and I braced myself, ready for fight or flight. Preferably flight. Leo said nothing but watched him as the man approached. He stumbled past, and I let out a sigh of relief. I was a grown adult, accompanied by another grown adult, and I felt trepidation to be walking these streets at this hour. What must it be like for a homeless, fourteen-year-old boy to be out here night after night, alone?

By then, the cold wetness had penetrated my jeans and sneakers, and Leo suggested we get a cup of coffee.

"Sounds good." I'd been sinking into a deepening depression with each block, soaking up the misery and despair of these streets. It would be nice to get warm and take a break from all this pathos and paranoia.

Chapter Eleven

A Few Bad Apples

[Portland, Oregon, April 1994]

We went into an all-night diner. I was grateful for the warmth and the light. Others were in there, also drawn, one assumes, by the warmth and light. From the looks of the place, it couldn't be the food. There was one waitress on duty, a peroxide blonde, more peroxide than blond, in her fifties, maybe sixties. Leo was right: in this world, age was relative. The cook in the back looked Middle Eastern, swarthy, wearing a three- or four-day stubble, cigarette dangling from his mouth as he cooked something over the grill.

We slid into a booth with cracked plastic seats, and I removed my wet jacket and cap as the waitress came over with menus. No water. Leo pulled off his hood, unleashing his curly black hair. She smiled at him. "Hey, handsome. What can I get you tonight?"

He gave her one of his angelic smiles. "Hi, Marge. Two coffees?"

"You got 'em."

When she left, he sniffed the air. "Is that you?"

I nodded, holding out the front of my flannel shirt. "Eau d' turpentine."

"Nice. Subtle, yet distinctive."

Marge delivered two mugs of coffee. It wasn't Starbucks. It wasn't even Folgers, but it was hot and it was liquid. As we drank and got warm, Leo told me more about street culture.

"Do-gooders want to 'save' them, but for what? American middle-class culture? A divorce rate over 50 percent. Domestic violence that's finally come out of its own closet. Addiction to alcohol, or prescription drugs, or nicotine, or food. We have an epidemic of obesity in this country, and it's not because people are hungry. Middle-class culture may work for the majority—maybe—but it's not for everyone. But I think you know that."

Yes, I thought, *for some of us it doesn't work*. But I wasn't so ready to buy the street as an alternative. "Middle-class culture has its dysfunctional aspects and negatives, granted, but it also has its strengths and values. I'm having a hard time seeing any positives to this . . . culture."

"No? How many days do you think you'd survive on these streets?"

I nodded. "Point taken." Survival skills were important. "But surely these kids want a better life than this, than what they're living."

"They aren't really that different from most people. There was this cartoon in *Willamette Week* awhile back of a stereotypically cartoonish blind man: dark glasses, white cane, tin cup for begging. He's standing before his fairy godmother who's offered him three wishes, and the guy's all excited, telling her, 'I want a new pair of glasses, and a new cane, and a new cup.' Like most people, he didn't have the imagination to wish for vision. Think of the people you know: Do they imagine *a better life* for themselves? My guess, probably not. Most only want more of what they've got. More money, bigger house, better job, different spouse, better sex."

I sat there, truly in awe. "How does one so young possess such insight?"

He appeared embarrassed by my comment. "As I said, age is relative out here. One year on the streets is probably equal to ten years in suburbia."

"Perhaps. But I doubt there are many we've met tonight who possess your understanding."

"Are you familiar with Krishnamurti?"

"I read him some in college."

"I stumbled onto his writings when I was living with one of my patrons. I'd never read anything like it before. There was all the mess and muck of life, but he seemed to be observing it from some higher perspective, seeing in a new way. I knew I wanted to see life through Krishnamurti's eyes, so I read everything I could find by him . . . . Those books I didn't return to the library."

I made a mental note to get books by Krishnamurti, then asked, "Why did you invite me out here?"

"I was hoping you could help me and these kids. Steve and the others don't understand."

"I have no experience with the street world either."

"It's not experience. I've watched you with the prevention team and the counseling and testing volunteers. Chad's hypersexuality, Lionel's beer obsession, the colonel's homophobia—you don't judge. You observe. You learn. And I've seen what you're doing with the testing program, how you're putting it together. I need your help turning my work into a program with 'measurables' to get Steve and the county off my back." He paused. "And I sensed it when I first met you."

"Sensed what?"

"You're like me and these kids. You don't belong anywhere either."

Before I could respond, a different patrol car pulled up to the curb and parked, both officers staring at Leo through the window. This time he ignored them, but I could not.

"Is it my imagination, or do the police gaze at you with a certain lack of love?"

He took a drink of coffee. "Yeah, I don't like them much either."

"What have they got against you?"

"I know too much."

"Know what?"

"I'm onto their game."

"Game?"

"Shaking down the flophouse owners. Taking money from bar owners to look the other way, to not see the drugs, the underage patrons. They rough up the street people, demand hush money from the pimps and prostitutes, confiscate drugs, then sell them themselves."

"You make it sound widespread."

"I only know what happens down here. Probably doesn't happen that much in the West Hills."

Maybe I was looking skeptical again.

"Let me tell you about the police. Danny and another kid named Elliot were picked up by two cops late one night last week in a secluded area of Washington Park. They found a small bag of pot on Elliot. But instead of taking them in, one cop drags Danny to a side of the car and jerks him to his knees. Then the cop opens his pants and grabs Danny's head."

I winced. "Did Danny resist?"

"What's the point? Better to just get it over with. So, Danny opens his mouth and lets it happen. He was more bothered by Elliot's cries."

The other cop had taken the little fellow to the rear of the car (symbolic?), thrown him face down onto the trunk, yanked his jeans down to his ankles, and taken him from behind.

"The cop used a condom. For *his* protection, not Elliot's," said Leo. "It took less than five minutes. Then the two cops took the marijuana and turned them loose."

I experienced a gag reflex at the story and swallowed a gulp of coffee.

"Each of these kids has stories to tell about their run-ins with the police. They aren't human to the cops. They're lowlifes, deadheads, junkies, vermin. It's even worse for the girls. If it's night, they take off running at the sight of a cop car."

"Surely you're not saying all police are bad."

"No. But these kids aren't going to wait around to see if they've got a good cop."

"Still, it's kind of hard to believe cops would be that . . . cavalier."

"Yeah, so was police brutality until someone captures Rodney King being beaten senseless on video, then it's no longer hard to believe."

I took another drink. "How are they doing?"

"Danny and Elliot? They're fine. Elliot's still sore. It was a first time for him. There's the difference again. Living on the street, sex is just something you do for money or a place to stay or to get a hit. There's no feeling. You get it over with, and move on. Sure, they're pissed at the cops, but they aren't 'traumatized.' If this happened to your typical high school kid their age, he'd be messed up for life, probably undergo years of therapy and be left with psychic scars. Danny and Elliot just brushed themselves off and got back out there, probably more ticked off at the police for the theft of their pot. See the difference?"

"I think so."

"The cops were just lucky they didn't try that with Danny. Danny'll give blowjobs, but he won't let anyone fuck him."

"Does he always have a choice? Like with Elliot and the cop?"

"Danny's got a switchblade. He's never used it, but if the time came, he would. I taught him how."

"That cop?"

Leo said flatly, "Danny would've used it." Then he said, "You look pale."

I cleared my throat. "Yeah. The fumes from the turpentine must be getting to me," and I took another swallow of coffee. "Did they report this?"

"Danny and Elliot? They won't testify. I've reported other incidents to the Sexual Minorities Roundtable. But as long as the kids won't say anything, the police won't take me seriously."

"When's the next Roundtable?"

"This Tuesday."

I pulled out my notepad and pen. "Give me all the facts. And as much detail as you can get from Danny and Elliot—time, exact location, any identifying information on the two police officers, badge numbers, license plate."

He studied me. "They should have that. I've taught them to

95

note those things."

"We'll write it up to present at the Roundtable, give them enough details to make a case, even if the boys won't come forward. And then we'll work on some measurables for you."

Leo smiled gratefully. "Thanks. I was hoping you would."

I went home that night—actually, three the next morning—home to my hot shower, home to my warm bed in my safe house. But in spite of my fatigue, I couldn't sleep. I lay awake thinking of the street kids, seeing their faces again. When I finally did fall asleep, I dreamt I was wandering on the Bogong High Plains, once again searching for someone. It was night, and at some point in the dream the dark plains and stars overhead morphed into the streets and night lights of Portland. I was searching for Danny.

Chapter Twelve

The Freak Show

[Portland, Oregon, April 1994]

On Tuesday afternoon, Steve and I met with Arthur and the county medical director, Harry Caulfield, who had taken a personal interest in our counseling and testing project. He seemed a friendly, relaxed man, and I was not surprised when both Steve and Arthur addressed him as "Harry." We were well into the training and Arthur, typical bureaucrat, was typically cautious, suggesting it was too soon to tell if the experiment would work, while Steve, typically enthusiastic, assured Dr. Caulfield we were off to a great start and he had no doubt it would be successful. I sat quietly, letting Arthur and Steve do the talking, as I assessed Dr. Caulfield and sensed he was assessing me.

As it was approaching three, I excused myself. "I'm sorry. I need to leave. I promised Leo I'd meet him at the Sexual Minorities Round-table today." He had gotten additional information from Danny, and I had helped draft a statement and wanted to be there to support him when he read it before the police chief and his staff.

"It's good for you to know the players at the Roundtable," said Steve. "You'll probably meet Jake Caulfield."

"Jake Caulfield?" I asked, turning to Dr. Caulfield.

"My older brother. You should prepare yourself. He's a character."

"Is he in medicine, too?"

"No. Professor of political science at Reed College. Now retired."

"Jake's the dean of AIDS activists here in Oregon," said Steve. "And one of my heroes."

"One of mine, too," said Dr. Caulfield.

"He's also something of a legend around here," added Arthur. "A medical anomaly."

"How so?"

"He's one of a very select few who've been infected for years yet continues to remain asymptomatic."

"His partner, David, died five years ago," explained Dr. Caulfield. "We know Jake's been infected for at least nine years, ever since the test was developed, and probably years before that. Yet, for whatever reason, the virus remains dormant in him, not advancing to AIDS."

"There are only a few hundred cases like Jake in the entire country," said Arthur.

"If we can crack the code, figure out why my brother has remained asymptomatic, we may be able to find a vaccine that could save others."

"It's just about the only hope those of us who're HIV-positive have," said Steve, "that we may be an anomaly like Jake."

I arrived twenty minutes late. Leo met me outside the municipal building, looking relieved. "I was afraid you weren't going to make it."

"Sorry. The bridge was up, and then I had a heck of a time finding a parking place." We hurried up the steps and slipped into the chamber, settling into the back row. The meeting was underway. Around a large oak table sat the chief of police with one of the city commissioners next to him and a host of colorful characters: men, women, and some I wasn't sure of; there were Latinos, Asians, African Americans, gay men in leather, lesbians with Mohawks and nose rings, all listening as a representative of the transgender community was speaking on behalf of one of their members who was in jail, requesting that she have a cell away from the male prisoners. Behind the chief sat a bank of his officers, watching the proceedings.

The speaker was biologically male, dressed in a poorly fitting dress, with muscular hairy arms and a five o'clock shadow appearing through her makeup. If that ensemble wasn't unsettling enough, she was also wearing an ill-fitting wig. I felt embarrassed for her. As she spoke in a deep baritone voice, I saw one of the police captains exchange a look with another officer and silently mouth, *Fucking freak show.* The other captain smiled, nodding as the speaker ended her presentation.

"Thank you for bringing this to our attention," said the chief. "I'll raise the issue with the county sheriff who runs the jail."

She stood there a moment longer, obviously wanting something more than this, then reluctantly returned to the row in front of ours.

At that point, a large bulldog of a man sitting at the table spoke up. Probably in his mid-sixties, he was dressed in a tweed coat over worsted sweater and dark slacks. Bulky in build with close-cropped hair, he resembled a former heavyweight contender gone to seed, but wore a genial smile as he addressed the police chief.

"Now, Hiram, the request seems pretty straightforward. I'm sure the sheriff will go along with your recommendation. May we receive a response?"

Leo whispered, "That's Jake Caulfield. One of my heroes."

The city commissioner spoke up. "I don't understand the issue here. Why shouldn't this fellow be locked up with other male prisoners? He was caught in the act of prostitution in a no-hooker zone."

"*She,* Commissioner."

"She, he. Just because *he* was wearing women's clothing doesn't make *him* a woman. We can't have separate cells for every transvestite our officers bring in."

"I think it would be helpful to define our terms," said Jake Caulfield. "A transvestite is a man who dresses in women's clothing because it turns him on. Most transvestites are heterosexual men. Women, of course, have dressed up as men for decades. Nothing wrong

99

with them wearing jeans or boots or even a suit and tie. Think Annie Hall."

"Was she a transvestite?"

"I don't believe so. Now, a transsexual, or transgender, person is one who is biologically one gender, but psychologically the other. In this case, a woman in a man's body."

"So, this fellow's gay?"

"Not really. Because he identifies as being she."

"Still, if he's sexually attracted to men, he must be gay."

"No," corrected Jake patiently, "if *she* is sexually attracted to men, then *she* must be straight."

The commissioner was shaking his head. "I don't understand."

"Precisely the problem, Commissioner."

"So, what about drag queens?" he asked. "Are they transvestites or transsexuals?"

"Usually neither. Drag queens are largely gay men who dress up as women to be entertainers. The transgender man dresses in women's clothing because he experiences his essence as female. Psychologically female, though biologically male."

The police chief interjected, "Regardless of gender nuances, we have a practical problem of space."

"Hiram, imagine for a moment: How would you like it if you were locked up with a bunch of women?" The room broke into laughter, including the chief. "Never mind," said Jake. "I think the logic of my argument just collapsed." When the room settled down, Jake continued. "The male prisoners, like our commissioner here, are going to see a gay man, a 'fag,' and we know what happens to gay men in jails throughout the world."

The police chief asked, "So, what are we supposed to do, put him—er, *her*—in with the women prisoners? They're going to see a man, not her 'essence.'"

"I totally agree. The best solution is that she be given her own cell."

"Jake, our jail's overcrowded now. We have three prisoners in cells that are supposed to hold no more than two. Inmates sleeping on the floor on mattresses. And you want me to find a cell for this person?"

"Yes."

The chief sat back in his chair. "Do I have to provide room service as well?"

"That's up to you. Now, Hiram, let's stop taking the Roundtable's valuable time. You know you're going to give her a safe cell because it's the fair and decent thing to do, and you're a fair and decent man."

"Plus, if I don't, your ACLU friends are going to slap the city with a lawsuit."

"Well, yes, there is that additional incentive to do the right thing."

Leo whispered, "He knows more about the law than many lawyers."

I nodded but was thinking Jake Caulfield knows a lot more than the law.

The police chief turned to his assistant taking minutes and said, "Note to the county sheriff to arrange the transfer of 'Ms. LaRue' to her own cell."

"Yes, sir."

The chief then asked, "Are there any other issues anyone would like to bring up before we adjourn?"

Leo stood, holding the statement I had helped him prepare.

"Yes, Leo?"

I could see he was nervous. I whispered, "Breathe deep. You're doing fine."

He began to read the account we had transcribed from the kids' memories. "On the night of March 28, at approximately 11 p.m., two boys, aged fourteen and fifteen, were stopped by two police officers in the Washington Park area." He provided their badge numbers and the police car's license plate, which Danny had memorized. "The police officers questioned and searched the teenagers. They discovered a small amount of marijuana on one of the boys, which they confiscated. Then in this dark and isolated area, they proceeded to commit indecent acts on their persons—" Leo's choice of words, not mine. His voice quavered as he continued reading. Everyone could see the paper trembling in his hands. He reminded me of a kid in school, terrified as he gives his report before the class. Listening, the commissioner wore a look of distaste on his face, as if handling garbage. The officers sitting behind the chief stared at Leo in the same manner as the cops I'd seen in the patrol cars.

When Leo finished, the police chief cleared his throat. "Will these young people who *allege* this happened testify in court?"

"No, sir. They're too scared."

The chief exchanged looks of exasperation with his captains around him. "Leo, we've been over this before. Without witnesses willing to testify, how can we take this seriously? These are mere allegations. Maybe these kids were trying to get back at a couple of officers who busted them several months earlier. You've got to give me something to work with. You can't just come in here and make wild accusations." Several of the officers behind the chief nodded approvingly.

Leo's slender shoulders slumped. He folded the piece of paper and sat in his chair as Jake spoke again. "Perhaps you could investigate whether similar accusations have ever been made against these two officers. At the very least, you could check the records to see where the police officers were at the time these events were *alleged* to have occurred."

"That would not constitute proof."

"No, no, of course not. But it may be worth investigating to see if there *could* be any basis to these allegations. To demonstrate the police did not dismiss the allegations outright."

The chief picked up his pen and began writing. "Yes, I suppose I could. Still, without substantiated testimony or witnesses—"

"Of course, it's all hearsay."

There followed several announcements, then with no further business to address, the chief adjourned the Roundtable until next month. People immediately got to their feet, clumping together into groups, like talking to like. The transgender woman was shaking Jake Caulfield's hand, thanking him for his help. After she had moved on, Leo went to Jake as I followed behind.

The two embraced, then, holding Leo at arm's length, Jake looked him up and down, exclaiming, "Emilio, I swear, you grow more handsome every time I see you."

"No, it's just that every time you see me you've grown more desperate."

"Yes, well, it could be that, too."

"Thanks for the help just now."

"No, no, you did fine. With a little more practice, you'll be great." Jake was buoyant and bubbly, a twinkle of mischief in his eye as he continued to hold on to Leo, admiring him like a work of art. "Ah, Emilio, we could make beautiful music, you and I."

Leo turned to me, smiling. "He flirts with all the young guys."

"Now, that's not true. Well, maybe 80 percent true. Ninety, tops." Then he turned to me. "But, really, Emilio's my type."

"Male," said Leo.

"I have very high standards. And you are?"

Leo introduced me as the new mental health specialist at CAP.

"Mental health! I love mental health! I look back on mine with fond memories."

Shaking hands, I said, "I just came from a meeting with your brother."

Jake immediately turned sober. "Now you mustn't believe everything Harry says about me. We had a very difficult childhood, you see, and he's still bitter."

"Actually, he spoke highly of you. Said you were one of his heroes."

"Oh . . . well, yes, we've always been close."

"And I hear you're something of a legend in Portland."

"Oh, no, no, no." He laughed lightly. "People exaggerate. Really, it's not *that* big."

Leo was shaking his head as I clarified, "I was referring to the fact you're a long-term survivor and have developed no symptoms."

"Ah. Yes, that too."

"It seems pretty significant."

"I hope so. I have donated my living body to science—since no one else here appears to want it," he said with a chastening glance at

Leo. "Which means I'm subjected to an endless series of tests. It's a wonder I haven't died from all the testing they've performed on me."

"Still, it's good of you. Many people are hanging their hopes on those tests and what they may discover."

"It does give my life some meaning and purpose," he admitted. "And what would life be without meaning and purpose?"

I offered, "'Nasty, poor, brutish and short'?"

His eyes lit up. "Thomas Hobbes!"

"Who?" said Leo.

Jake explained, "Seventeenth-century English political philosopher. Had a rather bleak view on the human condition." He turned back to me with new interest. "Literate, cultured, and attractive. A man after my own heart. What are you doing for dinner tonight?"

Leo said, "Don't mind Jake. Really, he flirts with everyone."

"Of course, I do. You never know when it might pay off. People tell me I bear a striking resemblance to the young Marlon Brando." He turned back to Leo. "I caught that eye roll, Emilio, and, may I say, it's most attractive on you."

Leo put his arm around Jake's broad shoulders. "Jake's a lech. But a sweet lech."

"Actually, an aspiring lech. I mean, with a mug like this, guys aren't exactly beating down my door. And there's really no need—it's always open."

"You do sound desperate," I said.

"Tell you truthfully, my work is nothing more than an advanced case of sublimation. If I could just get laid, I'd drop all this AIDS activism in a heartbeat."

"I have a class to get to," said Leo. He playfully kissed Jake on the cheek.

"Tempt not a desperate man!"

Leo turned to me. "Thanks for your help today." As he left the room, I saw a couple of police captains shoot him looks that could be considered lethal.

"You mustn't take me seriously," Jake was saying. "Emilio's right.

It's really just an act I put on. However, if you're free Saturday night, I am available."

I chuckled, and that mischievous twinkle came back in his eyes. "I bet you're trying to figure me out in your diagnostic manual, that DSM-III thing. Well, I'll give you a hint: I am a very fascinating page 55, and sometimes page 136. Occasionally, in my darker moments, page 207."

Before I could respond, the police chief came up, whereby Jake introduced us.

"Well, I'm all for mental health," said the chief as we shook hands. "It's in such short supply these days. Unfortunately, it's too late for Professor Caulfield here. But mental deterioration is a sign of age and to be expected, I suppose."

"People tell me I don't look a day over forty."

"Jake, you gotta stop listening to what people tell you." Then the chief lowered his voice. "About just now. Leo's one of your protégés. Talk to him. If he wants to help his kids, he's got to follow the rules. He can't just continue making these unproven accusations. All we need is one of our muckraking weeklies to pick this up and blow it all out of proportion." Then he added, "And you know making these charges isn't good for Leo's health."

"I know, I know," Jake sighed. "I'll speak with him."

"Please do." The police chief offered me a perfunctory smile— "Good to meet you"—and left.

Once he'd gone, I asked, "What did he mean, not good for Leo's health? Was it a threat?"

"No, no. Hiram genuinely likes Emilio. It was a warning. The chief knows he's got his bad apples on the police force, and he's aware of what bad apples are capable of doing."

"So why doesn't he do something about them?"

"Bad apples have strong unions."

Most of the people had left the room by now, and as we made our way out into the hall, Jake spoke more freely. "Hiram is a good man, and as chief he wants to do the right thing. He's cleaned up the department,

105

a vast improvement from the way it was under his predecessors. I can vouch for him and most of his captains. But he's right. For him to be able to get rid of the bad apples, he needs proof and witnesses who will testify."

We stepped out into a dusky April afternoon, the sky a slate gray.

"Portland's police are nothing like Chicago's, or LA's or New York City's, but still, you don't want the police pissed off at you anywhere. There are those cops who'd like to put an end to Leo's work, and to him. You know the type: If they weren't wearing a badge, they'd probably be in prison themselves. No, Hiram's right, Emilio's in danger. I plead with him not to go out on the streets at night by himself." Jake paused, looking away. "I dread to think what could happen to that pretty face if some bad apples got hold of him."

"You're saying they'd rough him up?"

"Oh, much worse than that. After they'd finished with him, he'd vanish. That is, what was left of him would vanish." All his witty banter now gone, Jake Caulfield was serious, scarily so. "I fear for the boy."

His words chilled me as we went down the steps, and I gave an involuntary shudder, as if already knowing Leo would vanish seven months later.

Chapter Thirteen

Black Mary

[Melbourne, Australia, April 1986]

"The 1936 skiing tragedy? Yes, I remember it. Remember it well. I was twelve when it happened."

I was sitting in a popular student pub with Arnold Begara, geology instructor at the Royal Melbourne Institute of Technology. After Gray told me of his experience of being lost on the high plains as a boy, I was intrigued and wanted to learn more of the "local lore" that Cleve Cole's spirit wandered that desolate region. As a part-time instructor in counseling at RMIT, I was on familiar enough terms with Arnold to invite him for a pint and to ask about the Mount Bogong tragedy. It turned out he had a personal connection.

"It was my father's search party that found Hull and Cole."

Short and wiry, bald with a bushy beard, Arnold was in his early sixties, yet after decades of walking and climbing all over the world, he possessed the muscular legs of a man half his age. Still a bachelor, he was dressed in walking shorts and hiking boots. But then he wore walking shorts and hiking boots everywhere he went, whether in the field or lecturing in class, embodying that informality that's a national trait among Australians. If the Queen were to present him with an Order of the British Empire, Arnold would no doubt receive it in walking shorts and hiking boots. His family had lived in Glen Valley for generations. As a boy, he loved to explore the high plains and never stopped loving them, and was now recognized as an expert on their flora, fauna, and social history as well as their geology.

It was late afternoon. There were a number of students in the pub, the continuous buzz-hum of their conversations and occasional bursts of laughter providing a backdrop to Arnold's story.

"When Michell stumbled into our township that evening, the alarm was immediately sounded and men organized to set out at first light. By mid-morning the next day, every able-bodied man in the vicinity was out searching for the two skiers. Michell was in pretty bad shape and confused from his ordeal. He could provide only the sketchiest details of where he'd left Cole and Hull. They may not have been found in time if it wasn't for an old aborigine woman named Black Mary. It was she who told her grandson, Black Curly, where to find the men." Arnold paused. "Black Mary. Black Curly. That's what we called the aborigines when I was a boy. It wasn't meant to be demeaning, but of course it was. They had their own names in their own language, but none of us White Fellas could pronounce them. Or at least, none of us bothered trying."

"How did she know where they were?"

"She said she'd seen them in her pipe smoke." He raised his bushy eyebrows.

"Kind of makes me wonder what she was smoking."

He chuckled. "She said she saw one of the two men wandering by himself, lost in the snow. She told Curly he'd find both holed up in a hollow log up the Big River Valley. Curly was around nineteen at the time, same age as my brother Patrick, working the sheep stations. They'd been best mates since childhood. Curly knew to listen to his grandmother. She was a healer, a kind of shaman among her people, one of the last of the Old Ones. Curly and Patrick were in Dad's search party and found the men in the area where she said they'd be."

I breathed out. "Wow."

"And that's not even the strangest part of the story."

"What else?"

I knew from my reading that Mick Hull was weak but still conscious when they found him, and that Cole never regained consciousness. Both men were unable to walk and needed to be carried out on makeshift stretchers.

"It's rough terrain up there," said Arnold, "and the searchers were fighting terrible conditions, snow and sleet and battering winds from the tail end of the blizzard. It took my dad's party the better part of two days to bring them down." The sun coming through the windows cast Arnold in its beam, highlighting his sun-burnished, leathery features and shiny dome.

"We—the women and children and old men who'd been left in the township—were all there when Sister Watson returned to Glen Valley with Cole. Me and my mates huddled around to get a look as they carried him into the church hall that'd become a base of operations. I still remember the smells in there—of pork and chicken, beans and baked bread that Mum and the other women had been cooking to send out to the search parties. We youngsters all crowded around, craning our necks and gawking, but couldn't see much. Cole was wrapped in blankets. All I saw was his nose protruding. I remember because it was black."

Arnold stopped to take another drink from his pint. Two students nearby were playing darts. I became aware of the *thunk* of the darts against the board, followed by typical young male commentary on what the game proved about each other's sexual prowess. But I was soon back in Glen Valley.

"A number of local aborigine women were there as well—their men out with the search parties—and I remember seeing Black Mary with her pipe. She was staring at the unconscious man, too. He'd been the one she'd seen wandering by himself in her pipe dream. She was shaking her head. But not like Mum and the other white women shaking theirs, out of sadness or concern. Even as a twelve-year-old, I recognized it was a

109

kind of disgust. According to my brother, Black Mary didn't think much of White Fellas who tried to cross the high plains in winter. Why? Just to prove you could? That, to the Black Fella, was crazy. *So you were the first to cross the plains in winter. Congratulations. And so what?*

"The doctor from Omeo shooed all of us out before he and Sister Watson unwrapped the blankets, and we went back to our chores. When Curly returned later that night with the search party, he told his grandmother they'd found the two men where she'd indicated they'd be. According to him, she said, 'I saw that White Fella with Sister Watson,' and shook her head. 'They brought back only his body.'"

Although it was warm in the pub, I felt suddenly chilled.

"Curly told Patrick all this, and Patrick told me." Arnold drained the last of his pint, setting it down. "It was some years later, after the reports started about seeing a man wandering alone on the high plains, that we understood what she meant."

"They brought back only his body," I murmured.

"And that's what I know about the Mount Bogong tragedy."

I gestured to his empty beer mug. "Another?" He waved no.

"So, as a man of science, do you put any credence in these reports of Cleve Cole's spirit wandering the high plains?"

"As a man of science? No."

I nodded, the rational skeptic in me reassured.

"But only part of me is a man of science."

"What do you mean?"

"There's another part that recognizes science can't fully explain the mystery of this multidimensional universe. Science goes only so far, taking us to the edge of that mystery, and says, 'Here's where what we know ends. For now.'"

"You're saying some part of you believes?"

He was thoughtful before answering. "I prefer to say some part of me refuses to *disbelieve* until all the scientific evidence is in." He gave me a smile. "Check back with me once all the evidence is in."

I chuckled, but was still feeling an uncanny chill.

They brought back only his body.

Chapter Fourteen

A Plan for Leo

[Portland, Oregon, April 1994]

I had started working out daily at the Princeton Athletic Club, in the afternoons once the lunch crowd had left and before the evening crowd arrived. Nicknamed "the Princess" because of its large gay clientele, the facility was clean and well maintained, three blocks from our offices, and open from early morning to late night, making it convenient for my shifting work schedule. Plus, CAP staff members were offered reduced rates due to a sympathetic manager whose partner had used our services prior to his death.

I headed for the locker room, confident I'd exercised enough to seriously ache in the morning. I was settling into my new normal since returning from Australia in January. Eating again, I had begun gaining back some weight and losing what Sandy called my "Buchenwald look." People were no longer assuming I was HIV-positive.

In the locker room, I found Lukas changing into his gym clothes. Even more string-bean skinny than when dressed, he was excited about the counseling and testing training, then in its fifth week. "I've been telling everyone we're going to start testing in June," he burbled.

"They're already getting in line!" He finished tying his bright, neon-pink gym shoes (Why was I not surprised?) and jumped up from the bench. "I'm going to go get buff!" And he dashed out of the room, leaving me to struggle with the image of a buff string bean.

I pulled off my sweaty clothes, wrapped a towel around my waist, and headed for the wet sauna before returning to the office. Besides Lukas, I'd also seen Chad, Lionel, and Reggie here. Lionel was usually in the free weights section, curling seventy-five-pound dumbbells in each hand. I tended to avoid that area when he was around, curling my own wimpy twenty-pound weights. I entered the sauna, less than half full at this time in the afternoon.

"Hobbes!"

Through the thick, gauzy steam I saw Jake Caulfield sitting on the top tier, waving. "Come join me up here in the Troll Section." Heads swung around to me as I climbed up next to him. He was sitting on his towel with his everything hanging out and grinning like some big jolly Buddha.

"Whew! It's hot up here," I said, the moist air burning my nostrils and throat.

"Yes, but the view's much better."

"You work out here?"

"It's how I maintain my svelte figure," he said, then looked down at his bulbous belly with disapproval. "But mostly I come for the eye candy." His statement was met with an assortment of smiles, chuckles, and groans. He added, "They all know I'm harmless. Unfortunately."

He had a big teddy-bearish quality, along with an impish grin and mischievous eyes that never ceased their roaming as we talked. Amid the buzz-chatter-sweat of the sauna, an attractive fellow entered and joined us on the top tier, immediately drawing Jake's attention and welcoming smile.

"People tell me I resemble the young Robert De Niro," he offered by way of introduction.

The fellow nodded. "Cool."

"I thought it was the young Marlon Brando people say you

resemble," I said.

He turned back to me. "Different people."

By then I was perspiring heavily. "Well, that's enough for me. I'm heading to the showers."

"I'll join you," said Jake. "I think I've filled up on enough candy for today."

We cooled off in the showers, Jake chattering the entire time, occasionally breaking off to flirt with some man who came in the shower room.

"Bill, you're in luck. My social calendar opened up for Saturday night and I'm available."

"Gee, I'd love to, Jake, but I'm having dinner with George Clooney this Saturday."

Jake watched him go, shaking his head. "George Clooney. How sad. The poor guy lives in his own fantasy world."

"Do you ever have any luck?" I asked.

"Haven't yet, but I remain hopeful. Besides, it's like fishing: If you love it, you go even when you no longer have bait. Or for that matter, a dependable pole. What about you?"

"What—what about me?"

"Why aren't you fishing?" He appraised me with his eyes. "You clearly have bait. And I assume your pole is dependable."

"Very dependable, thanks for asking. But it's been a long time since I went fishing." I turned off the faucet, grabbed my towel and stepped into the drying area. Jake followed, his eyes latching onto a handsome African American guy on his way to the sauna, the white towel around his waist in striking contrast to his deep brown skin. Jake mused as he dried himself, "Why is it the fat old guys parade around buck naked while the handsome young dudes always cover themselves up?"

"No clue," I said, wrapping the towel around my waist and heading to the locker room as he paraded buck naked behind me.

"I think we need new club rules," he announced to all within earshot. "Fat old guys should be required to cover themselves, and hot young dudes should be denied towels."

"Denied towels?" I hoped I sounded dubious.

"Yes. I say let them air dry!"

Back in the locker room, as we began dressing, Jake lowered his megaphone voice, leaning closer to me. "About our mutual friend."

Leo. "Yes?"

"I'd like you to deliver a message. Tell him he needs a new strategy. Don't bring his reports any more to the Roundtable. It's not doing any good. He presents these 'allegations' one at a time, and the chief and his officers dismiss them one at a time. Instead, I'd like him to start compiling a data file on what happens out on the streets. For each incident, record dates, times, locations, badge numbers and names of officers if he can get them from the kids, and license plate numbers of their cars. Detail everything that happened. He may need your assistance setting up the file and organizing the material."

"I can help him."

"Have him keep a coded registry of the young people's names separate from the file of incidents—Boy A, Girl A, Boy B, something like that. He can assure the kids he won't give their names to the police, and their identities will be kept confidential. Compile this data over the next several months. When the time's right, that file and the number of incidents will not be so easy to dismiss."

"You think the Roundtable will believe him if he has a file of multiple incidents?"

"This isn't for the Roundtable, or the police. Not even Hiram— that could place him in a difficult position. No, when it's time, we'll take the file to a neutral party."

"Neutral party?"

"A federal prosecutor. A sympathetic city commissioner, or a newspaper editor. I'm suspecting the data will show a pattern—which officers, which shifts, doing what. The coded registry will be evidence there are real people behind these claims."

I nodded.

Two men entered the locker room. Jake's voice went softer. "And he needs to hide the file where it can't be easily found. Only you should know its location in case . . ." He turned sober. "In case something happens to Leo."

Chapter Fifteen

Fathers & Sons

[Portland, Oregon, April 1994]

At the end of the fifth evening of counseling and testing training, most of the team, including Arthur and Steve, were going out to the bars to enjoy a drink together, extra team-building time I hadn't planned. They called to John, "Joining us?"

"No. You go on. Have a good time. Maggie will have dinner waiting for me."

"You mean Maggie will *also* have dinner waiting for you," called Lukas, bringing a laugh to everyone, including John.

Tyler came up to me as I finished putting away the chairs. "You going out with the group?"

"Ah, no," I said. "I'm not much into bars."

"Yeah, me neither." Then he remembered, "And I'm not old enough to go. So, would you like to get a hamburger and milkshake instead?"

After the evening's sharing about fathers and sons, I sensed he needed to talk. "Sure. I'm much better with burgers and shakes."

We went to Hamburger Mary's near the PSU campus. The funky setting seemed to relax him. He did need to talk. It poured out—about his family, him still living at home with his parents and two younger sisters, his excitement about the training. He talked nonstop, taking only occasional bites of his hamburger and slurps from his milkshake, so I ate and listened. His story was closer to mine than any of the other team members: straight-appearing boy, dated girls in high school because it was expected, and because he usually preferred being around girls, except in one significant way. Girls, he said, had always been his best friends. But by high school, he realized what that significant difference was.

"My parents have been great. They're very supportive. I mean, it's not easy for them, but they're trying to understand. They even went to see *La Cage Aux Folles,* and I love them for it."

"You're fortunate to have such parents."

"I know. It's still all new to them. And to me, too. I just came out last year."

I know we will have advanced as a society when "coming out" becomes an archaic expression, no longer used. What did it mean? Future generations will ask, generations who have a different understanding of sexuality and being human. They'll wonder that earlier people—us—divided sex and sexuality itself into such rigid and artificial categories, much as we wonder how earlier, seemingly intelligent people could have believed in phrenology, or that slavery was a natural part of God's order.

"What about your sisters?" I asked.

"When I told them, they said they love me and I'll always be their brother. But they're not sharing their dresses with me." He smiled, embarrassed. "As if I would ever want dresses."

It was a sixty-minute hamburger. Good that I was a slow eater. He'd barely touched his food. After an hour, he began to wind down, now talking about his new gay life, "such as it is."

"I've not really done anything yet—I mean with another guy. Well, with anyone." (Boy, that came as a surprise.) "There's so much I want to experience. I go home after each training and fantasize about what it would be like to do some of those things."

117

"Apparently, you and John both."

He grinned. "I asked John if he'd meet my dad. I think it might help my dad accept it . . . accept me. I mean, he does, don't get me wrong, it's just that . . ." He stopped.

"What?"

"I think it's harder for him than he lets on, me being his only son." His face flushed, tears welled up, and he looked away. I drank the last of my milkshake as he sniffed, wiped his nose, and composed himself.

"So, what did John say?"

He was happy again, eyes bright. "He said he'd be glad to. He said he would be *honored*."

"That's good. John's a good man." My view of the colonel had been changing over the past several weeks.

My biggest concern for Tyler, as for all young people hungering for experience, was that he take precautions. Over the past ten years I'd seen too many young men like him become infected through the lust and rush for first experiences. I knew it would break my heart (again) if this kid became infected.

"So, do you have any close friends?" I asked.

"Not really. I'm attracted to older guys. I had crushes on some of my coaches and teachers in high school. Loved it when my wrestling coach taught me a new move, when he held me tight against him. I had a crush on my physics teacher, too."

"You enjoyed physics?" I said, surprised. Tyler struck me as more the literary and arts type.

"*Hated* physics. But I'd have taken the History of Masking Tape if Mr. Jackson taught it."

I smiled, remembering. With me it was my Latin teacher, Mr. Clough. And people thought I loved Caesar.

We were wrapping up. Tyler took the remnants of his now cold burger and fries to go. As we stepped out into the chilly April night, he said, "Thanks for listening. I guess I needed to talk."

"Any time."

He lit up. "Really? Thanks. I really admire you. You're kind of a role model to me. Who I'd like to be someday."

Surprised at his comment, I shook my head. "Oh, Tyler, you are so far ahead of me when I was your age."

In the sixth week, Arthur was going over the ethics of counseling.

"You never counsel a current or former lover."

Lukas raised his hand. "What about *future* lover?"

Arthur looked at him. "Nor anyone with whom you are potential lovers. In other words, do not date the clients."

Lukas raised his hand again.

"Lukas?"

"What if we accidentally bump into them later that night in the bars?"

"What I'm saying is, don't use this program as a dating service."

"Right." He wrote in his notebook, murmuring, "Do not use program as dating service." He looked up and winked. "Got it."

Arthur continued, "Clients will be randomly assigned to you. If you find you've been given someone you've previously been intimate with—"

Lukas raised his hand.

Arthur sighed. "Lukas?"

"Define 'intimate with'?"

"Fucked."

"Oh. Thanks." He hunched over his notepad, scribbling. "Fucked."

"Then you greet him, explain that you are not allowed to counsel sexual partners, and that he will be reassigned to another counselor."

"Poor Chad's never going to get to work with anyone," said Reggie and everyone laughed.

Arthur drew the session to a close, admonishing them, "Remember, you are all role models. If people see you being unsafe, it discredits the program. We cannot afford to be hypocrites."

"I thought those were just Republicans," said Lukas.

"Ahem!" said John.

Lukas winced—"Oops!"—and sang out, "Sorry!"

As part of the training, all the counselors would be tested for HIV except Chad and Marco, who were positive; even John who was straight and married; even Tyler who was clearly a virgin. They all needed to go through the experience to better appreciate how their clients would be feeling. Arthur introduced us to Roy, one of the phlebotomists assigned to the program, and explained the procedure: Blood would be drawn tonight, results back in one week's time. With the exception of John and Tyler, most in the group had tested before.

And with the exception of Lionel, who had turned pale. "Uh, I've got this thing about needles . . ."

Roy smiled to reassure him. "Yeah, a lot of guys do."

"It's more common than you'd think," said Arthur. "I hope we come up with a test soon that doesn't require drawing blood. My guess is we've got a lot of men out there who've never tested because of their needle phobia."

"So, let's just get it out of the way, shall we?" Roy said to Lionel.

The group broke for coffee, snacks, and the lavatory as Roy escorted Lionel back to the room that had been set up. Chad and I tagged along to support Lionel, or hold him down. By the time he got into the chair, he was even more pale and light-headed. He gripped its arms like he might fall out of it.

"Why don't you talk with Chad?" suggested Roy. "Pretend I'm not here."

"I wish," murmured Lionel. He was breathing fast and shallow as he turned to Chad on the other side of him.

"Hey, big boy, come here often?" teased Chad.

Perspiration had broken out on Lionel's forehead. He turned back, watching Roy tie a rubber band around his bicep.

"Hey, look at me," said Chad. Lionel looked back, sweat rolling down his face. "Now show Mommy what a brave boy you are and I'll buy you a beer when this is over."

Roy turned over his arm, dabbed it with a cotton swab, and

Lionel passed out.

"Wow," said Roy, "that was record time."

"Okay, I think he's ready," said Chad.

Following the break, during which the rest of the team had their blood drawn and Lionel recovered, we role-played and discussed potential problematic counseling scenarios that could come up. As we were ending the night with our usual debriefing, Tyler had an announcement.

"I . . . I've met someone." The group erupted with cheers and applause.

"You sly dog, you!" said Lionel, throwing the boy into a headlock and kissing his hair.

"So, tell us about him," said Chad. "We're assuming it's a *him*."

The kid was beaming with the blush of first love. He appeared happy. And embarrassed. And nervous. And excited. Yeah, it was definitely first love. He stammered, "Well, he's a little older than me. We met recently. We kind of have a class together." Based on what Tyler told me, I bet it was one of his professors, who unlike his high school teachers may have had less hesitation reciprocating Tyler's interest. One could see the elation and relief on his face, to be able to talk about this with someone.

"It goes without saying," said Arthur, "but it's my job to say it anyway: Be sure you play safe."

Tyler's blush deepened. "We haven't . . . played at all."

"Details! Details!" shouted Lukas.

"We're still just getting to know each other. I mean, we don't need to jump into bed immediately."

"I advise jumping into bed immediately," said Chad. "It's a great way to find out whether you like someone or not."

"Is he negative?" said Arthur. "I hope he's negative."

"Doesn't matter if he's negative," said Marco. "You can be passionate and playful, *and you can do it safely*. Terry and I have great sex, and we're always safe. It also helps if you're monogamous."

"But," said Chad, "you can also have great sex and not be monogamous."

"The voice of experience," added Lionel. "Lots and lots of experience."

Marco continued, "Being safe is even more important to me than to Terry. I don't think I could live if I infected the man I love."

"Right," Arthur said to Tyler. "Always employ universal precautions. Do not assume the other man knows his status."

"'Employ universal precautions'?" said Chad. "Jeez, Arthur, why must you always be so clinical."

"Because I'm a clinician."

"There's more important things in life than 'being safe.'"

"Oh? Like what?"

"Like love! Like passion! Excitement! Sometimes I think we forget what we're surviving *for*. It's why people climb mountains, or race cars, or bungee-jump off bridges—to feel alive! To connect!"

"And I'm just saying connect safely." Arthur's volume was rising. They were both becoming heated. I decided to let this play out rather than intervene. It was important for the team to learn how to resolve disagreements.

"My God, Arthur, it's first love. *First love.* Tyler shouldn't have to be thinking about death and disease."

"Yes, he should! He *should* be thinking about death and disease. So should all young guys his age; otherwise his generation will end up decimated like ours. Romance is all fine and good, but the virus is real and it's out there!" He flung his arm to *out there*. We'd never seen him so worked up. Usually Mr. Placid, Mr. Calm and Steady, Arthur's face was now red, eyes bulging, veins protruding from his neck. "Three hundred thousand people have already died!" He was shouting. "And that's just in America. *Three hundred thousand!* And we still have no cure! We have no vaccine. We can't even slow down the progression of the disease. It's a death sentence!"

Said Chad softly, "I know."

Arthur sat back in his chair, obviously ashamed of his outburst. The color drained from his face. He composed himself as he looked down at his hands. "Of course you do. I'm sorry."

Silence; no one spoke.

Then Chad turned to Tyler. "Be safe," he said.

The boy nodded, still dazed by the ferocity of their argument.

Arthur raised his head to the youth. "And love like there's no tomorrow."

Chapter Sixteen

Pride

[Portland, Oregon, May-June 1994]

The night of Tyler's announcement ended with the team members taking him out to celebrate with milkshakes. ("Do they have beer-flavored milkshakes." Lionel wanted to know.) During Tyler's sharing, I had noticed John going from being happy for him to becoming distracted, to finally wearing a pained expression on his face—maybe sadness? As the group was leaving, I checked in with him.

"Are you all right?"

"What? Oh, yes. Fine. Good session tonight."

"You look, um, thoughtful."

"I guess it was Tyler's sharing. About falling in love. I realized my gay son never had that kind of support from his family."

"Oh?"

"He should have, like his older brothers did. We heard about their first dates in high school, met their girlfriends, went through their breakups, got to know their fiancées. The girls became part of our family even before the weddings; we were always there for my sons as a family." That flash of anguish crossed his face again. "My gay son never had that. He had to move away from us before he could explore that part of his life."

"Just wondering: Does your 'gay son' have a name?"

"Jonno, or Johnny."

"He's John Jr.?"

"No. I'm John. He was named Jonathan after Maggie's brother who died in Vietnam."

His face once again took on that pained expression I'd seen earlier. "I don't even know if he has a partner. He's never said. I never asked. Maybe I didn't want to know." He took a deep breath. "I'm glad Tyler has this group to support him."

"You're part of the group, too."

He looked at me. "Yes, I am. Tyler wants me to meet his father."

"Yes, he told me."

"I don't know what I'm supposed to do or say."

"I don't think you need to do or say anything, other than just be yourself: the father of a gay son who loves and accepts his son for who he is."

He nodded. "I can do that." He was silent a moment. "I hope Jonno had a group like this when he needed it. He should've had that support from his family."

"Well, you know, it's never too late for parents to offer emotional support."

"You're right, it's not. Maggie and I need to talk when I get home tonight."

"If she's waiting in her negligee with the candles burning, I hope Maggie's not going to be too disappointed."

He smiled. "Well, I'm sure we won't need to talk about it all night."

The next week, our seventh session, Arthur began with, "I'm happy to announce that tonight we are giving only negative results." There were immediate cheers. "Remember that feeling," he admonished them. "Help your clients remember that feeling." Then he proceeded to train the team in how to give negative results:

"Review the client's file, call his name, greet him, and take him into one of the rooms. Don't prolong the anxiety these guys will be under. No small talk. They've been waiting all week for that test result. Open the file, turn it around toward them, and point to the box marked 'Negative.' Let them *see* the result so there's no doubt in their mind. The visual confirmation is important. Celebrate with them—what a great relief it is to be negative!—and discuss ways they can stay that way. The post-test counseling is as important as the pretest."

Marco raised his hand. "What about giving positive results? How do we handle those?"

Arthur turned sober. "You will never have to give a positive result."

I took over. "This is the procedure: You greet your client and take him back to the assigned room. We'll be ready. Arthur will knock on the door and join you once you're in there. You will introduce him to the client, 'This is Arthur from the county health department. He's an epidemiologist and a gay man, and he's going to talk with you about your test result.' And then you leave the room. No *I'm sorry*. No *everything's going to be fine*. Arthur will take it from there. He's trained to deal with all the possible reactions to the news. He'll get them through the initial shock and hook them up with the services they'll be needing, as well as try to learn their sexual partners' names so those men can be contacted and tested as well."

Among the group there was an almost embarrassed look of relief. In time, Arthur would come to be known as the Grim Reaper. Once the program was established and running smoothly, he normally showed up only on those evenings when we had a positive result. There was a tension among the counselors when they saw him. It meant one of the clients sitting out in the lobby was going to go home that night with his life irrevocably changed.

During that night's wrap-up portion, the group was eager to know how Tyler's new relationship was coming along. Their eagerness was blunted by his awkward confession.

"He doesn't exactly know."

"Doesn't exactly know what?"

"How I feel about him."

The group was stunned. "You haven't told him?"

"Not really. No."

Chad said, "Scratch my advice about jumping into bed together."

"But why not, why not tell him?" the group pressed.

He shrugged, even more embarrassed. "What if he doesn't like me?"

Chad exclaimed, "How could *anyone* not like you, Tyler? You're adorable. You're sweet and kindhearted and cute. I can hardly keep my hands off you."

"Which places you in a select minority of the population," murmured Arthur.

Over these seven weeks, Tyler had become the group's gay kid brother, and now they flocked and flapped around him like a bunch of mother hens protecting their chick.

"I don't know if I could take it if he said, 'Piss off, kid.'"

Lionel was sitting next to Tyler. "If he doesn't treat you right, tell him your Uncle Lionel will take him into the back alley and break both his legs."

Tyler grinned and hugged him. "Thanks, Uncle Lionel."

"No." All heads turned toward John. "I've observed you during this time we've been together, Tyler. You've got a good head on your shoulders. And a good heart. And you've got a solid inner core. I would have you on my team any day. No, you'll be fine. Whether he likes you or doesn't, you'll be fine."

Tyler swallowed. "Thank you, John."

Psychologists have found that gay kids tend to be "delayed" in their social development. While their heterosexual peers were dating, having their first crushes, their first loves and first heartbreaks, gay kids were frequently on the sidelines watching, or mimicking their peers with the dating, the kissing—while sensing that something was missing, something they weren't getting. They would experience all this later, usually in their twenties. My concern for Tyler (other than he practice safer sex when the time came to practice) was that he not become too emotionally invested in a first relationship. But that's also part of growing up. And if he did fall, he would have a band of older brothers who would be there for him.

A week later, there was still no movement on the boyfriend front with Tyler, but John had something to share.

"Maggie and I called my gay son in LA. Well, Maggie called him. She's usually the one who calls him—inviting him home for Thanksgiving, and she said if there's someone special in his life, to bring him, too. That we'd like to meet him."

"How sweet!" said Lukas. "I can't remember the last time I had Thanksgiving or Christmas with my family."

The group congratulated John and Maggie in a kind of vicarious family bonding, and we moved into the training section for the night.

In the ninth session, we began to wrap up. Next week, the last week, would basically be review, evaluation, and graduation. As the other team members headed home or off to Scandal's for a beer, John hung back, wanting to talk to me.

"I'm going to miss these sessions."

"Well, in another two weeks, the fun begins and you'll be working together." But I knew what he meant. Only six counselors would be scheduled each night. They wouldn't be back together as a full team except for training updates Arthur and I planned to hold every quarter.

"I'll admit it was a challenge for me at first," he said. "I've always had a hard time with effeminate guys like Lukas. They've gotten under my skin, and I've been thankful that Jonno wasn't like *that*. But, you know, I'm glad I stuck with it. Once I finally got Lukas's sense of humor, I've really come to like him."

"Well, you're still ahead of Arthur. I don't think he's gotten Lukas's humor yet."

"No, I now realize how funny and fun he is . . . and free."

"Free?"

"To be who he wants to be. He doesn't allow himself to be hedged and wedged into a certain idea of what it means to be a man. I used to think effeminate guys really wanted to be women, and that they were failures as men. But I see them differently now."

"How?"

"They've defined for themselves what it means to be a man rather than what their society has told them a man should be. And that takes guts. Real guts." There was an undeniable tone of admiration in his voice. "Imagine, all those years in the military, and it took some effeminate guy to show me what true courage is."

"Could you ever tell Lukas that?"

"I'm not sure. I'm just getting used to the idea myself. But I would like to tell some of my old buddies in the service. I guess I'm not too old to learn."

"You were *willing* to learn, John, so you did. I think Jonno would be proud of his father."

He looked embarrassed. "Thanks. Well, see you next week."

In our last session, Arthur ran them through a review of key points. "These test results tell us you were negative up until three months ago. Not now. Why?"

Reggie jumped in. "Because of the virus's incubation period. It takes that long for the body to develop antibodies to the virus."

"And why is that important?"

"Because the test can't measure the virus itself," said Marco. "That's why it's called the HIV *antibodies* test."

Arthur was pleased. "Good. Very good."

I turned to him. "This weekend is Pride, and we launch the counseling and testing program. Arthur, are we ready?"

"More than ready." He grinned. "We are going to be awesome."

The group cheered. *Awesome* was not an Arthur word.

"I'll admit," he said, "I had my doubts about this whole enterprise. But I have no doubts now. I'll be proud to serve with each and every one of you."

I conducted the final team-building session, asking them to reflect on what they had learned and what they had received from the training. When it came John's turn, I sensed a tenseness in him.

"I called my gay son last night in LA. And I asked him to forgive me."

All eyes turned to him. His eyes were focused on the floor. It was so quiet you could hear a pin drop—and it was a carpeted floor.

"When he was a boy, maybe nine or ten, he wanted to dance ballet. I don't know where he got that idea. I said no. We were living on a military base in Utah at the time, and I was afraid for him, what others might think. I guess I was really afraid for myself, what others would think if my son was studying ballet. So, I told him no, and he didn't fight me on it. I told him to take up sports instead like his brothers, and he did—tennis and swimming, lettering in both. He was always an obedient boy. Of all my sons, he was the most obedient. I think, more than the other two, he was always seeking my approval." He looked over at Lukas, who had glassy eyes. "And we never spoke of it again. Until last night."

"What did you say to your son?" I asked.

John was red-faced. "I told him I was sorry. I told him I knew how much dancing meant to him. I told him I refused him because of my own fears. And . . . and I told him I loved him."

Lukas was noisily sobbing into Chad's shoulder.

"What did he—your gay son—say?"

John smiled at my gentle jab. "Nothing. He said nothing." Then we saw tears come into the colonel's eyes. "He just wept on the other end of the phone."

By now Lukas was howling, Chad's arm wrapped around his shoulders. "It's just so beautiful!" he sobbed. But most of us were feeling tears well up or a catch in our throats.

Then John said, "I want to thank you, all of you, for letting me be part of this team. I came for one reason: to volunteer, to see how I could help. But I've received far more from you than I could ever give." He was now looking at Lukas. "You have all taught me what it really means to be a man."

In the months ahead, John proved to be one of our most popular counselors. Guys requested him when they came in. Pretesting sessions usually averaged twenty to thirty minutes; his often ran forty-five minutes to an hour as these men opened up to him. To many, he was the caring and accepting father figure they'd never known and always wanted. He would often tell them as they left to have their blood drawn, "You'll be fine, son. No matter what happens, you'll be fine."

We ended the evening with a graduation ceremony. Steve was on hand to give out the certificates and to thank them for the commitment they'd taken on, for being willing to stand in the frontlines of this epidemic. He presented John his certificate, shaking his hand as we applauded. But before John sat down, Lukas shouted, "Wait! Wait! We're not done," and he withdrew a long lavender boa from a shopping bag, hopped up, and draped it around John's shoulders. Then he saluted. "*Mon colonel*, we are making you an honorary queer!"

John laughed as we clapped and cheered and whistled; then taking one end of the boa, he threw it rakishly over his shoulder, befitting a sultry torch singer, to which there were more hoots and cheers. "Woo-hoo! You go, girl!" Lukas shouted and gave him a big hug.

Afterward, as the group celebrated with cheese and crackers and soft drinks, I went up to Steve. "You were right about John. I wouldn't have given him a chance. Thank you."

"But you did. Thank *you*."

There was a toast from Reggie, his light brown face glistening from happiness and laughter and pride, his arm around Lionel's massive shoulders. "Here's to our brothers: nine bodacious queer white boys and one uptight, tight-ass, super-cool straight dude!"

They all laughed, and John, still wearing his boa, raised his soda in salute.

It was a good night. On Saturday, we would launch the testing program at Gay Pride. I was glad they'd become a team. Over these past ten weeks, they'd found a shared strength and support. Now the work was to begin, and they would need both in the months coming.

They began to leave, a number of them to continue celebrating at Scandal's. They called, "John? Joining us?"

"No, you go on. I've got to get back. Maggie's waiting for me."

"What position are you trying out tonight?"

There was laughter, and they called to me.

"Thanks, but I've got to leave, too."

"Because of Maggie?" More laughter.

"No. I've—" I saw Steve looking at me, "I've got an early morning."

Tyler was slipping on his jacket as he came up to me. "Do you have a minute?" He had that need-to-talk look in his eyes.

"Sure." We went into one of the counseling rooms. I was right. He was in a quandary how to confess his feelings to his special friend, whom the group had come to call "Mr. X." He was still in a state of wonder. "I can't believe it. That I'm in love. I mean, I've had crushes on guys before, but this feels different. This feels . . . so different. But I don't know what to say to him."

"What would you like to say?"

He thought for a moment and took a deep breath. "I would like to tell him I've never felt this way about anyone before. I want to be with you all the time. I think about you when I'm not. I admire you. I love you. I . . . I want to make love with you."

It was your pretty typical first-love romanticism, idealizing the other, going in head over heels, all-or-nothing type of love. Very age-appropriate.

"That sounds really good," I said. "Why don't you tell him that?"

His gaze dropped to the table. "I just did."

My mind jammed. "Oh . . . Oh, I see. Well, I mean, um . . . I'm . . . I'm honored."

Dumb word. Not honored! Don't be honored, you dimwit.

We sat in embarrassed silence, his eyes still down, staring at the table, his peaches and cream complexion flushing pink. "I've wanted to tell you for a long time."

"I'm at a loss for words . . ."

"It's okay if you don't feel the same about me—"

"No, no, I really do like you. You're a very attractive—" thankfully, I stopped myself from saying *kid,* "man. And any guy would be lucky to have you as a . . . as a friend." I was digging myself deeper and deeper. "It's just . . . it wouldn't be a good idea. Not where I'm at right now."

He nodded, composed, though still staring at the table's surface.

"I'm sorry, Tyler."

He looked up. "No, it's all right." Though he didn't look all right. "I've put you in an awkward position. I'm sorry."

He got to his feet. I remained sitting, not saying anything, certain that whatever I'd say would only make matters worse. He picked up his daypack, slinging it over his shoulder.

"Don't worry about it. Really. I'm not going to flip out or anything. Just something more to chalk up to experience, right? I'll see you Saturday." And he hurriedly left.

I came out of the room just as he was getting on the elevator. Steve was the only one still there. He watched the elevator doors close, then turned back to me.

"I hope you let him down gently."

"You knew?"

"I think over the last couple of weeks, you were the only one on the team who didn't know Tyler's feelings for you. It was pretty obvious. The way he fawned around you. You were the older guy who he 'kind of had a class with.'"

My face was hot. "He just took me by surprise, that's all."

"What, you're not attracted to him?"

"That's not the point. He's nearly half my age."

"So, is that the point? His age?"

I felt myself getting defensive. "I think it's a factor, yes. And I don't want to get emotionally involved at this time, and especially not with someone that young."

Steve paused. "I now see what Jerald meant."

"What's that supposed to mean?"

"You've been with us for five months, and you don't have one close friend here."

The words stung. I thought he and Sandy were my close friends, and realized that, for them, they weren't.

"It's not about age, is it?" he said. I was looking away. "Do you know why you keep people at arm's length?"

I turned back. "Body odor?"

"You don't let anyone get close to you."

"I didn't know it was part of my job description."

"Your job. It's ironic. You're great at team building, yet you're not part of the team. You're a natural community organizer, who himself has no community. You're always making things happen, but never part of what's happening. You're one of us, and yet you're not."

"Haven't I done a good job for you?"

"You've done an *excellent* job. I don't know anyone else who could've brought this program in on time. I wasn't sure it could even be done."

"So?"

"This isn't about your job," he said. "It's about you."

I grabbed my jacket. "Sorry, but I'm off the clock. And my life is mine." And I left.

Chapter Seventeen

Mickey O'Shaughnessy

[Portland, Oregon, June 1994]

It's cold out here.

I've been so cold for so long.

Can't stop shaking . . .

The night of the counseling and testing team's graduation, I dreamt I'd returned to the Bogong High Plains. It was winter and I was caught in a blizzard, knee-deep in snow, unable to see anything around me, body slowly shutting down. I could no longer feel my hands, no longer feel my feet. Soon the numbness would reach my heart. I knew the search party wouldn't find me in time . . .

Didn't need Freud to interpret that dream, thank you very much. I'd become one of the living dead.

I sought out Sandy when I arrived at work and told her what happened the evening before, what Steve had said to me. I wasn't seeking sympathy, although if she wanted to offer some, I would have graciously accepted it.

"He's right, you know."

I felt less gracious about her sympathy for Steve's point of view. "Oh, fine, so you're taking his side?"

"I just think you've got some issues."

"Issues? I don't know what you're talking about."

"Well, for one—"

"Yeah-yeah-yeah, okay. I know what you're talking about."

"You don't let people get close to you. We've all noticed."

I considered how an adult would handle this situation—listening respectfully, hearing her out, thanking her for her candor—but decided to be a child and sulk instead.

"Take it as a compliment," she said.

"Compliment?"

"Sure. Steve cares about you—we all do—otherwise he wouldn't have said anything. Franklin doesn't let anyone get close to him either, but then no one wants to. I can recommend a good therapist if you're interested."

"Thanks," I said, heading for the door. "I've got to get to work. Maybe I'll check with you when I'm ready."

Steve arrived late and came into the prevention team's room. I was the only one in there. The others would be working that evening, so they normally didn't show up until late morning. He dropped into the chair next to my desk, looking pale, his eyes tired, shoulders sagging. I was immediately concerned for his health.

"Are you feeling all right?"

"I couldn't sleep last night," he said.

"Why?"

"I was out of line yesterday."

"Oh, that."

"It bothered me all night. I overstepped professional boundaries. I had no right to speak to you that way. I'm sorry." With Steve, one never doubted his sincerity.

"You spoke to me as a friend. Because you care."

"I do care," he said. "Many of us would like to know you better. But, like you said, your life is yours."

"Well, judging from how defensively I reacted, there must be some truth in what you said. The truth is sometimes uncomfortable to hear." Actually, I'd found the truth *usually* uncomfortable to hear; it seems to be one of the hallmarks of truth. "But thanks for caring enough to tell me. I'm sorry you lost sleep over this."

He shrugged. "It was an emotional night. After you left, I locked up and hurried to see if I could catch Tyler before his bus arrived."

"You went after Tyler?"

"Yeah, I needed to make sure he was okay." That was so Steve. "I found him and suggested we get a hamburger and shake."

"How was he?"

"A little teary at first, but he'll be okay. He just needed to talk."

"Let me guess: He took his hamburger and fries home in a doggy bag."

Steve smiled. "Yeah, he needed to talk more than he needed to eat. He was basically ashamed—of putting you in an awkward position, feeling he made a fool of himself, embarrassed by his feelings of affection. But as he talked I think he realized the love he was feeling was really admiration, along with a healthy dose of sexual attraction thrown in. Mind you, I've known people who thought they were in love for far fewer reasons. After we ate, I drove him home."

"You went to check on Tyler," I murmured. "Thank you for doing that. I should have."

"You weren't exactly in a position to do that right then. But don't worry. I really think he'll be okay. He's still at the worshiping-from-afar stage." Steve pulled himself wearily to his feet. "I just wanted to tell you that I heard you." He placed a hand on my shoulder. "And you're doing an outstanding job for us."

I nodded without saying anything more, and he left for his office. I sat there for a time, lost in my thoughts about what he said, what Sandy said, then pulled out a sheet of stationery and wrote Tyler a letter. He had given me a great gift, I wrote, of his respect and affection, and in offering me his love. Anyone would be honored and would consider oneself tremendously fortunate to be offered such a gift. As was I. But I regretted that I was not able to accept such a fine gift—from him or anyone—because of "where I'm at in my life right now." I apologized for causing him disappointment or any awkwardness and said I would always value him as a friend. Finally, I signed it, then sat back in my chair, wondering, Where *am* I at in my life right now?

Lost in a blizzard. Unable to see what's ahead or behind or around me. Unable to feel any longer . . . slowly dying.

Sandy looked up from her desk to find me standing at the door.

"Um, about that therapist you know . . ."

On Thursday afternoon, I was climbing three flights of stairs in one of Portland's older buildings: no elevator, narrow stairwell, bare walls, all looking clean and dowdy.

"His name's Mickey O'Shaughnessy," Sandy had said as she wrote his phone number on a Post-it. "His office is near here. He's the best counselor I know. But I have to warn you, he's not for the fainthearted."

I took the Post-it. "Why? What do you mean?"

"He's very direct. Even blunt. He considers most therapy so much mind-fucking, a waste of time and money. He doesn't coddle. If you're looking for a warm and fuzzy therapist, this ain't him."

"Oh, good, because, you know, coddling is for wusses." I had gone back to my desk and called the number, his answering service, and was able to schedule an appointment for the next afternoon.

On the third floor, amid a row of identical office doors with frosted windows, I found one with MICHAEL O'SHAUGH-NESSY, PH.D. That was all. It opened onto a small outer office that served as a waiting room. Spare and undecorated, it had a few chairs, no desk, and another door opening to a larger office.

"Hello?" I called out.

A deep baritone voice sounding like Darth Vader without the breathing apparatus called my name, and then "Come in, please."

I walked into the office where he was writing at his desk and stopped abruptly.

He looked up. "You seem surprised."

So surprised, I blurted out, "You're Black," and died a thousand deaths the moment the words left my lips. Or wished I had. The comment in all its vast stupidity and possible racism had slipped out of my mouth before I could stop it. He stared at me as I stammered, "I mean it's just that Sandy never mentioned it."

He put down his pen. "Sandy probably never noticed. If it's an issue, I can refer you to any number of colleagues. We come in a variety of colors."

"No, no. No-no-no, it's no problem." I stumbled around in the labyrinth of my mouth, trying to find the way out. "Really. It's just the name threw me. You aren't, you know, what one would expect for a Mickey O'Shaughnessy."

"You're thinking maybe Kunta Kinte?"

I could feel my blush going deeper. "No, but, c'mon, seriously, *O'Shaughnessy*?"

"It was the name of the man who once owned my great-great-grandfather."

"Of course. And *Mickey*?"

"My father was a Yankees fan. Any other questions?"

I thought of an exceedingly funny joke about the black Irish but wisely decided to drop it. "No. No, no. None. Thanks."

"Then please take a seat," he said, motioning me to a chair in front of his desk. I did. Quickly, before I said something else I'd regret for the rest of my life.

"Did you bring the client information form I faxed you?"

"Yes, yes, I did." I withdrew it from my shirt pocket, unfolded and handed it to him.

The office was spartan, no framed photos, no cozy knickknacks, no mementos; it was as warm and cheerful as the inside of a cardboard box. I sat, waiting as he perused what I'd written. *Well, this got off to a really bad start. Now we'll probably have to spend the first twelve sessions dealing with my latent racism.* I watched him as he read. *By the way, Dr. King is one of my heroes. And Rosa Parks, too. I've read* The Souls of Black Folks. *Twice. Very compelling book. Also* Soul on Ice. *Also everything James Baldwin ever wrote. Did I mention I have a number of friends who are African American? Truly, truly wonderful people. We're very close.*

He went to the second page as my mind jabbered on.

I took several courses in African American studies at university. I should have added that. Morgan Freeman is one of my favorite actors. And Denzel Washington. When I was a teenager I had a crush on Sidney Poitier. Saw To Sir, With Love *four times—probably better not to mention that.*

He laid the sheets aside. "So, what brings you here?"

I noticed his wedding band, and although I was pretty sure Sandy wouldn't set me up with a homophobic therapist, I wanted to be clear from the start.

"I don't know if Sandy mentioned it, but I'm gay. Is that a problem for you?"

"No. Is it a problem for you?"

"Me? Uh, no, not really."

"Then what do you want to talk about?"

"I'm not sure where to start."

"Start wherever you want. You must have a sense of why you came here. I don't."

I took a deep breath. "Sandy thought it might be a good idea for me to see you. She says I'm suffering from battle fatigue."

"Post-Traumatic Stress Syndrome?"

"More like *Ongoing* Traumatic Stress Syndrome."

"Meaning the AIDS epidemic."

"Yes. Sandy thinks I have some unresolved grief issues. She says I keep people at a distance. She thinks it's because I'm afraid of losing more people I care about."

"So, what would you hope to achieve in coming here? Or should we ask Sandy?"

"I'm not really sure."

He sat up straighter in his chair. He was a husky man, with a muscular upper torso and large biceps, a his white short-sleeve shirt and tie. "You should know that I have no philosophy of life to impart. I have no words of comfort to offer." Sandy was right. This guy was not going to coddle. "If you want to work on your issues, fine. If you don't, it's better not to waste my time and your money. You can undoubtedly find better and less expensive ways to distract yourself."

"Distract myself?"

"People use different ways to distract themselves from their pain, from their fears, from the loneliness and emptiness of their lives. They use work, or relationships, or religion, or serial life crises, or different forms of 'entertainment,' everything from sex and drugs to shopping. Some use therapy. How do you distract yourself?"

"Uh . . . work, I guess."

"It's very popular in our culture."

Nope. No warm fuzzies dispensed here.

"So, Sandy says you keep people at arm's length. That you don't let them get close to you."

"Well, that's her impression."

"Is it true?"

"Um . . . kind of."

"Yet I read in your statement you had a partner in Australia—Grayson? Now deceased."

"Yes."

"You were together how long?"

"Ten years."

"I assume this impression people have of you didn't start just since the death of your partner."

"No, I've always been kind of a loner."

"Nothing wrong with that, if that works for you."

141

"It works for me."

"Then why are you here?"

"Sometimes it doesn't work for me."

He picked up his notepad and pen. "So, let's hear how it *doesn't* work for you."

Chapter Eighteen

The Names Project

[Portland, Oregon, June-July 1994]

"How'd it go with Mickey?" asked Sandy, when I returned from our first session.

"Fine. He hates me."

"No. He's like that with everybody."

"You know, you could have mentioned that Mickey O'Shaughnessy was African American."

"Would it have mattered?"

"Not in the least. But I wouldn't have gotten off to such a bad start. And why, out of all the therapists in Portland, did you refer me to the one misanthrope?"

"He just has no time for bullshit."

"I wouldn't mind a little bullshit. You know, like some 'Nice to meet you' bullshit. Or 'How are you feeling today?' bullshit. He didn't even get out of his chair to shake my hand."

"He can't."

"What? Why?"

"He's in a wheelchair."

"Wheelchair?"

"I know it looks like a regular leather desk chair. That's intentional. He's one of the last people in this country to have had polio as a child."

"But three flights of stairs? How does he get to his office?"

"He uses the freight elevator in the building."

Oh fine. Now I was going to feel even worse when I ended the relationship with O'Shaughnessy. Which I had already decided to do.

"I'm surprised he has any clients."

"He does because he's effective. He normally gets the job done in half the time of most therapists. Doesn't allow himself to play any codependent games, doesn't enable one's issues. Like I said: For him, you're either there to work or not. There's no in-between."

Over the next three sessions, my relationship with O'Shaughnessy did not improve. I told him everything, holding nothing back: about my childhood, my adolescence, my suiciding years, my searching. I thought he might at least ask what I was searching for. He didn't. About my coming out, meeting Gray, our years in Australia together, Gray's illness and death. About Steve's allegation, apparently supported by Sandy and most people in the greater metropolitan area, that I didn't permit anyone to get close to me. I tried to sound a little miffed at that. O'Shaughnessy didn't seem to notice; indeed, he didn't seem to notice much; didn't ask questions, didn't express anything as I poured out my heart and spilled my guts—though admittedly I didn't really have my heart or guts invested in any of it. He sat behind his desk, notepad and pen before him, poised to write something noteworthy, something insightful whenever I got around to saying it. But nothing seemed to engage him, nothing seemed to warrant why I was here, pouring out my not-really heart and spilling my not-exactly guts.

Along with not asking questions, he made no observations, never requested clarification or more information. I began to feel guilty, like maybe I was keeping him awake. In truth, I didn't care for O'Shaughnessy's attitude; his brusque impersonal manner verged on rudeness. He managed only the most basic courtesies—"Good day," when I arrived—as if they were social requirements he was obliged to fulfill.

He offered no smile. No warmth. No connection. Didn't make the least effort to establish rapport or empathy. I considered his behavior unprofessional. Therapists are like mothers: by definition, kind, patient, understanding, and bestowing unconditional love whether they want to or not. Was he this cold with everyone he worked with, or did he have a particular dislike of me?

After each session, I railed at Sandy about his manner. "I have known more sensitive Marine drill sergeants!" I actually didn't know any drill sergeants except in the movies, which I felt should nonetheless count. "Really, your cat Fernando has better social skills."

I knew what I was doing. I was building a case for my eventual decision (which I had already made) to end therapy. And maybe, after our disastrous start, I also wanted O'Shaughnessy to know that my decision would have nothing to do with race. It was simply a waste of my time and money, though admittedly only a minor ten-dollar co-pay.

It was near the end of our fourth session when he abruptly flopped his notepad onto the desk. "I get so damned bored listening all day to what people *think* are their problems."

Excuse me. Bored? He gets bored?

"Isn't that like an occupational hazard for a therapist?" I said. "Isn't that what you're getting paid for?" I was irate. Here I had been baring my soul (not really) and he was *bored?*

"No. I get paid to help people move on from where they're stuck. But too many seem content to wallow in their stuckness. Endless recitations of what happened to them, what others did to them, what they did to others. I just want to say, 'When are you finally going to forget all this stuck-stuff and get on with living your life?'"

"You're saying I'm stuck."

"To quote my son, 'Duh.'"

"Well, I *know* I'm stuck, okay? That's why I'm here. If I wasn't stuck, I wouldn't need to come here listening to you telling me how stuck I am!" I realized I was shouting and dialed it down a notch. He'd gotten me riled.

"Honestly now," he said, "aren't you as bored as I am in these sessions?"

"I don't know. Just how bored are we talking about?"

"On a scale of one to ten, I'd say a solid eight."

"Yeah? Well . . . well, I'm only a seven." *So there!*

He sat back in his chair. "That's the first genuine emotion I've seen you express in the month you've been coming here."

I fell into a silent funk. I was not paying an admittedly minor co-pay to be told I was *boring!*

Then O'Shaughnessy asked, "Just wondering: Did you ever weep for any of those people you lost to AIDS?"

"Weep?"

"You know, tears. Crying. Sobbing uncontrollably."

That night on the Bogong High Plains, lying naked in the dust, weeping next to the bonfire as the flames leapt into the black sky . . .

"Once."

"Once." He pondered this for a moment. "How many people did you say you lost to AIDS?"

"Thirty-one." *Cal and Jerald.* "Thirty-three."

"Thirty-three. Do you remember their names?"

"Of course I remember their names," I said moodily.

He slid his notepad and fountain pen across the desk toward me. "Write them down."

I looked at the notepad, then at him. "Why?"

He sighed. "Because I want a sample of your handwriting."

"Okay-okay. Jeez." I took the pad and pen. "How do you want them? First names, last names? Alphabetically? Chronologically?"

"First names will suffice. However they come to you."

"However they come to me," I muttered, and I began to write,

Wystan—one of the organizers of what would become the Victorian AIDS Council; fiery, passionate advocate, knowing it was a matter of life and death. His life, his death.

Donald—professor of classical studies at Melbourne University, all pipe-smoking and tweed, erudite with a wonderfully wry sense of humor.

Down, down, down into the darkness of the grave . . .

Wesley—raging queen who accosted the Minister of Health on the steps of Parliament, dressed in full gown, heels and tiara (Wesley, not the Minister of Health). I smiled, remembering. It made front-page news with photos in both *The Australian* and *The Age*. Wesley was so proud.

Anthony—who died angry, raging at the dying of the light.

Nicholas—who died at peace with where life had brought him. (Note: Dying at peace is preferable.)

Rupert—gentle smile, gentle soul, generous spirit.

Gently they go, the beautiful, the tender, the kind . . .

Barry—sweet-faced kid from Barongarook. So much like Tyler . . .

I choked, tears suddenly stinging my eyes, and put the notepad back on the desk.

"I changed my mind. I don't want to do this."

"Keep going," he said brusquely.

I sat there, staring at the name, remembering a kid with his life before him. We called him, "Barry from Barongarook." A beautiful boy, barely a man, in so many ways like Tyler: kind, innocent, open to the world, lusting for experience. He'd escaped his small town in western Victoria for the big city, finding there the life he'd dreamt of . . . and it was where the virus found him.

O'Shaughnessy's voice breaking in, but this time with a surprising gentleness: "Please. Continue."

I picked up the pad and pen and resumed writing.

Jonathan—proud, willing to stand up to his Church, confident in God's love for him as he believed God created him.

David—shy fellow, shunning the attention, always working behind the scenes for others.

Pressure built in my chest. It was becoming harder to breathe.

Laurence—the only one who wept for us as he lay dying, for we who would be left behind.

Eyes filling with tears. I breathed out slowly.

Trevor—forsaken by his family who refused to come to Melbourne even as he was dying, even as he begged his mother and father to come, begged to see them one last time . . .

I broke into a sob, covering my eyes with my hand, and wept silently.

"Keep going."

After a moment, I wiped my eyes on my shirtsleeve, and continued writing.

Rodney—funny, funny fellow, like Lukas, outrageous sense of humor, who kept everyone laughing to the very end . . . when he left everyone crying.

Joe—bravely continuing to care for his dying partner even as he himself was failing by the day.

Quietly they go, the intelligent, the witty, the brave . . .

It was hard to see the names as I continued writing, tears dropping onto the notepad.

Martin—trying to find some meaning, some purpose or plan in all this suffering and sorrow.

Stefan—so matter-of-fact about it: shit happens; so does life; so does death.

Some names were now blue-black blurs, made anonymous by tears and ink running together, as if already erased from memory, as if they'd already become indecipherable in time.

"All right," O'Shaughnessy's voice, "that's enough." He reached for the notepad.

I jerked it away, holding him in a steely gaze, whispering fiercely, *"I'm. Not. Done."*

He stared for a moment, nodded, and sat back in his chair. I wiped away tears, and continued writing names as the faces rose up before me, like a moving queue from my past.

Alex—died feeling betrayed by life, all his hopes and dreams and immense talent made suddenly irrelevant.

Giles—indefatigable punster to the very end. ("I've no appetite, but my doctor said I must eat something. He gave me a raisin to live.")

I chuckled even as I continued crying and writing, writing and crying . . .

Cal—finding an ancient God in the midst of a modern plague.

Jerald—lusty sinner, late-blooming saint. In the end, so hard to tell them apart.

Until, finally, in the quiet of that small, austere office, I sat exhausted, all wept out, no more tears to shed, staring at the last name on the list.

Gray—who I loved.

The room was silent. Dust motes casually danced in the sunlight coming through the window. I placed the notepad and pen back on the desk.

"Thirty-three lives. Really pretty minor when compared to what's happening in Rwanda or Bosnia."

"But you're not living in Rwanda. Or Bosnia," O'Shaughnessy said softly. "And it does little good to compare one's suffering with that of others."

A box of tissues had magically appeared in front of me. I took several, wiping my eyes and blowing my nose. "A friend once asked, 'How can you remember all their names?' I asked her, 'How can you *not*?'"

We continued to sit in silence with the dust motes and sunbeams swirling around us, until O'Shaughnessy asked, "How are you feeling now?"

"Lighter. I feel lighter. I suppose this is what we call catharsis."

"I suppose it is."

I wiped my eyes with another tissue. "For catharsis, I expected some insight. Some reconfiguring of my world. Suddenly seeing it differently, but it's the same world."

"People often expect a revelation—why they are like they are, why they do what they do—but for many it's an emotional release, breaking the blockage of emotions dammed up for so long."

I nodded heavily, then looked at him. "So. Is that it? Now that I've 'catharsized,' are we done?"

"You tell me."

I gazed at the list of names. "No, I don't think we are."

"Then I'll see you next week."

I pushed the pad and pen back across the desk to him, got up and left the office without another word, went out the door and down the stairwell (*Down, down, down*) stepping in time to the slow cadence of my heart—

Wystan,
　　Wesley,
　　　　Trevor,

　　　　　　Quietly they go,

Donald,
　　Rodney,
　　　　Martin,

　　　　　　Gently they go,

Jonathan,
　　David,
　　　　Barry,

　　　　　　I know. But I do not approve,

Cal,
　　Jerald,
　　　　Gray,

　　　　　　And I am not resigned.

　　　　　　Not resigned.

　　　　　　I am not resigned.

I walked out onto Eighth Avenue, into the pulsing noise and light and warmth of a July afternoon in downtown Portland, back among the daily living, back into the swirl and color and beat of life, and stood there a moment, taking it all in.

No, never resigned.

Chapter Nineteen

The Dreamtime

[Bogong High Plains, Australia, May 1986]

"Mind the snakes," said Arnold as we set out on the path.

"Right." I tried to sound nonchalant. "So, what kinds are there?"

"Mostly black snakes, brown snakes, and tiger snakes."

"Ah. Which ones are poisonous?"

He turned back, grinning. "They all are."

"Grand," I muttered under my breath. Australian fauna can be generally divided into two broad categories: the cute and cuddly, and the deadly poisonous. Following our meeting at the student pub, Arnold invited Gray and me to join him on one of his geology treks into the Bogong High Plains. He made these periodically to check gauges he'd placed at different stations measuring rainfall, wind velocity, and the rare seismic readings. This was May in the antipodean autumn of 1986, three years still before Gray would become infected, four years after the first case of AIDS appeared in Australia, and only four years since homosexuality had been decriminalized in the state of Victoria.

Gray had been eager to meet Arnold, and Arnold was intrigued to hear Gray's experience lost on these plains as a boy. The two hit it off immediately. I knew they would, mostly because Gray hit it off with everyone he met. Naturally gregarious and outgoing, he could make friends with a statue. Good friends. ("How did Gray manage to break through your formidable defense system?" O'Shaughnessy once asked. "He wouldn't go away," I said.) Gray had pursued our relationship with the subtlety of a Panzer division. Later, I asked him why me? With his looks, intelligence, charm and social standing, he could have had anyone he wanted. He answered, "I need some darkness in my life." To this day, I don't know whether he was joking or serious. But it's true, we balanced each other: his sunny, extrovert nature with my own more saturnine, indrawn character.

We hiked most of that first day, Arnold maintaining a fast clip. Though half his age, we struggled to keep up. Along the way, he pointed out aspects of the high plains' geomorphology. We were seeing the land through his eyes—the eyes of a scientist, and the eyes of a lover. Gray was delighted with this guided tour by someone who shared his passion for the region. At one point, he turned back to me. "I hope this is changing your view of the high plains."

"Definitely," I said, panting. "I'm developing a whole new appreciation for scrub brush."

With his bristling beard, sun-burnished face, and weather-battered hat, Arnold looked like some old gold prospector in the Outback. Victoria had its own gold rush history, similar to California's, even had their own gold rush towns, like Ballarat and Bendigo.

He, like Gray, was a talker, happy to have someone along to talk to, and we learned his story: He'd sneaked into the army in 1941, misrepresenting his age, and became one of the "Desert Rats" who fought Rommel's North Afrika Korps. To a kid who'd hardly been outside his small township of Glen Valley, the war was an entry into the greater world and sparked in him a wanderlust to see more of it, to see *all* of it. After the war, he studied geology at the University of New South Wales, then used every opportunity to walk around another part of the planet doing fieldwork until well into his forties—through the

Middle East, into Nepal and the Himalayas, the Gobi Desert, even my own Pacific Northwest, in British Columbia. Eventually, he wound up back in Australia and the Bogong High Plains, his first terrestrial love, which became his specialization.

We returned to our base camp as dusk was coming on. I started dinner while Gray built a fire for the night. With a chill to the air, the two of us changed into long pants, while Arnold remained in his walking shorts. I admired his indifference to the weather. I myself preferred the cold, if for nothing else than to keep the bugs down. As the fire took off, Gray brought out a couple of Fosters beers for himself and Arnold.

"You don't care for our Aussie brew?" Arnold asked me.

"I don't care for brew."

"Can I help with dinner?"

"No, you two enjoy your talk. I'll handle it. That's how Gray got me into Australia, as an indentured servant."

"That's how my great-grandfather came to Australia from Ireland," said Arnold. "It's a noble profession."

"Yeah, that's what Gray keeps telling me."

Dinner was easy. I went to the ice chest, removing the vegetarian curry bake we'd prepared at home and brought with us. Our own hearty Indian-Australian concoction, it was a kind of curry quiche, with Tabasco sauce giving it a smoky bite. As the kerosene lantern cast its shadows over the makeshift kitchen, I placed the curry in the camp oven and prepared a salad, listening as Arnold and Gray talked about the indigenous peoples and their concept of the Dreamtime.

"No one can be sure with certainty what it meant to the First People," Arnold was saying. "Even *Dreamtime* itself is a mistranslation of the word *alcheringa* from the Aranda people of central Australia. It might be better rendered as 'the Eternal Uncreated.'"

I already knew this. In fact, the "ancient" concept of the Dreamtime was introduced as recently as 1938, by Adolphus Peter Elkin, an Anglican clergyman and early Australian anthropologist. It suggested the time before time, or time beyond time, or even time out of time. In the 1970s, it became popularized by another Australian anthropologist,

William Edward Hanley Stanner, who coined the term *Everywhen* to try and explain the concept; then the Dreamtime was appropriated by the New Age movement in the 1980s.

"It's a difficult concept for us moderns to grasp," Arnold was saying as he and Gray sat next to the robust fire. "Modern lives are circumscribed and defined by time. Most of us can't imagine existence without it. Indeed, time is what existence *means*, the canvas on which our lives are played out."

I knew Gray was fascinated by such talk. The no-nonsense Melbourne barrister was really a mystic as well as a romantic at heart. All he needed was to see God. Actually, he was the kind of mystic who didn't even need to see God. It's why I remained mildly skeptical about his boyhood account of encountering the ghost of Cleve Cole. I know how the mind can play tricks on itself. It's my business. Not that I thought Gray was lying. I never doubted *he* believed it.

"We are time-locked beings," Arnold was saying. "It may not be possible for us to even conceive of life without time. I don't mean like leaving your watch at home when you go on holiday. I mean where there is no sense of past and future, where there is only this eternal present. Only now. Only ever *now*."

I brought over their plates with the salad. "*Now* is time for dinner," I told them, and served up the spicy, savory bake, slices steaming in the chilly night air.

"Smells wonderful," said Arnold.

"It's our own culinary creation," added Gray proudly.

Arnold took a bite. "Delicious!"

"The secret ingredient is Tabasco sauce," I said.

"Tabasco sauce?"

I held up the small bottle we'd brought along since Gray always liked to splash it lavishly on his slices. "Gray tasted it the first time he was visiting my family in the States and became addicted. My mother sends us a case at a time. He uses it on everything: on his eggs, meat dishes, vegetarian dishes, breakfast cereal."

"Well, now I'm addicted, too," said Arnold.

As we ate by the fire, Gray resumed their discussion. "Do you think we moderns can ever experience the Dreamtime consciousness?"

"Most of us do it every night."

"You mean our dreams?"

"Yes. Elkins may have mistranslated the aboriginal word, but I think he captured the idea. In our dreams, we are outside of time. Past, present, future can be all happening at once."

"But what about being *consciously* aware of such a state?"

"The only way we can do that is by standing outside our ordinary consciousness. Every culture has found ways to induce that state, through chanting, drumming, dancing, sleep and food deprivation, intoxicants, psychotropic plants . . ."

"Have you experienced it?"

"Once, many years ago when I was on a geology expedition in central Mexico. My one experience with peyote."

"What was it like?" Gray was so intrigued he'd stopped eating.

Arnold paused, staring out into the black night, a smile coming to his lips like remembering a past love. "The universe opened itself up to me. I entered a different dimension. No, that's not right. I seemed to enter *all* dimensions at once. I was beyond time, beyond my body and this sense of self. It's impossible to describe because the experience is beyond words, but it remains the most extraordinary experience of my life."

"You tried peyote only once?" asked Gray. "That kind of experience, I think I'd want it daily."

"Only needed the one experience. Unlike other drug highs, you don't wake up and come out of it sober the next morning. You come out of it . . . *changed*, and you can't go back to seeing the world in the old way. Something fundamental has been altered, like the structure of your DNA."

I'd read accounts of people using peyote, mescaline, LSD, and other psychotropic drugs, and, though I had no personal experience, I remained skeptical. To me, it still seemed ultimately a matter of chemicals and neurons interacting felicitously in one's brain. Gray and I often had these conversations.

"I just know how the mind can dupe itself," I once told him, and recited,

"The mind is its own place, and in itself
Can make a heav'n of hell, a hell of heav'n."

"Milton. *Paradise Lost*," said Gray. "And I'd argue it's possible to glimpse beyond the veil of this material reality,

"To see a World in a Grain of Sand,
And a Heaven in a Wild Flower.
Hold Infinity in the palm of your hand
And Eternity in an hour."

"William Blake. *Auguries of Innocence*," I responded. "To which *I* would argue: It's all mental, man."

He had smiled. "Groovy, man." Most of our arguments ended in a draw.

"I've never tried peyote," Gray was telling Arnold, "but I think I've had such moments. Moments when I realize we're participating in some grand mystery, vast and far beyond our understanding, and incredibly wonderful." In the firelight, his eyes and face glowed. Fires brought out the mystic in Gray. "In those moments, it's as if I were seeing the face of God." He paused. "And as if God were seeing me."

The night hung in silence about us, the only sound coming from the crackling and popping of the campfire.

I held out the small bottle. "More Tabasco sauce?"

Gray sighed, turning to Arnold. "He does that on purpose."

"What? I asked if you'd like more Tabasco sauce."

"You deliberately break the mood." He explained to Arnold, "He also does that when I'm feeling romantic."

Arnold was laughing.

"Okay then, so no Tabasco sauce." I set the bottle aside and resumed eating.

157

"You're just afraid of being thought gullible. But I know you. You aren't the philistine you pretend to be."

"I didn't know I was pretending," I mumbled.

Arnold was laughing even harder.

"My partner, the agnostic who tries very hard not to believe in God."

"When God speaks to me, I'll believe."

"Have you considered maybe you're not listening?"

It was my turn to address Arnold. "It's not easy living with a Melbourne barrister who was captain of his university's debating team. And for the record, I prefer to think of myself as a rational skeptic rather than an agnostic. Agnostics know nothing, and are usually proud of it."

Arnold was still grinning at our exchange as he picked up his Fosters. "Myself, I like skeptics. They have to see, touch, and experience for themselves to believe."

"Please, Arnold, don't encourage him," said Gray, returning to his food. "As you see, we have our differences."

The older man's grin softened. His voice became wistful, maybe envious. "I wish your kind of relationship was available when I was your age." Both of us noted the change in tone. "I think you're very fortunate to have each other."

Gray turned back to me, now serious. Even in the firelight I could see it in his eyes and steeled myself for what I knew was coming. He was going to embarrass me.

Sure enough, still gazing with those love-struck eyes, he said quietly, "He is my life. It would be no life without him."

Arnold nodded, also looking at me.

Thusly embarrassed, I murmured, "I guess I kind of feel the same way."

Apparently, I broke the mood once again. Gray turned to Arnold. "And that's about the closest he comes to a profession of love. Apparently, it's considered unmanly for gay men in America to say 'I love you' to each other. He can't say it."

"Of course, I can say it."

"You haven't in all the time we've been together."

"I'm . . . waiting for the right moment."

Arnold was again laughing.

"I rest my case," said Gray, whereby he leaned over, throwing an arm around my neck, and gave me a big, sloppy kiss on the cheek. As I pulled away, he informed Arnold, "He also hates PDAs."

"PDAs?"

"Public Displays of Affection. Another beer?"

"Sure."

Gray got up, went to the ice chest, and returned.

"Ta," said Arnold, taking the Fosters.

They began talking about the latest football game, Australian rules rather than American football with its Iron Man armor and thuggery. Aussie "footies" wear only shorts and jerseys and bounce the ball on the ground like an ovoid basketball. As they talked, I again noted Arnold's legs—strong muscular legs, not as hairy as I would have expected—and hoped I'd be in such good shape when I was his age.

And that's when I saw it.

One of his thick wool socks had slipped down, clotting around his ankle, and there on the calf, not much bigger than a quarter, was a dark spot. Maybe a shadow? I stared at it in the flickering light as Gray tossed another branch onto the fire. The flames flared, momentarily brightening the sea of darkness around our island of light, and I knew what it was. I had seen such black lesions before.

I returned to eating my curry bake, now without appetite, staring into the fire as the talk of football muted around me.

Chapter Twenty

We Are Compadres
(Or, how team building almost destroyed our staff)

[Portland, Oregon, July 1994]

Following Cal's death, the board set about searching for a new executive director, and in July they hired Marti Michaelson. Marti had a proven track record as a crisis manager, working with financially precarious organizations like ours. The board had also wanted an executive director who wouldn't die on them. Cal had been the third. They decided this was a tradition they wished to change. The staff was wary of Marti's appointment: She had no HIV experience, she was very white, very straight, and very middle class. How would she work with a bunch of queers? they wondered. But at her first meeting with us, she scored points by admitting all of this.

"I still think I can help this organization," she said, because she had skills, experience, and expertise that could stabilize the agency and benefit the people we cared about. Then, after a pause where we saw her flush and momentarily tear up, she told us her teenage son was gay, and that as a mother she was determined to do everything in her power to protect him and other young gay men from becoming infected. That clinched it for the staff. Marti was in.

She was definitely high energy. It was going to take some time, getting used to this new executive director and her style. Where Cal had been mellow, Marti was wired; where Cal was cerebral, Marti worked from an intuitive gut-instinct; where he had been a calming presence, she was a double shot of caffeine, the kind of person who thrives on crisis. One suspected she needed it, maybe was not above creating it herself. She made quick, snap decisions, and before she completed her first month on the job, she'd decided the staff needed to pull together and become a team. It wasn't one of her better ideas.

She wangled a small grant for us to participate in a one-day outdoor challenge experience and made it mandatory, announcing there would be no exceptions, no emergencies, no sick leave granted, no deaths of distant relatives allowed. If anyone's grandmother died, she wanted to see the body.

The staff was not excited about the idea, feeling this was an indirect way of addressing the real problem, which was the dysfunctional relationship between the Finance Director and the Client Services Department, and between the Finance Director and the Prevention Department, and between the Finance Director and—well, I think we've identified the problem.

The staff felt they were having to go through this physical hardship simply because Marti couldn't manage Franklin. She and the board were too scared he'd resign, so it was couched as "team building." There was also much grumbling that the $5,000 grant could have been put to better use when all of our budgets were so tight. Some suggested it could have purchased fifty hours of intense psychotherapy for Franklin; others, that it could have bought a world cruise ticket for him—one way. Lionel particularly had been aghast at the frivolous expenditure. "Do you realize how many beers we could have bought for $5,000?" he exclaimed.

Steve defended Marti's decision as he, Sandy, and I were having lunch soon after the memo went out to staff. "She wants us to pull together as a team."

"I thought we already were a team," said Sandy.

"Well, she can't just single out Franklin."

"Why not? The rest of us do."

"Oh, he's not that bad." Steve preferred seeing the good in everyone.

Sandy did, too, though she was willing to make an exception in Franklin's case. "Of course he's that bad! He has absolutely zero people skills."

"But we all have personality quirks."

"No. You have quirks. I have quirks. Franklin has psychopathologies."

Brilliant with numbers, he was lousy with people. He tended to hold his head high, nose in the air, with a certain aristocratic tilt. This gave him the appearance of being condescending, which he generally was, making no effort to hide his disdain for lower life forms like our staff.

But he had performed miracles with the agency's finances, leveraging funds to maximize their impact, renegotiating loans, stretching every dime to its limit. As much as people disliked him, everyone admitted he was holding the agency together.

Like most of us at the chronically understaffed organization, he had double duty, also serving as the human resources director, and he was famous for his terse rejection letters to job applicants:

> *Dear Applicant:*
> *Thank you for your interest in the position of _____.*
> *We have selected a candidate.*
> *You are not he.*
> *Cordially,*

"Franklin believes courtesy is inefficient," Sandy explained. "At least he's an equal opportunity snob. He despises everyone."

So, it came as a surprise to me, as well as others, that Franklin made an effort to become friends soon after I arrived. I wondered why.

"Probably your graduate degree," suggested Sandy. "Franklin doesn't deign to speak to anyone with less than a master's. That puts you at least one step above the rest of us, who he considers barely potty-trained."

"He must be very lonely," I offered.

"I certainly hope so," said Sandy.

Now, after being with CAP for six months, I thought maybe I could be a bridge between Franklin and the rest of the staff, helping to create a better working relationship. This team-building day could be a good opportunity.

Some doubted Franklin would even show up, though Marti had communicated to him in no uncertain terms that he was required to attend. He was clearly the non-team player on our team and she was determined to forge us into a cohesive and coordinated unit. Eventually, the staff got into the spirit, starting an office pool, placing ten-dollar bets on whether Franklin would even show, and if he did, how many hours he would stay. By the time the big day arrived, the pool was up to $350.

It was a Wednesday in late July when we gathered at Camp Harmony, one hundred acres of wooded area, thirty minutes outside of Portland. We stood around in a circle, shivering from the early morning chill and drinking our lattes, except Lionel, who had gotten off work from his moonlighting job as a bar bouncer a few hours earlier and was secretly drinking beer from his Starbucks cup.

I had greeted Franklin as soon as he arrived, wanting to make him feel welcome, and was now standing with him on one side of me and Sandy on the other, already assuming my "bridge" role. Each spoke to me, ignoring the presence of the other. Still, it was a start. Marti was going around, high-spirited, high-fiving and joking with everyone, and discovering that a majority of her staff were not morning people. Indeed, a number were irrepressibly glum—it was too early, it was too physical, and some had already lost their chance at winning the pool because Franklin had shown up after all.

Our "event coordinator" was a bright-eyed, bubbly, and very earnest young woman who looked to be about thirteen. Her face beamed—s*he* was clearly a morning person—as she welcomed us, introducing herself as Shanti, which she explained means "peace" in Hindi. She was a student at the University of Oregon, majoring in Peace Studies. Camp Harmony was owned and operated by a co-op of people, probably all named peace in different languages, who were committed to the peaceful resolution of conflict. They had created this space, she told us, as an oasis of tranquility and love and understanding in a hostile and violent world. The staff stared at her. No one cared.

We would be divided into six teams of approximately five staff members each, with a mix of people from the three departments: Client Services, Prevention, and Administration. As Shanti read off the names, I hoped to be on Franklin's team. Something told me he was going to need a friend; but I was assigned to a team with Sandy, Carla and Jeremy from Client Services, and Elspeth, our bookkeeper, from Administration. Franklin was assigned to a team made up primarily with prevention people: Lionel, Chad, and Leo, and Annie from Client Services. Since I knew he considered Lionel and Chad to be over-age juvenile delinquents, I had a bad feeling already.

After the teams were announced, Shanti laid out the challenge. "Today you are going to become more than mere employees to each other. More than just people working in the same building. You are going to become companions on a grand adventure. Teammates on a glorious quest. Partners in peace." Her eyes turned misty. "Today you are going to become *compadres*." Thirty-some sleepy-eyed, shivering people glanced at each other. *Compadres?* What was Little Miss Sunshine on?

"Look around you. Your life will depend upon the other members of your team. Together, you're going to cross crocodile-infested rivers. You're going to walk over deep gorges. You're going to climb dangerous mountain peaks—"

Sandy murmured to me, "I think I saw that movie. They all died." Then Shanti went over the basic rules. First: No one leaves before the end of the day. Second: No one leaves with anger in his or her heart. Third . . .

After that, she led us into the woods and around the twelve "challenge stations" that made up the course. We would be required to walk across a deep gorge (narrow plank), swing on a rope across a treacherous river (mud puddle), and scale steep mountainsides (a concrete wall). Each team would start at one of the stations and then progress to the next when they'd accomplished the task—assuming they survived the crocodiles and hadn't plunged into the deep gorges. Without a doubt, the most challenging station was going to be The Wall. The upright slab of concrete was twelve feet high and covered with a net of thick, knotted ropes.

"Imagine it's surrounded by a swamp of deadly crocodiles," Shanti told us. "Your task is to see that everyone on your team gets over the wall."

Carla stared at it. Five feet tall, a perfectly spherical 220 lbs., she was not a happy camper. I'm sure I wasn't the only teammate wondering just how we were going to get her over that wall.

But Shanti was there to inspire us, to encourage us to be all that we could be. "We had a group here last week," she said excitedly, "and one of their members was in a wheelchair, and they were able to get *him* over the wall."

"With or without the wheelchair?" Sandy asked amid snickers.

"It just goes to show anything is possible when you think creatively as a team."

"Can't we just walk around it?" asked Charles. Our volunteer coordinator was far too fastidious for something as inelegant as clambering over walls.

No. The crocodiles.

Ah, yes. He'd forgotten the crocodiles.

Typical of the prevention staff, their solution was to not get themselves in that situation in the first place.

"Be creative! Think as a team!" Shanti enthused. "None of us is as smart as all of us."

"Franklin is," said Chad, bringing guffaws from our little group of team builders. Franklin glared at him, suggesting that regrettably Chad's next paycheck was going to go missing. Most likely an accounting error.

We'd have approximately twenty to thirty minutes for each station, breaking for lunch around noon. The menu was tofu burgers with alfalfa sprouts on whole-wheat sesame buns, steamed broccoli, and fresh fruit for dessert. By the looks on their faces, the staff was thinking lunch was the thirteenth station. Sandy smacked her lips. "Sounds yummy."

Lionel was prepared for just such an eventuality, whispering to us on the prevention team that he had brought an ice chest of cold beer and leftover sandwiches from the bar in the trunk of his car.

Shanti summed up, "And at the end of the day, after you've shared these experiences that will forge new bonds as a team, your group will be presented with the Camp Harmony Fir Bough Award of Team Building." She held it up. It looked like something your five-year-old made out of last year's Christmas tree.

"Remember," she reminded us, "leave no one behind!"—which sounded way too militaristic for a group committed to world peace and tofu burgers—and sent us off with a rousing, "You are *compadres!*"

Steve was his typical gung-ho cheerleader self: "Yay, team! Let's do it!" he shouted. Inspired, his team scampered off to their first creative challenge.

"Yay, team," said Sandy with a voice as flat as Australia. "Let's do it, too," and we left for our first station.

As the staff headed off into the forest, there was much parodying of the earnest young event coordinator.

"Last week we had a group here that included a member in a coma, and they got *him* over that wall."

"Well, the week before that, *we* had a group with a woman nine months pregnant, expecting quintuplets. She gave birth just as she

166

started climbing, and we got all *six* of them over the wall!"

In truth, we did all right as a team, even enjoying the first five stations, though some were loath to admit it. There were losses. At our second station, Elspeth broke a nail while swinging on the rope and wanted to know if that qualified for an employee personal injury claim. It was when our team reached The Wall that we knew we faced our greatest challenge. While Sandy, Jeremy, Elspeth and I stood there, contemplating how in the heck that other group got the wheelchair over, Carla took it upon herself to stomp around to the other side, unmindful of crocodiles, and stood defiantly, hands on her prodigious hips, daring us to drag her back. We stared at her, until I said to the others, "Works for me." The four of us climbed the rope wall, joining Carla on the other side, then moved on to our next challenge.

Everything had been going well until fifteen minutes before lunch when the whole endeavor fell apart. Franklin's team came to the concrete wall. He immediately jumped in front of the others and began climbing. Just as he neared the top, his foot slipped, becoming ensnared in the thick ropes. He twisted, trying to free it, lost his grip, and fell backward. And there he was: our finance director, hanging upside down six feet off the ground.

"Well, don't just stand there!" he shouted at his team. "Get me down from here!"

His team—Lionel, Chad, Leo and Annie—immediately huddled together to consult. Now *here* was a challenge to be sure. As Franklin dangled from the ropes, they discussed the daunting task before them; they weighed options; they brainstormed strategies; they considered the problem from every conceivable angle. Then, determining that the situation was utterly hopeless and there was nothing they could do, they all left for the parking lot to drink Lionel's beer, eat his sandwiches, and grieve the loss of their *compadre*.

We heard Franklin's shouts coming through the trees. "Come back here! Get me down from here, you fucking morons!"

In the team's defense, Franklin had been his usual insufferable self, disparaging and dismissing their ideas and suggestions as they tried to

167

figure out each challenge station. On top of that, he was one of those irritating people who is usually right. He had a keen, analytical mind good at solving puzzles. He definitely worked best as a team of one.

"We should go help," I said.

"Why? He's not on our team," said Sandy. "And besides, we're in the middle of crossing this treacherous mud puddle."

I stared at her.

She sighed. "Oh, very well."

So, Jeremy, Elspeth and I hurried toward the sound of the cursing, while Sandy and Carla hurried at a more leisurely pace. Other teams had converged on the wall by the time we got there. Charles's team, first to arrive, had done nothing to assist Franklin, concerned about rumors of crocodiles lurking everywhere, but Father Paul's team was trying to untangle him from the ropes. We joined them, and it took both our two groups, employing some effective coordination and very creative problem solving, to free our finance director. Pleased with ourselves, we wished Shanti had been there to see it. *Last week, we had a group that saved a member's life without tearing his seventy-five-dollar Abercrombie & Fitch T-shirt!*

Now back on terra firma, Franklin was red in the face, fuming and hurling invectives at his "team" and at this whole stupid idea. *So much for gratitude.* That was it for him. He'd twisted his ankle and, still cursing and now threatening a lawsuit, limped off to the parking lot where he climbed into his car and drove away, breaking both the First Rule (No one leaves until we all leave), and the Second (No one leaves with anger in his heart). Stunned, the staff watched him drive away, then checked their watches: two hours and fifty-three minutes. Chad won the pool.

About that time, a bell tolled, signaling lunch was being served. Once we gathered together in the mess hall, Marti expressed her disappointment in us. Franklin's team, back from the parking lot, hung their heads in contrition as Lionel offered a sincere apology, punctuated by deep beer belches. Marti left to see after Franklin, fearing he was going home to write out his letter of resignation. Sandy asked whether this meant we wouldn't get the Camp Harmony Fir Bough of Team Building Award. Shanti decided to use this experience as a "teachable moment." What was our responsibility? How could we have handled this differently? How could we heal this situation?

But with Marti's departure, the staff unanimously voted to leave for Hogies for beer and hamburgers, which actually turned into a pretty neat team-building experience. Chad treated us to lunch with the office pool he'd won; food and fellowship flowed; and, among other benefits of the day, we learned that Annie had scored a date with Shanti.

How did she manage that? we wanted to know.

"I asked her if she'd like to go with me to the march for social justice this weekend."

What march this weekend?

She shrugged. "I dunno. But this is Oregon. There has to be a march for social justice going on somewhere."

All in all, everyone agreed it had been a great team-building experience. We'd grown closer together as a staff and considered the money, or at least Chad's $350, well spent. The day's final toll: one broken nail, several scrapes and scratches requiring Band-Aids and antiseptic, and one twisted ankle. On the positive side, we lost not one of our *compadres* to crocodiles.

Chapter Twenty-One

Befriending Franklin

[Portland, Oregon, July 1994]

*"Hi, Franklin. It's me. Just calling to say sorry about how
today turned out and hoping your ankle is better. Call me at
the office when you get this message. I want to know you made
it home okay."*

After the disastrous team-building experience at Camp Harmony,
followed by the highly successful staff luncheon at Hogie's, I returned
to the office. Officially, we were closed for the day, and I appreciated
the opportunity to catch up on work without interruptions. I left the
voice message on Franklin's home phone, fearing that whatever progress
had been made in recent months with the humanization of Franklin
Youngson III had been lost.

Initially, I'd suspected that Franklin wasn't reaching out to me as a
friend so much as conscripting me as an ally. But over time, I realized
he did want more than an ally. We talked regularly in the office my first
month. Then in March he invited me to lunch, where he gave me his
opinions on everyone at CAP, none of them good.

On Sandy: "More butch than most of the men here."

On Steve: "Pollyanna-Man. Our very own cheerleader."

On Chad: "An Eveready sex toy whose battery never runs down."

On Cal, while he was still living: "Already dead. Just doesn't have the good sense to lie down and get it over with."

"Oh, c'mon," I'd protested, "he isn't dead yet."

"Isn't he? Look at him." Like Sandy, Franklin resented Cal's staying on as executive director when he couldn't do the job that needed to be done.

Even Father Paul, who was universally loved, drew Franklin's withering assessment: "Father Feel-Good. He's hiding something. Nobody's that nice without hiding something. Probably diddling the choirboys."

He had a favorable opinion of no one, liked no one—including, I suspected, himself. Being taken into his confidence gave me the uneasy feeling I was an accomplice. Sometimes I would challenge him.

"Why do you look for the worst in people?"

"Maybe because it's so apparent?"

"Or maybe that's all you're looking for? I mean, look for the bad, sure, you'll find it. Look for the good, and you'll find that. Sort of depends on what you're looking for."

Typical of tactless and insensitive people, he excused his behavior by saying, "I'm just being brutally honest." But from my experience, such people use honesty to justify being brutal.

In my third month at CAP, he invited me to dinner at a favorite restaurant of his, the Mongolian Grill. If I wasn't mistaken, he was being actually charming. I found it discomforting. Offering friendship was one thing, but I didn't want to go any deeper than that.

"Don't worry," he said playfully as if reading my mind. "I'm not coming on to you. You're not my type."

I admit I was relieved. "Ah. And what's your type?"

"Wealthy."

Over dinner, he let down his guard more than ever before, revealing the person behind the persona. The three glasses of wine probably also contributed to his candor.

"As a general rule, I don't trust people."

"No kidding," I said as I ate the spicy beef dish. My gentle sarcasm elicited a smile from him. "And why is that?"

"People can't be trusted."

"Always?"

"Statistically, I'd say one hundred per cent of the time."

"That's not been my experience. Not with everyone."

"Then you haven't waited long enough."

It was somewhat like making friends with a wild tiger. So far, so good. But you never knew when he might turn on you. I discussed this tenuous relationship with Father Paul.

"Franklin is intellectually brilliant and emotionally crippled," he said.

"So why is he here? I mean, why does he stay if he hates it and despises the staff?"

"For some people, if they can't be loved, being needed is the next best thing. And we do need him. He's performed financial miracles keeping this agency afloat." Father Paul encouraged me in my efforts to befriend him. "For whatever reasons, Franklin is reaching out to you."

Franklin had continued initiating these get-togethers. (I refused to call them 'dates,' as Sandy suggested.) One weekend he invited me to the opera. "I was given two free tickets. Want to go? Most of these clods can't appreciate music that doesn't *twang* or *screech*." Opera was not my strong suit, but I agreed to go as long as it wasn't Wagner's complete Ring cycle. (It was Puccini's *La Boheme*, and I was surprised to find Franklin quietly weeping when Mimi dies.)

Then, amid June's spectacular prelude to summer in the Pacific Northwest, we were having lunch together one day when he said a friend had offered him his beach house and suggested we "get away" for the weekend. I squirmed in my chair. It had begun to feel like we were dating.

"As you said," I offered gently, "I'm not really your type."

He immediately backed off, dropping the topic, yet we maintained our collegial friendship at the office—maybe not surprising since I was the only person there he could casually speak to—and I felt we were making progress in his relationships with the staff.

Then came the team-building fiasco at Camp Harmony.

At 5:00 p.m., I was finishing up at the office. Franklin hadn't returned my call. I tried again. Got his answering machine. So I decided to drive out to his condo in Beaverton, stopping at the Mongolian Grill and getting a takeout order of his favorite dish. I rang the doorbell, heard a *limp-thump, limp-thump* coming to the door, and held up the bag of food, along with a big smile, at the peephole, which I knew he'd be checking.

He opened the door, looking suspicious. "Yes?" He was still dressed in the shirt and walking shorts he'd worn at Camp Harmony, his ankle wrapped in a tight bandage.

"I thought I'd stop by and see how you're doing. I brought some of your favorite food from that Mongolian place you like."

"I'm not hungry."

"Oh . . . well, mind if I come in and eat while the food's still hot? I'm famished." A lie. I was still stuffed with Hogie's hamburgers and fries.

He opened the door further, standing aside and shaking his head. "You are so transparent."

"Thank you."

"I didn't mean it as a compliment."

"No, I didn't think you did, but I wanted to leave open the possibility."

I went into his dining room and began opening the cartons. "Nice place," I said, looking around. The savory smells of the spicy-hot beef and rice immediately filled the small area as he limped into the kitchen to get a dish and silverware for me. I spooned out the contents onto my plate. "Gosh, this sure smells good. Thanks for introducing me to that restaurant."

"You want something to drink?"

"Water'd be great. Thanks."

173

He brought back a glass of water for me and a glass of some kind of alcohol for himself, then pulled out a chair and lowered himself into it. I looked at the amber liquid. I could tell by the slight slur of his voice it wasn't his first. He said, "It's for the pain. I'm self-medicating."

"How's your ankle?" I asked as I began eating.

"The nurse in the ER said I'd live, much to the staff's disappointment."

"Oh, no, they really feel bad about what happened."

"How bad?"

I stopped chewing. "How bad?"

"Yes. On a scale of one to ten, how bad do they feel?"

"Oh. Um . . . maybe two? But a strong two."

He chuckled in spite of himself, then resumed his aggrieved look. "Marti was here earlier, begging me not to resign."

"Probably a good time to ask for a raise."

"I would if we could afford it." I could see his eyes salivating as I ate. "Are you going to eat it all?"

I sat back in my chair, holding my stomach. "Whew, I can't. It's delicious, but I'm already full. I'll just take the rest home and have it for dinner tomorrow night . . . unless you want some?"

He got up and limped to the kitchen for another plate, murmuring, "You are so transparent."

He was clearly hungry and dug into the food. As we continued eating, I asked, "I'm interested: Why are you at CAP?"

"What do you mean?"

"I mean, what are you doing at a lowly nonprofit that's always financially shaky? You could be working for a bank or investment firm and making three or four times what you're making here."

"More like ten times what I'm making here," he grumbled.

"Exactly."

"It may be hard to believe, but I care about people, too."

"No, I don't find that hard to believe. Though you do hide it well beneath that cynical front you put on."

"My cynicism is well earned."

"You know what they say: Scratch a cynic and you find a disappointed idealist."

"Scratch a cynic and you have a lawsuit on your hands." He took another drink and set down his glass. "We do what we can. You're good at community organizing and making things happen. Marti's good at fundraising. Steve's good at inspiring and getting people excited. Sandy's good at . . . well she must be good at something. And I'm good at finances. So, it's what I do."

I watched as he finished the last of the cartons. When he was done, I said, "Why don't you go into the living room and elevate your leg? I'll rinse these plates and put them in the dishwasher."

"You don't have to do that. Just leave them on the table."

"No, I'm pretty sure this Mongolian sauce will permanently stain if not rinsed off right away."

He didn't argue, refreshed his drink and carried it into the living room. After I cleaned up, I joined him on the sofa where he'd elevated his foot on a cushion.

"You should probably put ice on that for the swelling."

"That's what the nurse said, but I couldn't be bothered to stop on the way home, and I had other priorities for the ice cubes here." He held up his glass, clinking the cubes.

I returned to his spotless kitchen, opening the freezer and removing a couple packages of frozen vegetables, wrapped them in tea towels and brought them back to him, placing them around his ankle. "I'm applying peas and carrots and broccoli. They're known to have strong healing properties, especially the broccoli. You should probably stay off your ankle for a couple of days."

"I told Marti I'm taking tomorrow off. I'll be back Friday."

"Good. People'll be glad to see you."

"Oh, please. I know they hate me."

"People don't hate you."

"Sandy does. The prevention team does. Most of the client services staff do."

Some things are hard to deny. "Okay, but still, when considering the Earth's total population? The number of people who actually, *truly* hate you make up only a small fraction—probably no more than 10 or 20 percent. Thirty tops."

In spite of himself he chuckled and took another drink.

I ventured, "It's that you don't let people get close to you, Franklin."

"Yes, we have some things in common, don't we?" he said. "The difference being that you don't *want* people to get close to you"—he turned sad—"and that people like you." He drained his glass, then fixed his eyes on me like a laser beam. "I've watched you. You give the *illusion* of intimacy. People open up to you. Confide in you. But you don't let anyone get close. It's a very effective guise, like my cynicism, but you're just as damaged as I am."

"Can't argue with that."

"So, why then do people like you and don't like me?"

"Maybe if you gave them a chance."

"Give people a chance, and they'll betray you. I believe we've had this conversation before."

I saw the hurt child, the brilliant, perceptive, hurting child. One needn't try very hard to see the lonely little boy he'd once been. And was still. I paused. "You must have really been hurt."

He flared. "Don't practice amateur shrink with me."

"I'm not. Sorry. It was just an observation. I meant, you seem wounded."

He closed up. "You'd better go. You and Steve have an early morning meeting with the county."

"Yes, we do."

I got up, walking to the door, then turned back to him. "We're all wounded, Franklin. Just in different ways."

Without looking at me, he said, "Thank you for bringing dinner," and I left.

When I arrived at work the next morning, I went immediately to Sandy's office. "Franklin's in a lot of pain."

"Good."

I was becoming exasperated with her attitude. "Would you do me a favor?"

"Sure."

"I would like you to try and be nice to him when he returns tomorrow."

"Be nice to Franklin? I have an image to protect, you know."

"Okay, then I'm not asking you to be *nice* to him. Just don't be *un*-nice. We need to help him."

She sat back in her chair, crossing her arms. "Why?"

"Why? Because . . . well, how about because he's another human being?"

"I want proof."

"Will you just do it for me? Please?"

On Friday morning, as Franklin came hobbling off the elevator with a cane, Sandy was at the front desk with Connie. She looked up and said, "Good morning, Franklin. Welcome back."

He stopped, eyeing her suspiciously. "What?"

"What *what?*"

"What do you want?"

"Why do I have to want anything? Can't someone say 'good morning' without wanting something?"

He moved on to his office without further comment.

Later that morning he came limping into the prevention room, easing himself into the chair next to my desk. Since the rest of the team would be working that weekend, they hadn't yet arrived.

"All right," he said, "what's happening?"

"What do you mean, what's happening?"

"Sandy is trying to be nice to me. None too convincingly, I might add."

"Why not give her a chance?"

"Because it's not her. She's not being authentic."

"So, let her be *in*authentic for a while. She's making the effort, okay? Trying out new behavior can be awkward at the start."

"She's trying too hard."

"At least she's trying. Why not try it yourself?"

"Try what?"

"Being inauthentic. *Pretend* to be nice to her."

"That's a stretch."

I shrugged. "See what happens."

"And then my 'team' from Camp Harmony left a box of Godiva chocolates on my desk with a note: 'We feel terrible about our bad behavior.' Misspelled of course."

"Behavior?"

"Bad. *B-O-D*."

I had purchased the chocolates, which I knew were his favorite, and given them to the team to give to Franklin. Sounded like I should have also written the note.

"I think they're saying they're sorry for what happened."

"Well, you can call off the Nice Initiative."

"Why don't you just accept it?"

"Because it's not honest. People trying to play like they care."

"Then accept it as not honest, but they're trying."

"Very trying," he murmured, pulling himself back to his feet, and left for his office.

The staff did try, but the "Nice Initiative" wore thin after a couple of weeks because Franklin didn't respond in kind. He continued to see Sandy's and the staff's gestures as inauthentic, which was true, I admitted, but he didn't give them any points for effort. After four weeks, the staff stopped trying.

But there was now a chill between Franklin and myself. I had seen him emotionally vulnerable that evening in his apartment, and he couldn't forgive me for having witnessed it. He stopped stopping by my desk, and always had excuses when I invited him for coffee or lunch. As we moved into September, finally, sadly, I had to admit our attempts to befriend Franklin had failed.

—◠◠◠—　—◠◠◠—　—◠◠◠—

"I would like to see Mum and Dad again. One last time."

Strange how past vigils bleed into the present, how certain ghosts hover. I was thinking of Trevor in Fairfield, the infectious diseases hospital outside Melbourne. Most people with AIDS grow old before their time. Jerald was thirty-seven when he died, and Cal was forty-five, yet both looked in their sixties. For Trevor, it was the reverse. He seemed to grow younger with each passing week in the hospital. He'd always been slender and small in stature. He'd joke about his "runt genes," back when he still used to joke. Though in his mid-twenties, he resembled a sick little boy lying in his hospital bed, like he should have been in the children's ward. He sat with a large-print Bible open before him when I came to visit. His vision had deteriorated due to the cytomegalovirus, one of many viruses that had been ravaging his body over the past year. I knew his time was approaching.

"Is there anyone to contact?" I asked. I'd seen friends visit, his pastor and members of the Metropolitan Community Church, the "gay church" in Melbourne, but never saw any family.

"I would like to see Mum and Dad again," he said. "One last time."

"Of course. Is there anything I can do?"

"Would you call them? Tell them I'd really like to see them?"

"Sure. Where do they live?"

"In Ballarat. They may not come. We haven't spoken in seven years. When I came out, Dad said he never wanted to see me again."

"People say rash things when they're upset." I looked at his small, bird-frail body, his face and arms splotched with dark lesions from Kaposi's sarcoma. "Things . . . change."

I'm brought out of my memories as a hospital staff person enters the waiting room, pushing before her a cart loaded with cleaning supplies, and quickly reorient myself. Providence Hospital, not Fairfield; Portland, Oregon, not Australia.

"Sorry for disturb, sir." Very thin with a very thin face, cheekbones prominent and skinny arms, she looks Sudanese, maybe Somali, wearing a hijab headscarf.

"You're not disturbing me." I smile at her. "Thank you for your work. You keep this room very clean."

She smiles shyly, slightly bobbing her head. "Thank you, sir." And she begins wiping down the plastic chairs.

"Tell me if I'm in your way."

"No problem, sir."

As she quietly cleans, collecting and restacking the back issues of *Bon Appetit!*, my mind drifts, remembering another tentative voice.

"Hello?"

"Mrs. Ellis?"

"Yes."

I introduced myself as a friend of Trevor's and conveyed his request to see her and her husband. "It would mean a lot to him," I said.

"Oh, I'm not sure that would be possible." Her voice was soft, hesitant. I pictured a timid woman cringing on the other end of the phone.

"It's serious, Mrs. Ellis. I'm sorry to tell you that Trevor is quite ill. This will probably be the last chance you'll ever have to see your son." I paused. "He would really like to see you."

Her voice went whispery. "Yes, I see . . ." I strained to listen. "Uh, thank you . . . I, uh, I'm not sure that we—"

Suddenly an angry male voice came on the phone. "Who is this? What do you want?"

I again introduced myself and explained why I was calling.

"We have nothing to say to him. Understand? Don't call again!" He slammed down the phone.

I hung up with a sigh. Some things apparently don't change.

When I returned to his room the next day, Trevor raised himself up from his pillow, his eyes expectant like those of a child. "Did you speak with my parents?"

"I did. Last night . . . spoke to both of them." I pulled up a chair next to his bed and sat. "It didn't go well."

He slumped back onto his pillow, his eyes going dull, as if dusk had settled over them.

"I'm sorry, Trevor."

"I knew they wouldn't come. It's my father. He's a deacon in our church, and our church said I was damned if I didn't change."

He turned away from me, staring at the wall.

"I'm sorry," I repeated, having nothing better to offer.

"I did try. To change. Tried everything. Counseling. Prayer sessions. They sent me away for a month to a conversion camp led by a Christian psychiatrist from the States. He said God could change us if we really wanted to change. And I did. I wanted God to change me so badly. Prayed each day asking. But He didn't. After a time, I knew it was no good. When I told my parents, Dad said to leave and never come back."

"How old were you?"

"Seventeen."

He looked down at his spindly arms, spotted now with the lesions. "Maybe I am damned."

"It's a virus, Trevor. A virus. It's biology. Not theology."

He whispered, "I feel damned."

And I felt helpless. What does one say to the damned? Even when I first met him years before, serving on a care team together, Trevor carried a deep sadness in him. But then, most of us did.

"What about your mother? I sensed she wanted to say more. Maybe your mother would come to Melbourne."

"She doesn't drive. Dad wouldn't let her."

"She could take the train down."

"She'd never take the train by herself. She's always been scared."

My mind raced through different possibilities. "All right. If you call your mother and she wants to come to Melbourne, I'll drive to Ballarat and bring her down."

He turned his head back to me. "But that's almost two hours from here."

"I know. I've been to Ballarat before. I'll do it."

"Really?"

"Really . . . I'll even take her back."

It had been months since I'd seen his smile. It would be worth the hours of driving to see it again when his mother arrived.

"What do you say? Shall we call her?"

"My dad . . ." His voice drifted off.

"Is your father at work now?"

He nodded.

Five minutes later he held the receiver to his ear with both hands as if it were a heavy dumbbell.

"Ready?"

He nodded again. I dialed the number. It rang several times, then . . .

"Oh, hello, Mum? Hi, it's me. Trevor?" His voice was tentative, soft and timid like his mother's. "H-how are you?"

I sat next to his bed. I could hear the sound of her voice, though not the words.

"I'm glad to hear that. Myself, I'm . . . I'm not doing too well."

There was silence on the other end.

"I would really like to see you again, Mum. I was hoping maybe you could come to Melbourne?"

Her voice.

"Yes, I know Dad won't, but I thought maybe you could come? I really want to see you."

I tapped my chest.

He looked at me. "My friend—you spoke with him on the phone?—he said he'd drive up there and bring you to Melbourne. . . . He said he'll even take you back." He smiled, but his smile faded when there was no response. I know what it feels like to have a joke fall flat.

Her voice again. I didn't need to hear her words to know what she was saying. I saw the tears filling his eyes as he clung to the phone receiver. "I've missed you. I would really, really like to see you."

Her voice. He looked at me, shaking his head. *No.*

"Mum, I wanted to say I'm sorry. I never wanted to be this way. I don't know why I'm like this. If I could change, I would. You know how hard I tried to change."

Her voice.

"I know Dad won't, but can you forgive me?"

There was silence.

He swallowed loudly. "I love you, Mum."

Silence. Nothing came back.

The tears were now sliding down his cheeks. "Mum, I love you." In that hospital room his mother's silence was deafening. It hurt my ears. I dropped my head, closing my eyes, not wanting to witness this as he pleaded, "Mum?"

"Sir? Please, sir."

I look up.

"Be okay. You see. Be okay."

The cleaning woman's holding out some tissues to me, and I realize I'm crying. Tears rolling down my face. "Oh, I'm sorry," I say, embarrassed. "Thank you." I take the tissues. "Sorry about this."

She smiles sympathetically. "Be okay. You see."

"Yes. Yes, I'm sure it will." I wipe my eyes with the tissues, too embarrassed to look at her. I can only imagine her story, what she has experienced . . . what she has survived, and she's the one comforting me. "Be okay," she says softly once more, then turns and leaves the room. I slump forward in the chair, still embarrassed, holding the tissues to my eyes as I hear her cart trundling down the hallway, silence closing behind like water in a boat's wake. I give myself to the widening silence, where Trevor's voice is now steady, sounding grown up, "Well, I'd better go" even as the little boy is quietly crying before me. "I just wanted to say thank you. For everything. And that I'm sorry. That I'm really sorry. Please tell Dad I said I'm sorry."

Her voice again.

"I know. Good-bye, Mum . . . I love you."

Silence.

" . . . Well, good-bye then."

He handed me the receiver and lay back against his pillow,

exhausted. "She doesn't think it's a good idea."

I hung up the phone and placed a hand on his shoulder. It was like touching bone under his hospital gown.

"I'm sorry, Trevor. Can I get you anything? Or anyone? Your pastor?"

He slowly shook his head. He had become an active member of the Metropolitan Community Church when he first arrived in Melbourne seven years earlier. The pastor who visited and prayed with him preached that God loved Trevor as He made him—in His own image. It seemed to make a difference, and Trevor had seemed almost happy with his new life and with his new church family. But in the end, it was the harsh, cruel god of his father that he bowed down before and worshipped. Contrary to what scripture tells us, love is no match for hate.

The next day he fell into a coma and died two days later.

Chapter Twenty-Two

The Mother Brigade

[Portland, Oregon, July 1994]

Walking back from my work out at the Princeton, I was excited about the evening, the first weeknight I'd had free in four months. Like all the staff, I was working fifty-plus hours a week—in the nonprofit world there is no such thing as overtime—and I savored the anticipation of the coming evening like a delicious memory: *First, I'd prepare a baked potato for dinner, smothered in cheese and chives and savory bacon bits; then I'd lovingly take down a novel from the bookshelf, curling up on the sofa with a cup of hazelnut milk tea, and blissfully lose myself in its story for three or four uninterrupted hours.* It had been months since I'd been able to so immerse myself in a book. My reading these days was grabbing thirty minutes here, fifteen minutes there, whenever I could. I already had the book in mind, too, had been keeping it for just such a free night: Caleb Carr's historical novel, *The Alienist.* Yes, I was so ready for this evening!

Lionel was on the phones when I stepped off the elevator. The staff took turns relieving Connie, our receptionist, for her breaks and lunches. He was punching buttons and shouting, "Will ya *HOLD*?" in a tone suggesting dire consequences if the caller didn't. He waved me over, hand covering the mouthpiece, and whispered, "Annie needs to see you."

"Thanks."

Annie was at her desk in the Client Services Department. "Hi, what's up?" I said, pulling up a chair. She was immediately apologetic. "I hate to do this to you. Sandy's sending me home sick and wants you to take my care team training this evening." She did look pale, not her usual rosy complexion.

"No problem. Happy to do it."

"Really?"

"Really. Hope you're feeling better soon."

"Oh, it's nothing serious, just a case of gonorrhea in my throat." I continued to admire and be amazed, at times unnerved, by the candor of the young people on staff. "I went to the doctor this morning and started a course of antibiotics and I'm feeling fine," she said, "but Sandy still wants me to go home and rest."

"I agree. And it's not a problem for me to take your training tonight." *I'm putting* The Alienist *lovingly back up on the shelf.*

"Thanks a million. I owe you."

"Don't worry about it." *But gonorrhea in the throat?* I leaned forward, lowering my voice though no one else was in the room. "I don't mean to be too personal, but ..."

"What?"

"Um, how does a lesbian get gonorrhea in the throat?"

Without the slightest hesitation, she said, "Well, I'm not always a lesbian."

I sat back up. "Ah. Of course. Got the visual. No need to say anything more." Along with their candor, I admired how "sexual orientation" for younger people was such a fluid thing, not a rigid socio-psychological category or political statement. When Annie was with another woman, she was a lesbian; when she was with a guy, she, well, wasn't. She suggested I speak with Father Paul about tonight's training—he was in the kitchen—and thanked me a hundred more times before I left.

Stashing the gym bag under my desk, I headed back to the kitchen. *So, okay, I'll postpone* The Alienist *until Saturday night. That's better anyway.* I had a New Volunteer training session Saturday for those who'd managed to run the gauntlet of Charles's intake procedure, and then I'd go home, fix dinner, and relish my novel for the entire evening. That feeling of anticipated contentment carried me into the kitchen where I found Father Paul talking with Steve and Chad, the three of them enjoying small savory quiches donated by Valentino's Delicatessen. A number of restaurateurs often donated food items for the staff in appreciation of our work.

"Try one of these," said Steve. "They're delicious."

"Thanks. Maybe later. I just need some water."

"You'd better get one now before Carla discovers them," said Chad. Carla had an obsessive relationship with food. If she knew about them, she would sit in there, consuming one after another until they were all gone.

"I hear you're helping out tonight with the support groups," said Father Paul. "Thanks for stepping in."

"Happy to do it," I said, going to the water cooler. "I enjoy the Mother Brigade." They were a care team that had begun a number of years ago as a grief support group for mothers whose sons had died of AIDS. But, being mothers, they needed to do something more than just grieve. Over the years, the group had continued to grow, until now it comprised several active care teams.

"They are indeed remarkable women, these mothers," he said, "and we need to support them however we can."

"You'll meet another remarkable mother this weekend," said Steve.

I looked up from the water cooler. "This weekend?"

"You're going out with Lionel on his bar blitz Saturday night, right?"

"Oh. Yep, sure am." I'd forgotten.

Friends going through my things decades from now, sorting and settling my earthly affairs, come across a copy of The Alienist. *In pristine condition. They remark on it. Looks like it's never been read. Probably can get a fair price for it at Powell's Used Books.*

"Christine Levinson is one of our most popular volunteers on the bar blitz team."

"She's a hoot," agreed Chad. "I'll probably see you out there."

Steve returned to their conversation. "So, I made my flight reservations this morning."

"Going somewhere?" I asked.

"Home for a visit."

"That's nice. Where's home?"

"Western Montana."

I'd found that no one actually comes *from* Portland. Portland is a city of immigrants. Everyone I knew was from somewhere else: Steve from Montana, Chad from Colorado, as was Sandy. Lionel was from New Jersey, Andie from Ohio, Franklin from Los Angeles, Father Paul from Michigan, and even Marti was from Boston originally. People seem drawn to Portland for a host of different reasons: progressive politics, funky laid-back lifestyles, scenic beauty, physician-assisted suicide . . .

Steve talked warmly of home, one of those small towns where everyone knows your name—as well as your salary, current financial situation, medical history, marital relationship, *extra*-marital relationships, drinking habits, criminal record (when applicable), and where 90 percent of your high school graduating class still lives, married to each other.

"Sounds like my hometown in Colorado," said Chad. "Mormon country. I was lucky to have gotten out alive."

"No, it's good to be part of a community like that," said Steve. "They're good people. Generous, kindhearted. Family means everything to them."

"Unless you're a gay member of their family," said Chad.

"Mormons are hardly the only people who condemn homosexuals based on their religious beliefs," Father Paul reminded him.

"I go home twice a year," Steve explained to me. "For Mother's Day and Christmas."

I was not surprised. I knew he carried his mother's photo in his wallet. (Yes, he was that kind of son.)

"Your mother is my hero," said Chad, munching on another quiche.

The story was well known among the staff. Steve's mother was part of her church's knitting group, a sweet-tempered woman. One could see where Steve got his whole-wheat-goodness personality and sense of decency. The eight women met each week to knit caps for Head Start children and blankets for new babies at the local hospital. A typical Western community, they took care of their own. In one of the knitting sessions, someone had started talking about "those gays," and the others began chipping in: "I hear they have no morals whatsoever and will sleep with anyone." "Yes, highly promiscuous, I've heard. It's no wonder this AIDS spread so quickly among them." "I'm told they volunteer for Scouting programs to prey on young boys."

It went on for five or six minutes like that, with a fair amount of head shaking and cluck-clucking of their tongues to accompany the click-clicking of their needles, when Steve's mother, without looking up from her work, remarked, "Well, my Steve's gay, and he's not anything like that." An unnatural silence had descended over the group, broken only by the ceaseless sound of the working needles as the other women, heads down, glanced sideways at each other, eyes wide, as they continued their knitting.

"That must have taken guts," I said, "especially in a small town."

"Mom said no. Not guts. She said all it took was her love for me."

"Then your mother's my hero, too."

"What about your mom?" Steve asked.

I hesitated. "We have some unresolved issues. She doesn't like to talk about it."

"It?"

"Me. She lives in mortal fear the neighbors and people at church will find out I'm gay. We just pretend a part of me doesn't exist, and so we don't talk about it."

"Did she meet your partner?" asked Steve. "I think it helped my

Mom and Dad when they met Mark and liked him."

"How could anyone *not* like Mark?" offered Father Paul.

"Yes, she met Gray. And she liked him. He was my 'Australian friend,' and she didn't want to know or hear any more than that."

"Almost three," said Chad, pointing at the wall clock. "We've got the meeting with the ACT-UP people."

"Right. Let's go," said Steve. He and Chad left the kitchen, while Father Paul and I remained behind, briefly discussing the training that evening. It would be easy, not requiring any preparation on my part. As we began to leave, he said, "You know, you're going to need to forgive your mother someday."

His statement caught me by surprise. "I don't think my mother feels she needs to be forgiven."

"No, not for her sake. For yours. You'll need to forgive her to be free of this."

"Free of what?"

"Of not being able to love that part of you she won't talk about. For not being able to love . . . who you are."

After a pause, I said, "She may not be the perfect mother. But then, I'm hardly the perfect son. So we love each other in our own imperfect ways."

Father Paul smiled and patted my arm. "Thank you for helping out tonight."

Chapter Twenty-Three

Queen of the Bar Blitz

[Portland, Oregon, July 1994]

God created mothers because He couldn't be everywhere at once.

Apart from its treacly sentiment and patriarchal sexism, the statement is theologically problematic as well. All the monotheistic religions assert that God *is* everywhere at once, immanent in His creation. And yet, many would probably still affirm the statement's metaphorical truth. We called them the Mother Brigade. Marjorie Wood, who led the care team, summed up their credo: "It's a mother's duty to love and care for *all* children." Marjorie believed, first, that everyone deserves a good mother (that's where her group came in) and, second, that it was never too late to become a good mother. Yes, there is the Gorgon type, like Gray's, but for every Gorgon there are twenty mothers like Steve's, and even a greater number like my own, those who love their sons and daughters, though confused and embarrassed at how we could have turned out *that way*.

And then there are mothers like Christine Levinson.

"Christine! Christine!" men shouted as we entered the Silverado. She was the hit at every bar we visited that night. "Christine!" guys would call out when they saw her, and she loved it. "Have you been a good boy?" she'd ask. "I have! I have!" the man would insist like some eight-year-old before a doubting Santa. "Really?" she'd respond. "Why?"

Short and matron-like in build, hair coiffed in a stand-up 'do and dressed attractively in casual business attire, she wasn't so much an extrovert as a one-woman kamikaze squadron, a cross between Mother Teresa and Bette Midler. She spoke in a loud South Bronx accent, cackled, smoked cigarette after cigarette, knocked back every drink bought for her (and there were plenty) and thoroughly enjoyed herself.

It was Saturday night, and I was not thoroughly enjoying myself. I've never felt comfortable in the bar scene, the smoky, seedy, noisy meet/meat markets, but Steve wanted me to become familiar with all their prevention programs. I had already attended a number of the men's discussion groups Chad coordinated, had accompanied Leo on his late-night walks on the streets and helped him develop his street outreach program, so I felt compelled to join Lionel and his team of five volunteers on this Bar Blitz.

They called themselves the Merry Fairies, and no doubt about it, of all CAP's volunteers they had the most fun. They would go in, occupy a bar for an hour or so, blitzing three, sometimes four bars in an evening. Since I didn't care for alcohol, they were delighted to make me the Designated Driver of the van.

I stood on the sidelines at the first bar, watching Lionel and his team of revelers flirting, joking, and gossiping, while passing out condoms and safe-sex information. "Here's a condom," offered Lionel to one attractive bar patron. "Would you like me to show you how to put it on?" He and his volunteers were perfect for this work, about as far as one could get from the Morality Police, playful, teasing, while conveying the serious message of, "Play Safe, Protect Yourself, Don't Infect Your Brothers."

But without a doubt, Christine was the queen of the bar blitz. Brassy, ballsy, and brazen, she handed out raunch as easily as she received it, hugged a hundred men in an hour, all types, all ages, all levels of inebriation, with the same message: "You keep yourself safe, you hear? I care about you and want to see you still here in ten years. I need your hugs." She was Coach, Cheerleader, Mother Confessor, Barroom Philosopher, and, as I was to discover that night, in some cases, Tempter. She played the mother role to these men as John, in time, had come to play the father role to those testing in our program.

At our second bar, she was out on the floor, dancing right in the thick of the frenzy, syncopated lights flashing, heavy music-beat deafening—*thud-thud-thud-thud*—producing a major headache as I nursed my third Pepsi for the evening, already exceeding my limit.

She came up to me, out of breath, fanning herself.

"You're very popular," I shouted above the music. It was the first time we had talked.

"I love these guys," she shouted back, looking out over the crowd. "I really do. Each is like a son to me. I know their fears, their insecurities, the loneliness they try to cover with alcohol. I know their desperation to hook up. It's not just about sex. They want to connect with another human being, to feel alive!"

Once she regained her breath, she lit another cigarette. By this time, my sinuses had packed up and left for home without me. The heavy beat continued pounding—*thud-thud-thud-thud*—the lights continued flashing, the darkened room a gyrating mass of bodies.

"Why aren't you out there dancing?" she asked.

"Come dance with me!" Flames reflecting off Gray's white naked body as he danced around the fire, circling, leaping, stomping, again and again shouting, "Come dance with me!"

I turned back to her. "Sorry?"

"I asked, why aren't *you* dancing?"

"Oh, I never really got the hang of it."

"What's there to hang? You just get out there and shake your booty."

"Yeah, I've never been very good at booty-shaking."

"My God, look around you. *Good* isn't an issue here. It's the shaking that's important."

"Sorry," I shouted back. "Hard to hear you in here," I lied.

The Merry Fairies moved on to our third and final bar for the night, thankfully a quieter scene. After making her jolly rounds of hugs and banter, Christine came up to me with her latest drink and what must have been her twentieth cigarette.

"You don't join in?"

I began to fear I'd become her cause for the night.

"I'm on the clock. Working. Just here to observe, thanks."

She studied me for a moment. "You're polite. You should meet my son, Martin. He's polite, too." It was the way she said *polite*, as in *He has a brain tumor, too.* Or, *He's in recovery, too.* Or, *He died several years ago, too.*

"He's still in the closet. I tell him, 'My God, Martin, you're thirty-five. When are you going to come out already?' He says, 'Mother, it's just not that simple.' 'Well, at least march with us in the Gay Pride parade,' I say. 'Someone might see me,' he says. 'Like that's kind of the whole point, isn't it?' I say."

"Doesn't sound like he's ready yet," I offered.

"Yeah, but will he ever be ready? I mean, c'mon, he's too *old* to be a latent homosexual. When he was growing up, it never bothered me he might be gay. I knew he was gay by the time he was five. My fear was he might be a latent Republican. I'm not sure I could have handled that."

She took another drink and another puff for sustenance. "But he's been scared of life as far back as I can remember. He gets that from his father, Maurice. Maurice always had a basic fear something bad was going to happen. I'd say, '*Of course* something bad's going to happen! Bad things are part of life as much as good things. Protect yourself from the bad and you block the good as well. The point is to live, to feel fully and deeply and muchly.'" She was slurring. "Why live life halfheartedly, you know?"

I was thinking, *Because sometimes half a heart is all we have left.*

Just then Chad came up to us.

"Christine!" He gave her a big hug and kiss.

"And how are you tonight, my little prince?" she asked.

"All good," he beamed. "It's always all good."

She laughed, stroking his hair. "That's my boy."

"Christine is my spiritual mother," he told me.

"And Chad is my spawn."

They chatted a bit more and laughed a lot. I was grateful for the reprieve from the Godmother's grilling.

"Well, I'm off to the hunt!" said Chad. "See ya!"

She watched him go with a warm smile. "In my next life, I'm coming back a gay man like Chad. They throw the best parties, have the best fashion sense, and get the most fun—except for you, honey. You sure you're gay?"

"Pretty sure." I was watching the crowd, but sensed a laser beam on my forehead. Fortunately, I was saved by the show starting. A young guy clad only in a G-string was up on one of the platforms, dancing to the driving beat. Caught in a web of swirling, flashing lights in the darkened room, he was the physical embodiment of the music, twisting and turning his slender, sinuous body, grinding his hips around and around and around.

"Mm-mm, look at the buns on that kid," said Christine.

But I was already looking. And he did have perfect buns. One of those guys who seems overdressed in a G-string. The music possessed him as he pumped his hips to the pulsing, pounding rhythms, now drowned out by the cheers and whistles of an appreciative audience.

"Makes me hot just watching him," said Christine. She turned back to me. "In case you hadn't noticed, I'm the female equivalent of a dirty old man."

Interesting. I was just thinking she was Jake Caulfield's female equivalent. A coincidence? I think not.

Amid the syncopated lights, I saw the kid's grin. He was clearly delighting in the crowd's enjoyment of his lithe, smooth body, of being visually caressed by a room full of men and one horny older woman. He maintained his rhythmic gyrations on the platform while sinking down so men could stuff bills into his G-string.

Christine nudged me. "Why don't you go up and, you know,

slip in a bill?"

"Oh, he looks . . . busy." At the rate the boy was raking in the bills, he could have single-handedly put a dent in the national debt. "Besides," I said, "he's not really my type. You know, young, cute, sexy."

"What are you, a eunuch?"

I nodded, watching him. "For all intents and purposes."

"But why? You're a good-looking fellow. You've got a nice body."

I am being checked out by a woman my mother's age?

"What's holding you back?"

I nodded to the kid. "The law?"

"Besides that. And he's legal." She turned back to the boy dancing on the platform. "I mean, probably."

By this time, she was a little loopy, maybe one or two or ten too many free drinks.

"Honey, life is too short. Too beautiful and sexy not to play. Is that really the way you want to spend your time, sitting at home jerking off?"

Oh, great, so now we're getting into my autoerotic behavior?

"Don't you want more from life than being Designated Driver?"

I joked, "You make it sound like a bad thing."

Didn't work. "Ever hear the motto, 'Life was meant to be lived'?"

"Hmm, sounds familiar. I think I found that in a fortune cookie once."

"It's true. I live by it. Hell, it's part of my family legacy."

"Family legacy?"

"My maternal grandparents were killed in the Holocaust."

I swung around to face her. "Oh, gosh, I'm so sorry, Christine!"

She was again watching the dancing kid, nodding her head in time with the beat, then turned back to me. "What? Nah, I just made that up. My grandparents lived in Hoboken all their lives. Died in their nineties within months of each other."

By now I was thinking this woman is not drunk; this woman is nuts.

"You're probably thinking I'm nuts."

"No, no," I laughed lightly, not even convincing myself.

"I just like to try on different ideas. Like trying on different lives. See how they feel. Know what I mean?"

But I was irritated that this sixty-some-year-old, more than a little inebriated, extrovert woman who makes up lies as it's convenient was telling me how to live. Or . . . *to live*. She was a cross between Bette Midler and Mother Teresa all right. A right cross. How arrogant, how presumptuous of her to make these judgements of me based on this highly artificial social setting filled with secondhand carcinogenic smoke! My defensiveness also told me that truth was lurking somewhere in the vicinity.

Sensing my withdrawal, Christine offered, "Of course, I could be totally wrong about you."

"Well, maybe just a litt—"

"Though not likely. I'm an excellent judge of character." She checked her watch.

"We're almost done for the night. Why don't you let me buy you a drink? One drink? Just to loosen up a bit."

"Thanks, but I don't like alcohol."

"You're afraid of losing control."

"No, it's not about control. I've just never cared for the taste of it."

"My son Martin doesn't like to lose control either. Martin's been risk-averse since he was a toddler. Just like his father, Maurice. We'd go to Baskin-Robbins and my husband would order vanilla ice cream."

"Maybe he preferred vanilla."

"How would he know? He never tried any other flavors. But that's okay. Some people can't handle risk."

"Oh, I take risks."

"Like what?"

"Huh?"

"What risks do you take?"

"What risks?"

"Yeah, you know, like: 'risks recently taken by you.'"

In that moment, all I could think of was being the first kid in our neighborhood to ride a bike without training wheels.

"When was the last time you took a risk? I mean, a big risk?"

She was definitely getting too close to the Forbidden Zone of Terrible Truths.

"Gosh, gee, there's been so many. It's hard to know where to begin. Oh, look! Here comes Lionel." I waved him over.

"How you two getting along?"

"Fine," said Christine. "I'm trying to seduce him to the Dark Side, but the force is strong in this one."

Lionel turned to me, grinning. "I should warn you, with Christine, resistance is futile."

"You're kind of late with the news, but thanks anyway."

I returned home around 2:00 a.m., reeking of cigarette smoke—on my clothing, on my skin, on my hair, coating my eyeballs—and went directly to the utility room, where I stripped off my clothes, tossing them into the washer for a soak and cleaning in the morning, then took a long hot shower to steam out my pores and become reunited with my sinuses.

When was the last time you took a risk? I mean, a big risk?

Under the jets of hot water, I kept hearing Christine's question, her prodding, her poking, her nosing into my life, so irritating! So, I decided to think instead of the dancing kid, which was far less irritating. Yet her voice continued to nag over the music's beat and the boy's seductive bumps and grinds and grin.

Finally, I turned off the water, leaning my forehead against the shower wall with a sigh. The last big risk I took? I knew the answer even back in the bar with Christine. Ten years ago. I said yes to Gray. That was the last big risk. Me performing without a net. And look how that turned out.

Chapter Twenty-Four

A Philosophical Fable

[Bogong High Plains, Australia, May 1987]

Once upon a time, Gray told me a fable. It was autumn, the land sere and dry, the evening quickly chilling as we had our evening meal next to the campfire. It went like this:

"There once was a Chinese philosopher—"

"Which part of China?"

"What?"

"China's a big place. Which province did he come from?"

"It's a fable. Does it matter?"

"I like to know these things."

"He was from . . . um, Hung Chow."

"You made that up."

"Anyway, there once was this Chinese philosopher—"

"Any particular school?"

"What do you mean 'particular school'?"

"Ancient China had a number of different schools of thought. Confucianism, Taoism, Ch'an Buddhism—"

"He had an online degree."

"Oh, one of those schools."

"So, this Chinese philosopher, he once dreamt that he was a butterfly—and no, I don't know what kind of butterfly."

"Too bad. It would have added authenticity to the story."

"Okay, he dreamt he was a monarch butterfly."

"I didn't know they had monarch butterflies in China."

"The butterfly was visiting."

"So, he wasn't a real Chinese butterfly."

"No, but the philosopher was a real Chinese philosopher."

"With a wonky degree."

"Do you want to hear this fable or not?"

"All ears. Shoot."

"So, this Chinese philosopher with a wonky degree from Hung Chow dreamt he was a monarch butterfly visiting China on a tourist visa."

"I appreciate the details. They make the story more interesting."

"I realize you're a concrete thinker. The dream was so real—"

"Must have been at the REM stage of sleep."

"The dream was *so real*—and this is the important part—he couldn't tell whether he was a Chinese philosopher who'd dreamt he was a butterfly, or was actually a butterfly now dreaming he was a Chinese philosopher."

Gray exhaled. He seemed relieved the telling was finished.

"That's it? That's the whole fable?"

He shook his head, "I'm sorry I bothered," and resumed eating.

"No, it was okay . . . though it didn't have much of a narrative arc. And the character of the Chinese philosopher was kind of one-dimensional. He could've been developed a bit more—"

"Just pass the Tabasco sauce."

"Here. So, what's the point of the fable?"

"The point?" Gray put down the bottle and recited, "All that we see and seem is a dream within a dream."

"Edgar Allan Poe. Really deep." And I recited back, "Something unknown is doing we don't know what."

He creased his brow. "Who said that?"

"Sir Arthur Eddington. His explanation for how the universe works."

"Eddington was a poet?"

"Physicist. All physicists are poets. They just use mathematics instead of words."

"I call foul." Gray handed back the Tabasco sauce. "The fable suggests we can never be sure of who we are."

"Well, at least I'm sure I'm not a butterfly... Pretty sure."

"Philosophers have been trying to answer that question for thousands of years."

"Whether we're really butterflies?"

"No, what's real. Descartes set out to doubt everything he could, to take nothing for granted, until he found that which he could not doubt."

"Descartes. He that 'I think, therefore I am' guy?"

"Right. *Cogito ergo sum.* He eliminated everything down to the one thing he couldn't doubt: that he was thinking. And if he was thinking, then he must be real."

"But he assumed he was thinking."

"Huh?"

"I'm saying maybe he stopped doubting a step too soon. He could've been hallucinating, or merely dreaming that he was thinking."

Gray considered this. "Okay, but either way, it's still proof that he exists."

"What, 'I hallucinate, therefore I am'? Doesn't seem as persuasive an argument."

"The question is, how do you really know what's real, whether you're a philosopher dreaming he's a butterfly, or a butterfly dreaming he's a philosopher?"

"Are those the only two choices?"

"For the purposes of this discussion, yes."

"Then I'd rather be a philosopher. With tenure."

He sighed. "I think we're losing the point here."

"Remind me again."

"That we can't ultimately know what's real. This, right now, could all simply be a dream I'm dreaming."

"But if you're in the dream, how would you ever know whether it's a dream?"

Gray erupted in excitement. "Exactly! That's the whole point! Brilliant!"

I stared at him. "I think I missed the brilliant point I just made."

"That we can't tell whether we're really dreaming or not. This may all be a dream I'm having, and you're just part of it."

"You're suggesting I'm not real, that I'm part of your dream?"

"Could be." He looked at me expectantly.

"Great. If this is your dream, you do the dishes, and I'll dream I'm reading a book."

With a grim smile, he leaned over, kissed me, and took my empty plate. "Read your book. I'll do the dishes. You are so lucky to have me."

"I know. Though it may only be a dream."

"Read your book."

What's strange is that now, years later, my time in Australia does seem more like a dream than a memory. A dream where I was lucky to have Gray.

Chapter Twenty-Five

One Regret

[Portland, Oregon, September 1994]

"Hey, Tyler."

"Hi!" The first counselor to arrive for that night's testing, he came off the elevator bubbling with his usual excitement. And now from being in love.

"How's Dean?"

"We're doing great! Really great."

"Glad to hear it."

I had been right about Tyler. Given his youth, his looks, and his sweet personality, he was hit on by a number of guys who came in to test. And Steve was right: the boy learned to politely but firmly fend off invitations. Then, in the second month of the program's operation, he met an older man who came in to test, a professor at Portland State University, whose invitation he chose not to fend off. When he told us, he quickly added that Dean was *not* one of his instructors. Dean, he said, would never permit that with a student. And since Dean taught microbiology, it was unlikely Tyler would be taking any of his classes. They began a friendship, which became a relationship, and the team watched their gay kid brother blossom into first love.

I saw his grin evaporate as Arthur came down the hall from the phlebotomy room. I quickly added, "We're good tonight. All negative results. Arthur just came by to check up on us."

"Hi, Tyler," said Arthur. The youth returned to his full-throttle smile. "Hey!"

The counseling and testing program had proved to be a tremendous success. Almost immediately gay men were coming in to test. As summer slid into early September, we had a full house every Tuesday night and were getting the data the feds wanted. Along with the epidemiologists, we were relieved that most nights the results were negative. Hopefully, this meant Oregon gay men were getting the messages about safer sex.

"Are we all set up back there?" I asked Arthur.

"We're good. Roy couldn't make it tonight so I'll be doing the blood draws."

The test results were guarded as tightly as the Price Waterhouse envelopes delivered to the Academy Awards. They came sealed, the results known beforehand only to Arthur and to me. When we did have the occasional positive result, Arthur would join us, meeting with the counselor and reviewing the protocols. It was important the counselor not show alarm or excessive concern. "Just act as natural as you can," Arthur advised. Once the counselor took the client into the assigned room, Arthur would knock on the door, enter, and the counselor would introduce him and leave the two alone. At the end of each night, we debriefed the evening over pizza donated by a local restaurateur who himself used our services.

By six o'clock all the team had arrived and men began to come off the elevator. I was at the front desk, signing people in and preparing the files for the counselors, when a tall man with thinning hair came to the desk. He wore glasses and a tie, very proper and professional looking. "I'm here to get a test."

"Sure. First time with us?"

"Yes."

"Then welcome." I handed him the one-page explanation of our program. "Everything's confidential here. You can use a false name to sign in, if you wish. The counselor will ask your real name when he gets the rest of your personal information. What name would you like to use?"

"Oh, that won't be necessary. My name's Martin Levinson."

"Levinson. By any chance is Christine your mother?"

He groaned, rolling his eyes heavenward. "Oh, God, what has she done now?"

I laughed. "No, no, I really admire her."

"I know. Everyone does. You can't imagine what it's like to have a mother everyone admires."

I laughed again at his pained expression. "And just to re-emphasize: We don't tell *anyone* you came here to test."

"Thanks. But I'm sure she already knows. Can't keep anything from her."

He took a seat, waiting to be called.

Unlike Martin, a number of men preferred to use fake sign-in names, and initially we got a number of "Oscar Wildes," "Dorian Grays," "Rock Hudsons," and "Bart Simpsons." In time, the proxy names became more inventive. I handed Reggie the first file for the night. He looked at the name on the folder, and called out, "The Reverend Jerry Falwell." There were snickers and chuckles among the men waiting in the lobby as the client rose from his chair. Reggie shook his hand. "Hi, Jerry. Please follow me." National homophobes became especially popular, and on any given night we could expect to have "Billy Graham," "Pat Robertson," "President Ronald Reagan," "President Nancy Reagan," and various and sundry popes.

"Pope Pius of the Eternally Damned," Chad called out.

"Mr. Phyllis Schlafly," called Tyler.

The humor helped cut the somber-thick atmosphere. But once inside the counseling room, the volunteers were strictly professional. I gave John the next file. He looked at the proxy name, then at me, shaking his head as he called out, "President Reagan's ballet-loving son—the cute one."

Much else was happening. I linked up Lukas with the transgender group I'd met at the Sexual Minorities Roundtable, and over the summer he conducted several workshops for their members on dressing, make-up, and wigs "to bring out your Inner Woman." Following my tour of the streets with Leo, I'd helped him develop "measures" for his program to satisfy Steve and the county. We built a needle exchange into his street outreach. Leo would give out two clean needles for each used one. He also freely distributed condoms (didn't want the used ones back, thanks), and we opened the counseling and testing program to the street kids. Leo was there every Tuesday night. Only he was designated to work with any minor who came in. As a further incentive the health department provided Subway gift vouchers each time the young person returned for his or her result. This gave the epidemiologists an insight into the occurrence of HIV among the street population. Surprisingly, HIV wasn't showing up. We aimed to keep it that way. The county was happy, so Steve was happy, so Leo was happy. I had also been working with Leo to collect the data and build a file on police activities, according to Jake's instructions.

And, except for the occasionally recurring dream of wandering lost on the Bogong High Plains, I sensed my therapy work with O'Shaughnessy was coming to an end. We had used the post-weep sessions following my catharsis in late July to mop up remaining puddles of grief, discussing the losses in more detail and without tears. I'd entered a calm period in my life, where wounds began to heal and scars to bleach and blend in, becoming part of my soul's landscape.

I was still frustrated by O'Shaughnessy's cold manner. He had lowered his impenetrable emotional shield that one time when I wrote out my litany of the dead, but then the shield was raised again.

"Really, I don't need warm and fuzzy," I complained to Sandy, "but *approachable* would be nice; *empathetic* would help. He's the least sympathetic person I've ever known."

"He doesn't give sympathy because he doesn't allow it for himself."

"He's alone, too, isn't he?"

"Pretty much."

"But he's married?"

"Was."

"And has a son?"

"Did—well, technically *does*, I suppose. He pays child support back in Delaware, so I suppose that counts. He hasn't spoken with his son for several years. The boy's now a freshman in high school."

"My god, he sounds more messed up than I am."

"What, you wanted a perfect human being for your counselor? Someone who's got his act all together? Good luck with that."

"Yeah, but still . . ."

"You're both similarly wounded," said Sandy.

"What does that mean?"

"I felt you'd understand each other. I think one needs to be deeply wounded to recognize and help heal the wounded-ness in others. And, in that regard, he really is the best therapist I know."

I saw O'Shaughnessy Thursday afternoon at our regular time.

"I don't really have much to talk about," I started. "Everything's been going okay."

"Is that your goal: Okay?"

I shrugged.

"So, do you feel done?"

I thought about it. "Not sure. But I don't know where to go from here. Or what else to explore." We'd discussed the recurring dream, my grief over Gray's death, my mother's inability to accept a kind-of-important-part of who I am, my trauma as a five-year-old when my sister revealed there was no Santa Claus. What was left to talk about?

"What is it you haven't told me?"

"Haven't told you?"

"Yes."

"Hmm, let's see. Thirty-seven years. I might have missed something."

"What is it you've *avoided* telling me?"

"You mean like sexual fantasies?"

"Are they important?"

"Not really. Pretty tame."

"Tell me one thing you regret."

"Come dance with me!"

I stared at O'Shaughnessy, but was looking out over the Bogong High Plains. Early autumn in the southern hemisphere, 1991. Stars especially bright that night, an early chill settling over us as we huddled close to the fire. The band Gondwanaland playing on the boom box Gray brought from the car. I was reading a book cradled in my lap, holding a flashlight in one hand, nursing a mug of hot tea in the other—

O'Shaughnessy said something.

I blinked. "I'm sorry. What did you say?"

He studied me for a moment. "I asked you to name one regret."

Looking out once again across the dark expanse of the high plains, I whispered, "I wouldn't dance."

"Wouldn't dance?"

I felt my face reddening, my throat tightening. I swallowed. "We were camping. It was about a month after Gray received his diagnosis. He'd graduated from being HIV-positive to officially having AIDS. He wanted to dance and I wouldn't."

"Why not?"

"I'm a terrible dancer."

"I'm guessing we're not talking the foxtrot."

"Come dance with me!"

"You know I don't dance."

"Yes, at the gay gala. Around people. But out here? Just the two of us?"

He pulled on my arm, sloshing tea on the ground. "C'mon, I want to dance."

"No. I do not dance on principle. Anywhere."

"What principle?"

"On the principle . . . that I do not dance." I returned to my book.

"C'mon, there's no one else around within fifty kilometers. Dance with me! I want to get in touch with my aboriginal roots."

"What aboriginal roots? Your great-grandparents came from Liverpool."

"My family may be English, but I'm 100 percent Australian. This is my land. This is my sky." He turned his gaze upward. "And just look at it."

"So I did. One vast, blue-black canopy. Sky everywhere. In all my travels, I've never found a sky to compare with Australia's. Immense. Unbroken by mountains or trees or anything but the horizon. And that night, with no moon, dazzling with stars, the Southern Cross the only constellation I could recognize, it was like looking out into a different universe, and reminded me of a poem—

"There was just a continent without much on it, under a sky that never cared less."

"Your Oregon poet, William Stafford."

"It was a game we played, Gray and I, quoting pieces of verse for the other to guess the poet. And he recited back:"

"Everything mortal has moments immortal, Swift and God-gifted, immeasurably bright."

"Hm. Whitman?"

"Lowell."

"Robert?"

"Amy."

"How does an Aussie barrister know American poets better than I do?"

"Remember, I majored in American Literature at university, and you're using poetry as a diversion. Unfair. It almost worked."

Gondwanaland's pounding, throbbing music was making the night air pulse around us.

"Just listen to that beat," he said. "Don't you feel it? Doesn't it make you want to get up and move?"

"Mm, it's a little difficult to hum along to. Maybe if it was Enya."

"You don't dance to Enya. You meditate to Enya. You light candles and share a hot bath to Enya."

I perked up. "Sounds good. Want to go home and share a hot bath together?"

"No, I want to dance," whereby he spread his arms and began to sing, "Let your fantasies unwind! Let your spirit soar! Listen to the power of the music of the night!"

"I'm warning you, Grayson. Break into a medley of Andrew Lloyd Webber show tunes and I'm packing up the car and leaving you here."

He pulled on my arm again. "C'mon, just you and me. No one's watching."

I fended him off. "Really, I can't. It goes back to a traumatic experience I had as a teenager."

"What traumatic experience?" he scoffed.

"It was my senior prom. Mom insisted I go, so I invited Mary Ann Cartwright and she wanted to dance."

"So, what, you were clumsy?"

"A total disaster. She wears a prosthetic leg to this day."

Gray was shaking his head as he got to his feet. "You are so full of it."

"My mother's convinced it turned me gay. She blames herself." I went back to my book.

He pulled off his thick wool sweater and threw it at me. "I want us to dance naked, wild and uninhibited around the fire."

I looked up as he peeled off his T-shirt, his torso marble white against the Australian night. "Do you have a permit for that?"

He threw his shirt at me and began unbuckling his jeans. "I want us to dance together, you and me, to become one with the music until we merge into each other's being."

I mumbled as I watched him strip, "Well, I'm certainly all for merging."

He turned up the music as loud as it would go, and now, fully naked, flames reflecting off his marmoreal body, he slowly raised his face and arms to the glittering night sky arcing above us, his hands reaching for the stars. From where I sat on the ground, gazing up, he appeared to be touching them with his fingers. There was something eerie and mystical, something holy and chthonic about the moment, as if he were drawing power and life from that magical sky, a human conduit connecting the vast starry tapestry

211

overhead with the vast earthly terrain below.

O'Shaughnessy sat, watching me.

"Of my many memories of Gray, that's the one that remains with me most vividly. He seemed to have slipped into a different consciousness. Unworldly, or *other*worldly." I took a deep breath. "But I wouldn't dance. So, he danced alone, to the drums and the didgeridoo and the bullroarer of Gondwanaland. Well, it really wasn't a dance, more this wild frantic flailing of arms and legs, leaping and jumping and twirling around and around the fire. And the whole time he kept shouting . . ."

"Come dance with me!"

"You're scaring the dingoes and jackrabbits."

"I don't care! Come dance with me!" He continued around the fire in his solo Dionysian frenzy. "C'mon!" he shouted.

"I can't dance with a hard-on," I shouted back, and watched him circle the fire, again and again, until his body shone in the firelight, glowing, glistening with sweat, like something newly born and pulled wet from the womb.

"He kept dancing like that until the tape stopped, and I watched him the entire time. He was so . . . happy. Not pleasantly, contentedly happy. *Ecstatically* happy. Laughing, breathless, until finally exhausted."

The silence in the room seemed to pulse in my ears as I remembered. I was staring at the desk surface. "But I wouldn't dance. I had my principles—that, and absolutely no sense of rhythm."

I quietly summed up. "We made only one more trip to the high plains after that, two years later in 1993. And neither of us felt like dancing then." I nodded, more to myself than O'Shaughnessy. "So, yeah, that's what I regret."

He turned to the clock on the wall, that circular island of time, and said, "We can continue discussing this next week if you wish."

I got to my feet to leave and paused. "I understand now why Sandy referred me to you."

He looked up from writing his notes. "Oh?"

"You don't let people get close to you either."

212

He hesitated before speaking. "Let's just say, I think we understand each other."

I nodded soberly and left his office. But once outside the door, I skipped down the three flights of stairs, whispering loudly, "*Yes! Touché! Touché! Touché!*"

～～～ ～～～ ～～～

I watch her slow, steady caressing of the rosary beads, one after another, after another. This simple act of faith calms and lulls me as the beads make their prayerful circuit.

Gray ... Trevor ... Jerald ...

Tactile prayers in sync with silent lips.

Cal ... Giles ... Stefan ...

I myself no longer believe in prayer, or that there's anyone or anything to pray to, yet still find a kind of solace and peace being around those who do. I realize I'm piggybacking on her prayers and hope she doesn't mind. I wonder who she's saying the rosary for.

"Mi hijo," she whispers. Her son.

Did I voice my thought? I'm not sure. But we now seem to have a conversation, the two of us, so I ask, "¿Que pasó?"

"They shot him. They shot my son."

"Ah. I'm sorry. How is he?"

"It is serious," she says, still working the beads, eyes still unseeing. *"The doctors say very serious."*

"Lo siento," I repeat.

"And you? You wait for someone, too?"

"Sí. Un amigo."

"It is serious?"

"Yes. Also very serious."

We sit in silence, each weighted by our worries, when she says abruptly, *"I say the rosary for my son. Not for me."*

"Ah."

"When he was small, I held him as I prayed. He would touch the beads with me. It helped him to sleep. So, I've continued my prayers, all these years I've been looking for him."

"You've been searching for your son?"

"Sí."

To my unasked question, she answers, *"My husband, he sent me away. He would not let me take my young son."*

"Why did your husband send you away?"

"He learned this youngest wasn't his."

"Oh, I see. Forgive me, I shouldn't have asked."

Her fingers continue working the beads as she says softly, *"He was kind to me."*

"Who?"

"The little one's father. The farm owner's son."

I'm embarrassed to have intruded into her private past. *"You don't need to tell me more. I shouldn't have asked. I'm sorry."*

But I don't think she heard me.

"He was young, my age, and very gentle with me."

A smile appears on her lips. I can see the beautiful girl she once must have been.

"When he saw the bruises on my face, he was angry. He wanted to tell his father, but I begged him not to. I cried. I was used to the beatings, and it would only make things worse. So, he held me close, and he cried, too. He cried for me."

Her smile fades. *"Still, I think he must have said something, for the beatings stopped. My husband was angry. But he no longer beat me."*

From my limited knowledge of Mexican culture, I knew Latina women wouldn't share such personal matters, especially not with a man. But she wasn't speaking to me; it was as if I were hearing her innermost thoughts, as if eavesdropping on her private confessions to her soul.

I'm drawn back to her voice.

"He was always reading some book."

"The farmer's son?"

"When he wasn't working, I would see him under a tree, or in the hayloft, or in the meadow—wherever he could get away—always with a book. He was unhappy. He wanted to go to college, but his father said he must take over the farm. He sensed I was unhappy, too, so far from my family. He saw that I, like him, was trapped."

215

Her leathery face glows, her blank eyes shine. *"He would read to me. I couldn't understand much, but I loved to listen to the sound of his voice. Loved to sit next to him as he read by the stream, loved that he cared about me."*

He took advantage of you and your loneliness. Did I say this, or only think it? But she doesn't seem to notice, so I'm hoping I kept the bitter thought to myself.

"I told my husband this youngest son was his. And he believed me. At first. But as the baby became a boy, one could see he was different from his brothers. By the time my little son was four it was clear he was not my husband's. And so I was sent away."

"What happened to the farmer's son?"

"He went to college that fall, somewhere in the East. He returned only a couple of times those first two years. He and his father did not get along. He never knew he had a child."

That slight smile resurfaces. She is back on the high plains of Oregon. *"It was the happiest time of my life. I would wake each morning, eager to see the farmer's son, and when he saw me, his smile brightened my world. And when he went away, he left me with a beautiful gift. My son, and my son's father, gave me the only happy moments in my life."*

I was wrong. The farmer's son hadn't taken advantage of her, hadn't callously used and cast her aside. He had given her the only moments of love and happiness she'd known.

But her smile has vanished. The light has gone out of her eyes. *"My husband would not let me take my son. He hated the boy when he found out, but he would not let me take him. He was punishing me. So I had to leave my son there on the farm across the mountains."*

The beads lie still in her hands, Christ suspended on his cross between heaven and earth.

"I'm so sorry." I can think of nothing comforting to say; there are no comforting words to offer.

"I worked many jobs. Saved any money I could. And years later I returned to buy my son. But my husband had moved on. And my youngest, they told me, had run away. Or been sent away. That's when I began looking

for him." She sighs. *"And after all these years searching, I find him here."*

She resumes her worshipful fingering of the beads. *"I committed a grave sin, and this is God's punishment for my sin. That is why I do not say the rosary for me. I say it for my son."*

Why do people always think they need the gods to punish them? We're quite capable of doing it ourselves.

"I hope you will hold your son once again and say the rosary for him."

But before she can respond, a change comes over the room. We both feel it. An icy chill. Something's happened. She raises her head as if catching a scent on the air. I'm shivering from the sudden cold, like inside a refrigerator or a morgue—probably refrigerator; I've never been inside a morgue. She, too, is shivering. She draws her shawl more tightly around her and is now gazing past me, her eyes large, and now there's terror in them. She hurriedly makes the sign of the cross, whispering, "Que Dios nos cuida . . ."

I turn to see what she's asking God to protect us from, and I freeze.

A man stands in the room, tall and thin, his bloodless face ensconced in a hood, all the more unsettling for being without expression as he stares at us.

I turn back to the old woman. *"Who is he?"*

She says softly, *"El Angel de la Muerte."*

The Angel of Death? That doesn't sound good. I look again. The specter is slowly moving toward us. The woman cowers at his approach, putting out her hand with the crucifix to ward him off. Oddly, I'm feeling no fear. I recall the phrase, *No temo más que la muerte:* "I fear nothing but death." But I don't even fear death. I am calm as he approaches. I am fearless.

The specter now stands before the poor terrified woman. I want to reassure her, *Fear not. You have nothing to fear.* I watch as the figure raises his hand over her as in bestowing a blessing, watch her eyes slowly close, her arm drop into her lap, watch her slump in the chair, chin resting on her chest, and she whispers, *"Mi hijo."* She's dead.

Okay, so I was wrong.

I want to call for help but am unable to speak, unable to make any sound whatsoever. I'm frozen in my chair as the specter slowly turns and looks down on where I'm sitting. His face is as immobile as a mask, a mask I don't want to look behind. He lowers himself until we are face to face, his eyes glowing as they gaze into mine. I realize he's from the other side. Except I don't believe in "the other side"—which seems kind of irrelevant at the moment.

Why are you here? I ask.

I've come to guide you. It's a voice flat, monotone, dead.

Death as my guide? I'm thinking I saw this in a Woody Allen movie once, and it all starts feeling suspiciously like a dream. I ask, *Is this real? Or am I dreaming?*

He answers, *Yes.*

Yes? How can it be yes to both?

The mask offers a thin smile. *It's all mental, man.*

I remember those words. Where have I heard them before?

"I'm sorry. What did you say?"

"I asked if it's okay to turn on the TV."

There's a shift: I'm gazing at a skinny young man, maybe early twenties, a pimply kid dressed in black jeans and wearing a dark sweatshirt, brown curls poking out from under the sweatshirt's hood. His smile is polite and respectful. His eyes are green and not glowing. He is not from the other side. So, he's probably also not my guide.

I pull myself up in the chair, blinking awake. "Oh, yeah, sure, go ahead."

"Sorry to wake you," he says. "Your eyes were open, but I couldn't tell if you were asleep or awake."

"No, it's okay. I have the same problem."

"Thanks."

As he stands, I ask, "What are you in for?"

He laughs. "You make it sound like we're doing time." *Well, yes, that's one way to think of existence: as a kind of waiting room where we're all doing time.* "I just brought my girlfriend in. She went into labor 'bout half hour ago. They think it'll be at least another hour," he says. "I'll keep it low."

"What?"

"The television."

"Oh, yes, right. Thanks."

He goes to another chair, pulls off his hood, and points the remote at the TV suspended from the ceiling. *Nice kid,* I think as he switches it on. Well-mannered, courteous. But way too young to be a father. I glance around the room. The blind woman is gone.

Why am I not surprised?

Chapter Twenty-Six

When Plague Becomes Personal

[Portland, Oregon, September 1994]

Marti had been with the agency two months when the epidemic suddenly got personal. Hired as executive director in July, she'd already brought in several large corporate sponsors by late August and was bolstering the agency's always shaky finances. She was making AIDS respectable in the general community. Franklin was delighted, of course, being able to develop a reserve rather than worrying whether he'd make payroll that month. We were at the weekly management team meeting—Marti, Franklin, Sandy, and myself. (Marti had asked that I attend the meetings.) Steve was away at a conference at the Centers for Disease Control in Atlanta. Increasingly, she was having him attend such conferences, freeing her to chase down major donors and more corporate sponsors. The two of them had developed a close working relationship, so much so that Steve had become the unofficial deputy director of the agency.

She opened our meeting looking pleased as she provided an update. Funding was stable, at least for the short term, there were a couple of new contracts coming up we could go after, and she'd signed on two more substantial donors. When first hired, she had told the board of directors that she typically stayed with an organization five years, long enough to get it out of crisis and on firm footing, which was fine with the board. She was already thinking of her next move. Marti was always looking ahead.

"In five years, I'll be ready to move on," she said, "and Steve will be ready to step in as the new executive director."

The three of us—Franklin, Sandy, and I—remained silent, all thinking the same thought, I'm sure. Marti caught the shift in the atmosphere. She searched our faces. "What? You don't think Steve would make a good executive director?"

After a pause that none of us wanted to fill, Franklin, departing from his usual snarky tone, said in a gentle voice, "It's not that. It's . . . well, he may not be able to."

We saw the realization dawn on Marti's face. Her jaw flexed. She flushed pink. "Let's take ten for nature." She got up and left the conference room.

Once she'd gone, Franklin said, "How could she not know?"

"She's still new to all this," said Sandy.

I rose from my chair. "Excuse me."

Her office door was closed. Since she had an open door policy, I knew it meant she was in there. I rapped lightly. "Marti?"

There was no answer, so I softly opened it. She was sitting at her desk, eyes red, nose red, tissue in her hand covering her mouth.

"Are you okay?"

She shook her head. I closed the door, came over, and sat in the chair in front of her desk. "We thought you knew."

She wiped her eyes with the tissue, then took several more from a box. "I'm not sure I can do this. I thought I could, but now I'm not sure." She blew her nose. "My first job was fundraising for a hospice. People were dying all the time. But most were old. Most had lived a full life. There was an appropriateness to it, a time-for-every-season sense about it. But here . . ." She shook her head slowly. "I thought I was stronger."

"You will get stronger," I said. "This work, it makes you stronger."

She looked at me with her teary eyes. "Really? How?"

"Each time you lose someone you care about, you get stronger."

She was quiet before speaking again. "Do we know how long he has?"

"It varies from person to person, but common wisdom says you have five to seven years after the first opportunistic infection."

"Five to seven years," she murmured. Then she asked, "How long did your partner have?"

"Two years."

"I'm sorry." She was composed again, natural color returning to her face, breathing, normal. "I don't want to be here when Steve gets ill. I don't think I could handle that."

I said nothing. There was nothing to say to that.

She took a deep breath and gave me her professional, confident smile. "I'd better go fix my face and get back to the meeting."

"Yes." I stood. "For everything there is a season, and a time for every purpose under heaven, including a time to fix one's face and get back to the work before us."

She smiled, a smile I recognized as a *thank you.*

"And I've got to start setting up for counseling and testing. It's going to be . . . a heavy night."

It was busy, the lobby full ten minutes before we were to begin. Fortunately, I'd scheduled an extra counselor for the evening. I was working the front desk, signing people in and preparing the folders, when I saw Marco step out of the elevator with his partner, Terry. They came up to the reception desk and we greeted each other.

"I wasn't expecting you tonight," I said to Marco. "You're not scheduled this week."

"No, I came to support my man," he said, his arm around Terry's shoulders. "We're always safe. I won't take any chances on infecting the one I love, but I want him to get tested every six months just to make sure. I insist." He looked around the lobby. "You've got a full house. I can help if you want."

"Thanks, but I think we've got it covered. I have seven counselors on tonight."

John came up to us. "Hey, Marco. Nice to see you again, Terry." They shook hands. "I've got your results. Ready?"

Marco and Terry briefly touched hands before Terry followed John to the first counseling room. As we watched them go down the hall, Marco said, "It's a little ritual we have. Each time, after Terry gets his results, we go out to a favorite restaurant and celebrate with a nice dinner and bottle of wine."

We saw them enter the room and close the door; then Marco studied me more closely. "Are you feeling okay? You look pale." Before I could answer, we heard three soft knocks. He turned back to see Arthur open the door to the counseling room, enter, and close it after him. Marco stared at the closed door, then turned to me with a questioning look on his face.

"I'm sorry, Marco."

The door clicked open and John stepped out into the hallway. His face was ashen; he looked sick. He saw Marco staring at him, dropped his gaze to the floor, and left for the break room. Marco watched him go, then, his voice edging toward anger, said, "Why wasn't I told?"

"You tell me why you weren't told."

The anger immediately collapsed, leaving him looking hollow. "Because results are confidential and can only be shared with the client."

"Leo," I called, "will you handle the front desk?" I took Marco by the arm. "Let's go in here. Terry's going to be a while." He let me guide him into an empty office where he dropped into a chair. He appeared in shock, kept repeating, "I don't understand. We're always safe. There were never any breakages. I always checked."

I sat and listened as he continued talking in the same dazed manner. "We use double condoms, for godsake. Terry jokes that I 'double-bag'

223

everything, like I do our groceries in the supermarket." Time limped on, with Marco repeating over and over, "I just don't understand. We're always safe." Finally, he looked at his watch. "I need to be there when he comes out."

"Terry's going to need your support tonight. You're going to need each other's support. Go home. Here's my phone number. Call me if you need to, okay? Any hour." He nodded dumbly as he took the slip of paper.

When Terry emerged from the counseling room with Arthur and came back to the lobby, his eyes were bloodshot. He looked shaken. Marco immediately went to him and they embraced, their eyes squeezed shut, foreheads resting against each other, saying nothing as they clung tightly together. A hush fell over the crowded lobby, the usual chatter-buzz-hum ebbing away like a receding tide, leaving a hollow silence as those sitting there averted their eyes. After a moment, Marco kissed Terry on the cheek. "Let's go home," he said hoarsely. Terry nodded, and they left.

The counselors ate very little of the donated pizza that night. Arthur and I encouraged them to talk about the experience as we did each evening, but no one felt like talking. It must be like losing one of your men during wartime. Reggie and Chad looked dazed. John remained ashen and kept staring at the carpet. Tyler was close to tears several times. Leo maintained his usual placid calm. It seemed everyone just wanted to leave, so I put the pizza away in the refrigerator where Carla would find and finish it in the morning, and we went home.

It wasn't the worst night the team ever experienced. That would come several months later.

Chapter Twenty-Seven

Dancing on the High Plains

[Portland, Oregon, September 1994]

Clinically, it's called seroconversion. Terry's turning positive cast a pall over all of us. Marco seemed to be taking it even harder than his partner, as if he himself had become newly infected. I suggested he might take a break from the program, but he wanted to continue, and I understood he needed to continue, needed helping other men remain uninfected.

Two weeks later, in mid-September on a slow night, John asked to speak with me alone. We went into one of the counseling rooms. He, too, had been shaken by the experience. It was the first time someone he personally knew was diagnosed with HIV, and he had handed that person his death sentence. I knew he needed to talk, but I wasn't prepared for what he needed to tell me.

"Marco didn't infect Terry."

"What? How do you know?"

"He told me. In the pre-counseling session. He cheated on Marco. It was a one-time thing. He and another man had been drinking, and this man didn't use a condom. Terry doesn't want Marco to know. Monogamy's always been so important to them, he's afraid what it will do to their relationship, but I see how it's tearing Marco up. It's tearing me up, knowing this. But confidentiality prohibits me from telling Marco. Right?"

"Right. In this case, Terry is your client. Not Marco. And we need to keep Terry's confidence."

John nodded heavily. "I know. I just hate to see Marco suffering like that, thinking he infected his partner. I had to tell someone." He looked up at me. "Isn't there anything we can do?"

"Let me talk to Arthur. He's continuing to work with Terry. I'll confide this information to him—he doesn't need to know how I found out—and see if he can convince Terry to 'fess up to Marco. If for no other reason, we need to contact that other guy so he can begin treatment and not infect others."

Like John, the knowledge of how Terry became infected weighed heavily on me, far more than I'd have expected. It brought up strong emotions from deep places in my subconscious. Twice that week I dreamt I was searching for someone on the high plains.

"I know why I wouldn't dance with Gray that night."

O'Shaughnessy's eyes studied me, but he said nothing.

"I was angry at him."

"Angry for . . .?"

"For so much. For getting infected. For dying. For leaving me behind. Angry for—" I stopped.

"What?"

My head dropped. "Angry for betraying our relationship . . . for betraying me."

I could hear the clock on the wall *tick-tick-tick-tick* off the seconds of silence, kept staring at my hands in my lap, avoiding O'Shaughnessy's eyes. "It was a fling. It was just a fling while he was at a conference in Sydney in 1989. It's how he became infected. He'd had too much to drink. There was a momentary attraction to another guy who was flirting with him. And they . . ." My voice trailed off as I stared at my now-clenched fists.

"I see."

"He was so genuinely sorry when he returned from the conference and told me. He cried, and Gray never cried. It was clear how sorry he was. How bad he felt."

I pulled out my handkerchief and blew my nose.

"Did you express your anger to him?"

"No. I couldn't."

"Couldn't? Or wouldn't?"

"There's not always a difference."

"Isn't there?"

"Maybe there is. I don't know. Anyway, I was never able to express it. He kept apologizing, for weeks afterwards, saying how sorry he was. How badly he felt. Promising it would never happen again. Always promising it would never happen again. He raked himself over the coals so much, there was nothing left for me to rake."

I put away the handkerchief. "He immediately got a test, and each month after that. We started taking precautions, something we'd never had to do before. And then, three months later, when his test came back positive, we understood what his 'fling' meant to our lives. And any anger I felt turned to panic, then to dread."

I cleared my throat. It was hard to swallow. "We went into practical mode, doing what needed to be done at each stage. There never seemed the time or the place for anger."

O'Shaughnessy considered this, then asked, "What would you like to say now that you couldn't—or wouldn't—say then?"

Something exploded within me. I slammed my fist on the desk. "A fling! It was so stupid of him. He knew the virus was out there. So stupid and reckless! Goddamn fool!" I shouted. "Goddamn fucking fool!" I hunched over, weeping in my hands.

And thus, Catharsis Number Two . . .

It was soon over. Passing quickly like an Australian summer storm.

O'Shaughnessy moved the box of tissues across the desk toward me. I took several. "I seem to be doing a lot of crying recently."

"You have a lot of crying to catch up on."

"Yeah, I guess." I wiped my eyes, back in control of whatever emotions I was still capable of. "I just hope you're not charging me by the tissue, that's all."

He sat forward in his chair. "So, along with your grief, you've been carrying a lot of anger all these years."

"Apparently," I said, taking another tissue and blowing my nose. "Who knew, huh?" I looked away. "I knew."

He let me go through a few more tissues, then said, "You have found your way to the center of your sorrow. Congratulations. Now you need to find your way out."

I stared at the crumpled tissues in my hands. "It's just that . . ."

"Yes?"

"It's just so hard to be the one left behind. To be the 'survivor.' You want to ask, survive *for what?*"

But instead of answering my unanswerable question, O'Shaughnessy recited softly:

"I have no will to weep or sing,
No least desire to pray or curse;
The loss of love is a terrible thing;
They lie who say death is worse."

I recognized the African American poet. "Countee Cullen," I said, again wiping my eyes, and added, "Another fine old Irish name."

And then the most extraordinary thing happened. O'Shaughnessy smiled. I was stunned. I didn't know it was possible. He might have also chuckled. I seem to remember a chuckle with the smile, but that could be memory's later embellishment; however, the smile I would swear to. I felt I should contact someone, *The Oregonian* or KGW-TV maybe, but they'd probably require a photo as proof, and by then he'd recovered from the experience, restoring his usual stern expression, yet his voice was . . . almost friendly. "So, shall we continue this next week?"

"Sure," I said. "Why not." I stood and took another tissue.

"One for the road?"

He nodded with what I think was a suppressed smile, and I left.

There is a coda to this memory. The weekend before I left Australia forever, I took one last farewell trip by myself up into the Bogong High Plains. There was a strong breeze blowing as I arrived at our base camp. Dusk settling. I took the container from the car and went walking amid the scrub brush and rock until I found a clearing. I stood a moment, listening for ancient songs on the wind, but heard nothing except the rustling brush. Perhaps understandable. They weren't my ancestors. They weren't my songs. Then I opened, lifted and tilted the box, its gritty contents bursting away from me in a dusty cloud of ashes, dancing on the wind as if set free. As if joyful in reuniting with this land, with this sky, with their aboriginal roots.

It was a night much like that night we'd shared two years before, stark, dark, and cold. I returned to the campsite and built the kind of fire Gray would have enjoyed; brought the cassette player from the car, slipping in his favorite Gondwanaland tape, and turned up the volume as loud as it would go. I took off my clothes and stood before the flames, watching the sparks swirl, twirl, and ascend like fireflies into the night; then, stretching my arms to the star-peopled sky overhead, I took a deep breath ...

And I danced.

I danced to the didgeridoo's low rolling guttural growl—*Yawr-rrrrYawrrrrYawrrrr*—danced to the bullroarer's barks—*Yeowp!-Yeowp!-Yeowp!*—danced as the modern synthesizer overtook the ancient indigenous sounds, and recalled *that first date. A restaurant in Shinjuku. So thrilling! So scary!*—danced to the pounding-throbbing drums, like spirits pulsing up from deep within the earth—*Hiking these plains in springtime, skiing them in winter*—The fire crackled and popped—*fixing a thousand dinners together*—sparks carried aloft, brief bursts of beauty against the night's blue-black sky—*sharing a hot bath in the glow of a dozen candles*—I circled the fire, again and again—*snuggling toasty warm against each other under the doona*—stomping my feet and yelling at the top of my voice, "Come dance with me!"— *Climbing Mount Fuji in autumn. Exploring Milford Sound in New Zealand. Making desperate love atop Wilson's Promontory*—around and around I went, driven by the music's beat—*watching Gray reach up, touching the unfamiliar stars*—passing through veils of smoke, eyes stinging, throat burning, skin hot, then chilled, then hot—*Watching his desperate, naked death-defying dance*—and somewhere, amid the music's rhythms and the fire's tempo and the night's chill, I danced outside of time, where my wild dance merged with his, the two joining together . . .

Until I realized the music had stopped.

I collapsed to the ground, breathless, panting, sweaty, smudged with dust and ash and smoke, and wept as I had never wept before.

Just wondering, O'Shaughnessy had asked, Did you ever weep for any of those people you lost to AIDS?

Once, I said. Once.

I cried, naked and alone in the Australian night, until the fire burned down to a heap of glowing yellow-orange-yellow embers, radiant heat caressing my skin, bringing with it a strange physical solace. And there, amid unbearable grief, I discovered an opening through my grief, became one with it, and found it suddenly bearable.

Still panting, I turned over onto my back, staring up into the canopy of stars overhead *(So many! So vast! Older than the Ancients, whispered Gray)* and a great peace came washing over me. The cosmic tide, rolling in and out, in and out, over and over, gently in time with my breathing, each wave carrying me toward that multitude of lights overhead, slipping into the sacred where the stars were no longer distant, the sky no longer foreign, and I no longer a stranger. The vast unknowable universe had become suddenly, intensely intimate, enveloping and holding me in its earthly cradle. And in that moment, in that brief, eternal moment,

I, mortal, became immortal,
swift and God-gifted,
and immeasurably bright.

230

Chapter Twenty-Eight

Getting in Bed with the Devil
(And he isn't even your type.)

[Portland, Oregon, September 1994]

"You've been invited to present at the National HIV/AIDS Conference in Washington, DC, next February," said Harry Caulfield, the
county health director. "There's a lot of interest in your volunteer counseling and testing program. The county'll pay your expenses, of course."

Steve and I were meeting with Arthur and Harry and Dr. Thomas
Jenkins from the state health department. They were congratulating
us on the success of the program. Only into our third month, and
already high numbers of gay men were coming in to test, giving the
county's epidemiologists a better picture of the AIDS impact in the
greater Portland area. The Centers for Disease Control was following
our work with real interest, added Arthur.

Steve said, "Thanks, Harry. That's great news."

Unlike Harry, Dr. Jenkins, the only one dressed in suit and tie,
was clearly the kind of person you addressed as "Doctor," his chilly
professional demeanor suggesting he wasn't on a first-name basis even
with his wife.

Harry then got to the point of the meeting. "Now we want you to take your program to the next level."

"The next level?" said Steve.

"We'd like you to begin testing men in the bathhouse."

Portland had only one gay bathhouse, the Excalibur Nights. We knew anecdotally that a lot of unsafe sex happened there and among men who didn't identify as gay, married men and guys in denial who wouldn't be caught in a gay bar but could anonymously slip in, have sex with other men, and then go home to their wives and girlfriends. These men wouldn't be showing up at our testing clinic, and certainly not at the public health clinics, admitting to homosexual behavior.

Steve glanced at me, then turned back to them. "Sure. It's important to reach that population. But it's not just up to us. The bathhouse owner, Delmore Kratz, may not agree. He's permitted us to install and stock condom bins, but he's not been very open to outreach or even distributing HIV prevention materials in there."

At that point, Jenkins interjected, "He will this time, or we'll close him down. I've had the state legislature on my back for years, wanting to know why we permit a gay bathhouse to operate while other parts of the country have closed theirs."

"And, of course, you've told them that closing the bathhouse would only drive that population underground and beyond our reach," said Harry in a tone intimating he and Jenkins had had this conversation before.

"Yes, I've told them. But I'm not sure how much longer they'll go along." He turned back to Steve. "We'll tell Kratz he can cooperate with you or he's out of business."

"I'd like to see if we could convince him to cooperate without threatening him," said Steve. "The manager at the bathhouse has been sympathetic to our work. Maybe he'll help."

Harry added, "If anyone can convince the owner, it's Steve. I suggest we let him and his team make the approach. If they're unsuccessful, we can step in with the big stick."

Jenkins was agreeable, so that afternoon Steve contacted the bathhouse manager and set up a meeting in two weeks.

On the afternoon we were meeting the bathhouse folks, I joined Steve in the elevator, coming back from my workout at the Princeton. "By the way," he said, "I thought it'd be good to have a member of the counseling and testing team with us, so I invited Tyler."

"Tyler?"

"Yeah, is that okay? Most of the other counselors work during the day."

"Sure, I guess."

I was at my desk, checking phone messages and emails when Franklin stopped by.

"Heard you're meeting with Delmore Kratz today."

"Yes, in about fifteen minutes."

"Be sure to wash your hands afterward. Or better yet, delouse."

"You know him?"

"Only by reputation, which is all I want to know. But he is wealthy."

"One of the A-Gays?"

"Hardly," Franklin sneered. "He'd never be admitted to that club no matter how much money he had."

"Because of his business?"

"That, too, but mostly because he's a vulgarian. Lots of money and no class. He has a large mansion overlooking the Columbia River where he throws parties with handsome young guys that'd make Hugh Hefner's Playboy events look frumpy. In summer, you'll see him out on the river in his mini-yacht bedecked with naked boys."

"Boys?"

"Oh, they're legal. Just. The likes of Brandon Chittock would die before being associated with Delmore Kratz. But if your meeting goes well, try to convince him to make a financial contribution to our programs. He should. His bathhouse certainly contributes to the number of our clients."

"We don't know that. That's what the county wants us to find out by testing there."

Tyler showed up as Steve, Arthur and I waited in the conference room. I greeted him. "Hey, Tyler. Thanks for joining us."

He was all bright eyes and eager. "I'm honored to be invited." He was that kind of kid who is "honored" to be invited.

Soon Delmore Kratz arrived with his manager, introduced only as "Tork." We all shook hands and sat around the table, Tyler next to me, sitting across from Kratz. I studied the bathhouse owner as Steve made the introductions and offered coffee and water. It's always uncomfortable encountering a stereotype. Kratz was a man in his fifties, trying hard to appear in his thirties. His face glowed like Tyler's, but from the plastic sheen of Botox rather than the blush of youth. Hair was at least three shades too brown, and he dressed in that expensively tacky style associated with Las Vegas: coat and slacks, open shirt with wispy chest hair and gold chain around his neck. The fleshy throat-wattles further ruined the effect. Tork was large like Lionel, but where Lionel was mostly muscle, Tork was mostly *formerly* muscle, looking like a biker who'd fallen on hard times: shaved head, beard, tattoos covering both arms, black leather pants, and vest pulled across a stained white T-shirt straining across a huge beer belly. Meeting him in a dark alley, you'd probably hand over your watch, wallet, credit cards, and gold teeth fillings without him even asking.

Steve thanked them for coming. He began by noting that the bathhouse had a "select clientele," including a number of men who did not identify as gay and could be at risk for HIV. Delmore was smiling at Tyler in a way that made me cringe, while Tyler, in all his sweet innocence, smiled back. And I suddenly realized why Steve had invited him: Tyler was bait.

I silently fumed at Steve as he laid out the proposal. "We'd like to offer HIV counseling and testing in your bathhouse one evening a week."

Kratz abruptly shifted his attention away from Tyler. "Testing in the bathhouse?"

"Of course, it would be free to your patrons. Blood would be drawn there, and the men could choose to receive their results a week later back at the bathhouse, here at CAP, or at the county health department. The testing and the results would be anonymous and totally confidential."

"But if they want to test, they can come here to CAP or with their private doctor."

"It's highly unlikely that your patrons who don't identify as gay would come to a testing clinic for gay men, or go to their family doctor asking for an HIV test. That's why we'd like to bring testing to them on Saturday nights starting in November."

"Saturdays? But that's our busiest night."

"We know. We would need two adjoining rooms, one for people to drop by and talk—we'll provide snacks and beverages and HIV prevention materials—and the second room for the confidential counseling and blood draws."

I could tell it wasn't going well. Kratz shook his head. "I hate to sound mercenary." *Heaven forbid anyone think you mercenary, Delmore!* "But that's two rooms I'm not being paid for on the busiest night of the week. Is CAP or the health department going to compensate me?"

"No," Steve said flatly. "We realize you'd be making somewhat of a financial sacrifice, but we're hoping you'll want to help stop the spread of HIV."

"I think my support for your organization is well known," he said. *Damn, this is where I need one of Franklin's Donor Pledge Cards for Tyler to hand him.* "I'm already making condoms freely available in the bathhouse."

"Condoms that we provide," Steve reminded him.

"But to have testing *in* the bathhouse?" He shook his head again. "I'm concerned for our clientele. We pride ourselves on discretion at the Excalibur Nights. How can our patrons relax and enjoy themselves with people from the county in there?"

"The counseling will be done by trained volunteers who are

themselves gay men. Tyler here is one of them." Tyler smiled at him. "Our program has been very successful in large part because of our counselors like Tyler."

"I can see why," said Delmore, smiling again at Tyler in a way that made my skin crawl.

Arthur added, "And the phlebotomy—the blood draws—will be performed by a county nurse who is also a gay man wearing street clothes."

Kratz was not sold. "I'm sorry. My clientele doesn't want to be reminded of AIDS when they come to relax and enjoy themselves. I don't mean to appear crass," I bit my tongue, *Now, how could anyone think you crass,* "but it's not good for business."

At that point, Tork spoke for the first time. From his appearance, I would have doubted him capable of more than a series of grunts, so I was surprised when the large, bald, tattooed man spoke in a soft voice.

"Actually, it might be good for business, Mr. Kratz."

"Oh? How so?"

"It would show the gentlemen who visit your establishment that you care about their health and well-being. That you're trying to make a difference in this epidemic."

"Well, I *do* care. I mean, good heavens, I've lost dear friends, too."

"Exactly, sir. I think it would show our clients, and the entire Portland community, that Excalibur Nights, and you in particular, are committed to preventing the spread of AIDS."

I was stunned at how well Tork spoke, how respectful, how intelligent he sounded. I could see Kratz was considering his manager's words.

As if on cue, Tyler said, "It's really important work. We're helping to keep our brothers safe. It would mean a lot to us to offer testing in your bathhouse, sir."

Kratz was clearly charmed. "Oh, please, not 'sir'—Delmore."

"Delmore," Tyler repeated. He gave the older man the most beautiful, winsome smile, and I realized Tyler was no longer the innocent kid who'd come to us in March. I felt proud of him, and at the same time sad for his lost innocence.

"I would love to give you a personal tour of the bathhouse, my boy, and we could discuss your project further," said Delmore, apparently forgetting there was anyone else in the room with him and Tyler.

"We'd love a tour," said Steve, inviting himself to Delmore's party.

"Yes, that would be great," added Arthur.

Kratz looked momentarily befuddled, but Tyler quickly said, "When could we visit?"

Somewhere, though I'm not sure at what point, and clearly neither was Delmore, the decision had been made. Steve, Arthur, and Tork were already discussing details and scheduling a time for a tour of the bathhouse as Delmore continued smiling at Tyler while pretending interest in what they were saying.

At the conclusion of the meeting, everyone shook hands once again, Delmore clinging to Tyler's beyond the socially prescribed limit. "If all the volunteers are as attractive as you, I predict your program's going to be a stunning success."

"Thanks," said Tyler. "Your support means a lot to us. Really."

Delmore handed him his personal card. "We should get together for dinner. My treat. I'd love to hear more about this wonderful program and the important contribution you're making to our community."

Tyler took it. "Wow, thanks!" I glanced over his shoulder. The business card bore the Excalibur Nights logo—a hand rising out of the water, but in place of the Arthurian sword it held aloft a rigid phallus. *Classy.*

Once Tork, Delmore, and Arthur departed for the elevators, Steve turned to Tyler. "Thanks for joining us today. Here, can I have that card?" Tyler gave him Kratz's business card whereby Steve tore it in half, then tore the halves in half, tossing the pieces in a trashcan, and patted him on the shoulder. "You did great," he said and left for his office.

Tyler was staring at the shredded business card as I said, "Yes, thanks for your help."

He turned back, his eyes once again bright. "Sure! Anytime. Just ask." He'd been in his relationship with Dean for two months now and was obviously happy, yet he still often acted toward me like a young pup eager to please. All he needed was a tail to wag.

I said to him, "During the meeting I realized you're growing up."

He rolled his eyes. "Yeah, finally, huh?"

"What I was thinking is, someday this epidemic's going to be over, and it will fall to your generation to continue the struggle for our rights and respect as human beings." I paused. "I think you're going to be one of its leaders, Tyler. And I'm going to be proud to say that I knew you. That I worked with you. That you were my friend."

His eyes glistened, tears threatening to pool up. "Thank you," he said softly and left for the elevators.

Steve, I was less proud of. Once Tyler had gone, I stormed into his office where he was checking his emails. "You used Tyler as bait! Please note the accusatory tone in my voice."

"Yep," he said without looking up from his computer. "And it worked out swell."

Swell? I hadn't heard that in decades.

"Doesn't that strike you as just slightly, oh, slimy?"

"I can live with it."

"He's a volunteer in my program. Why didn't you ask me first?"

"Because I knew you wouldn't approve."

"I wouldn't. I don't."

"There you are. This was too important, and I didn't want you to compromise your values, so I asked him myself."

I was still angry. "He idolizes you and you used him!"

Steve looked up. "No, he respects me. He *idolizes* you, and he knew exactly why he was there."

"He did?"

"I told him we had a very important meeting, and I needed him to come and look innocent and adorable. Yes, he was typecast. And he totally understood within the first five minutes why he was invited."

"With Delmore Kratz visually groping him the whole time."

"He'll survive. And let's not get too self-righteous, okay? Tyler *is* a handsome young guy. We've all visually groped him. And don't pretend you haven't."

Ouch.

"Okay, so maybe I have," I mumbled, "but at least I feel conflicted about it."

Steve chuckled, returning to his computer.

I was frustrated that he refused to feel any remorse for his actions. Even a smidgen of guilt would've given me a handhold to layer on more recriminations. But I could see it wasn't worth the breath, so I started to leave. As I got to the door, I turned around.

"People still say *swell* in Western Montana?"

He grinned at me, and I left.

~~~ ~~~ ~~~

I'm listlessly turning the pages of *Bon Appetit!*'s Christmas 1991 issue. Who knew there were so many different kinds of macaroons? I toss it into the chair next to me and notice the television is turned off. When did the young man with the girlfriend in labor leave? Maybe while I was engrossed in "The Secret of Soufflé Success"? Or maybe when remembering how we got HIV testing into the bathhouse with Tork's help? I had so totally misread the big guy. He gave Steve, Arthur, and me a tour of the bathhouse two days after our meeting with Delmore Kratz. In contrast to the fabled bathhouses of San Francisco and New York City—those clean, brightly lit pleasure palaces offering wet and dry saunas, Jacuzzis, swimming pools, massage rooms, lounges where the likes of Bette Midler once performed—Portland's Excalibur Nights occupied an old three-story building like a squatter. Constructed in the forties, the building had served many purposes before its current incarnation. Drab and derelict from the outside, it was even more depressing inside. A smell of disinfectant pervaded every floor, partially covering other smells I didn't even want to guess at. Dingy and dimly lit (the windows had been painted black so it was perpetually night in there), its dubious claim to being a "bathhouse" relied solely on a single grotty shower room on the second floor. You couldn't get me to take off my shoes, much less anything else, in there.

We climbed to the third floor where Tork had set aside two adjoining rooms for our program. Unlike the rest of the facility, these rooms were well lit and freshly painted a bright lemony yellow, and decorated with a number of attractive HIV Prevention posters of smiling men, tenderly embracing. "Keep your love safe." "Share only your love," and the iconic message from the earliest years of the epidemic, "Be Here for the Cure." It was a cheery island of light in a dark and fetid universe, and we were relieved to find it. This wouldn't be too unpleasant for the volunteers.

"I thought we'd try and brighten it up a bit," Tork said in his soft voice. He and his staff had removed the bed from each room and installed cabinets for our supplies and a small refrigerator for the blood specimens, as well as for soft drinks we'd offer when men dropped by. There was a coffee table with chairs around it in the "meeting room," as well as two chairs and a small desk in the next room where the private counseling and blood draws would happen.

"You did all this since we met on Wednesday?" asked Steve.

Tork answered shyly. "Well, no. I was hoping Mr. Kratz would agree, so we began working on these rooms a couple of weeks ago when you first told me about your project and asked for the meeting." He added, "Mr. Kratz rarely comes in the bathhouse anymore, and never up here to the third floor."

"Well, this is much more than we expected," said Steve. "Thank you for all your help in making it happen."

The man was embarrassed by Steve's expression of gratitude. "No, no, it's worth it if we can keep other guys from going through what . . ." He stopped, choked up, and, to our surprise and alarm, began crying. We stood there awkwardly as he pulled out a handkerchief. "I'm sorry," he said, wiping his eyes. "It's been five years, and I still miss him so much."

Steve placed a hand on his shoulder. "You don't need to apologize to us."

Arthur and I both nodded, with Arthur adding, "We've all been there."

Tork replaced his handkerchief, too embarrassed to meet our eyes. "Just let me know whatever you need." And the four of us headed downstairs.

Yes, we've all been there . . .

I glance again at the wall clock, 2:53, and pull myself out of the chair, heading for the nurses' station. I need to get the blood circulating and to see if there are any updates. The nurse I spoke with earlier is still on duty, writing in a file as I approach. Behind her stands a male nurse, reviewing a chart. She looks up, offering a friendly smile. "No change,

241

I'm afraid, which is also good news, considering."

"Yes, I suppose it is."

"I can tell you he's been moved out of the ICU into a private room. That's hopeful."

"Great," I say. "Thank you."

This is the first vigil where I've not been allowed to be in the room. Sitting with a person, even when unconscious, offered a sense of shared presence. In the silence, one becomes aware of deeper soundings we're not usually attuned to; the vigil becomes an occasion for the busy, workaday mind to listen to its own depths. But not this time. Of course, it would have to be this vigil, where the relationship is . . . more complicated. Again, I feel the urgency: *Don't let him die before we make peace.*

Then I remember. "Oh, the young man who was in the waiting room with me. Did his girlfriend's delivery go well?"

The nurse looks quizzically at me. "I don't believe there've been any deliveries this morning. At least not since I came on duty at twelve." She turns to the male nurse behind her. "There weren't any births tonight, were there?"

He leans over, checking the computer screen. "Nope. It's been a pretty quiet night. People probably staying away with all the police hanging around."

"That's strange," I say. "He said his girlfriend was in labor."

"I haven't seen anyone else in the waiting room tonight other than you," she says.

Her comment surprises me. "You didn't see a young man—late teens, maybe early twenties, slender, dressed in black jeans and a black hooded sweatshirt?"

She shakes her head. "No. Oh, wait, there was a police officer in there briefly, about two hours ago."

"Yes, I remember him . . . too. But I'm surprised you didn't see the young man."

"I wonder if you may have been dreaming. It looked like you were asleep when I walked past the room."

I try to laugh it off. "Next you'll be telling me I dreamt the cleaning woman in there."

"Someone was cleaning the waiting room?"

"Yeah. Dressed in hospital scrubs. Looked Somali. Maybe Sudanese, with a, you know"—my hand circling my head—"hijab thing."

The two of them are looking at me strangely now. They glance at each other; the male nurse says, "The cleaning staff don't come on for another couple of hours."

By now, I feel like I'm making a complete fool of myself, a feeling I'm not totally unfamiliar with, and decide it's probably better not to bring up the blind woman with her rosary beads.

They're still staring at me.

"You know, I think I'll go back to the, ah, waiting room, and, um, wait."

They smile professionally, like they're wondering if maybe they should call security and have me committed to the psych ward upstairs. I head back down the hallway, confused and a little creeped out, trying to come up with some explanation that I can buy.

Clearly, the nurse must have missed seeing the hooded young man in the waiting room as he watched television. After all, he wasn't there that long. And no births tonight? Simple: The hospital sent his girlfriend home. False alarm. That happens. I'm sure that happens. And I know I didn't dream the cleaning staff. I was thinking of Trevor's last days and his parents' refusal to visit their dying son, and the kind lady found me crying. *"Please, sir. Be okay. You see."* I was embarrassed by my tears and—

She gave me tissues! I know there were tissues. I used them. Evidence!

I hurry to the waiting room, straight for the two wastebaskets.

No tissues.

I check my pockets.

No tissues.

I search around the area where I'd been sitting.

Hmm, strange. No tissues.

243

I stand there, confused, feeling a little dazed. A mental health specialist doubting his own mental health. Sad. The nurse had a point. Other than dozing briefly here and there, I've been without sleep for more than thirty hours. I've read studies on sleep deprivation. One's grasp on reality begins to slip after a time, and one can start hallucinating.

But no, I did not dream them! I insist to myself. I've had vivid dreams all my life, but I can tell the difference between my dreams and what's real, though admittedly I'm becoming less certain about what's real. But still, *I DID NOT DREAM THE CLEANING LADY!* No more than I dreamt the police officer, or the blind woman, or the Angel of Death—

Okay, I probably dreamt the Angel of Death. Yeah, that was probably a dream.

This seems like a good time to reconsider my earlier decision against vending machine coffee. So yes, get some coffee, then maybe turn on the television and see what's playing in the early morning hours. I don't care what, anything to keep my mind focused on something other than my mind.

Chapter Twenty-Nine

Into the Fall

[Portland, Oregon, October 1994]

Lukas was attractive as a man; as a woman he was stunning.

At the annual fall gala, the largest of our fundraisers, he arrived as Lady Bianca, his stage personality, wearing a luxuriant dark wig and dressed in a slinky glittering gown that probably only 2 percent of the adult female population could fit into.

John was amazed at the transformation. Sporting a tuxedo and carrying his glass of wine, he said, "Lukas, I swear, if I was thirty years younger and single—"

"And gay."

"—and gay, I would probably be asking you for a date."

"Well, if you were thirty years younger and single and gay, I'd probably accept."

"You look phenomenal!" exclaimed our retired military colonel.

"Thanks. But you can tell Maggie you're safe with me because I never play around with married men. Unless they insist."

"You can tell her yourself. She's here with me tonight."

Lady Bianca's eyes lit up. "Oh, goody! Where? I've been dying to meet her!"

Maggie was a bubbly, bighearted woman in her mid-fifties. When John introduced them, she gazed at Lukas in his gown and moaned, "How could I ever compete with that!"

Lukas hugged her. "You don't need to. You're far more beautiful than me."

Maggie had been looking forward to meeting the Counseling & Testing Team. "John's told me so much about all of you," she said repeatedly. "My, but aren't you a handsome couple!" she said to Marco and Terry in their matching tuxedos, both looking well, both looking happy. Terry had finally confessed to Marco how he'd become infected. Over a difficult two weeks, they'd worked through their feelings, and Marco told me he was back to "double-bagging."

Maggie absolutely fawned over Tyler. Dressed in his rented tuxedo, he looked like he was on his way to the senior prom. "Oh, you're just as adorable as John described you!" He was accompanied by Dean, a professor in his mid-forties at Portland State University.

She met Reggie, dressed in a white tuxedo contrasting handsomely with his rich, dark skin. "The computer programmer and dancer! Our youngest son always wanted to dance." He had brought his sister, elegant and poised in a deep red gown.

When John introduced Maggie to me, her effervescence softened. She took my hands in hers, saying, "Thank you for letting John on your team. This has been the best thing that's happened to him since he retired." Her eyes misted. "You brought our son back to us." John smiled, nodding, as Maggie gave me a hug. Unprepared for the depth of her emotion, I stumbled over my tongue. "It's been wonderful to have John on the team ..."

She was one of those people who lights up a room, and she danced with all of the team members—except those who didn't dance on principle—exclaiming, "I've never danced with so many handsome young men in one night!"

It was a fine evening. The ballroom dazzled in its autumn reds, golds and umber tones. I'd delivered the registration materials earlier in the day as final preparations to the room were being made. So typical: fifteen gay men fussing with the elaborate decorations while Annie, our petite, ninety-pound sometime-lesbian, lugged in the twenty-pound bags of ice. The governor of Oregon was present with her husband, as were the mayor, several city commissioners, and two congressional representatives with their partners. Marti, accompanied by her husband, equaled Lady Bianca in being stunning. It was all so glorious, we could momentarily forget why we were here. Steve came up to me as I stood observing on the sidelines. He and Mark made another handsome couple in their matching tuxedos. We watched the crowd together, man and woman couples, male couples, female couples, mixed race couples. He was happy. "Someday"—he paused—"someday this will be normal."

I chuckled, shaking my head. "You're such an optimist."

He added quietly, "I hope I live to see that day, where this will be normal."

I looked into my ginger ale, not knowing what to say. At that moment, Sandy entered the room, dressed very elegantly in a non-butch gown. Her eyes searched the ballroom. I smiled and waved to her. She spotted me, and I could tell from her face something was wrong. I left Steve and went to her.

She was out of breath. "Leo just called. Something's happened. He needs you."

"What's wrong?"

"Something about one of his kids. He wouldn't tell me, but he sounded upset, and you know Leo doesn't get upset."

I set my glass on the table next to us. "Where is he?"

"He said to meet him at a coffee shop he once showed you."

"I know the place. I'll go now."

She gripped my arm. Her eyes looked frightened. "Call me. He didn't want me to come. Said he didn't want me to see him 'like this.'"

I placed my hand on hers. "I'll call. I promise."

I arrived at the coffee shop fifteen minutes later. Several heads looked up as I entered. Marge, the waitress, said in her gravelly smoker's voice, "He's back here."

She led me through the kitchen. The same cook was standing at the grill, wearing the same three- or four-day stubble, the same cigarette dangling from his mouth. As we passed through, Marge said to him, "Mo, you didn't see nothing."

"I never see nothing," he said, working the grill.

As we walked past the counters, sinks, and shelves stocked with food products, I said, "I'm surprised you remembered me from before."

"I didn't. But we don't get that many customers dressed in tuxes these days."

She opened the door to a small back office, large enough for only one metal desk and two chairs. Leo sat in one of them, holding an ice pack to his face. As I entered, he looked up, removing the pack. It stopped me.

"*My God.*"

His right eye was swollen shut, his face covered in bruises, a cut on his cheek, a large purple lump on his forehead.

"You want some coffee?" Marge asked me.

"No. No, thanks."

"Anything for you, Leo?"

He shook his head. Marge closed the door, leaving us alone, and I sat in the other chair.

"What happened?"

He spoke slowly, enunciating the words. "I had a run-in with our local constabulary." I could see blood in his mouth, his top lip split open.

"Let me take you to the ER to look after that eye."

He shook his head. "There's no time for that. I need your help."

"What can I do?"

"The police know about my file."

"How?"

"That's not important now. We need to make it public, and we have to do it quickly."

His jaw flexed. He wouldn't meet my eyes. "I'm going to bust the police bureau wide open about what goes on down here. The drugs, the deals, the payoffs, the kickbacks. I've got names, badge numbers, dates and times—"

I placed my hand on his knee. "Leo, will you just tell me what happened?"

For the first time since I'd met him, I saw him tear up. His voice broke. "It's Danny." And he began crying.

Chapter Thirty

Danny

[Portland, Oregon, October 1994]

Another, older boy told him they could make easy money. The kid said he knew a couple of porners who would pay cash to shoot them. Take off your clothes. Smile for the camera. Get dressed. Earn two hundred bucks. Don't gotta do nothing. He and Danny could go together, he said. The kid, Brad, took Danny to a run-down hotel on First Avenue where rooms rent by the hour. They entered the lobby. The night clerk, a gaunt old guy with uncombed hair reading a newspaper, didn't bother to look up as they passed through. Danny followed Brad upstairs to a dimly lit hallway where Brad knocked on a door.

A large, unshaven man opened it. "Ah, come in, come in, gentlemen. Welcome to Universal Studios' satellite office. Glad we can do business." A thin, weasel-faced guy was setting up lights.

Creep One closed the door, eyeing Danny. "You're kind of small. You got a big dick?"

Danny put on his tough, cocky façade. "Big enough."

"Yeah? Show me."

"Show me the money first," said Danny, "then you can see

all you want."

The man smiled, turning to Creep Two. "That's the problem with the world today. No trust." He withdrew his wallet. "So, let's see"— addressing Brad—"that was two hundred together, right?"

"Two hundred each."

He stared at Brad with his wallet open. "Oh, so we're paying union wages. Okay, then, two hundred each." He handed over the money, muttering, "I hope we're dealing with professionals here. I got no time for amateurs," first to Brad, then four fifty-dollar bills to Danny, who counted them and tucked them into his back pocket.

The man put away his wallet. "Okay, so are we good? Can we get on with it? Time is money, you know."

"Yeah, yeah, we're good," said Brad.

"Okay, we'll start with you," he said to Danny. "Beauty before the beast." Brad was a thick, lumpish kid with terrible acne and bad teeth. "Get undressed and go take a shower." He gestured toward the bathroom. "There's a towel and some soap and shampoo we brought along. These dumps never provide the amenities."

The other man snickered as he stood, fiddling with one of the lights. He had a half-moon scar over his right eyebrow.

Brad said to Danny, "Go and take your shower. I'll stand watch here till you get back, then you do the same for me."

Danny nodded, kicked off his sneakers and quickly pulled off his clothes, stripping down to gray underwear that must have once been white, and went off to the bathroom.

When he emerged five minutes later, a towel wrapped around his waist and carrying his shorts, there was no sign of Brad. The larger man was fumbling with one of the cameras. "Oh, your buddy had to leave. Said he had some pressing engagement he just remembered."

Danny's alarms were going off—way too late. He'd been set up, and he wondered how much Brad was being paid to bring them pretty boys. Just wait until he found Brad . . .

"Anything wrong?" asked the man. "I mean, if you don't want to do this, just give back the money and we'll forget all about it, and you got a free shower out of the deal."

Danny thought for a moment, then shook his head.

"Okay, so let's do it. Not bad money for twenty minutes' work."

There was nothing to do but get the photo shoot over with and get out of there as fast as he could.

"Go on over by the bed."

The weasely one turned on the two klieg lights, immediately revealing how seedy the room was. Danny stood next to the brightly lit bed, the sheets clean but dingy gray. He unwound the towel from his skinny waist and tossed it aside.

"Ah, that's much better," said the man as he squinted through the camera. "All spic and span."

Danny stood there, hands on his hips, while the man continued to fiddle with his camera settings, then looked back at the boy. His sex hung long and limp between his legs.

"You need something to help get you in the mood?" He reached in his shirt pocket and held up a white capsule. "Here. No charge."

"What is it?"

"Newest designer drug out of LA. It'll get you going fast."

Danny walked over, took it, and popped it in his mouth.

"No water?" asked the man. "So let's get started."

While his assistant adjusted the lights and shields, the man took a series of still shots, directing Danny through a variety of poses on the bed. Danny could already feel the drug racing to his heart and head. And dick. It was hard as iron. He felt his blood heating up. It wouldn't be difficult keeping a hard-on.

"Good. Good," said the man, as he continued to guide Danny through different shots. "Yeah, hold that. Ah, there's something about skinny boys with big dicks."

He moved in close, shooting every inch of Danny's body.

"Good. Let's do the live action now." He put down the SLR and took up one of the video cameras, looking through it as he directed his assistant in adjusting the light.

"There. That's good, Lonnie. Keep those lights like that." He came over to the bed where Danny was lying on it, hands behind his head, hard-on red and pulsing from the drug coursing through his system.

He sat on the bed and positioned Danny how he wanted him, on his back, one knee up. "Okay, let's get you started," he said, reaching for the boy's crotch. Danny swatted his hand away. "I can do it myself."

"Sure, sure. Just wanted to lend a helping hand." He picked up the video camera and stood, focusing on the boy. "Okay, ready? So begin."

Lightheaded from the drug, Danny began stroking himself. It was hot in his hand. He closed his eyes to block out the two goons and the dingy hotel room and the bright lights shining in his eyes, focusing on the intense sensations. Every part of him felt horny, every nerve in his body hypersexual. He was floating on a sensual ocean, his head swimming, cheeks burning, his breathing coming more and more rapid as he continued pulling on himself.

"Good. That's good." The voice echoed in his head, coming from far away. "Let me know when you're about to come. I need a close-up."

Danny's face was hot, heart thudding, breathing deepening, and he felt the first seismic tremor. "Okay," he whispered.

Even with his eyes closed, he sensed the camera moving closer. Then, with a sudden gasp, his body arched, head pushing back into the pillow, legs reaching down the length of the bed as he shot a thick, white stream stretching from throat to belly, and groaned—and then was back in the dumpy room as he finished pulling off.

"Beautiful," he heard above him, the camera still running. "Great shot."

He opened his eyes, the room swimming around him. He noticed the two men had hard-ons straining through their pants. Creep One switched off the camera. "A star is born." He put down the equipment. "Jeez, kid, you did that like a pro. You done this before?"

But Danny wasn't there for social conversation. He'd done what he was paid to do and wanted to leave. Pulling himself up into a sitting position, he grabbed the towel, wiping his chest and stomach as Creep Two turned off the lights and the other man put the camera in its case. Tossing the towel on the floor, he reached for his underwear and sat on the edge of the bed, pulling them on, when the large man came over and sat next to him.

"Hey, what's the hurry? Now the work's done, we can get better acquainted."

He noticed the man's erection hadn't subsided. Neither had his, still hard as iron. As he reached for his jeans, the man put his big paw on the boy's bony shoulder. "Looks like you're ready to go again."

He tried shrugging off the hand, but it remained glued to his skin. "No need to be unfriendly." Danny stood to step into his jeans, but the goon swept up his slender frame and threw him back onto the bed, tossing his jeans on the floor, and straddling him.

Danny struggled. "C'mon, man, I did what you wanted."

"Not everything."

He sat on the boy's stomach, pinning his shoulders to the bed. Danny bucked under him, trying to kick him from behind with his feet. Lonnie the weasel came over and held his ankles, and Danny felt his shorts being pulled down his legs.

"No!" he screamed.

The big man put a hand over his mouth and in the other hand appeared a switchblade, his switchblade. Holding Danny's face in his grip, the man leaned close, clear menace in his voice. No more Mr. Congeniality.

"Now listen, you little bitch, play along and keep quiet or I'll cut off your dick and stick it down your throat and your days of working the streets are over. You're a beauty, but who wants a dickless beauty to play with? Understand?"

His jaw aching in the vise-like grip, Danny nodded.

The pressure eased, and the man's jovial mien returned. "That's more like it. No hard feelings. Consider this just one of the perks of the job."

He released Danny's face, placed the knife on the lamp table next to the bed, and got onto his knees, flipping the boy over onto his stomach. Danny's eyes were burning with fear and rage. "No, don't do this." His face in the pillow, he heard the sound of a belt being unbuckled, a zipper opening. "Please. I don't do this," his voice quavering, now sounding like a scared kid in place of the tough pseudo-adult before.

"Don't worry. There's nothing for you to do. Just lie there and think of England, or whatever."

"No, wait. I'll give you a blowjob. I give good blowjobs."

He felt his buttocks being massaged.

"Nah, I'm no fag. But if there's no pussy around, a boy's ass'll do."

The man's meaty paws clamped onto Danny's hips, pulling him up onto his knees.

"No, really, I've never done this."

"First time for everything, sport."

He felt hairy thighs spreading his hairless legs apart, then lube being rubbed back there.

"No, please."

"Sh-sh. You're breaking my concentration. Now just relax and enjoy it."

A hand thrust his face down into the pillow and the hard thing was forcing its way in, the pillow muffling his cries, the pain excruciating as it continued pushing in. Then broke through. He screamed. The bulky weight was on him now, stubbly cheek rubbing against the boy's smooth face, breath stinking of cigarettes and garlic as the man began rocking over him, nuzzling his neck and hair. Pain ripped through him as the rocking got faster and faster, pumping, pressing him deeper into the mattress, when at last he heard the man grunt, a final thrust, a groan, and the weight on him froze. They lay like that for what seemed several minutes. Danny hurt but it was no longer excruciating. He felt the hardness in him begin to melt. The puffs of rank breath on his face became slower, more regular, a kiss on his cheek.

"Now, then, that wasn't so bad, was it?"

The thing pulled out of him, pain once again, but he was beyond crying out. He lay there, sinking, disappearing into the sagging mattress, as the bed rocked and swayed with the man getting up, like being buoyed and carried along on the ocean. He was at Seaside with one of his foster families, floating on an air mattress, lazily feeling the sun and the salt on his skin, as the gentle waves rocked and lulled him to sleep.

Voices came drifting over the waves from shore.

"All yours, amigo."

"Why do I always get sloppy seconds?"

"Because I'm the pathfinder. I clear the way for you. You should be grateful."

The bed rocked again, hands pulling his thighs apart, then the hot hard thing again entering him, less pain this time, no resistance. He lay still, face in the pillow, the weight on him bucking the bed, as he heard whistling elsewhere in the room. His eyes fluttered open. The large man was folding up the shields, putting them away in the suitcases. He closed his eyes, heard the cases snap shut, a chair scrape on the linoleum floor, the grunts of the man on top of him. He was floating again on the waves, couldn't have said for how long, was hardly aware of the man's climax, then his withdrawal. The boy lay limp on the sheets, the voices in the room unintelligible as he drifted away out to sea . . .

Gradually, the voices became more audible, people talking. He was lying on the bed, his anus feeling ripped open, when he felt his buttocks being massaged.

The man's voice, softer now. "You might want to take a shower and clean up before you leave."

He lay there without moving. The hand stopped, resting a moment, then patted him. "You're a good kid. You'll be fine."

The hand left and he felt a sheet drawn over him.

"You need to be out of here in about thirty minutes. Okay? . . . Do you understand?"

Face still buried in the pillow, he nodded.

"Good boy."

A big hand ruffled his hair like his foster father did (*which one?*) when he was small. He lay still as he heard the voices, footsteps on the linoleum, door opening, door shutting, footsteps going down the hallway. He didn't know how long he lay there like that—it could have been a minute, it could have been an hour—before he pulled his aching, broken body into a sitting position and threw off the sheet. He stood uncertainly on his feet, the backs of his thighs wet and sticky; his rectum hurt. He picked up his shorts from the floor and slowly stepped into them, then his jeans. His switchblade was missing from the bed stand. He remembered the money and quickly checked his back pocket. The fifty-dollar bills were gone. It was only then he sat back onto the bed, dropping his face in his hands, and wept.

It was one of those times in my life when I wished I drank. I said softly, "Where's Danny now?"

"He's safe." Leo's voice was flat, his face expressionless, but his good eye was steely cold. "I took him to the ER. There was some internal tearing and bleeding, but they released him. They tested him for HIV to get a baseline reading. We'll test him monthly for three or four months to see if he's infected. But don't worry about Danny. He's somewhere where he'll be cared for."

"So how did you end up like this?"

"I went back out to pick up a prescription for when the hospital's meds were gone. On the way back, I ran into a couple of cops on the beat. I knew them. I was angry. There were words. (*Your days are up. I've got a file of all the shit you've been pulling down here. Got your names, your badge numbers, dates, details. You're fucked.*") "I told them I had enough evidence to put them and their buddies away."

I said nothing, but he knew what I was thinking.

"I know, I know," he sighed, leaning heavily into the ice pack. "I wasn't at my most rational. I might've also thrown the first punch."

"What happened?"

"We got into it, right there off Burnside. They would've killed me if another cop hadn't come along."

Leo lying on the sidewalk in a fetal position, trying to protect himself as both cops kicked and beat him with their nightsticks. He hears a car screech to a stop, a car door opening, radio voice squawking from inside. Someone shouting, "Lay off, Durbin!"

"Fuck off, O'Connor! Leave this to us!"

Leo raises his head, hurting everywhere, sees a young cop pushing at the other two officers. "I said lay off him!" More shoving, then fists.

"That's when I managed to get to my feet and run," said Leo. "If that other cop hadn't come along, I know they'd have killed me. They weren't interested in taking me in."

I breathed out slowly. "Okay, if they know about the file, we'd better act fast. We need to talk with Jake."

"I already tried. That was weird."

"What?"

"I made it here to the cafe and called him. But it was like he didn't know me. I kept saying, it's me, Leo. Emilio. He was polite, like you'd be with a stranger, then suggested I make an appointment with his department's secretary at Reed."

"But he's been retired for years."

"I know. So that's when I decided to call you. I reached Sandy, but couldn't let her see me like this. She'd probably go hunting down the cops herself."

"So, what do we do?"

"Can you drive me to my apartment?"

"Of course. But you shouldn't be alone tonight. You could have suffered a concussion. Please let me take you to the ER."

"No. The police could be watching the hospital."

"Then why not stay at Sandy's? Or, if you don't want her to see you like this, stay at my place."

"I'll be okay. I just need some sleep. Then let's meet at noon tomorrow. At the Starbucks in Pioneer Square. You bring the registry. I'll bring the file, and we'll go over to Jake's house and see what's the best way to handle this." Following Jake's suggestion, Leo had kept the file hidden at his place, and I'd kept the coded registry of names at mine.

I knew it was no good to insist. "Okay. What about the two goons? Shouldn't we report them?"

Leo's voice turned eerily flat. "The street will take care of them."

Marge gave Leo a bag of ice to take home with him. I brought my car around back and helped Leo into it—he was wobbly on his feet—then drove him to his apartment in Northwest Portland. As we

pulled up in front, I tried again. "I really wish you'd stay at my place."
He opened the car door. "No, I'm fine. Thanks for everything. See you tomorrow at noon."

"I'll be there."

I watched him weave unsteadily up the walk, watched him mount the steps, unlock the door, and enter. Once he was safely inside, I left for home to call Sandy. There was no way I could manage a gala after this.

That was the weekend Leo vanished.

Chapter Thirty-One

On Filing a Report
(Or, Who knew it was so hard to become a missing person?)

[Portland, Oregon, October 1994]

I had a bad feeling when Leo didn't appear at noon on Sunday. I called his apartment from Pioneer Square, concerned he might have had a concussion. No answer, so I waited impatiently until 1:00 p.m., then drove to where he lived. The building had once been a large and impressive house in the 1930s, probably for a large and impressive Portland family. In more recent decades, it'd been converted into a number of less impressive apartments. I went up the steps and knocked on the door. No response. So I knocked again, and again, eventually banging on it, until I saw movement through the window: someone descending the stairs. A college student-type opened the door, barefoot, skinny and hipless, dressed only in a pair of gravity-defying jeans hanging so low, downy brown hair poked out the top of them. He had a thin hairless chest, the first wispy attempt at a beard, and looked groggy. He also looked irate.

"Dude, what *is* your problem? People are trying to sleep!"

But I was feeling too desperate to be apologetic. "It's after one," I said.

"Exactly."

"In the afternoon."

"Huh?" He blinked, squinting over my shoulder into the dull daylight.

"Look, I'm really sorry to wake you, but I need to speak to Leo. It's urgent."

I had clearly not made a new friend. He grumbled, "Wait here," and closed the door. I watched as he went up the stairs.

He was back in a minute. "He's not there."

"Are you sure? Maybe he didn't hear you knock. He might have suffered a concussion last night."

"I looked in his room," he said wearily. "Leo doesn't lock his door. He wasn't in the john. He's not here, okay?"

I left a note with him, along with a ten-dollar bill for his troubles, asking Leo to call me as soon as he got the message. Next I called Sandy, trying to keep my own fears tamped down and not alarm her. I returned to Pioneer Square and waited through the afternoon, hoping maybe he had first gone to check on Danny. Sandy kept trying his phone. When he didn't show up for work on Monday morning, we spoke with Steve, and the three of us decided to call the police. We thought it would carry more weight if we reported a missing employee rather than just as "concerned friends."

Sandy made the call as Steve and I listened. The person on the line suggested we wait. People sometimes don't show up for work, she said, especially on Monday mornings. But Sandy wouldn't take no for an answer. "We are very, *very* concerned"—enunciating each word—"and we don't want to wait." The person acquiesced, saying an officer would come to our office that morning. Two hours later, a policewoman, Officer Herndon, was sitting in Steve's office, writing in her notepad.

"When did you last see Mr. Saavedra?" she asked.

"Saturday night, around nine-thirty," I said. "I dropped him off at his apartment. We were to meet the next day at noon, and he never showed up. I went to his apartment building, but he wasn't there."

261

"Do you have any idea what might have happened to him?"

Bad apples, I thought, but said, "No."

"Has he ever disappeared before?"

"Yes," admitted Sandy. "At times, he needs to get away for a while. But he's always let me know he'd be gone."

After a few more questions, she recapped her pen and closed her notepad. "We normally recommend waiting. You'd be surprised at the number of reports of missing people we get each month. Most show up. There's no law against people disappearing if they choose. Maybe he's just sleeping off a bender somewhere."

"Leo doesn't drink or use drugs," said Sandy.

"You're sure of that?"

"Hasn't in over two years."

Steve interjected, "How long do we need to wait before you consider him officially missing?"

"Typically, two or three days."

She must have seen our alarm, adding, "Unless there's suspicious circumstances."

"There could be," I said. She looked at me. "He had a run-in with two police officers the night before he disappeared."

"What kind of run-in?"

"They got into an argument—a fight, actually."

"Over?"

"He's our street outreach worker, and he doesn't always see eye to eye with the police on how to work with street people." I decided not to tell her about the file. "A third officer came by and broke up the fight. Leo left while the three officers were still . . . discussing it."

She reopened her notepad. "What time did this happen, and where?"

"Probably around eight. Near Burnside and Third Avenue."

"And you believe Mr. Saavedra's story?"

"I saw him afterward. He was in pretty bad shape—swollen eye, split lip, purple bruises on his face."

"Then I'd also suggest you check the area hospitals. When I get back to the office, I'll review the incident reports for Saturday night. Did he get the names of the officers?"

"Probably. But he didn't tell me."

Sandy was clearly anxious, edging on anger. I hoped she could keep it together. "When you finally determine that Leo's missing, what can you do?"

"We'll check his car registration."

"He doesn't own a car. He uses public transportation and walks everywhere."

"We can check his cell phone records."

"He doesn't have one."

"Then recent credit card transactions."

"He doesn't use credit cards."

Officer Herndon looked exasperated. "Bank account?"

"Yes, he has a bank account."

"Then we can check to see if there's been any activity. If necessary, we can get his dental records for possible identification. But for now, we'll hold off on filing an official report until it's certain Mr. Saavedra is missing. He's only been gone about a day." She gave each of us her card. "Be sure to let us know if he calls you or if you hear anything about him."

"Thanks for coming over," said Steve with a smile, which was good since neither Sandy nor I was smiling. "We appreciate it."

"I'm sorry I can't be more helpful at this time."

I sensed we were racing against time, and feared we were already too late.

Chapter Thirty-Two

Looking for Leo

[Portland, Oregon, October 1994]

Officer Herndon called Steve later in the day. She'd found no reports of any interaction between police officers and Leo on Saturday night. But I already knew she wouldn't.

Tuesday morning Sandy and I drove to Leo's apartment in Northwest Portland. The leafy streets were clogged with parked cars, and we kept circling around, trying to find a place to park until she swung into an empty space.

"You can't park here," I told her. "It's disabled parking."

She switched off the engine. "So, *limp* when you get out."

We went up the steps and knocked on the door. There was no answer, but we knew at least one of the tenants was there. The pungent odor of marijuana wafted from an open window on the second floor. There was an "APT FOR RENT" sign next to the door with the manager's phone number and Sandy called it on her cell phone. She got a voice recording and left a message, saying she was at the apartment building and wanted to speak to the manager. We resumed knocking on the door, hoping to rouse the happy smoker upstairs. After five more minutes of intermittent knocking, we concluded the smoker was too happy and gave up. As we turned to leave, a man came down the sidewalk. "You the people who phoned?" He was of that indeterminate age called "old," somewhere between sixty and eighty, wearing rumpled gray slacks and a green cardigan sweater over a loud Hawaiian print shirt, a sartorial ensemble causing one to shield one's eyes.

"Yes," said Sandy. "We work with Leo Saavedra. We're concerned that he's not shown up for two days now. We'd like to check his room."

"Nah, I got no authority to let you in his room."

We stood on the covered porch as it began to rain.

"We've filed a missing person report with the police," said Sandy. "Would you rather they come and search his room?"

"They were already here."

Both of us looked at him with surprise. "The police?"

"Yeah, two cops yesterday morning. I'm not sure I should be letting people in his room."

Alarm bells that had been ringing in my head since Sunday just got louder. We hadn't met with Officer Herndon until 11:00 a.m. I doubted the police worked that fast.

Sandy made a show of sniffing the air, the pungent smell from the second-story window still strong. "Would you like the police to visit again?" she asked, smiling at the man. No need to be unpleasant when threatening someone.

He smelled the illegal scent, too. "I guess it'd be okay for you to look around, you being Leo's friends and all." It must have been Sandy's smile.

He unlocked the front door, and we followed him up the stairs to the second floor and Leo's apartment. It was a shambles. "The cops did this," he said. "Leo's very neat. Likes things clean and orderly."

"He was always neat when he lived with me, too," murmured Sandy.

It was your basic college student décor. Mattress on the floor, table, two chairs, small kitchenette with microwave, mismatched furniture from Goodwill, an old beat-up sofa, chest of drawers,

265

jerry-rigged bookcase of wooden boards and concrete blocks. The police had definitely been looking for something: The mattress and bedding were turned over, drawers of the dresser open, clothes lying on the floor, books pulled off the shelves. I went directly to his desk, its drawers already open, papers and folders on the floor. The third drawer had a false bottom, where Leo had told me he hid the file. I lifted out the panel, revealing the hidden compartment, then looked at Sandy, shaking my head. *It's not here.*

"Did the police officers take anything?" I asked.

"They were in here by themselves, but I didn't see them take anything when they left."

"Could you describe them?"

He looked at me like I was crazy. "They were cops. What's to describe?"

"Badge numbers? Did they leave cards?"

"Nah. They were just cops."

"Did they have a search warrant?" asked Sandy.

"Hey, cops say they wanna search, I let 'em search. Don't want no problems with the cops."

"Did they say why they were searching or what they were searching for?"

"Didn't ask. None of my business."

I squatted before the bookcase, studying the titles on the floor—college texts, several paperback novels, five well-thumbed books by Krishnamurti—while Sandy went through the closet. The manager stood at the door, watching. "Leo pays his rent two, three months in advance. Keeps his room clean. Seems like a good kid."

I went to the open chest of drawers. The usual: underwear, socks, T-shirts. The second drawer had several pairs of jeans. I pulled out a pair, holding them up and stared at them . . .

Something knocking at the back door of my mind.

Sandy noticed. "What is it?"

"Nothing." I refolded and returned the jeans to the drawer. Whatever it was, it should have used the front door.

"Like I told the cops, Leo takes off from time to time," said the manager. "I wouldn't worry. Haven't seen the other one, neither."

Sandy and I both turned to him. "The other one?" I asked.

"His roommate or whatever. I don't inquire too closely. None of my business."

"Do you know the other fellow's name? Or how we could contact him?"

"Nah. He comes and goes. Probably went with Leo. Maybe they took a vacation, you know?"

"Is he a cosigner on the lease agreement?" asked Sandy.

He shook his head. "Just Leo. They're both quiet. Keep to themselves. Never no problems. Wish all my tenants were like them."

"Okay. Well, thank you for letting us look," I said, and the three of us went downstairs.

Once we were back inside Sandy's illegally parked car, I said, "He wasn't very forthcoming, was he?"

"None of his business."

"Did Leo say anything to you about having a roommate?"

"No, but he's always been private. I respected that."

Before returning to the office, we stopped at a coffee shop on Northwest Twenty-Third Avenue to discuss next steps. Sandy was clearly anxious as her hands gripped the cup. "It's not looking good, is it?"

"I think it's too early to lose hope," I said quietly.

"He could be badly injured. He could be lying somewhere."

I didn't meet her eyes.

"You think he's already dead, don't you?" she said.

"I don't know what to think." I was trying to be rational, calm, trying not to let my own fears seep out. "Let's assume he's alive until we learn otherwise, okay?"

"If the cops were searching his apartment for the file, it must mean he took the file with him, and that they didn't get him." She was reaching for any hope. I couldn't blame her, but I also could think of different, less hopeful scenarios.

"Or maybe they did get the file," I said, "and they went to his apartment, looking for the registry."

"What registry?"

"Leo recorded the different incidents in his file, but he coded them so there were no names. The street kids, the pimps and prostitutes, the bar and flophouse owners—they were each given a code. You need the registry to identify those people. *If* the police got the file, they know they need the registry as well."

"Where's the registry?"

I lowered my voice. "At my house. We decided to not keep the file and registry in the same location."

Sandy was quiet. "If the cops did get Leo and the file, they'd have realized they needed the registry, too. And if they hadn't killed him already, they could have made him tell where the registry is, and who has it."

I shrugged. "That's a lot of *ifs*."

"I'm saying, watch your back."

"I know. I know."

It seemed both of us wanted to change the topic, so I asked, "How did he wind up living with you, anyway? I didn't know that."

"Two years ago. Father Paul found Leo on the streets and brought him to me."

"Father Paul?"

"Yeah, he was doing his own street outreach, trying to get the young people into treatment or safe homes. He'd talked with Leo a number of times, convinced him to turn his life around. When Leo reached that point, Paul asked if he could stay with me. He knew I'd taken in several foster kids. Leo was in pretty bad shape. Hooked on heroin. I normally don't accept addicts. Too much heartache and disappointment. But Leo was determined to get clean. That's what he had going for him, that and Father Paul's commitment to him, so I gave him a chance and a room. Told him he could stay as long as he worked to get clean. And he did."

"That was amazingly generous of you."

"I knew he was a good kid. Just really messed up. Ever see someone going through withdrawal?"

I shook my head.

"Not pleasant to witness. It was a rough two months. He'd lie on his bed, curled up in a fetal position for hours, sweating, feverish, shaking. And silent. I never heard him cry or whimper. He'd learned to tough it out on the streets. Father Paul came and sat with Leo every day of those two months, talking him through the withdrawal." Sandy's cup sat steaming in her hands. "I'd bring him food, water, juice—leaving them in his room—but they were usually untouched. He lost so much weight, I became concerned. When he was going through the worst of it, he closed even me and Paul out. Didn't want anyone to see him like that. The only one he'd let in was Fernando. He'd leap up onto the bed and curl himself next to Leo for hours, through the sweats, the shaking, just lying next to him, purring softly. I think it had a calming effect on Leo. He seemed to rest more easily when Fernando was lying next to him." She took a drink of her coffee. "Maybe Fernando sensed they were kindred spirits. Both were abandoned when young."

"I take back every mean thing I've ever said about Fernando."

I was glad to see her smile. We talked about what to do next. Sandy would contact Officer Herndon, ask if she knew about police officers searching Leo's apartment. We'd already contacted area hospitals as Herndon suggested. I would go to the Sexual Minorities Roundtable that afternoon to tell Jake what had happened and seek his help in getting the police to investigate.

Chapter Thirty-Three

Who's President?

[Portland, Oregon, October 1994]

I arrived late to the Sexual Minorities Roundtable, coming from a meeting with Arthur and Tork. We were making final preparations to launch the counseling and testing program in the bathhouse in November. I slipped into a back row, relieved to see that Jake was there. I had tried to call him several times Monday but only got his answering machine. I left messages, saying it was urgent, but never heard back. We hadn't talked in a couple of months. I usually worked out at the Princeton mid-afternoon, while he preferred the busier times "when the voyeurism is better."

He was addressing the roundtable in his usual jovial manner, the discussion about enhanced police patrols around the downtown area where a number of gay bars were clustered. I knew there'd been several incidents of bar patrons followed and attacked by young thugs. Jake was summing up. "In the interest of public safety, it would be helpful for police cars to be seen in the vicinity when the bars close around 2:00 a.m."

"That's a matter of scheduling and, of course, available manpower at that hour," said the police chief, "but I'll have my staff look into what's possible and we'll get back to you at the next roundtable. Thank you for bringing this to our attention."

"That's our porpoise," Jake said affably.

Porpoise? I leaned forward in my seat, wondering if I'd heard correctly. Or was he making a joke? Then I noticed the chief and a number of people in the room were looking at Jake with quizzical expressions.

The chief spoke again. "You said *porpoise*. I think you meant purpose."

Jake grinned at him. "Hiram, I think you need to have your heart checked."

"My heart?"

Jake stopped, momentarily flustered. "Well, no, not your heart. I meant your *hearing*. Nothing wrong with your heart, I'm sure."

"Are you feeling all right, Jake?"

"Of course. Why wouldn't I feel all right?"

"You just haven't seemed yourself lately."

"Well, I don't know who else I would be." He now appeared uncomfortable and made an attempt to return to the matter at hand. "So, I believe we were discussing accommodations for transgender persons at the county jail."

The chief spoke evenly, "No, we were discussing police patrols when the bars close on the weekends."

Jake looked like he was trying to recall something. "Well, yes. That, too."

The chief checked his watch. "You know, I have to get to my next meeting. Why don't we leave further discussion for next month, shall we?"

"As you wish, Hiram. As you wish." Jake opened his arms expansively. "We aren't going away."

"Then we are adjourned. Thank you, everyone." As he stood, the chief looked directly at me—we'd spoken several times since meeting in March—and tilted his head toward Jake. I nodded back, then made my way up to Jake as people were leaving the chamber.

"Hobbes! I haven't seen you in eons."

"Hi, Jake. Have time for coffee?"

"For you I'm always available."

We left the building for a nearby coffee shop, Jake chattering away as usual, though I thought he seemed distracted, like a person with something weighing on his mind. Not fully present. Once we'd settled into a booth and ordered our coffees, I told him what had happened to Leo Saturday night and of my growing concern. "He's vanished. Didn't make our meeting on Sunday. Didn't show for work yesterday or today, and hasn't notified anyone. We're very worried." Jake listened with a kind of detached interest, where I would have expected more alarm. I paused. "You know we're talking about Leo?"

"Mm, yes . . . Do I know him?"

I sat back in the booth. "You know him very well. He's one of your protégés. Emilio?"

By the look on his face, he was processing the name. A light suddenly came on. "Oh, Emilio?"

"Yes."

"He's missing?"

"Yes." Thank God, I was finally getting through. "He said he called you Saturday night, but you acted like you didn't know him."

"Didn't know him? Emilio?"

"That's what he said. You don't remember him calling?"

"No. But if the boy needed my help, I'd have gone to him in a . . . in a . . . you know . . ."

"Heartbeat?"

"Exactly. Oh, I was afraid this might happen someday. I told him to be careful. I told him not to go out on the streets by himself."

"We're getting nowhere with the police. We tried to file a missing-person report, but they want to wait to see if he shows up."

Jake was incensed. "Well, thank you very much, but we are *not* going to wait to see if he shows up. We'll raise this with, um . . . oh, you know, the police chief."

"Hiram."

"Yes, of course. Hiram. We'll raise it first thing at the roundtable today."

I stared at him. "We just came from the roundtable." His face took on a vacant look. "Don't you remember?"

Jake's coffee remained untouched. "Oh, yes, that's right." But he didn't sound convinced, or convincing.

"Jake, are you feeling all right?"

"Of course. Why is everyone asking if I feel all right? I feel perfectly fine."

I studied him for a moment. "Do you know what day it is?"

"Tuesday. The roundtable's always on Tuesday."

"Yes, it is. Can you tell me who's president?"

He looked at me as if it were a joke. "Oh, c'mon."

"No, I'm serious. Who's president?"

As he tried to remember, his face changed. "I . . . I . . . ." First a look of perplexity, then of growing alarm, then panic.

"Can you tell me your mother's name?"

"Gloria," he said quickly. "And her maiden name was Wishram." He appeared relieved.

"Good. How about your father's name?"

That lost look came over his face again. He was struggling to recall, his forehead moist, his eyes darting here and there as if trying to work through some problem.

Then he waved his hand flippantly. "Well, we were never close anyway." But his forehead remained damp, his eyes round with what looked increasingly like fear.

"I think it might be a good idea for you to check with your doctor."

He nodded, realizing the implications of what I was suggesting. "What . . . what do you think's happening?"

"I don't know. You may have suffered a slight stroke that's affected your memory." There was a worse-case scenario, but I didn't want to think about it, much less mention it.

"Okay. I'll call her office when I get home."

"You remember your doctor's name?"

"Cecilia Jacobs. One of the best AIDS docs in Portland."

"Tell her you can't remember the president's name, or your father's. She'll know what to do."

He nodded, looking at me.

"Maybe I should drive you home."

"No, no, no. I'm perfectly capable of driving myself."

"You remember where you live?"

"Of course. In Laurelhurst. Lived there over forty years."

"Okay . . . May I call you in an hour, just to ease my mind that you made it home safely?"

"Oh, I never refuse calls from attractive men." He grinned broadly, but the quip fell flat, lacking his usual flirtatiousness.

"I'll call you before five."

He nodded again. I could see he was shaken.

"Sure I can't drive you home?"

"No, I'm fine, thanks." He bid me good-bye and rose from the booth, and I watched him go.

Just as he got to the door, he abruptly swung around, shouting throughout the coffee shop, "Clinton!"

Chapter Thirty-Four

We Carry On, Like Always

[Portland, Oregon, October 1994]

It was now the third week of October, and for the next two nights I walked the streets, seeking out the street kids. "I work with Leo," I would tell them. "I'm trying to find him." But strangely, everyone I asked had never heard of Leo, even though I recognized some from the underworld tour he gave me back in March and others who had tested at our clinic. I also said I was looking for a fourteen-year-old boy named Danny, trying not to sound like a pervert. I wanted to make sure he was okay. "Nope, never heard of him neither." Now clean-shaven, dressed as I was, I realized I had all the street credibility of Reagan at an AIDS conference.

Walking for several fruitless hours, I dropped into the coffee shop off Burnside. It was eleven-thirty by then, and there were only a scattering of people in the café. I took a seat at the counter, and Marge brought over a pot of coffee, pouring me a cup.

"Personally, I think you looked better in the tux."

I smiled. "Thanks." Then I turned serious. "Leo's missing."

"Yeah, I heard."

"You haven't seen him?"

"Not since Saturday night when he left with you." She lowered her voice. "The word on the street doesn't sound good."

"What are they saying?"

"Leo's gone."

"What does that mean?"

"Just gone. On the street, you don't ask for details. It's generally better not to know."

I took a swallow of coffee. That wasn't the news I wanted.

"I knew something was up," said Marge. "The cops been comin' 'round now, happy as clams."

"Did they ask about Leo?"

"Nah. I don't think Leo's on friendly terms with them, so I say nothing. I give 'em free cups of coffee, but that's all I give 'em."

"Do you know who Leo hangs out with? Do you know his roommate?"

She shook her head. "Leo pretty much keeps to himself." I appreciated her using the present tense. I was fighting to not slip into the past tense myself.

"I'm looking for one of Leo's kids named Danny. Maybe five foot two, slight build, pale, reddish-blond hair. He was hurt the night Leo disappeared. I need to make sure he's all right, and I'm hoping he might know something."

"I don't know Leo's kids. He sometimes brings in one or two who're especially hard up and buys them dinner, but I don't know names."

I finished the coffee. "Okay. I'm going to keep walking the streets. See if I can find out anything more. Here's my card with my office number, and on the back my home number. In case you hear anything, I'd appreciate a call."

"Sure."

I pulled out my wallet.

"It's on the house."

"Thanks." I put down a five-dollar bill. "A tip for the house."

She picked it up. "The house says thanks."

As we entered the final week of October, Steve, Sandy, and I were getting nowhere with the police, so we appealed to Marti to contact them in her role as the agency's executive director. We sat around her desk as she called Officer Herndon, putting her on the speakerphone.

"I'm calling about my staff member who's been missing now for over two weeks. Leo Saavedra?"

"Yes, I took the report that he'd disappeared."

"We don't believe Leo disappeared voluntarily," said Marti.

"I'm sorry but we usually don't investigate unless there's reason to suspect foul play."

"Like what, his dead body?"

Officer Herndon was patient, her voice remaining calm, her tone level. I'm sure we weren't the first distraught people she'd had to deal with. "I appreciate how distressing this must be for you and your staff, Ms. Michaelson. I'm sorry there's not more we can do at this time."

"I heard he had a fight with some officers the night he disappeared."

"We have no record of that happening."

"He'd been threatened by police officers before."

"Did Mr. Saavedra file a report that he'd been threatened or harassed by the police? Do you have anything in writing to support that?"

Marti looked up. I shook my head.

"No," she conceded.

"Again, I'm sorry. There's really not much I can do at this time."

Leo's disappearance hit the staff hard. A new anxiety among people familiar with anxiety, who lived daily with the expectation of bad news. Without saying it, we were bracing ourselves for what we expected was coming. Life resumed its routine. We went about our work. There was still an epidemic on, meetings to attend, trainings to conduct, cases to manage, potential donors to cultivate, so we carried on, returning to what we could do since it seemed there was little we could do for Leo. It's what we'd become good at in this epidemic: carrying on.

On Tuesday, Steve joined us in the conference room for the prevention team's weekly meeting. "Chad's going to be a little late," he said as he took his chair. "He's at the doctor's office." So, it was just Steve, Andie, Lionel, and myself.

"Any word on Leo?" asked Andie.

"No," Steve said grimly. "No word. But a heads-up about Chad. He's started a new treatment regimen. Beta carotene. It's experimental. The docs don't know yet what side effects there'll be, but it's already turning his skin kind of orange. He's self-conscious about it, so just pretend you don't notice, okay?"

We nodded soberly. It was clear to all that Chad's health was becoming more precarious. The eighty-plus pills he was taking daily didn't seem to be as effective as before. It's why he signed up for this new experimental drug protocol.

The agenda for the team's meeting was to develop prevention messages for the general population, based on questions our information hotline staff were receiving. For those of us who'd been involved on the front lines for a decade, the extent of the public's ignorance and misinformation about HIV and AIDS was disturbing: "No, ma'am, you can't get HIV by touching someone who's infected"—nor by kissing your gay son, or breathing the same air on long passenger flights, or from mosquitoes. No, ma'am, not even from gay mosquitoes. *Thanks, Fox News.* Then there was the elderly woman concerned for her and her husband. She'd heard on the radio that one could get HIV from "annual intercourse." Could that be true?

We were still brainstorming prevention messages when Chad arrived, carrying his cup of coffee and notebook for the meeting. Given his light complexion, his skin tone did have an orange-ish cast. We all greeted him, pretending not to notice. Except Lionel.

"Well, look who's here," he said, grinning. "If it isn't the Great Pumpkin!"

Chad offered a sheepish smile as he settled into a chair. "Yeah, and Mom always said orange wasn't my color."

We chuckled politely, except Steve who stared at Lionel with an *I-can't-believe-you* look on his face, whereby Lionel dropped his head, mumbling, "I forgot."

The counseling and testing team was no less affected by Leo's disappearance than the staff, and they, too, were subdued yet determined to carry on doing what they had volunteered to do. They were reviewing their files when Arthur joined us for the evening, although there were no positive results to deliver. It'd been more than six months since the team had gone through their own HIV testing experience back in April, he pointed out, and those members who weren't HIV-positive (except for John) should test again, if for no other reason than to be good role models. Tyler blushed as he told us he finally had a legitimate reason to get tested. There were immediate cheers and slaps on his back, which only deepened his blush, but one could also see he was pleased to share this information with his brothers.

"I just hope . . ." began Arthur.

"Dean and I are *very* safe," Tyler said.

"Then I'm *very* pleased."

I looked over the schedule. "Lukas, why don't you take Tyler for his pretest counseling session before the crowd arrives."

"Oh, goody!" exclaimed Lukas, jumping up and grabbing the folder out of my hands, then taking Tyler by the arm. "I'm dying to hear all the dirty details!"

As they headed down the hall to a free room, Arthur called after them, "Let's maintain professional standards, Lukas, shall we? Professional standards, please?"

Lukas swung around, all wide-eyed innocent. "Of course. *Always.*" And he slipped into a business-like demeanor as if greeting a new customer at his salon. He gestured Tyler to one of the rooms. "This way, if you please, young sir." He smiled at Arthur, then followed behind

Tyler, whispering excitedly, "I want to know absolutely *everything!*"

I headed back to the staff room for some water before clients began arriving. Chad was in there by himself, sitting at the table, eating a slice of the donated pizza and reading a textbook for one of his classes.

"Hey, how's it going?" I asked.

He looked up. "Great. There is an upside to my skin tone."

"Oh? What's that?"

"Lukas wants to help me select a new wardrobe to go with the New Me."

I chuckled as I filled a cup from the cooler, then said, "You know, I've never asked you how you're handling all this."

"Fine." He was his usual upbeat self. "I'm determined to remain positive." He laughed at the tired joke, a little too forced, I thought. "Really, everything's going fine. I have more friends and a better sex life than ever before. I'll get my BA in one more year. Then I'm going for my master's degree. Always planning for the future."

"Good for you." Then I repeated, "And how are you handling all this?"

It was like he slipped off a mask, revealing the face that always lies beneath, a face a little sad, eyes slightly hollow, and said softly, "It's like living with a ticking bomb inside me. Each morning I wake up, and it's ticking."

"I continue to be amazed at the courage I see from you, from Steve and others. Day after day. I don't know how you do it."

But by then he'd replaced his mask. "I'm not sure it's courage. I just try not to think about it. I seem to handle it better that way. Or is denial unhealthy?"

"I'm a pragmatist in these matters. Use whatever works for you until it no longer works. Then find something else." I placed a hand on his shoulder. "If you ever want to talk when denial isn't working for you that day, I'll take you to lunch. Meanwhile, I'll continue to admire your courage." I left for the front desk and for the evening to begin.

According to common wisdom, you had maybe five years after your first opportunistic infection. And they wouldn't be your best years.

I was concerned for Chad. I'd seen the signs before. Gray was dead two years after his first symptom, and I was pretty sure Chad's decline was starting.

When I arrived at work the next morning, I went into Sandy's office and closed the door. She looked up. "Closed door? This can't be good."

"No," I said, taking the chair in front of her desk. "It's not."

"Leo?"

"Chad. I think he'll be needing your services soon. He's developing symptoms. The whole team's noticed."

She put down her pen. "I've noticed, too. We're ready."

"This could be hard on the staff. I've seen it before. It's like one of your own family."

"Yes," she murmured, "it will be hard. Chad's special to me."

I smiled at her. "Steve. Leo. Chad. Is there anyone here who's *not* special to you?"

"Franklin. No, wait. He's special to me, too."

I turned somber. "Just between you and me, I think Chad'll go fast. I see the same pattern as with Gray. Doing fine, and then the symptoms begin, followed by a steep, rapid decline."

I was surprised to see Sandy's face flush and tears well up, to see such emotion from a hardened veteran. "I could be wrong, of course," I offered. "It's only a hunch."

She took out a handkerchief and wiped her eyes. "No. I've seen it, too. And I think you're right."

"I know it's hard when it's one of your own staff," I acknowledged.

She folded the handkerchief, putting it back in her pocket. "No, it's hard when it's your kid brother."

"What?"

"Chad's my younger brother . . . my only brother."

"Sandy, I'm . . . I'm so sorry. I didn't know."

"Only a few people here do. Steve knows. Father Paul knows." She rolled her eyes. "Franklin as personnel director knows. We keep it to ourselves."

"But you have different last names."

"I still use my married name."

It was one of those O'Shaughnessy moments. I blurted out before I could stop, "*You* were married?"

She stared at me. "Yes. To a very nice man, who, it so happens, has excellent taste in women. And we're still good friends."

"That's nice," I mumbled, wishing my brain had an automatic shut-off switch whenever I was surprised. Once she said it, I saw the resemblance: same hair color, eye color, Chad's short, compact body. Sandy was taller, huskier, but the same build. Probably the same hairy legs, what Chad called his "hobbit feet." Both came from Colorado.

"It's how I got involved with AIDS. I was running a women's shelter in Boulder when Chad tested positive. I left to come out here to be closer to him. CAP was looking for a client services manager. I had the qualifications. It seemed like a good fit."

"I'm sorry," I repeated. "How long has he been infected?"

"Four years."

Four years. He was right on schedule, but I kept that thought to myself.

She sat up in her chair, once again in control of her emotions. "When the time comes, we'll deal with it. Like we deal with every-thing else here."

Chapter Thirty-Five

As If Death Summoned

[Portland, Oregon, October 1994]

It was also on Wednesday morning that I received a call from Jake. He was to meet with his doctor that afternoon to receive the results of his tests. Would I accompany him? I said of course. I'd pick him up and we could drive to the medical center together.

At 4:00 p.m., we were sitting in the waiting room, talking about this and that. No word still on Leo. Jake had called the police chief. Hiram was concerned, but there wasn't much he could do except follow police procedures. I was relieved that Jake seemed lucid. I was still hoping the tests would indicate a minor stroke.

At 4:10, a medical assistant took us to Dr. Jacobs's office. She was writing at her desk as we walked in and looked up, smiling. "Hello, Jake," then looked at me. "Is this your partner?"

"I'm working on it," he said.

I introduced myself as a friend, and we shook hands and took our seats. She was younger than I'd expected, probably late thirties, early forties. The no-frills type—straight hair to her shoulders, no jewelry, little makeup. No time for a social life was my guess. She opened the file in front of her and studied it. Putting off the bad news for as long as possible?

"By the way," Jake offered, "Bill Clinton is president."

She smiled again. "Very good. And who's the vice president?"

Jake's eyes went vague, searching. Then he turned to me. "It's always the trick questions, isn't it?"

She began, "Jake, I'm afraid the news is not good."

"How much not good?"

"The tests indicate you have AIDS dementia."

It was the worse-case scenario I had feared.

Over the next ten minutes, she discussed the nature of the tests, their results, range for error—not much—and went over the diagnosis, the prognosis, the practical concerns, but I could tell Jake, while staring directly at her, wasn't listening. So I listened for him, nodding to her as she talked that I understood, that I would convey what she was saying at a later time when he was ready to hear it.

When she finished, Jake said, "So, all this time we thought the virus was dormant in me, it's been messing with my brain?"

"Not really. The virus can enter the brain at any time. It doesn't need to incubate. It could affect the brain when one is first infected, or, in your case, many years later. For whatever reason, it chose this moment."

"Treatment options?"

"There's been some limited success with AZT, but the benefits are only temporary. I'm sorry, Jake. There's nothing else available at this time. I would suggest you begin making arrangements while you can. Do you have someone who can help with your legal affairs?"

"Yes," he said. "My sister-in-law. She's an attorney. We've always been very close . . . Um, her name will come to me."

"I'd recommend you attend to these matters as soon as possible," said Doctor Jacobs. Translation: the dementia was advancing rapidly.

Jake was silent as I drove him home. When we arrived at his place, a lovely old stone house built in the 1920s, he asked me to come in, and we went into his book-lined study. The late October sun streamed through the windows, lending the scene a bright cheeriness that belied the occasion.

"Have a seat," he said. I settled into one of two comfortable leather armchairs as he opened his liquor cabinet. "What do you drink, by the way?"

I wanted to tell him I didn't drink alcohol, didn't like the taste, didn't like the fuzzy-headedness it produced in me. "Whatever you're having," I said.

He poured two glasses of whiskey, handed me one, and settled into the other armchair. He was understandably subdued. "You're familiar with this condition?"

"I've known several people with AIDS dementia, yes."

"I'm not sure what to expect. What *should* I expect?"

"I'll pull together some articles for you. You can read them at your leisure, when you're ready to."

"I'd rather hear it from you."

"Okay." I put aside my glass. "Based on the people I've known, and from what I've read, you can expect to become increasingly forgetful. You will find yourself remembering selectively—recalling your mother's name but not your father's, remembering events from childhood, but not what happened yesterday. You will forget more and more . . . until eventually you no longer have a memory."

He nodded soberly. "This could actually have been useful during the Reagan years." He sipped his whiskey, then asked, "How quickly does it progress?"

"It varies from person to person." *As soon as possible,* Dr. Jacobs had said. "Yours appears to be advancing rapidly. I'm sorry, Jake."

"Well, it could be worse. At least I still have my dashing good looks."

I smiled out of courtesy, and because I didn't know what else to say. Then I offered, "The one positive thing I've found with dementia is that, as your memory goes, most likely so will your fears and anxiety."

"How's that?"

"The people I've known experienced panic, anxiety, grief, as you'd expect. But as the dementia progressed, and their memory evaporated, most settled into a contented, eternal present, pretty much oblivious to all that was happening to them."

"Well, there is that, I suppose." He downed his whiskey and set the glass aside, shaking his head. "So, now it's my turn. This whole epidemic, it's as if death summoned an entire generation of gay men."

I nodded as he lapsed into a personal reverie. "If so, I would have to commend death for an ingenious plan. I mean, you have to admit, it's brilliant. No need for the messiness of war. No blood and carnage. All death needed was a microscopic virus, a masterpiece in design that mutates, making it a moving target for researchers. Just when they think they've got it, it changes on them. And then you tie the vehicle for the virus's transmission to sex, one of the most primal urges in our nature." He looked at me. "Think about it: What if death had tied its transmission to—oh, I don't know—filing our income taxes, or remembering to vote? But no, it was tied to something so *basic* to our humanity: our need to connect with each other."

The late afternoon sunlight was seeping away, the study growing progressively darker as he talked. How appropriate, I thought.

"And then, to ensure that this little demonic virus has a chance, you release it among a despised minority—so despised the general public doesn't even like to think about them—so nothing will be done to try and stop it. I mean, who cares if it's just a bunch of queers. This is God's retribution against their abominable abominations. Good riddance!"

He gave a bitter chuckle. "Can you imagine if there'd been some strange, mysterious illness killing, say, Boy Scouts? Or Southern Baptists? Can you imagine the same level of disinterest? Oh, no. Funds would be found. It would be a priority for the CDC. University research teams would be competing for big federal grants to stop it. The media would be running daily news stories. "WHY ARE BAPTISTS DYING?" But it was only a bunch of queers who probably deserved it anyway."

He suddenly looked sad. "Except now it's no longer just queers. Now it's women and babies and hemophiliac children who are dying as well. Now we have 'innocent' victims." He slowly shook his head. "And the sad thing is we could have stopped this back in 1981. We had the science and the expertise. We could have isolated and quarantined the first cases, as we did with Ebola in 1976. *We could have.* But now it's too late." He looked at his empty glass. "Now the plague is within the city walls."

We sat in silence in the darkening study.

Before I left, I called his brother Harry at Jake's request, updating him on the test results and on Dr. Jacobs's emphasis that arrangements should be made quickly. Harry said he and his wife would be right over. Then I left Jake and went down his stone walkway to the street. As I got into my car, the weight of the epidemic, the weight of all these years, pressed down on me so heavily I was too exhausted to turn the key. Thirty-three names. Thirty-three of more than three hundred thousand. And growing.

As if death summoned.

Death was now summoning Chad and Jake and Steve, and Marco and Terry, and countless others whose names I'd never know.

I started the engine, wondering, *Could things get any worse?*

But one must never ask that. The answer is always yes.

Chapter Thirty-Six

Something Worse

[Portland, Oregon, November 1994]

In early November, Portland experienced one of its rare snowstorms before Thanksgiving. A major front swooped down from the Arctic, dumping a heap of the white stuff on the city. Commutes were canceled, students were sent home, and offices closed early. Yet all my counselors scheduled that Tuesday evening called to say they would make it in. They knew the guys who were anxious about their test results would as well. I was never more proud of these volunteers. It was going to be a difficult night, so I decided to splurge on our small budget. With still thirty minutes before starting, I left Reggie in charge and slipped out to purchase carafes of Seattle's Best Coffee and some tasty, savory treats from Valentino's. The team deserved it.

Reggie was organizing the front desk when Marco and Frank got off the elevator with Lukas, who was bubbling like a schoolboy with the first snow of the season.

"Well, you look happy, Sunshine," said Reggie.

"I am, I am!" Lukas sang, unwrapping his scarf. "I was just telling Marco and Frank I woke this morning to nine inches."

"Whoa, nine inches? Where do you live to get that much snow?" Lukas stopped his unwrapping, staring at Reggie. "Who said anything about snow?"

Before Reggie could respond, Darren and John came up to the front desk, each carrying a file. Darren said to Frank, "Want to get your results out of the way before people start arriving?"

"Sure."

"And I guess I've got your results tonight," John said to Lukas.

He saluted briskly. "*Oui, mon Colonel!*"

They went down the hall and into the counseling rooms. Lukas was chattering away as he and John took seats at the table. "I love the snow. A nice fire, cup of hot cocoa, someone to cuddle with—"

There came a knock on the door. They both turned as it opened and saw Arthur standing there.

Lukas was surprised. "Well, hi, Arthur! What are you doing . . ." Then his face fell. "Oh."

"Hi, Lukas," said Arthur, closing the door quietly behind him.

Lukas turned to John. The colonel's eyes were cast down at the folder lying on the table, face red, and he looked back to Arthur.

"I'm sorry, Lukas."

He continued staring at the county epidemiologist, then flopped back against the chair, crossing his arms. "Damn. It must've been that mosquito bite last summer, huh?"

Arthur gave him an obliging smile.

"I mean, I haven't done anything unsafe since I've been in this program, and my test result in April was negative."

Still standing at the door, Arthur spoke softly. "Most likely you became infected prior to the program's start, and the antibodies hadn't yet developed by the time we tested. That's why those results showed up negative."

"Well, say what you will. I maintain it was a gay mosquito that bit me."

John began to rise from his chair. "I'll just step outside and leave the two of you—"

Lukas turned to him. "Could you stay?" He'd gone pale and now looked scared. "Would you? Please? I'd like you to stay."

John nodded, sitting back down as Arthur pulled up a chair and opened the file John slid across the table to him.

I was waiting when Lukas came out of the counseling room with Arthur and John. It had taken much longer than I expected to get the coffee and savory treats, and Lukas had arrived earlier than usual. I'd wanted to be there when John gave him the results. To support both of them. When they emerged from the room, Lukas was composed, subdued compared to his usual flamboyant self. Arthur followed with his calm, placid gait, as if he'd just returned from a quiet walk in Waterfront Park. He'd later give me an account of what happened in the room. John followed Arthur, looking devastated. I might need to send him home.

Lukas was smiling as he came up to me. "Well, how about that? Looks like my dad's prayers were finally answered."

"I'm so sorry, Lukas. I'm so very sorry. Why don't you go home? Take care of yourself tonight."

"No, I'm scheduled."

"It's okay. I called in Marco as an extra counselor for the evening. He'll take your place."

But he was adamant. "No, really. I *want* to stay. Please."

"You're sure?"

"I need to be here tonight"—he looked around the lobby where men were gathering —"with my brothers."

And Lukas did fine throughout the evening. All of us were amazed. He was his usual bantering self, joking and teasing and flirting with the clients. No one would have guessed he'd just been handed his own death sentence.

Later, as we wrapped up the night with our debriefing session, he said, "I think you all know. So, I just want to acknowledge it."

There were words of support, words of comfort, words of sadness, lots and lots of words. There were hugs; there were tears, though not from Lukas. Paradoxically, his role seemed to be to comfort and reassure the rest of us. He remained strong, stable, and calm.

We ended the session early. There were buses to catch, and we didn't know how bad the snow was getting outside. In spite of the arctic conditions, Frank, Reggie and Marco invited Lukas out for a late dinner. The four of them were heading toward the elevator when John was putting on his coat and called, "Lukas."

Lukas stopped and turned around. "You want to join us?"

"No. No, thanks. I need to be getting home to Maggie."

"Another candlelight dinner and negligee waiting for you?"

John offered a polite smile, but it quickly vanished. "I just wanted to say . . ." He stopped, stumbled over his words, started again. "I just wanted to say that what you did tonight . . . it took courage, true courage, and, uh . . ."

Lukas searched his face.

"Well, if you were *my* son, I would be proud to be your father."

For once Lukas had no quick comeback or flip remark, but said quietly, "Thank you, John."

The elevator door opened and Marco called out, "Going down?"

Lukas swung around. "On whom?"

There was more laughter. I watched the four of them get into the elevator with John, and the doors closed.

Chapter Thirty-Seven

Hitting Bottom

[Portland, Oregon, November 1994]

It was the night Lukas tested positive that I hit rock bottom, forgetting that grief is bottomless. It happened as I was driving home. The roads were a slushy mess, the snow pale orange in the streetlights. The few cars on the freeway slogged along cautiously at thirty miles an hour in the snow ruts. Like John, I was proud of Lukas. He had soldiered through the evening with a regal courage truly befitting a queen, and once again I realized how much our lives are these brave fronts we show to the world.

I didn't want to go home yet. I knew ghosts would be there waiting for me so, on impulse, I swung off the freeway on the Washington side of the river, heading for its waterfront park. The parking lot was empty, a pristine field of white. At the single lamppost, large fluffy snowflakes swarmed around like hundreds of glowing butterflies. I sat in my car, transfixed by its beauty. Add snow to any setting and it suddenly looks Norman Rockwellian. Usually the walkway was filled with people, any time of day or night, any kind of weather—lovers hand in hand, young families with strollers, sleek runners running, cyclists cycling, kids skateboarding, seniors shuffling age-appropriately along—but tonight there was not another soul out. I set off on the river walk, the path covered in snow. Fortunately, I'd brought my hiking boots, down coat, cap, and gloves to work that morning. With coat collar turned up, I set off at a brisk pace, leaving the bridge and its light for the darkness stretching upriver.

Leo had now been missing for more than a month. The staff were speaking of him in the past tense. The police had added his name and photograph to a national database of missing persons. They'd accessed his bank records, which showed no recent activity. I'd checked with Marge at the café, asking what "the street" was saying. She said the street no longer talked about Leo. (I had also heard nothing about Danny and could only hope the boy was safe.) At yesterday's management team meeting, Steve had raised the awkward question of filling Leo's position. "We have contract obligations to the county," he said. I knew how difficult this was for him to bring up. Marti looked at Sandy, whose eyes were focused on the table, and said, "Let's wait another couple of weeks. Till after Thanksgiving, okay?" There was a finality about posting his position, an admission that we didn't yet wish to admit. Probably would be necessary, yes, but ... not just yet. The meeting finished on that low note, and we started to leave the conference room, all except Sandy, who remained sitting, appearing ashen. Franklin stopped next to her and, quite out of character, said gently, "He could still show up." Sandy raised her eyes to him. "Thank you, Franklin."

The snow had stopped, the wind died down, a breeze now coming off the river. I kept walking into the darkness, my boots crunching in the soft, cushiony snow, my breath puffing out in front of my face. The exercise felt good, what I needed. I might not stop until I reached Idaho.

Sandy still encouraged us not to give up hope. Hope? I had passed that point long ago. I knew Leo was never coming back. At best, we might learn what happened to him. And maybe it was better not to know. I was more concerned for her. It's always harder on those who maintain hope—hope against reason, hope against the evidence, against what we know. And now I was doubly concerned for her: Chad had entered the hospital with his first bout of pneumonia over the weekend. The clock was ticking.

Breathing deeply from the brisk walk, I stopped a half mile up, where the path arched out into the river, and rested on the railing. Now far from the bridge's luminescence, everything glowed in the eerie snow-light. Strange how snow mutes some sounds (cars on the bridge) while magnifying others (water lapping against the rocks below).

Following his diagnosis, I'd checked in with Jake regularly, usually by phone, updating him on Leo—that there was no word. Sometimes he couldn't recall who "Emilio" was, or me, and I needed to remind him. Then yesterday, a caregiver had answered the phone. Professor Caulfield was no longer receiving calls or visitors, she said. I was directed to contact his brother, Dr. Harry Caulfield, if I had questions. She could give me the telephone number. "Thank you," I said. "I have it." Jake, Chad, Lukas . . . soon Steve. It was now only a matter of time before they would be joining the long litany of names I had long committed to heart.

Resting next to the river, I pondered the strange paradoxes of grief and grieving. Grief is universal, yet the loneliest of experiences. Everyone goes through it, but no one can really know what you're feeling. Grief is cumulative; and there comes a point where you just want to stop accumulating. You know you *can* go on another day, but wonder why you'd want to. You're surviving on a daily ration of hope, but it's a meager meal and eventually can no longer sustain and nourish. After a time, you realize you're just going through the motions—and emotions—of living without your heart really in it. You've died in all but name only. Somehow you missed reading your obituary in the newspaper.

The snow began falling again. I remained at the wooden rail, wrapped in the moment's soft snow-glow, gazing out over the dark river. I couldn't remember ever feeling so low. But the mind has a short memory. Along with a short memory, it's also prone to hyperbole: This is the *lowest*, the *saddest*, the *worst* you've ever felt. Face it, the mind's a drama queen. At such times, I fall back on my professional training, counseling myself, trying to put me in contact with my rational, wiser mind to bring some perspective to the drama queen.

"You're just having a bad day," I say.

Yes, but it's been a bad day for a very long time.

I gripped the railing through my gloves, closing my eyes, and whispered, "Bear it, Heart. You have borne worse."

I had. Almost exactly one year ago, November 1993. I had borne worse. But instead of late fall with unseasonable snow, it was late spring on the high plains with unseasonable beauty. Gray really wasn't strong enough, but he wanted to go up there. He knew it would be his last trip. We both knew it would be his last trip. He slept most of the drive from Melbourne. By then he was sleeping much of the time. We arrived at our favorite campsite late in the afternoon, midweek, with not another person about. I unpacked the car, set up the tent, organized the camp, and built a fire. Dinner would be easy. Gray drank only half a glass of Ensure these days, and I'd lost my appetite months ago. When everything was ready, I carried him from the car to a camp chair in front of the fire. He was experiencing wasting syndrome by then, and we'd been unable to halt the weight loss. At one time weighing a trim 170 pounds, he now barely weighed a hundred. The evenings were still cold at this elevation, and I bundled him in a down coat, wrapped him in a blanket, with a knit cap to keep his head warm. I brought over two mugs of hot milk tea to where he sat, bathed in the sun's dying light.

He watched with his large hollow eyes as I approached. "You're losing weight," he said, his voice now a raspy whisper.

I handed him the mug with the straw. "Look who's talking."

"Yes, but I have an excuse."

I sat in the chair next to him, gazing into the fire. "So do I."

He cradled the mug in both hands for its warmth. "You should eat something," he pressed. "You need to keep up your strength for both of us."

"Maybe later." I took a drink of tea.

It was still, not the slightest breeze. We watched the sun low on the horizon, its light turning the distant hills soft lavender. He sighed. "It's so beautiful out here, so quiet. Thank you for bringing me. I know it was a hassle."

"Not a hassle, really. Just against doctor's orders. For some reason, they think you're medically fragile."

He grunted. "Screw the doctors."

"Screw the doctors? You're thinking of young Dr. Amir, aren't you?"

He smiled. "He is handsome, isn't he?" He sucked some tea through his straw as the golden light softened the bleak harshness of the high plains, then said, "You've never liked it out here, have you?"

I surveyed the landscape. "Dust, flies, snakes, scrub brush—what's not to like?"

He smiled again. "I thought so."

"It's an acquired taste," I admitted. "Like Vegemite."

"You'll return to the States after . . ." his voice trailed off.

"Yes," I said. "Unless your mother begs me to stay."

He chuckled. "Good. You belong among mountains, just as I belong here on the high plains."

We sat listening to the fire's crackle, the only sound amid the vast silence around us. I felt the heat on my face, the chilly nip of the coming night on my ears.

"Nice fire," he said. "If I die out here—"

"Don't you dare."

He half-laughed, half-coughed. "I was just saying, if I died out here, you could spread my ashes and we could eliminate the middle-man altogether. Save some bucks."

"The service is already paid for."

Then he said, "My ashes . . ."

"Will be spread here. I promise."

"Thank you." He released another deep sigh. "I am at peace. Out here, I'm finally content and at peace."

Yes, well, you're not the one being left behind.

I suppressed the bitter thought. I'd been suppressing a lot of bitter thoughts over the past four months as Gray continued to decline; and I was feeling envious, maybe resentful, because I was so far from anywhere approximating peace and contentment.

But I was glad to see him happy. He'd been moody and non-communicative for several weeks. The last year had been rough on him. On us. As his T-cell count continued to drop, measuring the erosion of his immune system, he was hit by one opportunistic infection after another. As soon as we got on top of one (thrush in his throat), another cropped up (lesions on his back.) Then in the past few weeks, he'd developed Kaposi's sarcoma in his lungs, and his doctor advised Gray he had maybe four months. Privately, Dr. Amir told me he was being optimistic in his prognosis. Gray fell into a deep depression, so deep, that I feared he'd never climb out of it and that this was how I would forever remember him.

But out here he was his old self again, talkative and joking and whimsical. The land was restoring his naturally buoyant spirits.

"Don't suppose you feel up for a dance," he said.

I rolled my eyes. "Can we just please forget the fucking dance?"

He was grinning. "I was trying to cheer you up."

"Yeah, well, good luck with that," I muttered, taking another drink of tea and recalling that night two years before. "But you did look hot, dancing naked around the fire like that."

"Oh fine. I was off communing with the ancestors, entering the Dreamtime, becoming one with the universe, and all you could think of was sex . . . Good for you."

Both of us fell quiet, probably remembering the sex life we'd once enjoyed long ago, centuries ago. Then he said, "You know, this isn't sad."

"Oh, good. For a moment there I thought it was."

Chuckling again, he said, "I'm going to miss your sense of humor."

"No," I said, "you're not going to be the one missing *anything*." Wasn't quick enough on that one; the bitter thought slipped out before I could catch it. Ashamed, I looked away, not wanting him to see the tears in my eyes.

"No, I suppose not," he said, gazing into the fire. He was quiet for a moment. "Still"—he turned back to me—"I'm going to miss your sense of humor."

In spite of the circumstances, I had to smile, and shook my head.

He began coughing. I took his cup, placing it with mine on the ground. "Lean forward." I gently tilted him as he continued coughing for another minute. With the KS in his lungs, he'd been bringing up blood, but at least there was none this time. Once he recovered, I put the mug back in his hand. He sucked some tea through the straw, exhaled deeply, and recited,

"Dark mother always gliding near with soft feet,
Have none chanted for thee a chant of fullest welcome?
Then I chant it for thee, I bring thee a song
That when thou must indeed come, come unfalteringly."

"Whitman," I murmured.

When I didn't reciprocate, he prompted, "Your turn."

"Can't think of anything," I said and took another drink.

So, he recited again,

"Because I could not stop for Death—
He kindly stopped for me—
The Carriage held but just Ourselves—
And Immortality."

"Emily Dickinson."

He waited. I shook my head.

"Nothing? I don't think you're trying."

I looked down into my cup. "Poetry has gone out of my life."

"It's just death, you know," he said matter-of-factly. "It's going to happen to all of us eventually."

I turned to him. "I'm sure you meant that to make me feel better."

"In the stages of dying, I've come to Acceptance."

"Congratulations. Some of us are still working on Denial."

"You need to get with the program," he joked.

Bitterness tinged my words again. "Maybe I don't want to get with the program."

"It's going to happen," he said, "whether you get with the program or not."

We sat quietly, listening to the silence darkening around us. In Australia, the sun doesn't so much set as it just suddenly drops from the sky, and it's dark. Like it forgot to dusk. Then he said, "Don't get stuck here."

"No, I'll be going back to the States."

"That's not what I meant. Don't get stuck *here*."

I had nothing to say to that, so he continued, "I worry about you. I don't want you to be alone. And you don't make friends easily."

"I've got plenty of friends."

"You have plenty of colleagues. Coworkers. Associates. You need a friend who loves you. Everyone needs a friend. And I know it will be hard for you to let someone get close. Not everyone is as persistent as I was."

"*No one* is as persistent as you were."

He chuckled again. "Exactly my point." Then he became quiet. "You need to move on with your life. We both need to move on. Let someone else in. Please."

I continued staring into the fire. "Tell me again how this isn't sad."

"This isn't sad," he said. "This is life."

But I was in no mood to be philosophical and remained silent.

So, he mused, "'We are such stuff as dreams are made on.' On the drive up here, I had a dream—"

"I hope this isn't about that Chinese philosopher again and his butterfly fetish."

He smiled. "No. I dreamt I was caught in a snowstorm. Lost out here on the high plains, blinded by the blizzard and unable to see in any direction. In the dream, I knew the search parties weren't going to find me in time. That I wasn't going to make it."

I said nothing. It was a textbook example of a dream symbolically mirroring one's situation.

"But then, in the midst of the blizzard, I saw a figure. A man coming toward me. And I felt this immense, this overwhelming sense of relief . . . and joy."

Okay, now he was demonstrating Freud's idea of dreams as wish fulfillment.

"Because you were going to be rescued after all?"

"No, that's what was so strange . . . and so wonderful." His eyes had gone glassy staring into the flames. "I knew the man hadn't come to save me. He was coming to take me home." And he began to weep.

"Oh, Gray . . ." I set our mugs on the ground and took him in my arms, holding him tightly.

"I was going home," he whispered, and we both cried while the darkness engulfed us.

The great river sighed.

I was covered in snow. I brushed it from my coat, shook it from my cap, now chilled to the bone, and began the long walk back toward the lights. Trudging through the mounting drifts, I realized I had inherited Gray's dream. It was now mine. *I* was the one lost, unable to see the way forward. *I* was the one slowly dying in a blizzard.

But no one was coming to take me home.

And then the most miraculous thing happened ...

Chapter Thirty-Eight

Thanksgiving . . . and Giving Thanks

[Portland, Oregon, November 1994]

I rang the doorbell to John and Maggie's house on a crisp, clear autumn day. They lived on two rural acres east of Portland with Mount Hood shining white in the distance, and a large bank of blackberries forming their western boundary, one of those sprawling patches that threatens to take over the neighborhood; tomorrow, the world. Remembering Lukas's estrangement from his parents, John had invited him to join his and Maggie's family for Thanksgiving dinner. Lukas confessed to me some jitters, what he called "stage fright," about going. "It's been a long time since I've been around normal people," he said. Although celebrating the holiday with my family, I said I'd stop by in the afternoon to support him—or, given Lukas's flamboyant energy, maybe to support John and Maggie's family. And John had asked me to stop by, too. His "gay son" would be flying up from Los Angeles Wednesday night, returning first thing Friday morning, and he wanted me to meet Jonathan.

"Happy Thanksgiving!" said John when he opened the door, greeting me warmly. "Thanks for coming by."

"How's it going?" I asked. There came a burst of laughter from inside. "Sounds okay."

"Just fine," John said, closing the door and taking my coat. "It took my older boys some time to get used to Lukas, but it's good for them. It's *bracing*."

I followed him into a dining room filled with people sitting around a large dining table.

"My mentor!" shrieked Lukas, his arm above his head, flapping his hand like a windsock in a storm.

"Mine, too," said John, bringing an extra chair from the living room. He introduced me to his family, starting from my right. It was too tight to move around the room and shake hands, so I remained standing, nodding to each as John introduced them.

"My oldest son Joe, his wife Sarah, and their two kids . . ."

Joe was a big, beefy guy, his wife matching his girth, with two stout children, a boy and a girl. They offered friendly smiles.

"You know Maggie." Maggie blew me a happy kiss, beaming from having all her family together. Or maybe from the wine. Or both. Lukas sat next to her, also beaming. I was pleased to see he didn't need my support after all.

"James, my second son, and his wife Susan, and their daughter Charlotte . . ." James resembled his dad, though a bit thicker around the middle. Susan was an attractive woman, trim and athletic, as was Charlotte, a teenager. By the look on her face I could tell family Thanksgiving wasn't her idea of a good time.

"And this is Jonathan, my youngest."

But I'd noticed Jonathan the moment I walked into the room. Fine-boned and slender in contrast to his meatier brothers, light brown hair, and quite handsome, he offered a disarming smile. At least, I was totally disarmed by it. I nodded to him, quickly sitting next to John for fear my eyes might betray me.

I had not been so knocked off my feet by someone in years— many, many years—and was grateful Lukas held center stage as I felt my heart racing. Lukas resumed his monologue which my arrival had interrupted, most of it PG until relating the incident where he was performing on stage as Lady Bianca, belting out a particularly energetic rendition of "I've Gotta Be Me!" when one of his breasts popped out of his gown and went flying into the audience. His pantomiming of the experience was hysterical in itself. Maggie was laughing so hard she had tears in her eyes, as did the other two women. The stout little ten- and twelve-year-olds watched wide-eyed; John was chuckling and Jonathan grinning. Only the two older sons looked uncomfortable, wearing tight, steel-reinforced smiles, like given the choice, they would have preferred undergoing dental surgery at that moment.

"Really, I don't know how you girls manage it," Lukas was exclaiming. "If you have trade secrets, please let me know!"

Throughout this, my heart had been going pitter-pat, like pistons on a steam locomotive, as I maintained a constant peripheral view of Jonathan, sitting on the other side of his father, and thought—imagined? hoped?—he was side-staring at me as well. I've met a number of handsome men over the years, some even more handsome than Jonathan, but none had such an effect upon me, literally taking my breath away and causing light-headedness. Blood pounded in my ears as I tried to control the timpani drum solo in my chest and hoped the others didn't notice. *Could you please lower the beating of your heart? You're upsetting the dog.*

Over pumpkin pie with ice cream and coffee, I remained focused, though still peripherally, on Jonathan. He was the quiet one in this raucous group, ate only a few bites of dessert. Wasn't a big eater. *He must work out at a gym, or maybe he's a runner. I could get back into running.* I wondered if he liked hiking and backpacking, wondered what books he liked to read (it was somehow a given that he was a reader), what music he listened to, what films he enjoyed. I really, really hoped he wasn't into sports and cars. Even as my mind rattled on, powered by a heart in overdrive, I recognized my fantasies had totally hijacked my reason: *He lives in LA, for godsakes! And with his looks, he most likely already has a partner, or anyway a lover. Or a long line of lovers. You probably need to take a number.*

And yet reason could not rein in my excitement. *Yes, yes, yes, I know it's only fantasy. But can we just please enjoy this a bit longer?* I liked feeling this way again . . . feeling alive. It had been a long time.

Nearing 2:00 p.m., "the big game" was about to start—football, I think—and Maggie, Sarah, and Susan began stereotypically clearing the table as the men stereotypically began moving toward the television in the living room. The same was happening, I was sure, at my house and millions of homes across the country. Lukas excused himself. He was joining friends to help serve the Thanksgiving meal at the Portland Rescue Mission, as they did every year. He was on the later shift. After he'd hugged and kissed Maggie, thanking her for a wonderful time, he came around the table, taking Jonathan's hand in both of his, and said, "You're just as adorable as I knew you'd be"—which clearly embarrassed Jonathan—"I mean, really, with a name like Jonno? How could you *not* be adorable?" Lukas kissed him on the cheek as he had kissed Maggie, and John got Lukas's coat, escorting him to the door.

"I should be going, too," I said.

Jonathan turned to me. "Oh, do you have to go?" They were the first words we'd spoken to each other, his eyes looking head-on into mine, jamming my brain.

"Yes, yes, I should probably be moving on."

Don't. You. Dare.

But nothing can come of this!

Who cares if anything comes of it? You've not felt like this in how many years?

Many, I admitted.

And just what do you have to do that's so important?

Um . . . escape?

As this conversation spiraled in my mind, he said, "I was hoping you might stay and keep me company. I can't stand football."

My God, he needs someone to keep him company!

I had to admit, it was a compelling argument.

"Sure. I could stay a little longer, I guess."

He broke into a beautiful smile that made me go weak in the knees.

"Here." He put a casserole dish in my hands. "Let's clean up the kitchen so Mom and the girls can watch the game."

"Sure." I seemed capable of little more than monosyllables at that moment. *Help him clean the kitchen? Of course! Help him clean the sewers of Paris? Love to! Whatever.*

"And call me Jonno. Jonathan's my LA name."

I don't remember a lot about the rest of that afternoon. Memories of it are now wrapped in a golden glow. Jonno and I sat at the dining room table, drinking cup after cup of an anise-flavored tea—I estimate one to two gallons each—and I remember talking partners, mine, deceased; he, currently without.

"I've not had a lot of luck with partners," he confessed. "Never really found a person I wanted to spend my life with." We shared monogamy in common. I wondered what else we shared in common.

Occasionally, there would come a burst of shouting from the living room.

"Who's winning?" Jonno once called.

"Are you really interested?" John called back.

"No." He smiled at me again.

He was thirty, a landscape architect, loved gardening and working in the soil. "Not very feasible in Los Angeles. I have garden boxes on my apartment balcony." He actually didn't care for the city, didn't like the congestion, the smog, the pace of living, the glitz and the glamour. He'd attended the Academy Awards a couple of years back in full tuxedo (he did love movies) with the man he was dating at the time, a Hollywood producer. The experience had been a bit much and over the top for him. "I prefer to watch the Oscars at home in my pajamas, eating pizza." I tried to imagine him in his pajamas eating pizza; then I tried to imagine him out of his pajamas, which was even more fun.

I can't recall much of my conversation. I do remember asking him, "Do you like hiking?"

"I love hiking. But you have to drive a couple of hours out of LA to get to anything approximating nature."

"Well, maybe some time when you're visiting again, we could go hiking. In Portland, you're about fifteen minutes from nature."

"That'd be great," he said. "Why not tomorrow? It's supposed to continue clear and sunny."

"I thought you were returning to LA in the morning."

He paused, giving me that winsome smile again. "I've decided to stick around a couple of days."

I think at that point I would have melted into a puddle right there on Maggie's shiny hardwood floors if John hadn't come out of the living room during a commercial break. He put a hand on each of our shoulders. "How are the two of you doing?"

"I'm fine," said Jonno.

I'm in love. I don't think I actually said that. I hope I didn't actually say that. But details are sketchy, and both of us were surprised when sometime later the sports enthusiasts broke up and began filtering back to the kitchen and the bathrooms.

"That was a short game," said Jonno.

His father gave him a wry grin. "They went into overtime."

"Oh." Jonno blushed. I knew that feeling. I was feeling it, too. Like when I was a teenager, returning home with bruised lips from an especially tempestuous bout of making out.

I rose from my chair. "Jeez, is that the time? I should be going."

Maggie hugged me. Joe and James gave me manly handshakes. When Jonno and I shook hands, I sensed neither of us wanted to let go. But did. John walked me to the door.

"I'm glad you were able to come by," he said, his hand again on my shoulder in a very paternal way.

I was grinning—too wide, probably. "Me, too!" And I felt a blush coming on. "I mean, it was great . . . the pie and meeting your family and everything."

The next day, a bright, beautiful November morning, I picked Jonno up and we went for a four-hour hike in the Gorge, climbing Table Mountain. Being that time of year, we saw no other hikers the entire day. And we talked continuously, covering our lives in great detail. The views became ever more spectacular the higher we climbed. The whole day was perfect, except Jonno got a nosebleed at the summit and had to lie on a flat boulder until it stopped. He'd been prone to nosebleeds ever since he was a child, he explained. Sitting next to him, gazing at his slender build, the breeze playing with his soft hair, sun highlighting his fine features, I had the strongest desire to lean over and kiss him. Instead, I told him what a great counselor John was, how men came in requesting his father by name.

On Saturday, we went to the Chinese Garden in Washington Park—not exactly the best season for it, most of the foliage being dormant, but Jonno loved the landscaping and liked to visit whenever he was home. By then, I'd have happily accompanied him to look at the Willamette mudflats. In the evening, we went to dinner and covered all the details of our lives we'd overlooked the day before. At one point, I said, "I feel guilty monopolizing your time while you've been home. I hope your parents don't mind."

"Are you serious? My father worships you. My mother wants to adopt you. They know if we hadn't met, I'd have been back in LA Friday morning. So, really, don't worry. My dad's been wanting me to meet you ever since he did your training. It changed his life . . . It changed our relationship."

Sunday morning, I drove him to the airport. At the terminal, we jumped out of the car, checked his bag with the curbside service, then stood awkwardly, suddenly unable to think of anything further to say. We fell back on tried-and-true formulas of parting.

"It was great meeting you," I offered.

"Yeah. You, too."

"Maybe we can do this again sometime."

"Definitely."

"Well . . . hope you have a good flight back."

"You, too—I mean, a good drive home."

A platitudinous farewell, we finally put ourselves out of our mutual misery by spontaneously embracing—a quick hug, immediately parting, as if we'd bumped into each other. Other than the handshake on Thanksgiving, that was the first time we touched. He smiled shyly one last time, grabbed his daypack, and went into the terminal. I left the airport, my heart thrumming. I wondered if it was safe for me to drive.

Is there a problem, officer?

Your heart was doing 140 in a 65-heartbeat zone.

Jonno decided to come home for Christmas that year.

Chapter Thirty-Nine

Infatuation, Possibly Love

[Portland, Oregon, November 1994]

It was apparent to people at work that something had happened. Something wonderful. By the time I returned to the office following Thanksgiving break, Lukas had managed to tell everyone in the Greater Portland metro area about Jonno and me. (Thanks, Lukas.) At the testing program Tuesday evening, he was still burbling about it to the other team members. "You should have seen it. It was love at first sight!" I was relieved John wasn't scheduled that evening.

"How would you know?" I said. "You left soon after I arrived."

He batted his long eyelashes at me. "Oh, honey, the way the two of you avoided looking at each other all through dessert? It couldn't have been more obvious."

When I told Sandy about Jonno and our weekend together, she said, "He lives in LA?" Then putting her fingertips to her forehead and closing her eyes like some fake psychic, "I see travel in your future. Lots and lots of travel."

Most of the staff were still in their twenties, so stories of falling in (and out of) love were a common occurrence at our agency, except unlike most workplaces, here they could talk freely about their boy-friends and girlfriends of the same sex. Jokes and ribbing were also standard fare, especially when playing to the stereotypes of lesbians' and gay men's dating styles.

Question: What does a lesbian take on her second date?

Answer: A U-Haul trailer. She's moving in.

Of course, the women gave as good as they got. Where lesbians supposedly are ready to set up a home together, gay men supposedly inhabit the opposite end of the commitment spectrum.

Question: What does a gay man take on his second date?

Answer: What second date?

But I was definitely looking forward to a second date with Jonno. And a third, and a fourth . . .

On Wednesday I received a card from him, addressed to the agency, thanking me for the hike on Friday, for the time together on Saturday, and for driving him to the airport on Sunday. He said he hoped we could connect when he came home for Christmas (in four weeks!) and included his mailing address. During my lunch break, I dashed off a card to him, already knowing the US postal service would be needing to put on additional staff because of us.

I was surprised to find myself. . . *happy*. Such a strange word when applied to me. Life took on a forgotten richness that week, everything cast in a golden hue. I thought of Jonno constantly, found myself smiling without realizing it until someone's expression told me I must be grinning like an idiot.

The rational, cautious part of me urged prudence.

—Don't get your hopes up, okay? This is just infatuation, which you know has a shorter shelf life than whipping cream.

But the irrational, giddy part wasn't listening. It was too busy being happy.

—Happy, happy, happy, happy!

—You don't even know him, cautioned Reason. You spent, what, a total

311

of maybe eighteen hours together over three days?

—Yes! Eighteen incredible, wonderful hours! And loved every second of it!

—It probably won't last. Nothing lasts. Life is transitory, imperma-nent, defined by constant change and . . . um, hello, are we listening?

But I was thinking about Jonno, wondering what he was doing at this moment. Was he maybe thinking about me?

—Great, we have a lovesick schoolboy at the controls.

—Do you think it would it be too forward of me to call him? Is it too soon?

—Aren't we a bit old for this kind of high school crush?

—Yeah, I wonder where Jonno went to high school. Must ask John. Also need to find out his favorite foods, his favorite books . . .

—You're not paying attention.

—Wonder what kind of music he enjoys. Or films. I should have asked—Hope not Tarantino. My god, there's so much I don't know about him!

—May I just point out that he lives in LA, which happens to be 965 miles from Portland. Or 1,552 kilometers, which sounds even farther.

—You're right, I could really rack up the frequent flyer miles.

—That wasn't my point.

—Maybe even earn enough to finally make that trip to Nepal. Wonder if Jonno would like to go trekking in the Himalayas.

—Hello? Is there anybody here with his feet on the ground?

—I'll have to buy some new boots. And a new backpack.

—Just promise me you won't make any major decisions in this state of mind, okay?

But I was too happy to pay attention to Reason. I could barely concen-trate on my work, so I took care of simple tasks not requiring much thought, like making up new files for testing night or cleaning off my desktop. Wow, my desk actually has a shiny wood surface! How cool is that?

—Right, so maybe I'll just check back when you come down to earth.

And amid all this giddiness, there was something else: My recurring dream of being lost in a blizzard, searching for someone on the Bogong High Plains had abruptly stopped . . . ever since meeting Jonno.

"Interesting development," said O'Shaughnessy at our next session. "Any idea why the dreams have stopped?"

"Nope," I said innocently.

He stared at me like a priest hearing a teenage boy's suspiciously lily-white confession.

"Well, now that you mention it . . ."

The priest continued waiting.

"I . . . kind of met someone."

"'Kind of met someone.' That may explain why you look lighter and happier than I've seen you in the six months you've been coming here."

"Yeah. That could be it." And I quickly told him everything about Jonno, about hiking together, about our walk in the Chinese garden, our dinner Saturday evening. O'Shaughnessy sat there, listening with his usual warm and caring manner. I could imagine what he was thinking about all this and felt myself becoming more and more defensive as I talked.

"And, yes, I realize it's probably just infatuation *(PROBABLY?* Reason shouted in my ear*)* and I'm not addressing the deeper, under-lying emotional issues we've been working on. And I know people rush into relationships, thinking they're in love as a way to *distract* them-selves, to use your word, from their sadness or whatever." I jabbered on. "Yeah, probably just deluding myself, that love will solve all my issues, or remove my grief, or change my life . . ." I stopped only because I was out of breath. "Don't you think? Infatuation, huh?"

O'Shaughnessy pulled himself up in his chair. "Could be."

"Yeah, probably is," I conceded. "I mean, it *is* infatuation. No 'probably' about it." I laughed lightly for his benefit. "I realize it's too early to think it's, you know, love."

Then he said something that surprised me.

"Love has to start somewhere. Infatuation seems as good a place as any, I suppose. And, no question, love is a game changer."

"Game changer?"

"Love can change everything."

I hadn't expected something so . . . well, *sentimental* from hard-assed O'Shaughnessy.

I said softly, "I'd forgotten what it feels like to feel this way."

"What way?"

"Just . . . to *feel* again."

One doesn't realize how empty one's soul has become until it's refilled once more. There was no denying that Jonno was an elixir, bringing me back from the dead. Could he maybe also help me get over my loss of Gray?

But no. Probably not that. I think one finally doesn't "get over" one's deepest losses. The soul is not healed in some restorative sense, not returned to what it was before grief's deep scars were etched into its landscape. What I was feeling was something else: a hope that new experiences, of love and passion, could alter and expand the very topography of the soul's landscape, to include both the old loss and the new love, and in the process become something more, something greater than it was before. A new soul.

Chapter Forty

Not Your Usual Message

[Portland, Oregon, December 1994]

"I don't know if I love him anymore."

It was a familiar confession. I'd heard it numerous times from guys caring for their infected partners. I had felt the loathsome doubt myself. We were sitting in one of the counseling rooms. We'd been talking for the last half hour, about his fears, his tears, his terrors, the deep sorrow he felt for his lover of six years, the admiration he felt for the way his partner was bravely carrying on. Now we'd reached the bedrock of his soul, beyond the sorrow and the admiration, where lay the feelings he didn't share with others.

"I'm twenty-seven, and I feel like my life is over." Typical of this epidemic: a young guy, old-seeming, weary from worry and the day-to-day drip-drip-drip of his life draining away. "Some days I just want to run, go back to Alaska. But I won't. *Can't.* I'd never be able to look myself in the mirror again."

"What's your greatest fear?" I asked.

His face flushed, voice going to a whisper. "That when he's gone, all I'll feel is relief . . . and hate myself for it."

The phone rang.

Now? The phone has to ring now? It was rare to call someone while in the counseling rooms. "Excuse me," I said, picking up the receiver.

Connie at the front desk. "Sorry to interrupt, but Steve needs you in his office. He said it's urgent."

"Okay. I'll be right out." I looked back at the young man. "See if Father Paul's available, will you, Connie? Tell him it's urgent."

I hung up the phone. "I'm sorry, I'm being called to another meeting."

"It's all right. I had nothing more to say anyway."

No, there's probably a lot more, I thought, and I hoped Father Paul was free; we had tag-teamed like this before.

"I lead a weekly support group for people who are going through what you're going through. You'd be welcome to join us. I think you'll find you're not alone in what you're feeling."

There came a knock on the door. I rose and opened it, introduced the young-old man to the priest, explaining that Father Paul coordinated the care teams and could answer more of his questions. I exchanged a quick look with Father Paul. *He needs to talk.*

I then shook hands with the young man, saying, "When the time comes, you'll probably feel relief *and* grief. If possible, allow yourself to feel both."

I went to the front desk. "What's up?" Connie was Information Central.

She whispered, "A reporter came in, asking for Steve. She said it's about Leo."

I saw the anxiety on her face. "Where's Sandy?"

"Out at a meeting."

"Okay, thanks."

I knocked on the door to Steve's office and entered. He introduced me to Amelia Sanchez, an investigative reporter with *Willamette Week.* I recognized her name from several *WW* articles about Portland's street youth, as well as a major exposé on apartment landlords jacking up the rent, putting renters out on the streets. That article had resulted in a state investigation and eventual legislation expanding tenants' rights and protections.

"Call me Amy." She smiled as we shook hands, but the smile seemed perfunctory, a courtesy. Not so much insincere as involuntary, like a social reflex or facial tic. She was small, slight build, with dark eyes that held you in their stare, and she wore her hair short, bangs over the forehead, probably more for convenience than style. Late thirties, I guessed, but her flat expression and the bags under her eyes made her appear older, intense and driven, the joyless crusader who probably has little cause for joy in her crusades. As we shook hands, I thought, *There's a backstory here. Sorrow, my guess. Lots of sorrow.*

As she resumed her seat, Steve said, "Amy worked with Leo on a couple of her articles."

"Oh?" I went over and stood by the window with my back to the Portland skyline.

"Yes, Leo was helping me with a story on street youth. He told me there was one person on staff here who'd walked the streets with him, knew the kids, and 'gets it.'"

Steve interjected, "I figured you must be the one here who 'gets it.'" I could tell he was miffed at Leo's insinuation that the rest of the prevention staff didn't.

Amy continued, "Shortly before he disappeared, he told me he was working on something I might be able to use. A special file he'd been compiling over the past six months."

I dropped my gaze to the floor. It had to be the file on illicit police activity. I hadn't told Steve about it.

"I was wondering whether he ever mentioned anything to either of you about it."

Steve shook his head. "I never heard anything about a special file."

I quickly hitched a ride on Steve's response. "I went out on the streets with Leo only a couple of times. Didn't really get to know the kids that well." It's an old trick: Let people think you're answering their question when you're really deflecting. It helps if you say it with a smile and look the person in the eye—whenever possible, look them in the eye—then ask your own question to deflect further. "Have you heard any news about him?"

"Nothing specific, but the word on the street isn't good."

"What are they saying?" asked Steve.

Her dark eyes dropped their professional neutrality. "Just that you probably shouldn't be expecting Leo to return."

Both Steve and I remained silent.

"Sorry," she said. "I have a bad habit of telling it like it is."

"No, it's all right," said Steve. "I think most of us have come to that conclusion, even if we don't want to admit it yet. Sorry we can't be of more help about this file."

She shrugged. "Just wanted to check. Something else: You have an HIV counseling and testing program here, right?"

"Yes," said Steve, nodding to me. "He coordinates it."

"I'm investigating a recent double homicide down on First Avenue two days ago. Coroner's autopsy revealed one of the men was HIV-positive. I wanted to see if either of them had come to your clinic. I've already checked with the county's clinic." She pulled out two mug shots from her breast pocket. "These are from prior arrests. About four and five years ago." She handed them to me. William "Bill" Murkowski looked to be in his late forties, maybe early fifties; heavyset; balding; swarthy, unshaven face. The second man, Lonnie Dickerson, probably in his forties, was skinny with a narrow face, giving him a weasel-like look. He, too, had thinning hair, and a scar like a half-moon over his right eyebrow. "Did either of them come here to test?"

After studying the photos, I handed them back. "Our confidentiality policies wouldn't let me tell you if they did. But they didn't."

"Okay, thanks." She slipped the photos back in her pocket. "Dickerson was the one infected. Needle tracks on both arms so probably an IV drug user and maybe not gay."

"You investigate homicides as well?" asked Steve.

"I investigate anything, but these murders might relate to my article. The deceased were two pornographers known to recruit street kids for their films."

I went cold and turned my head to gaze out the window so they wouldn't see my eyes.

"No great loss to humanity, but the police still need to investigate. Leo ever mention anything about pornographers and the kids?"

"No," said Steve.

I'd not told him what happened to Danny. Only that one of Leo's kids had been assaulted and Leo was upset about it, blaming the police for allowing such activity to go on in that section of town.

"The police think street kids did it?" Steve asked.

"No street kids did this. They weren't just murdered."

"What do you mean?"

"The two rented a room at one of the flophouses off Burnside for a couple of hours where they made their films. When a clerk went to check the room sometime later, he found their bodies." Her mouth pursed in disgust. "They'd been stripped and taped to a bed. Their eyes were removed, none too gently by the looks of it, and their genitals cut off and stuffed in their mouths. Coroner says actual cause of death was suffocation. Noses were taped shut and they choked on their dicks. Actually, each had the other's dick rammed down his throat. I didn't ask my source how the coroner determined that. Really didn't want to know."

Steve glanced at me. "You're pale. You okay?"

I cleared my throat. "Yeah. Yeah, I'm fine."

"I don't blame you," said Amy, misunderstanding the reason for my paleness. "It's a pretty ugly story. The clerk who found the bodies was just a kid. He threw up and shit his pants at the same time." She shook her head. "Talk about contaminating a crime scene."

"And people didn't hear anything?" asked Steve. "If someone tried to cut off my dick, all Portland would hear me screaming."

"Not a peep. And with people in the rooms on either side of them, too. One of the reasons the cops think these were professionals."

"The clerk didn't see who they were meeting?"

"No. Just the two of them going upstairs with their equipment. They were regulars. They'd come in, do their shooting, and leave within

319

a couple of hours. Whoever did this was waiting for them."

I took a deep breath. "So, not street kids."

"Definitely not street kids. All the camera equipment and lights were still in the room. Kids would have taken and fenced the stuff within an hour. No, this had the hallmarks of hired killers, with a certain sadistic twist. And that's what's interesting the police. This wasn't your typical gangland execution. Those're quick, efficient, and usually don't include swallowing your partner's dick. They think this was a showcase murder meant to send a message."

"What kind of a message?" asked Steve.

"Who knows? Maybe, 'You're not welcome here'? Both came from Las Vegas."

She stood. "Well, thanks for your time. If you hear anything, I'd appreciate a call." She handed each of us her card.

"I'll walk you out," said Steve.

After she left, I remained in Steve's office, again staring out the window. Crazy thoughts swirling in my head. Two pornographers preying on street kids. Eyes gouged out. Genitals cut off, stuffed down their throats.

"The street will take care of them," Leo said that night in the back of Marge's café.

I didn't hear Steve return, his voice jerking me out of my thoughts.

"Well, that's a grisly way to start the day, huh?" he said, sitting at his desk. "Sure doesn't sound like your usual message."

"No," I murmured, still staring out the window. "It sounds like revenge."

—

The waiting rooms begin to blur together. Thirty hours without sleep, and they come bleeding into my consciousness, bringing with them the shadows of other vigils . . .

I was thinking of Trevor again. His last days in Fairfield Hospital. Sitting next to him in his room, his eyes open yet unseeing, listening to his ragged breathing, mouth gaping like a final cry that won't come. I leaned close to his ear on the pillow and whispered, "*Let go, Trevor. Let go. There's nothing for you here any longer. Let go if you can . . .*"

He died at 10:16 on a Friday night. Good Friday. Given his deep religious convictions, I wondered if at some subconscious level, he'd held out to die on that particular day, like some people are thought to hold on until after Christmas or their birthday or an anniversary. But whatever, it was finally over.

Down, down, down into the darkness of the grave . . .

The nurse came back into the room to check on me. Earlier, she'd said, "Take your time. There's no hurry."

I looked up at her, "I suppose I should be going," and started gathering together my book, thermos half-filled with coffee from the hospital cafeteria, and the uneaten apple I intended for dinner, placing them in the daypack; then looked one last time at Trevor as the nurse stood patiently aside. Only five feet tall, always slight in build, and now so badly emaciated, he resembled the dried-out husk of a boy. During the past two days of sitting with him in his coma, I'd nurtured a thin hope that his mother might have a change of heart and make the trip to see him. It was a waste of a hope.

"Tell me," I asked the nurse, "what kind of parents refuse to visit their dying son?"

"I suspect, the kind who loves their church more than their child," she said.

I nodded, still staring at him. "Good answer."

"It's really not all that uncommon here," she added, "on the AIDS ward."

I hoisted the daypack onto my shoulder. "Thank you for the care you gave Trevor. And for caring."

In the lobby, I found a pay phone and called Gray.

"He's gone," I said.

"You know he's better off."

"I suppose." But I was thinking, *His death should have been witnessed by someone more than a casual friend, someone more than a fellow volunteer.*

"Hey," said Gray, "let's climb Wilson's Promontory tomorrow afternoon. We both need some exercise."

"Sounds good."

"And remember, we've got Susannah's recital Sunday afternoon."

"Oh, right. I'd forgotten."

There should have been someone who loved him there at the end, speaking last words of gratitude for his life, whispering words of affection in his ear in hope that some part of him was still aware, still listening. There should have been—

"Are you there?"

"Yes, sorry. What did you say?"

"I said we need to select the paint for the guest bedroom. Maybe first thing in the morning, then head down to Wilson's Prom?"

"Yeah, that's fine."

"When are you coming home? It's nearly eleven."

"Soon. I just need to make a couple of calls for him. Don't wait up."

Gray paused. "It's been two days."

I cleared my throat. "I know. He hung on longer than any of us expected." *Why? I wonder. His life had been unhappy and loveless. Why hang on? For what?*

"You're fortunate your supervisor lets you take off time for these vigils. I suppose it helps to work for an AIDS organization. One of the perks, huh?"

"Yeah. There aren't that many."

Gray was silent then. "I worry about you. What these vigils do to you."

"It just seemed that someone should be here to witness the ending of his life."

"But why you? You didn't even know him that well."

"He had no one else."

"I just don't think it's healthy."

"Can we talk about this later?" I didn't want to get into it then. And we'd already had this discussion before. Several times.

"Okay. See you when you get home."

After hanging up, I called Trevor's pastor. He thanked me. He would let the congregation know. "Trevor is now safe and loved in God's arms," he assured me.

Nice, I thought, *but too little, too late.*

And that was the extent of Trevor's *To Be Called* list.

I put down the phone, feeling exhausted, but didn't want to go home yet. I needed some time alone, needed to emotionally decompress before reentering the world of paint selections and piano recitals. I slipped into the waiting room next to the pay phones, grateful no one else was in there—Fairfield never had the crowds the metro hospitals did—and settled into a chair, feeling strangely numb as a hospital staff person came in, quietly pushing her cart of cleaning supplies. I nodded to her and smiled, and she smiled shyly back. I settled into my thoughts as she quietly worked around me, wiping down the other chairs and table, emptying the waste bins.

At that moment, what most concerned me was that Trevor may have died still believing he was damned by God for being gay. It could be kind of a big deal: *The Tibetan Book of the Dead* maintains that upon death, the person's spirit enters a transition zone called the *Bardo*. And in that zone between death and rebirth, the deceased still bears the beliefs and prejudices he'd lived with. In this after-death state, whatever he believes is real, not unlike when he was living. In the *Bardo*, one creates his own heaven, or his own hell. If this is true, I feared I knew where Trevor was at that moment.

323

I leaned forward, dropping my face into my hands.

You deserved better than this, Trevor.

It was a kind of prayer, I suppose. Just in case Trevor or anyone happened to be listening.

You deserved a better life. You deserved better parents. You deserved a better god . . .

"Sir?"

I raised my head. It was the cleaning woman.

"Please, sir. Be okay."

She was holding out tissues to me, and I realized I was crying, and I quickly sat up. "Oh, sorry about this."

"You see," she said, offering me a compassionate smile. "Be okay."

Chapter Forty-One

Good News. Not So Good News.

[Portland, Oregon, December 1994]

"Leo's alive!" Connie shouted the news as I stepped off the elevator.

"He's alive?"

"Yes! Isn't it wonderful?" She added, "He's also under arrest."

I went to the reception desk. "Arrest? For what?"

She didn't know. Franklin had taken the call from the police. Sandy, Steve and Marti were at a meeting with the county. Elspeth, Franklin's administrative assistant, had told Connie, and Connie had managed to tell everyone else by the time I returned from the gym.

I went directly to Franklin's office.

"I heard Leo was arrested. For what?"

He was running through a sheet of figures. He answered without raising his head. "Can't talk about it. Personnel issue."

I placed my hands on his desk, leaning over it. "Arrested for what?"

He looked up. I could see he was torn between lording it over me by withholding the information, and the glee he would feel in telling me, proving that he was right and I wrong about Leo. Glee won out, as I knew it would.

"For dealing drugs. To minors, no less."

"No. I don't believe it."

"Fine. Don't believe it. I'm sure that will change everything." He returned to his columns of figures.

"The police are framing him. He knows too much."

"Ah, yes, I'd forgotten what a police state Portland is."

I slumped into the chair in front of his desk. "What happened?"

"Apparently—or I think the proper term is *allegedly*—he was caught dealing dope. A detective was pumping me for information about Leo and his program. I told him he'd have to speak to Steve, or maybe you since you've worked with Leo on the streets."

"Does Sandy know?"

"She and Steve are with Marti at the county negotiating next year's contracts. I thought it might be best to let them sign the contracts before this little bit of good news hits the fan."

I was shaking my head. "No, I can't believe it."

"Great street outreach program you guys have going. We were *paying* him to deal drugs. Just wait until the Republicans get wind of this. You can kiss your funding for prevention programs good-bye."

I sat forward, face in my hands. How could such good news come with such bad news?

He put down his pencil, taking time from his busy schedule to gloat. "You are so naive. You obviously took the courses on Maslow and self-actualization and all that humanistic psychology crap and missed Basic Humanity 101. I warned Steve not to hire Leo. He's from the streets, and once a punk, always a punk."

I muttered, "Fuck you, Franklin."

The unaccustomed vulgarism coming from me stunned him momentarily into silence. Then he spoke softly. "Unlike you and Steve, I can't bring myself to some Pollyanna perspective on people. As I've said before, people invariably disappoint."

"Is that why you despise people so much? Because we'll invariably disappoint you?"

The question stopped him.

"Where's Leo now?" I asked.

"Being held at the county jail."

"Is it possible for me to see him?"

"You'll need to talk to Detective Williams about that."

"Will he speak with me?"

"I'll call and tell him you're our mental health specialist. I'm sure he'll be impressed."

It turned out Detective Williams *was* willing to see me, I suspect only in the hope of getting additional information about Leo. As I drove to his office, I experienced a mix of emotions: relief that Leo was alive (like others at CAP, I'd never expected to see him again), concern for his safety (it was hardly reassuring he was in police custody, given what I knew about some of the police), and bafflement (where had he been for the past eight weeks?) The allegation of drug dealing was a distraction. I was convinced it must be a trumped-up charge. The police had him where they wanted him. I needed to talk with Jake and hoped there was still enough of his mind left to help.

Williams was an older man with gray hair, his rumpled suit coat draped over a chair in his office. I wondered if they got them off the same rack at Sears: *Pre-rumpled Police Detective Suits*. He restated what Franklin had said. "Your employee's a dealer. We nailed him selling high-grade cannabis."

"I find that hard to believe."

He tossed the arrest statement onto his desk before me. "Believe."

As I read, he said, "It's solid. We have one of his buyers by the balls and he's willing to turn evidence."

Once I'd read the statement, he asked, "How long have you known Saavedra?"

"The past year. He's on the HIV prevention team with me."

"We heard you walked the streets with him."

"On two occasions. He asked my help in developing his outreach

327

program to street youth."

"Did he ever mention drugs and the kids?"

"Only in relation to drugs on the street."

"Do you know if he uses?"

"I'm pretty sure he doesn't. He kicked a drug habit a couple of years ago and, from all I've heard, doesn't even drink."

"Anyone where you work suspect he was dealing?"

"Never. I think people there would not believe it any more than I do."

"Then how do you explain that?" he said, nodding to the paper in my hand.

"I don't." I laid the statement back on his desk. "I would like to talk with Leo."

He picked it up and put it back into a folder, putting the folder into a desk drawer. "Not unless you're his legal counsel." He had turned perfunctory, it being clear now that he wasn't going to get any additional information from me. I knew I'd be wasting my time with him as well.

"I'd like to speak with the chief."

"Chief's a busy man."

"Tell him it's a friend of Jake Caulfield's."

The detective hesitated a moment. I'd seen him at a couple of the Sexual Minority Roundtables. He knew the chief's relationship with Jake. Maybe he thought the chief could get information out of me. "Wait here. I'll see if the chief's available." He stood up and left the office.

I was lost in a welter of disturbing questions. So much I wanted to ask Leo. Why had he vanished? Where had he been for the past two months? Had he been selling dope? What's the story with this buyer the police caught? Was he being framed by the police?

I heard the door open behind me.

"I had a feeling it might be you." The chief moved around the desk to the detective's chair and sat facing me. "How's Jake?"

"He'll be fine once he remembers who the president is."

He sighed, shaking his head. "I knew something was wrong."

"He's confined to his house. If he leaves, he gets lost and may not find his way back. Otherwise, he seems healthy, just becoming more and more demented by the day."

"Would it be okay for me to visit him?"

"Sure, though he may not remember you. Half the time he can't remember his own brother. You should call Harry Caulfield first." I paused. "What I really wanted was to talk with you about Leo. In Jake's place."

He sat back in the chair. "Yeah, I had a feeling that might be the case, too. It's not looking good for Leo."

"So I'm told."

"It's a solid case. One of the buyers is a very prominent citizen in the community. Comes from an old and wealthy family. Sits on several boards—a university, a charitable foundation. This would ruin him. So, he accepted a deal from the DA, giving names of some of Leo's other customers, and he'll testify against Leo to keep himself out of jail and the family name out of the papers. Now the DA has two other wealthy, upstanding citizens who'll testify they also bought dope from Leo."

"So, he wasn't selling to the street kids."

"The street couldn't afford the premium product he was hawking. This was high-grade quality for a select group of high-grade customers who could pay. From the testimony we've gathered, we think Leo must have made between sixty and eighty thousand dollars during the two weeks he's been back in town. As far as the courts're concerned, that puts him in the major leagues."

"Two weeks?"

"Yeah. He was laying low at a rich friend's apartment the buyer knew about. That's where we picked him up."

"But how could he buy it to sell it? That'd require a pretty hefty investment, and, contrary to popular opinion, we're not paid that well at CAP."

"That's one of several questions we have. We don't know where he was for the weeks he was missing. Don't know where he got the money to buy the product, and don't know what happened to the money he made. It wasn't on him or in the place he was staying. His bank account has less than two hundred dollars in it. And he's not cooperating." The chief leveled his gaze at me. "He could really help himself if he cooperated."

I understood. My role was to try and convince Leo to cooperate.

The chief added, "He's being represented by one of the most prestigious law firms in Portland."

"So, perhaps that's where the money went?"

"No. They're taking his case pro bono."

"Why would they do that?"

"I have my guess," said the chief, but he wasn't willing to share his guess with me.

"Would you let me speak with him? I want to find out what happened. See what he has to say for himself."

"Would you share that information with us?"

"If I thought it would help Leo, yes. I would encourage him, for his own sake, to cooperate with you."

The chief hesitated.

"I'll ask him about the money and I promise to tell you what he says." The chief still hesitated. "Ten minutes. That's all I need."

"Okay."

"And I need your word we won't be overheard or taped."

"I'll put you in a room where the lawyers meet their clients. It'll be confidential." He stood, and I rose from my chair as well.

"Thank you," I said. "When Leo first disappeared, I was afraid that . . ." My voice trailed off.

"I know. Me, too."

Chapter Forty-Two

Be Rid of Vengeance

[Portland, Oregon, December 1994]

I was sitting at a table in a small, bare room when the door opened and a guard escorted Leo in. He wore an orange prison jumpsuit and smiled in greeting when he saw me. The bruises on his face had pretty much healed. There was still a purple blemish around his right eye. He took the chair across from me.

"It's *so good* to see you," I said, once the guard left. "So good to see you alive."

"Thanks."

"I have ten minutes. I also have the chief's word we're not being overheard or taped. He let me see you because he wants me to ask you to cooperate."

"I'll cooperate through my lawyer," said Leo. He sat with his usual calm while I was sweating from anxiety. There were so many questions I wanted to ask him.

"Can you tell me what happened? Why you just vanished?"

"I knew I was in danger and thought it best I get out of town until things cooled down."

"You had us all worried sick. Couldn't you have let Sandy or me know where you were going?"

"I was afraid of putting you in danger, too. It was just better that people think I vanished. At least for a time." He did call Jake, he said, but his mentor had acted like he didn't know Leo.

"Jake has AIDS dementia."

Leo took in the information with a look of sadness. "I knew something was wrong."

"So, where were you?"

"San Francisco."

"And you've been back two weeks?"

"Yes."

"Where've you been staying?"

"A former patron lent me his *pied-a-terre*."

"Um, his what?"

"Small apartment. I knew I couldn't return to my place until I'd first straightened out a few things. At least I hope I still have an apartment. I was paid up through November."

"Sandy and I covered your rent for this month."

"Oh, thanks. I'll pay you back." Then he smiled. "Don't worry. Everything's okay."

"Really?" I looked around the small room. "Well, that's reassuring."

"Really, don't worry about this."

"The police say they have a solid case against you for selling drugs."

"They do." He said this without concern, as if I'd commented on the weather.

"They know you were selling premium marijuana to wealthy clients. They have at least one who's going to testify against you."

"I know."

I stared at him. "You don't seem particularly concerned about the situation."

"It is what it is. Living on the street, you learn to go with whatever comes your way. No point spending time wishing it were otherwise."

I sat back in my chair. "How can you be so relaxed about all this?"

"Meditation. Jail's a great place to meditate. I learned that from reading Gandhi."

I remained frustrated that I was more concerned for Leo than Leo was for himself.

"The chief wants to know what happened to all the money you made selling the marijuana. I told him I would ask you."

He was silent for a moment. "Tell him it went to a good cause."

"I'm sure he'll be pleased to hear that."

Then Leo leaned forward, lowering his voice. "Something's happening. Something big."

"Bigger than this?"

"This is nothing. When I returned, I gave my file on the police to the law firm that's representing me. They're considering the best way to make the information public so it'll have the greatest impact. I can't talk about it at this time. My lawyer will need the registry. I'd like you to photocopy it and send a copy to his office anonymously. I want to keep you out of this if at all possible. He'll be expecting it." He gave me his attorney's name and law firm.

"Okay. I'll send it tomorrow morning first thing." My time would soon be up and I wasn't going to have much information to give to the chief. As if reading my mind, Leo said, "Tell Hiram that I'll be cooperating fully. Soon."

"I'll tell him."

"And tell Sandy not to worry."

"Okay." I checked my watch. "Then I guess I should be going."

I stood, but hesitated a moment. There was one more question I needed to ask.

"Something else. Last week, two men—two pornographers—were killed in Portland. Actually, they weren't just killed. Police say they were tortured. Mutilated. I remembered your story about Danny being raped by the pornographers. Did you do it?"

For the first time since he entered the room Leo was not meeting my eyes. He stared at the chair opposite him, as if I were still sitting in it.

333

"Tell me you didn't do it, and I'll believe you."

He looked up at me. "I didn't do it."

I breathed out a sigh of relief. "Thank God. When I heard about the murders—"

"But I watched."

"What do you mean, you watched?"

"I paid. So I was entitled to watch."

I closed my eyes and slumped back into the chair, suddenly no longer concerned about the drug charge.

"What . . . how . . ."

He spoke quietly. "Through my connections in San Francisco."

"You knew who to contact to do this . . . kind of work?"

"I knew people who knew people who knew who to contact."

I was feeling sick to my stomach.

"And it wasn't cheap. That's why I had to go to California to get the best product. I knew where to go, who to get it from, and who to sell it to up here." He stated all this with his usual serene manner. "The former patron who lent me his apartment bankrolled the money for me to purchase the product. He didn't know what it was for. After selling it, I was able to repay his loan and pay for the work to be done."

I struggled to put my words together. "But . . . why? Because of what they did to Danny? After all your years on the street, surely you've seen this happen to other kids. And probably worse. I don't understand why you'd go to all that expense and effort to remove these two particular goons—"

Then it came to me in a flash. *That night in Marge's cafe, Leo's unshakeable calm finally shaken, the anguish on his battered face as he wept, describing what they did to Danny. Me holding up the pair of jeans in his apartment, knowing even then they were too short for Leo. "The other one comes and goes," said the manager. "They never make no trouble."*

The jeans belonged to Danny.

He said quietly, "That night of the gala, when you came to get me at the café and wanted me to stay at your place in case I had a concussion, I appreciated your concern. But I needed to get back to my apartment and care for Danny. Then during the night, I got up and saw a patrol car parked across the street. I knew the cops were going to be coming after me, and I'd probably never make it to meet you at Pioneer Square. So, I woke Danny, grabbed the file, and we sneaked out the back."

Leo had called the former patron who met and drove him and Danny to the man's *pied-a-terre* where they could stay. Knowing he was no longer safe in Portland, Leo borrowed one of the man's cars, and he and Danny drove to San Francisco where Leo knew another wealthy "patron." That's also where he bought the high-grade marijuana. He knew he could sell it for a healthy profit back here. And he knew why he was getting the money. He left Danny to be cared for by a friend ("Hannah, another earth-mother like Sandy," he said) and returned two weeks ago. Leo only went out when it was absolutely necessary, and then in disguise, to sell the marijuana and to meet with the law firm regarding the file. He had planned to resurface once the investigation into the police bureau was announced. But then one of his customers was stopped for a DUI, the police found the pot the man had purchased from Leo, and the man panicked. As part of a plea deal, he turned Leo in, as well as naming several friends who'd also been Leo's buyers. It was not long until the police found and arrested Leo.

I listened with a dull headache. When he finished, I asked, "Do your lawyers know about . . . ?"

"No one else knows. Only you."

It was all too much to take in. I realized I was in a kind of shock. "And so, Danny and you . . ." I didn't know where my sentence was going.

"I found him when he first came to Portland a year ago. Tried to get him off the street, into a foster situation. But he'd been in a couple that were disasters and refused to return to the system. So, I said he could stay with me for a while." Leo's tone shifted to a sudden tenderness. "Danny's smart. Street smart, but also highly intelligent."

"Like you."

"I'm all the family he's got. He's all the family I've got. I know it's not your usual relationship, and people won't understand. They won't even try."

"I'm not judging you. I just want to understand all this."

"What you need to understand is that Danny and I both belong to the streets. We're like feral animals living in a city. We adapt but we'll never be part of it. We'll never be . . . normal."

The guard appeared at the door and entered. Leo stood, once again composed and at peace, whereas I felt weighted to the chair, crushed by the gravity of the terrible knowledge I now possessed. As the guard took his arm, Leo said to me, "Thanks for your help."

I emerged out of my mental fog and looked up at him. "What does Krishnamurti say about revenge?"

"He says it's a poison, and that it's best to be rid of it." He smiled at me. "I am rid of it."

He turned and the guard escorted him from the room.

Chapter Forty-Three

When Reality's No Longer Reliable

[Portland, Oregon, December 1994]

Some things we can't explain even to ourselves. Which nonetheless demand an explanation. What Jake told me that afternoon in his muddled mental state left me uncomfortably suspended somewhere between belief and the impossible. We've all had experiences we might label uncanny. They're unnerving, unsettling, we try to dismiss them— *It was just a coincidence*, we tell ourselves, or *Must have been my imagination*—and most times the explanation works and we can dismiss what happened. But there are some experiences we can't so easily dismiss. We recognize we've stumbled onto something we don't understand, something that doesn't fit into our idea of how the universe works, and it shakes us to our core. In clinical terms, this is called cognitive dissonance: We no longer know what we believe, and no longer believe what we know.

After speaking with Leo at the jail, I felt the weight of the terrible knowledge I now carried and needed to share it with someone. Not Sandy. She was too close to Leo. Not Steve. Probably not even O'Shaughnessy. I'd not seen Jake in two weeks and badly wanted to tell him about Leo, that he'd been found, in one way, and lost in another. I knocked on his door in Laurelhurst. His brother answered. Harry Caulfield thanked me for visiting as we stood in the foyer. But the news was bad here, too.

"I'm sure he'll be glad to see you . . . if he remembers you," said Dr. Caulfield. "The mental deterioration has been rapid. Surprisingly rapid." He spoke softly, keeping his voice low. "We're making arrangements for Jake to be moved into an assisted care facility where he can be watched and cared for around the clock."

"I'm sorry, Dr. Caulfield."

"Please call me Harry."

"I'm sorry, Harry. For you, as much as for Jake."

"It's a strange experience. One part of me—the objective, medically trained professional—understands the physical mechanisms at work causing the brain's atrophy. But another part can't seem to comprehend what's happening, that I'm losing my brother by the day. His personality, his memory, our relationship, all is evaporating before my eyes."

"I'm so very sorry," I repeated quietly.

"He's in his study."

I remembered. "The police chief wanted to know if he could visit."

"Ask him to wait a week. Until Jake has a chance to settle in and adjust to his new surroundings."

As we walked to Jake's study, he said, "He still has lucid moments. Fewer and fewer of them. But today's been fairly good, though he's been agitated. Preoccupied with something he's working on."

Jake was bent over his desk, writing on a large sheet of paper, as we entered the study.

"Jake?" said Harry. "You have a visitor."

He turned, and his eyes lit up. "Hobbes!" And he rushed toward me with hands outstretched.

Harry Caulfield looked at me. "Hobbes?"

"It's a philosophical in-joke." But I took it as positive that Jake remembered me at all.

"So good to see you!" He clasped my hand in both of his.

"Thank you for coming!"

"It's good to see you, too, Jake."

"Yes, yes, of course, it is! Just the man I wanted to see. Perfect timing." He pulled me over to his desk. "Look, look, look!" He spread out several large newsprint sheets and turned to me. "This is big. I mean Nobel Prize big." The sheets were filled with scribbles and doodles, diagrams and arrows pointing to other scribbles. Each page was dominated at the top by the same four large letters: *A I D S.*

"Remember when I got my test results? Afterward we were talking, and I told you it was as if death summoned a whole generation of us?"

"Yes, I remember you saying that."

"I felt it then, something important, something *profoundly* important that I wasn't getting. But I *sensed* it. And then this morning it all came to me in a flash." He lowered his voice, struggling to contain his excitement. "AIDS. I know what it means. I've decoded it."

"Well that's . . ." I didn't know what to say. "That's great, Jake."

Harry looked somewhere between embarrassed and heartbroken. "Would you like a glass of iced tea?" he offered.

"That would be wonderful," I said. "Thank you." And he left.

Jake was as excited as a small child on Christmas Eve. "AIDS. It's an acronym."

I nodded.

"But an acronym for what?" His eyes were alight, eager for my answer.

"Acquired Immune Deficiency Syndrome."

"Ha, ha!" he laughed gleefully. "Yes, yes! The text! But what about the subtext?"

"The subtext?"

"Everything in the world has a text, what's there on the surface for us to see, but everything also has a *subtext*, that which lies below the surface, and wherein lies its true meaning and significance." He whispered breathlessly, his voice low. "Hobbes, I've discovered the subtextual code hidden within AIDS!"

"Ah. Really. Um, what is it?"

He smiled triumphantly, like one who's just found the doorway leading to the secrets of the universe. "Look here!" He took a black marker and turned back to me. "Watch—" then wrote beneath *A I D S*:

As If Death Summoned

He straightened up. "You see? The underlying subtext to everything that's been happening."

Harry brought me the glass of iced tea. "Thank you."

Jake was rushing on, his excitement undiminished. "This epidemic, it's not about retroviruses and T-cell counts. That's the text. Surface. But this"—he tapped the paper with his marking pen—"this is the key. *As if death summoned.*" His eyes glowed.

"Well, that's . . . that's great, Jake." I hoped I sounded at least somewhat convincing.

"It was suddenly so clear, so obvious. All this time, the true meaning of the epidemic was locked inside its acronym, but we couldn't see it. The virus is simply the physical manifestation, the microscopic mechanism, of the metaphysical cause. *We are being summoned.*" He stared at me. "And we cannot but follow." Then he turned to his brother standing aside. "Harry here doesn't understand, but you understand, don't you?" His eyes pleaded. "I mean, you must."

I put on the clichéd brave smile. "Sure. Of course. Good work, Jake. You did it. You cracked the code."

He appeared pleased, even a little smug, glancing at Harry, then asked, "Will you help me write this up? I want to send it to several journals immediately. We need to get the word out. It could change everything."

"Of course I'll help."

Harry looked at me quizzically.

With that, Jake became immensely relieved and gestured me to one of the armchairs. "Please, sit. Sit. And you too . . . um . . . ."

"Harry."

"Harry, yes, of course."

Jake slid down into his desk chair, looking exhausted but contented. "This is big, Hobbes. It's going to turn the epidemic around once word gets out. We need to write it up soon and submit it before that bastard Gallo tries to steal the credit."

I smiled. I hadn't taken a drink of the iced tea, the glass now warm in my hands.

Then Jake glanced at the clock. "Oh, is that the time? I must get dinner going. David will be arriving home soon. He's such a tyrant if dinner isn't ready and on the table."

Harry smiled. "Yes, such a tyrant, isn't he?"

I put down the glass and stood. "Then I should probably be going." There was no way, even if Harry hadn't been there, that I could talk to Jake about Leo.

Jake jumped up from his chair. "Do drop by again sometime. Lovely to see you."

"I'll show Mr. Hobbes out," said Harry.

Jake asked, "Who?"

I extended my hand. "Good-bye, Jake."

"Oh, good-bye . . . And who are you again?"

I paused. "A friend."

"Ah, of course you are." He pumped my hand vigorously. "Can't have too many friends, can we? So good to see you." Then he stopped and peered more closely at me. "But you look sad."

"Oh. Sorry." I forced a smile.

"No, no, you mustn't be sad," he said. "And you mustn't worry. Gray will be there to help you."

I went cold, feeling chilled and feverish at the same time, as if the temperature in the room had suddenly plummeted. My mouth was dry. One hoarse syllable escaped: "What?" —more breath than word.

"Gray will be there to help you," he repeated. "So, don't worry. He understands."

"Understands what?"

"Why you wouldn't dance with him that night. There in the desert? He understands. So don't be sad." And he gave me the kindest, most compassionate smile I'd ever seen on him. In my peripheral vision, Harry was slowly shaking his head, as if saying, *We've lost him again.* But I wasn't so sure. Jake seemed lucid. Indeed, he seemed . . . transcendent.

"I'll show you out," said Harry.

"Yes, show him out," said Jake. "I'll start dinner."

I followed Harry through the house in a daze as he explained, "David was Jake's partner, a professor of English literature at Reed and one of the gentlest, sweetest souls you'd ever meet."

"Yes," I said, my mind spinning.

He opened the front door and stopped. "Are you all right? You've gone pale." I was staring out onto a bleak, gray December day, yet blind to it, blind to the people passing by on the sidewalk, blind to the cars going by on the street.

"I know it's upsetting to see him like this—" Harry began.

"No, not that. It's just . . . it's what he said about my partner."

"Oh. Well, don't take anything he says seriously."

"But . . . I never told Jake about Gray. Not even his name. And never about that time in the . . . desert. Jake couldn't have known about it." I looked away, feeling lightheaded. "He couldn't have."

Harry Caulfield studied me, then said, "You *are* pale. Be careful with your driving."

Chapter Forty-Four

The Possibility of Redemption

[Portland, Oregon, December 1994]

I hadn't been this excited about the arrival of Christmas since I was a young child. But now it wasn't Santa Claus who was coming, but Jonno. In one week! We'd maintained a steady correspondence of cards, post-cards, and letters since Thanksgiving, making extensive plans for the nine days, six hours, and thirty-three minutes he would be here. Sleeping, we agreed, would be optional. I was counting the days.

But for the immediate present, I had more pressing matters than the breathless rush of lust, longing, and possibly eternal love. I was picking up Leo behind Marge's café. He had been released a day earlier on bail and was awaiting his arraignment. He went to the café, passing through the kitchen in case he was being followed, and left by the back door where I waited with my car. We were heading to Sandy's house in Southwest Portland to meet with her, his attorney, and Father Paul to map out Leo's legal strategy.

We drove in silence, taking a circuitous route, also to make sure we weren't being followed. Sandy met us at the door, hugging Leo. He clung to her for several seconds and then went into the living room, greeting Father Paul and the attorney, Lloyd Berkstrom.

"How is he?" she asked in a low voice as I removed my coat.

I couldn't meet her eyes. "He's fine."

At that moment, Fernando came walking regally into the foyer and stopped upon seeing me.

I made the effort. "Fernando! Buddy! How've you been?"

With utter disdain, he turned, tail in the air, and strutted from the room. I looked to Sandy. "You're my witness. I tried to patch things up."

"Cats are very sensitive to insincerity."

Over cheese, fruit and crackers, we discussed Leo's situation. Berkstrom did pro bono work for a number of our clients who had situations more complicated than dying. A dapper fellow preferring bow ties and beautifully textured vests with his lawyer suits, he possessed the jaunty manner of a jolly uncle. *Let's not take this too seriously.* It was all "manageable," he said.

It was decided Leo would plead guilty. They would make the case that this was his first offense, at least as an adult, his juvenile record having been expunged when he turned eighteen. Leo sat quietly listening as he stroked the cat on his lap. Fernando's low purr of contentment seemed to lend a mellowing effect to the setting.

It was uncertain what kind of sentence he might expect. Given the mandatory sentencing guidelines of the so-called *War on Drugs,* Berkstrom said Leo could serve anywhere between five and twenty years in federal court, but state judges had more leeway. The lawyer advised we arrange character witnesses to speak on Leo's behalf in hopes of swaying the judge toward leniency. Sandy quickly volunteered as a character witness, as did Father Paul. They'd ask Marti as the agency's executive director. One of Leo's professors was very supportive and had also offered. It was suggested that I speak as the agency's mental health specialist, but I declined. "I think we have enough people speaking on Leo's behalf," I said, not looking at him.

There was silence. I felt Sandy's disappointment.

But Leo agreed. "Yes, I think we have enough character witnesses. We don't want to overdo it."

It was also decided that until the hearing, Leo should not be staying in his apartment. There were still cops out there who would like to see him permanently gone. So he would move around, staying a few days with Sandy, then with Father Paul. Sandy knew he could also stay with Chad, who was now out of the hospital.

I was silent as I drove him back to his apartment to pack a few things.

"I know this is hard for you," he said.

I wondered if what he meant by "this" was what I understood by "this." I remained silent. It was difficult for me to look him in the eye. He asked, "Do you want to turn me in?"

"Do you want me to?"

"No. But I would understand if you did." He paused. "I *would* understand."

"*I'm* trying to understand."

"What?"

"How you could have done such a thing. I understand anger, rage. I can understand wanting revenge for what they did to Danny. I can even imagine myself striking out in anger if that happened to someone I loved. But this wasn't impulse. It was premeditated, cold-blooded murder."

"Someone once said, 'Revenge is a dish best served cold.'"

"Revenge is a dish best not served at all," I muttered.

"Would you prefer that I didn't tell you when you asked?"

"No. Yes . . . . no. I don't know." I was struggling with the turmoil inside me. "I can't reconcile what I know about you with what you did." I turned to him. "It makes me wonder. Are you really a monster? A psychopath? I mean, did you enjoy watching?"

His eyes fell away as we went up Burnside. "It was terrible. Far worse than I thought."

"Then why were you there?"

"It may sound strange, but I felt a kind of moral responsibility to be there."

"Moral responsibility? Yeah, I'd say that does sound kind of strange."

"Since I was the one responsible for what was happening, I felt obligated to be there."

We drove several more blocks. "Would you ever do it again?"

He shivered, though by then it was warm in the car. "No, never." From the streetlamps I could see he'd gone pale. "I told them to end it quickly. I thought I could watch, but I couldn't. I threw up twice."

"It was your vomit in the room?"

"There was no time to clean it up. No time to clean up anything. It was all over within fifteen minutes."

I was surprised. "That quickly?"

"They were drugged as soon as they entered the room, then suffocated while unconscious. Once dead, the cutting took place. They suffered very little, much less than Danny suffered."

"But the coroner said they suffocated on—"

"It was to appear that way."

"But . . . why?"

"I wanted word to get out on the street: This is what happens to goons who prey on the kids. And it worked. The news was on the streets before the media even heard about it. Several other goons cleared out of town within days."

"Do you think that mitigates the crime? Somehow makes it right?"

He answered wearily, "I left the realm of right and wrong years ago. You know that."

I returned to looking straight ahead as we entered Northwest Portland. "I don't know what Krishnamurti would say, but I know the Bible's pretty clear: 'Vengeance is mine, saith the Lord.'"

Leo nodded as he gazed out the window. "He can have it."

At work the next morning, I was in Sandy's office, door closed, discussing next steps.

Leo would be staying with her for the first two nights; then she'd take him to Chad's apartment.

As I got up to leave, she said, "You've changed toward him."

"Oh?" I decided to play dumb since I didn't have any other strategy but telling the truth, which didn't seem an option right then.

"I think I understand," she said.

"You do?" Had Leo told her, too?

"You're disappointed he was selling marijuana."

Nooooo, not exactly. But I decided to play it anyway. "Is that a problem for you?"

She thought for a moment. "No—and yes, I like to think of myself as generally a law-biding citizen who follows a good many of the laws. But I just don't put this in the category of serious criminal behavior. *I've* smoked marijuana. Most of my friends have. Heck, even our president admits he smoked in college, though he didn't inhale. I just don't see it as a moral failing. Can you accept that?"

I hesitated. "It's a little more complicated for me." And I left her office.

It still unnerved and upset me to think Leo capable of committing such a heinous crime and that he showed no remorse. Living outside of society's rules for so long, he didn't seem to experience the guilt most of us would. I realized that in some ways he was a primal man, able to exact terrible vengeance, and then he was over it. It was not so easy for me. I was experiencing the guilt of an accomplice simply by possessing this knowledge, and slept fitfully for the next several nights.

"Something's weighing on you," said O'Shaughnessy at that week's session. "I don't sense the joy that one would expect from a potential new relationship."

"No, I'm . . . I'm happy." I added a smile as an afterthought.

He stared at me. "Okay, we'll play the guessing game. Let's see: You're worried whether this relationship with Jonathan will work out."

"Not really. I'm very hopeful."

"You're wondering whether you can really love another person after Gray."

"No."

"Or that you're being in some way unfaithful to Gray and his memory?"

"No. We worked that out before he died. He *wanted* me to find someone to share my life with."

O'Shaughnessy pondered this. "Then there's something else weighing on you. Something blunting the joy of your joyous news."

I was silent.

"Ah. So, it is something else. Is it something you want to talk about?"

Hesitating, I asked, "What would you do if you were given information—in confidence—about a crime? A serious crime?"

"It depends on what I can live with. The world can be a morally ambiguous place at times. That's why we have laws and professional codes of ethics to help us decide what to do." He asked, "You're bound by professional codes from sharing this information?"

"It's a little more complicated than that."

Later that day, after most staff had departed, I turned out the lights in the prevention team room and headed for the darkened lobby. Light was coming from the Client Services department, and I looked in. Father Paul was still at his desk. We were the only ones there. It seemed fortuitous, and I rapped lightly on the open door.

He looked up from his paperwork and smiled. "You're working late, too."

"I'm heading home now."

"Then have a good evening."

I remained at the door. "Do you have a minute?"

He put down his pen. "For you, my friend, of course."

I immediately felt wrapped in this man's warmth and generosity even though I knew he would have time for anyone, and that he considered everyone his friend. I entered the room he shared with the other case managers and sat by his desk.

"Something on your mind?" he asked.

I began tentatively, "Have you ever—say, in confession—received information of a horrendous crime?"

"Yes."

"And did you honor the confidentiality?"

"Yes."

I considered this. "Under what circumstances would you break your confidentiality?"

He steepled his fingers in thought. "If others were in danger, or if the individual was a danger to himself. Or if I thought the individual might repeat the crime."

I sat there, staring down into my hands.

"But I don't think Leo will ever repeat his crime. Revenge leaves a very bitter taste in one's soul."

I looked up. "He told you?"

"Yes, he told me."

I felt an enormous relief, just knowing that someone else was aware of this besides me. Thank God, here was someone I could finally talk with! "I sense no remorse, no guilt in him for what he did."

"Oh, there is, but it's not so much remorse that he broke the law as it would be for you and me. It's more that he violated his own code. And that's why I don't think it will happen again."

"And you can live with the knowledge? You can live, carrying this knowledge?"

"Yes. Not comfortably. But yes, I can live with it."

"How? Tell me. I'm not sure I can."

"Because I see no good coming from locking Leo up for the rest of his life, or from his possible execution. And I can see much loss, of what he could still contribute to society."

"But can you excuse the severity of his crime?"

"No, I can't. But fortunately for me, it's not my responsibility to condemn or condone the actions of my fellow human beings."

349

"What about your legal responsibility? Your moral responsibility? Where does God come into all of this?"

"But you don't believe in God."

"No, but you do . . . uh, don't you?"

He smiled. "I do. And this is between Leo and God, for those of us who believe in God."

I was not finding the clarity I was hoping for.

Father Paul turned reflective. "I was a chaplain serving two tours in Vietnam. During that time, I heard the confessions of hundreds of men. Some terrible, horrible confessions. Difficult for me even to listen to. And I could see what agony the person was suffering for what he'd done."

"But that was war."

"War does not absolve one from one's conscience. That was so painfully obvious. And over these past twenty years, I've heard from some of those men, or about them. Some committed suicide. Some descended into their own private hells of drugs and alcohol. And some emerged from the fiery crucibles of their souls to make significant contributions to our society."

"So that's it? You believe in redemption?"

"I believe in the *possibility* of redemption. And that as long as one's alive, there is the possibility."

He returned to his gentle smile. "But I am explaining how I understand this situation. I'm not making moral prescriptions for you. You will need to come to your own understanding, and make your own decision that *you* can live with."

I nodded, staring at the mounds of papers on his desk, still not feeling any better, or any clearer.

His voice broke in again. "However, I would offer you this . . ."

I looked up.

"Whatever you finally decide—to turn Leo in, or to not turn him in—I can pretty much guarantee that it will not be a comfortable decision for you to live with. Either way, you will not feel good about it. You should probably prepare yourself for that."

Chapter Forty-Five

New Year, New Life

[Portland, Oregon, December 1994-January 1995]

The week between Christmas 1994 and New Year's Day 1995 is now a happy memory-blur. Jonno had told his parents he'd be staying at my place "so as not to crowd them," which I thought a bit lame, given that John and Maggie's large house wouldn't have been "crowded" even if all their sons and sons' families were staying with them. But they didn't act surprised. Jonno flew in two days before Christmas, and John and Maggie took us to see a performance of the Nutcracker ballet, followed by a late dinner at the Heathman Hotel. The restaurant reminded me of my long lunch there with Jerald in April. As they looked over their menus, I told them, "I can personally vouch for all the entrees here. The broiled salmon is excellent. So is the roasted pheasant and the braised lamb. And their pasta Alfredo has the best cream sauce on the planet."

"Oh," said John, "so you've eaten here before."

"Once."

Over dinner Jonno and I told them about our Thanksgiving hike up Table Mountain.

"I got a nosebleed, of course," he added.

"Of course," said John.

"Jonno's had nosebleeds ever since he was a small boy," Maggie explained. "Even in high school, he couldn't get through a tennis match without one."

"It did give me a psychological advantage, however," he said. "My bloodied white shirt seemed to unnerve my opponents." We laughed, and I thoroughly enjoyed the time we shared with John and Maggie.

Christmas Day we spent with our families. The next day, Jonno and I went snowboarding on Mount Hood (another nosebleed) then spent several days on the coast, nestling next to our cabin's fireplace as the winter gales roared outside. We were there on New Year's Eve, welcoming in 1995 as we sat before the fire with a bottle of wine and the remnants of dinner spread around us. It was a time of sharing more deeply than we ever had before. At one point, he said, "I know I can't compete with Gray and all he meant to you."

I pulled him closer. "You don't need to. That was another time and another life."

And another dream, I thought.

In the early hours of the new year, I woke, my body wrapped snug and warmly around his, and suppressed the urge to weep from happiness. *I never thought I'd feel like this again.*

It was a perfect break. It had also been a relief to not think about Leo. Sandy had hosted Christmas dinner at her house with Leo and Chad and some friends. But now the break was over. Jonno returned to LA, and I needed to return to my world.

Leo's appearance in court occurred during the first week in January. He pleaded guilty to the charge of selling marijuana, and the character witnesses spoke on his behalf. Sandy and I sat in the courtroom, listening to the testimonies. They were much the same: recounting the tough life Leo had been given, the adversities he'd overcome, praising his intelligence, his commitment to helping the street kids. Marti was speaking. "Your honor, twenty years ago, I could have been in Leo's place. I smoked marijuana when I was younger, all my friends did. True, I didn't buy or sell it, but only because I didn't know where to go to get it. I now have a husband and three children. I've served a number of organizations over the years as their executive director and believe I have made a positive contribution to our community. I ask that you not let this youthful indiscretion deprive Leo of a future, and deprive us of a young man with so much to offer."

Father Paul spoke movingly of finding Leo on the streets and how Leo had managed to turn his life around: getting clean, earning his GED, now in a degree program at Portland Community College, and doing outreach to street kids himself. When it came Sandy's turn, she related how she'd taken Leo in and never regretted it, how he'd beaten a heroin addiction, why she believed in him. His professor summed up well, "Considering Leo's background, and all that he's had against him, I find it extraordinary he's been able to create a new life for himself. Frankly, I would challenge any of us here to so dramatically rescript our lives and overcome what he's had to overcome."

I sat through the testimonies, watching uncomfortably, knowing what I knew. It was some small comfort that Father Paul was there, too, bearing the same terrible knowledge.

Leo sat upright next to his attorney with his usual quiet grace and poise, listening silently, smiling in appreciation, nodding his thanks to each speaker when he or she finished. The judge, a slight, small man, balding, with a white moustache and gentle eyes, listened thoughtfully, and I was hopeful. Leo's handsome, serene features probably didn't hurt his case either. It might have been different if he appeared as some coarse thug.

When the last speaker had finished, the judge asked Leo to stand.

"Mr. Saavedra, this court takes note of the character testimony that has been presented on your behalf today, and we have been moved by the personal challenges that you've overcome in your young life. We also believe in the promise that you may yet offer society. That said, we must also take seriously the laws that you have admitted to breaking. Respecting the importance and seriousness of these laws to our community's well-being, I hereby sentence you to one year in the county jail."

Sandy let out a slight gasp next to me. Leo stood calmly facing the bench.

The judge continued. "The court also takes note that this is your first offense, and, encouraged by the potential contributions you may yet make, I suspend all but forty-five days of that sentence, to begin serving immediately. I hope you consider this sentence just and will see it as one more challenge for you to overcome and to learn from."

Leo answered in a clear voice. "Thank you, your honor. The sentence is just, and better than I deserve." He raised his hands before his face in a *namaste* gesture, bowing his head once. I could see the judge was moved by his simple, graceful act.

"Very well. I am hopeful you will continue on your upward path. This court is adjourned." He pounded his gavel once. Leo was led away after shaking hands with his lawyer and turned back to all of us with a grateful smile. When his eyes met mine, I had to look away.

Chapter Forty-Six

The Feds Step In

[Portland, Oregon, January 1995]

There remained a tension between Leo and me. He felt it. I couldn't deny it. It was often difficult for me to look him in the eyes, and I found myself wanting to leave as soon as I got to the jail. Fortunately, Sandy, Father Paul and other CAP staff were regularly visiting him during those six weeks.

He'd asked me to get word to Danny in San Francisco. "Tell him I want him to stay with Hannah. And that I said he *must* go to the alternative school where she teaches."

I relayed his message. On my next week's visit, Leo asked, "How is everyone?"

"Everyone is fine," I said. Danny had followed through with his promise to stay with Hannah and attend school. "Don't worry."

"I don't worry."

"Right. I forgot."

"Still, it's good to hear that everyone is doing well. Thanks for your help."

I nodded.

After a pause, he said, "I know this isn't easy for you."

I was trying not to think about what I knew he was talking about. No great loss to humanity, the reporter Amy Sanchez said of the two goons, and I suspect she was right. Still, they were fellow human beings, and they'd been killed by someone I knew and admired through an act that was intentional and executed in cold blood.

"I'd better be going." I began to rise from my seat.

"One more thing," he said. "Tomorrow morning there's going to be a front-page exposé in *Willamette Week*. On police corruption in Portland. The Department of Justice will announce that it's opening an investigation of extortion, drug sales, and civil rights abuses by members of the police bureau. The mayor and police chief are being notified today. The DA's office will soon announce they're launching their own investigation."

I settled back down in my chair. "You know all this?"

"I know all this," he said flatly.

"How?"

"After I gave the law firm my file, they reviewed it, along with the registry you sent them. Once they organized it into a proper legal format, they saw that it got to the federal prosecutor for this district. After examining it, he notified the Department of Justice. The law firm also leaked the file to a friendly editor at *Willamette Week*, and they've been doing their own investigation, even had their reporters working on Christmas Day. They timed their exposé with the Department of Justice's announcement."

I was stunned at what had resulted from Leo's file. "How do you have those kind of connections?" I marveled.

He smiled. "When I first came to Portland years ago, I got to know one of the partners of the law firm—very well. He's still fond of me and very protective. He knows this investigation is going to be my insurance policy."

"What do you mean, insurance policy?"

"I won't be identified by the press as the primary witness, but when this story breaks, the cops will know it's me. It would look very suspicious if the primary witness was, say, found hanging in his cell, or killed by another inmate. I'm probably safer in jail than on the outside."

I nodded, still amazed and dazed at what was happening.

"This may help make up for . . . for other things I've done."

I averted my eyes, saying nothing.

He looked away. "Or maybe not."

"I've got to get back to work."

The news broke the next day. Leo's law firm had chosen the feisty little paper that had done some impressive investigative journalism in the past. Twelve officers were alleged to have been participating in an informal "ring of vice" that included extortion from local sex workers, flophouse and bar owners; confiscation of marijuana and other illegal substances that were never turned in; and random acts of brutality and sexual coercion against a number of street youth and sex workers. The unidentified rogue officers were placed on administrative leave until the investigations could be completed.

Willamette Week editors had also sent a prerelease copy to the police officers' union. If the union tried to strong-arm the investigators, they'd now have to deal with the Justice Department. Having seen the text of the incriminating evidence, listing specific dates, times, and identifying details of the officers, the union chose to remain quiet when the story broke. At that point, *The Oregonian* and local TV stations began their own daily coverage, highlighting the DA's statement promising immunity to those who came forward to testify about the cops' alleged abuses, and the chief released a statement pledging full cooperation with the investigators. The mayor, the chief, and the DA were confident it was only a few bad apples and wanted to clean it up and clear the name of the bureau as quickly as possible. They wanted no suspicion that the rot went any deeper. As we settled into a very cold January, the city heated up with the allegations.

The other big news was that Franklin was leaving for a position with the county. The staff was sincerely happy for him, and *ecstatic* for themselves. Sandy was managing her grief at his departure rather well, I thought. "I consider this Franklin's belated Christmas present to all of us," she told me.

I went to his office as soon as I heard. He was sitting at his desk, reviewing and signing checks.

"Hey, there's a rumor you're leaving for the county."

He looked up. "Yes. I'm sure the staff is celebrating in the streets."

"Oh, no," I protested. "No, that's not true." *Not in the streets, exactly.* "What's the position?"

"I'll be overseeing the finances on all health department contracts. It's a position that pays closer to what I'm really worth, decent hours, and I don't have to work two or three jobs like we do here."

"Sounds like a great opportunity. You'll still be making a difference."

He shrugged.

"We're going to miss you."

He scoffed. "Hardly."

"No, I'm serious. Marti, Steve, and I—even Sandy—we all know how hard you've worked to keep this agency afloat. And the board certainly knows the miracles you've performed here."

He allowed himself to be mollified. "Thanks. It's nice to know someone appreciates what I've done."

"When are you leaving?"

"End of March. I need to tie up loose ends, and I wanted to give Marti enough time to try and find someone to replace me. Good luck with that."

"Well, before you leave, let me take you to lunch to celebrate your new beginning."

"Sure. Why not."

"Again, congratulations."

I started to leave when he said, "By the way . . ."

I turned around.

"Just for the record, you are my type."

"Your type. You mean wealthy?"

He smiled in spite of himself. "Yeah. I mean wealthy."

"Good to know," I said and left.

Chapter Forty-Seven

Another Summons

[Portland, Oregon, January 1995]

I wasn't terribly surprised when Amy Sanchez called, asking to speak with me several days after *Willamette Week's* exposé hit the newsstands. I'd been expecting it. She was one of the reporters who had co-authored the article. Could we meet again, she asked, just the two of us, away from the agency? She proposed a neutral location, one of Portland's approximately 250,000 coffee houses. (I'm convinced the city's economy would collapse, romances cease, and political organizing come to a dead halt were it not for Portland's coffee shops.) It was a quiet, cozy place in the Pearl District, with customized-funk décor and soft jazz playing when I entered. Amy sat at a table in the back corner next to a bookshelf stuffed with used paperbacks. Dressed in jeans, thick wool sweater over a white shirt, and hiking boots—what's considered "business casual" in the Pacific Northwest—she rose as I approached. Her mouth flickered into a brief smile of greeting, like *There, got that out of the way,* and we shook hands. "I ordered coffee for us," she said. "They've got a Bolivian roast here that my system requires at least once a week."

"Sounds good. Thanks."

We took our seats. I complimented her on the article as our coffees were served. All the city was talking about it. She was modest as I'd expected. "Thanks. It was a team effort. Nice to see one's work actually make a difference." But I was feeling wary. While I sensed I could trust her, I chose not to. Probably because of her profession and training. I suspected she was fishing for a story, and I was the pond she was fishing in.

"Hey, good news about Leo's sentence, huh?" she said. "He'll be out by the end of February." She'd visited him just yesterday, she told me. "You must be pleased too, being his friend."

"Oh, I wouldn't call us friends," I said quickly. "We're more work colleagues."

She studied me for several seconds. "Something's happened between you."

I didn't want to shift my eyes away from her. To a trained reporter, breaking eye contact would be a dead giveaway that something was up. *Do not shift your eyes.*

She held my gaze, saying nothing.

Do. Not. Shift. Your. Eyes.

She kept staring, and I glanced at the bookshelf (*Damn!*) then she looked away, murmuring as if to herself, "So, something's happened between you." She seemed to brush the thought aside, or more likely, filed it away for future use, and got to the point of our little coffee klatch. "When I was in your office back in December, I asked if you knew about a special file Leo'd been keeping. Once I left, I realized you never answered my question." Her dark eyes bored into me. "You knew about the file, didn't you?"

"Yes."

She considered this a moment. "What about the murders?"

I hesitated. "Let's not go there."

"Fair enough." She picked up her coffee cup and drank. "The police are certain it was an outside job. Not local."

I said nothing, feeling her gaze on me, as if she were piecing together a story and wondering which pieces were still missing. I was again struck by her intensity, by her seriousness, like every day she woke to the eternal struggle between Good and Evil. And Gray thought *I* was serious!

"Anyway," she added, "because of that file, the police bureau is at last being investigated. It was a brave thing Leo did. He's a hero to me."

I suddenly felt sad. *Yes, he was once a hero to me, too.*

"I'm wondering what role you played in all this," she said.

"No role."

"But you knew about the file."

"I knew about the file." It was part of *my* training. When stuck, simply repeat what the other person says.

"Nothing else?"

"Nothing else."

She pressed. "What would you be willing to say off the record?"

"Off the record? I'd say this is an excellent roast. But don't quote me." It was no use being subtle with a professional like Amy. I felt her breaking off the fishing expedition and was relieved, then deflected her further with a question. "What were you and Leo talking about in your visit?"

"The article on the street kids. When he gets out, we'll resume working on it together. The kids'll never talk to me without him."

"Thanks for being interested in the street youth," I said sincerely. "Not many reporters are."

"It's personal for me."

I felt a shift in our conversation. It was my turn to stare silently, wondering what she wasn't saying.

Taking another drink and setting down her cup, she said, "My younger brother was one of them."

"Was?"

"Miguel—Mike to his friends—he was one of those kids who doesn't survive the streets."

Here was the sorrow I sensed when we first met in Steve's office. "I'm sorry."

"Over twelve years now," she mused. "When my father learned Miguel was gay, he kicked him out of the house. I was away at college in Berkeley at the time. Didn't even learn about it until I came home for the holidays, four months after he'd started living on the streets. My parents had kept it from me." Her jaw flexed. "I knew Miguel was gay. They didn't. I was so angry at them. Maybe at myself, too. I'd never spoken to him about what I suspected, and he never tried to contact me. Too ashamed is my guess."

"What happened?"

"I came home for Christmas and immediately went out looking for him. Day after day, night after night, for the three weeks I was home. No luck. So I returned to school at the end of the holiday break, hoping he was okay, wherever he was. Some weeks later my mother called to say his body had been found. In Seattle. He was fifteen." She turned her face away and whispered, "Fucking hell."

I was thinking again of Trevor and his parents, of their refusal to visit him as he lay dying. "Did your mother and father ever regret their actions? Ever feel remorse?"

She looked back at me. "I wouldn't know. When they disowned their son, they lost their daughter as well." *Yeah, here's the sorrow I sensed.*

She finished her coffee. "If Leo was doing his outreach back then, Miguel might have had a chance. So that's my interest in the street kids."

I nodded silently.

"I should be getting back to work." She stood, slipped on her coat, then looked down on me where I sat. "For what it's worth, the way Leo talks about you? I think you're more to him than just a work colleague."

She left the shop and I remained sitting there, staring into my empty coffee cup.

As with Leo, my visits with Jake had become distressing. In his first weeks at the care facility, he had been more lucid, and I still wanted to ask him about his comment, that Gray understood why I wouldn't dance with him. We sat in a cheerful activity room, decorated with boughs and wreathes and electric candles from the recent holidays.

"The last time I visited you in your home, you mentioned my partner, Gray."

"Did I?"

"Yes. You said he understood."

"Understood what?"

"That's what I wanted to ask you about. You see, he died a little more than a year ago."

"Oh, I'm so sorry to hear that," he said sincerely. "You must bring him around sometime. I'd love to meet him." He said that sincerely, too.

"But he's dead. He died."

Jake shook his head. "Yes, yes, so sorry. We've had so many losses in this epidemic. Still, I'd like to meet him sometime."

Okay, so maybe he wasn't that lucid after all.

On my last visit, he was sitting in the community room, watching television. The way he stared at the screen told me he wasn't really concentrating. It was Jerry Springer, so he wasn't missing anything. A number of elderly residents were scattered around the room, most of them oblivious to the television or much else.

I don't think he remembered me, though he pretended he did. At times, parts of the old Jake would resurface.

"People here tell me I resemble the young . . ." he stopped, struggling for the name. "Um, I resemble the young . . ."

"Marlon Brando?" I offered.

"No."

"Robert De Niro?"

"No." He continued searching through his damaged memory banks, then flipped his hand. "Well, you know, someone young."

I tried updating him about "Emilio," but he became distracted by the laugh track on the perpetual TV, laughing along with it, and settled back in his chair, staring mindlessly at the mindless television program. I invariably came away from these visits depressed and downhearted, and finally doubted I'd go back. It did him no good, and tore me up each time after I was with him.

It was also in late January that Steve went into Providence Hospital with a deep bronchial cough that became pneumonia. His T-cell count was plummeting.

Chapter Forty-Eight

Adrift on a Sea of Blood

[Portland, Oregon, February 1995]

"He asks about you," said Sandy. "He misses you."

It was late February, and I hadn't visited Leo in a couple of weeks.

"Yeah, I've been really busy, you know, with the testing program and organizing my presentation for the conference next week."

"He'll be released while you're at the conference," she said. "I thought maybe we'd hold a "Get Out of Jail" party on Saturday when you return. Invite a number of the staff and the counseling and testing team."

I was sorting papers as I sat at my desk, avoiding her eyes. "Sounds good. I'll go half on the expenses. But you might need to hold it without me. I don't remember what time I'll be getting in that day."

"Four fifteen. You're arriving at four fifteen, along with Chad and Lionel."

"Oh, that's right." I've never been particularly good at lying. It's one of my failings.

"So, you'll be able to make the party at seven."

"Yeah, probably," I said, still fumbling with the papers. "Unless I'm too tired. It's a long flight—" whereby Sandy put her hands on my desk and leaned into my face.

"I'll be *very* disappointed if you're not there. And the consequences would be dire."

I looked up. "Dire? Like, how dire are we talking?"

"Trust me, you don't want to be there when I go over to the Dark Side."

"Oh, that dire. So, yeah, I'll be there."

I had reached my decision about Leo, but as Father Paul predicted, I was not comfortable living with it, and I'd been finding excuses not to visit him in the jail. I could then almost forget what I knew by losing myself in the demands of work and the joys of a new relationship. Jonno had become the still point in my swirling, chaotic, and morally ambiguous world. I was now living and longing for the weekends when either he would fly up to Portland or I would fly down to Los Angeles. With all the frequent flyer miles we were racking up, we could make that trip to Nepal and go trekking in the Himalayas.

On my last trip to LA, I'd unloaded my frustrations about Leo, without telling what I couldn't tell. Up to this point, I had intentionally not brought these aspects of my life into our relationship, but on that occasion, I'd had two glasses of wine, which was one more than my limit. Three, and I would have become a sobbing idiot. Jonno listened intently as I told him about Leo, growing up on a farm in eastern Oregon, abandoned by his mother when he was young, despised by his father for being a *maricón*, and living on the streets in Portland since he was fifteen. I told him about Leo's intelligence, his ethereal calm, the poise and dignity with which he carried himself . . .

Oh, yeah, and he's also a murderer.

"Sounds like you really admire him," said Jonno.

Yes, I once did, and realized from Jonno's observation that perhaps I still did. This was a new kind of grief I was feeling: grieving the loss of a friend still living.

That weekend before the HIV/AIDS conference in DC, Jonno flew up Friday night and we spent Saturday afternoon helping John cut back the large, sprawling blackberry patch on his property. It was brisk outside, but no snow or rain, and for four hours we hacked away at the spiky, entwined vines, while John raked the cuttings together and burned them. Without their foliage, the thick stalks were easy to chop, and I enjoyed the exercise, swinging the machete and working up a sweat in the thirty-four degree weather. John was easy to be around, as relaxed and friendly as he was on the counseling and testing team. He and Maggie were clearly happy seeing their youngest so often, and I felt as welcome in their family as a fourth son.

As the light began to fade, we wrapped up our efforts. We'd made a substantial dent in the berry patch, while leaving plenty for Maggie's preserves in the fall. As we worked outside, she had labored indoors, preparing a large dinner for us, and their house was warm and rich with the aromas of roast in the oven and fresh baked bread as we washed up and gathered around their dining room table.

"Oh, dear," she said, carrying the pot roast in from the kitchen. "Look at your hands."

"The blackberries didn't give up without a fight," admitted Jonno.

It's true, the prickly vines had exacted their toll on us. Although we were wearing gloves and long-sleeved shirts, by the time Jonno and I were done, our hands and wrists were badly scratched, with torn, red, and swollen skin.

"Well, be sure and soak them with Epsom salts when you get home," said Maggie.

As we began filling our plates and passing the serving dishes, Jonno said to me, "You've met all my family. When do I get to meet yours?"

I poured gravy over the roast and mashed potatoes. "O Braveheart."

"Why?"

I passed him the gravy bowl. "Dad's fine. I think you'd like him. Mom . . . she might be a bit of a challenge."

"How so?"

"She's never been comfortable with her son being gay. She prefers not thinking about it. I mean, *me*." I saw a look on John's face that was hard to interpret. Concern? Sadness?

But Jonno persisted. "Still, I'd like to meet them."

"Maybe next time you're up."

After dinner, Maggie sent us home with a box of items: two tins of freshly baked cookies, one for Jonno to take back to LA, one for me; two jars of last year's blackberry jam; small loaves of still-warm bread; and a two-pound package of Epsom salts. "Take this and be sure to soak your hands in warm water tonight."

"Hot bath with Epsom Salt is my suggestion," said John.

Jonno accepted it from his mother with a kiss, then whispered to me as we headed for the door, "And I know how we can save on hot water and Epsom salts." We'd already found that my bathtub could comfortably accommodate two.

By the time we arrived at my place we were both aching and fatigued and ready for a hot bath and bed before Jonno returned to LA in the morning. We entered the kitchen through the back door, I carrying Maggie's food package, and Jonno the box containing our gloves, rain gear, and tools. I was setting my load on the table as he closed the door while balancing the box on his arm. As he turned around, it slipped and he fumbled it like a football, its contents clattering to the floor with him tumbling after it.

"Are you okay?"

"Okay I am," he said on hands and knees. "Graceful, I'm not." At that moment blood began streaming from his nose—not drip-drip-drip, but in runnels, falling and splattering onto the white floor tiles. He immediately sat up, holding his head back. "Must be my time of month."

"I'll get you a cold washcloth."

I went to the bathroom, wetting a cloth, and brought it to where he was still sitting on the floor, head back, like he was admiring my kitchen ceiling. He took it. "Thanks. This is so embarrassing."

"I hope you're not doing this just to get a psychological advantage over me," I said, gathering up the tools and gear, "because it's really not necessary."

He chuckled, holding the wet washcloth to his nose.

I put the box of tools aside, then tore off several sheets from the paper towel dispenser. As I knelt to wipe up the blood, his arm shot out to stop me. "No!" he yelled. "Don't touch it!"

The suddenness and alarm in his voice startled me. "It's just a little blood," I said.

"But your hands . . ." There was clear panic in his eyes. I looked down at my hands, at the raw, torn skin, at the open cuts and abrasions, and then again at the floor.

Blood.

I sat heavily on the cold kitchen tiles, facing him.

After a moment, I asked, "How long have you been positive?"

"Two years," he said softly, not looking at me.

We continued sitting there, the two of us now separated by the blood.

He reached for the paper towels. "Let me do it." Still stunned, I handed them to him. He continued to avoid my eyes as he held the cold compress to his nose with one hand and wiped the floor with the other. When he finished, we both remained sitting, not speaking. My mind was whirling, struggling to fashion a complete sentence.

"Your parents . . . do they—"

"No."

The room was so silent I could hear the soft ticking of the kitchen clock on the wall. A car drove past on the street outside. The tile's coldness seeping through my jeans.

"I wanted to tell you," he said. "Wanted to tell you on that first hike in the gorge, but I liked you too much. I hadn't liked anyone that much in years. And after what you'd gone through with Gray, I was afraid how you'd react. That I'd scare you off before we even got a chance to know each other."

Both of us stared at the smeared blood drying.

I could only mumble, "Why don't you go take a bath. I'll finish cleaning the floor with some bleach."

I know we talked that night, but I have little recollection of what was said. I remember he apologized, a number of times. I think I said it was all right, that I understood. I do remember him asking, "Are you angry?"

"No. I'm not angry," which was true. I wasn't feeling angry, wasn't feeling sad, or even anxious. Truth was, I was numb, wasn't feeling anything. My professional training should have helped me recognize I was in shock, but I was too much in shock to recognize much that night.

We both seemed to want to avoid talking and went to bed. I didn't sleep. He lay quietly next to me, but I sensed he wasn't sleeping either. *Put your arms around him. Hold him. Comfort him. He needs your support.*

But I couldn't. I felt sick, physically nauseated, and soon it was morning and we were driving to the airport. I pulled up to the curb at the departures concourse. We hadn't spoken a word since we left my place. We sat staring as if interested in the people coming and going through the concourse doors.

"I was waiting for the right moment to tell you," he said. "But I waited too long. I'm sorry. If you'd asked, I would have told you. But it was wrong not to tell you when we first met."

I sat, unable to fashion any response.

"After what you went through with Gray, I can't blame you for not wanting to go through it again." It was as if he were reading my thoughts. "I mean, if I were in your shoes? I wouldn't want to get emotionally involved with someone who . . ." He left the rest unspoken.

I felt hollowed out, as if something living—my heart, my soul, my spirit, *something*—had been removed, leaving this dried-out husk that was now me. At last, I said, "Maybe . . . maybe we should cool it for a while. Give us time to think about this." I hadn't prepared that. Didn't know what I was going to say before I said it. It just came out.

"Okay."

He got out of the car, took his pack from the backseat, and went into the airport. I wanted to say something more, but had no clue what it would be, so I watched him disappear through the departure doors.

The rest of the day was Numb Central. I couldn't believe that I hadn't asked him. *After ten years of living with the epidemic? After all my AIDS work? After Gray?* But it never occurred to me to ask Jonno his status. Nor did he ask mine. Safer sex had never even been a discussion; it was a given. So maybe I didn't want to know. Or maybe, feeling the way I did about him, I just *knew* he was negative. Like some men reported when they tested positive at our clinic. They loved the guy so much it never occurred to them he could be infected. Love is blind. It's also not too bright.

That night I wanted to call and make sure he was okay. But, honestly, how could he be okay? And what would I say? We'll make it work? Really? And just how would we do that? I didn't want to mislead him or give him false hopes. Could I manage a relationship with Jonno being HIV-positive? With Gray, yes. It had become part of our relationship. We grew into it together. But starting out with this hanging over us? Could I do it? Would there come a time, maybe in four or five years, or next year, when I would desert him when he needed me most? How could I live with myself? But how could I live with him? Or without him?

It was no good to call. I didn't have a clue what I would say and went to bed early, still feeling sick, where I dreamed:

Jonno is sitting across from me on the kitchen floor, both of us staring at the splatters and red puddle on the white tiles as the blood is spreading, like some blob from a science fiction B-movie. There's a shift: we're on separate ice floes, adrift on a red sea of blood "Three hundred thousand people!" Arthur is shouting as the space between us widens. "Three hundred thousand!" I reach for Jonno. "Take my hand!" I yell. "I'll pull you across!" But he doesn't move, just stares at my outstretched hand, red and torn from the blackberries, as our ice floes drift farther away from each other. "Please! Take my hand!" I cry. He slowly shakes his head, a terrible sadness in his eyes. "It's too late for

371

me," he says. "No!" I'm kneeling, still trying to reach him. "Too late for me," he says again, "but not for you," and I remain on the kitchen floor, hand outstretched as he continues floating away on a sea of blood.

The next morning, I was sick—vomiting sick, aching sick as with the flu—and was tempted to call the office, saying I couldn't make it in. But I was leaving Wednesday for the conference and still needed to prepare my handouts, and I knew it was all in my head. *So, like that doesn't count?*

Just as people had noticed the difference in me returning to work after Thanksgiving (clearly, something wonderful had happened!) they noticed the difference that morning. Something had happened, and clearly it wasn't wonderful. But no one mentioned it.

Except Sandy.

"You look terrible. What's happened?"

I shook my head.

"Jonno?"

I nodded.

"You had a falling out?"

I looked away.

"Would you please say something?"

Still not meeting her eyes, I mumbled, "It may not work after all."

"So . . . you want to talk about it?" she offered.

I shook my head. She knew not to push or pry.

"Well, you know where my office is."

I decided I'd call Jonno that night, to check in and see how he was doing, but I worked late and by the time I returned home I was tired and still sick and lay down for a nap first. It was past midnight when I woke, too late to call. *How convenient,* said that part of me that recognizes its own bullshit. Yeah, it was avoidance. I didn't know what to say to him, was afraid what he'd say to me. So I showered and went to bed, immediately falling asleep, and dreamed of the Bogong High Plains for the first time since meeting Jonno in November. In some ways, it was the same dream. *I was alone on the plains, searching for someone.* But it took a new and disturbing turn as if a layer of the dream had been peeled away, revealing what had always been there. What I had always known . . .

Chapter Forty-Nine

Stalked

[Portland, Oregon, February 1995]

The sun reflects off the snow, blindingly bright. I've at last emerged from the blizzard. I can see for miles and miles and miles in every direction. So clear. And so beautiful! (Must remember to tell Gray how beautiful it is out here.) A rocky outcropping lies ahead, looking like a half-finished chimney. It's familiar. I've seen it before, I'm sure. But then it was behind me. Confused, I look down and see my own boot prints stretching ahead in the snow and, with a sickening awareness, realize I've been walking in circles all this time. But there's something more, something even more unnerving. I see a second set of tracks, parallel to mine, in the snow. I'm being followed? I swing around, searching the plains again, looking for the person whose tracks these are, and I notice dark, churning clouds on the distant horizon—dark clouds all around me, and I feel a new despair. I've not escaped the blizzard after all. I'm in the quiet eye of the storm, and another is fast approaching from the west. I watch it roiling and boiling toward me, a much bigger storm, a great white tidal wave of billowing snow. I face it stoically, knowing that I can't survive another storm out here, and knowing that, all this time, someone has been stalking me . . .

O'Shaughnessy sat forward. "Stalking you?"

"Yes."

"Let me get this right: The person in your dreams whom you've been searching for all this time," he paused, "that person has been stalking *you?*"

I felt my face going red. "I know, sounds crazy, huh? I don't mean crazy in a clinical sense, of course. Not, you know, certifiable. Just your everyday, garden-variety crazy. Normal crazy." We usually met on Thursdays, but since I'd be at my conference, we'd rescheduled our appointment for Tuesday afternoon.

He repeated, "The person you have been searching for has been stalking *you.*"

"I hope we're not going to get, you know, all hung up on logic here."

He sat back in his chair. "We both know dreams have their own logic. But you're sure of the word you used. *Stalking?*"

"When I first returned from Australia a year ago in January, I needed time alone and stayed up at my parents' cabin on Lake Merwin for a week. One morning as I went out walking, I noticed my boot prints in the snow from the day before. They'd frozen during the night. And next to them was a parallel set of tracks, the padded paws of a large cat, and I realized that the day before I'd been stalked by a cougar. It was that same sense of alarm in my dream."

"And still no idea who this person is?"

"No."

"But not your deceased partner."

"No. Not Gray. I'm sure of that. I'm searching for someone else."

O'Shaughnessy checked his notes. "You said that in the dream you've been in the 'eye of the storm,' and that a new storm front is moving rapidly toward you. And that it will be an even bigger storm. One you doubt you can survive." He looked back at me. "Has anything happened recently, any significant event or changes in your life?"

"Funny you should mention that . . ."

By the time I'd finished telling him about Jonno being HIV-positive, the hour was up. Just as well. I had nothing more to say, and O'Shaughnessy had no words of comfort or counsel to offer. There *were* no words of comfort or counsel to offer. The next storm was already coming. I had reentered the blizzard.

As I stood to leave, I said, "I think I now understand the symbolism of the Bogong High Plains in my dreams."

"What's that?"

"They're a rendezvous."

"A rendezvous?"

"I'm going there to meet someone. And, all this time, he's been waiting for me." I headed for the door.

"I thought you'd like to know . . ." said O'Shaughnessy. I turned back to him. "I'm no longer bored."

"Oh. Um . . . good. Neither am I."

It was probably unrealistic on my part to hope that all the clients and all the counselors would fail to show up for counseling and testing that evening. I so very much did not want to talk with anyone. I scaled the hope down to more realistic dimensions: hoping that John wouldn't make it in for his shift. I didn't want to face him, knowing what I now knew. But that, too, wasn't realistic. John was the most reliable member on the team. If the apocalypse arrived and the end of the world was imminent, he'd no doubt leave a phone message. *I'll be there, though maybe a little late.*

So, instead I hoped I'd be run over by a TriMet bus.

All the counselors showed up that evening, including John (I should have spent more time crossing streets in front of buses), and I hunkered down for the night. It was busy, which helped keep me focused on what needed to be done. As we wrapped up at eight o'clock, all the counselors seemed eager to be off—all except John who held back, stacking the chairs, putting away the uneaten pizza in the refrigerator. He seemed like he wanted to talk. *Damn! Damn! Damn!* Had Jonno told him?

I stood at the filing cabinet, double-checking the evening's files before locking them away.

"Are you feeling all right?" he asked. "You don't look too well."

"I'm fine. Maybe coming down with a cold."

"Bad timing. Right before your presentation in DC."

"Yeah," I said, not meeting his eyes. "Is there ever a good time for a cold?"

"No, I suppose not. All ready for the conference?"

"Yes. We're meeting at the airport at six in the morning."

"Who all's going?"

"Arthur will present with me, representing the county in our non-profit/health department partnership. And Chad and Lionel will be presenting a workshop on their outreach programs."

I continued avoiding his eyes as I spoke, concentrating intensely on reviewing each folder to make sure that it was complete, trying to communicate in a non-communicative way how busy I was. *Busy, busy, busy. Oh, look how busy I am. Far too busy to talk.* I was almost finished with the folders, whereupon I'd need to find something else to be very busy with, when John said, "Last weekend . . . oh, thanks again for helping cut back the blackberries."

"Sure. Happy to do it."

"Last weekend, it kind of sounded like you didn't want Jonno to meet your mother."

I stopped, mentally sighed. "It's . . . complicated."

"Most parent-child relationships are."

I filed the last folder, then closed and locked the cabinet. "Mom would be polite. She would be *nice* to Jonno. But, trust me, the time would not be enjoyable like it is with you and Maggie. At best, it would be endurable."

John considered this. "Well, you have to start somewhere." I didn't respond, so he continued. "My father's and my relationship was . . .

377

complicated, too. We were never able to talk, never able to express, well, much to each other. I wish he was still alive. After my experience here on the team, and what I've learned with Jonno, I would have tried to reach out to him. But I don't have that chance now, so I'll never know what might have happened."

"That's too bad," I murmured.

"I think I'd be more understanding of him now, being a father myself. When you realize where you've failed as a parent, where your own fears got in the way of being the perfect father you wanted to be, well, then you can only hope that your child will forgive you and give you a second chance."

He pulled on his coat. "You taught me it was necessary to step out of my comfort zone so I could have a new relationship with my son. It probably also works in reverse, where the child might step out of his comfort zone to find a new relationship with his mother."

I gave him a half smile. "It probably does." Then I felt the smile fade. "But as for Jonno meeting my mother, it might be a moot point anyway."

"Oh?"

"He may have told you, we've decided to cool things for a while."

By the look on John's face clearly Jonno hadn't told him.

"I'm sorry to hear that." He looked genuinely sorry. "No, Jonno didn't mention it. But he's always been a private boy. Never shared his feelings much."

There was an excruciating silence between us. Then he said, "But I will say, and Maggie can vouch for this, over these last two months he's been happier than at any time since he was a child. I'm really sorry." They weren't just words. He looked anguished.

"It's not over between us," I said for his benefit. "We're not necessarily ending the relationship. I just . . . I just need some time to think about it."

"Because he's HIV-positive."

I met his eyes, but said nothing. It hadn't been a question.

"After volunteering here for almost a year, I was pretty sure."

Another awkward silence. "Does Maggie know?"

"No. I'll wait until Jonno's ready to tell us."

"I'm sorry, John. I'm so very, very sorry." For a moment I thought I was going to throw up, or worse, burst into tears.

"I know you've been through a lot with your partner in Australia. And I can understand why you wouldn't want to go through it again."

I remained standing at the filing cabinet, now holding on to it for support.

He slipped on his gloves. "Don't worry about Jonno. He'll be fine. He has a strong inner core."

I nodded silently, not meeting his eyes because of the tears in mine.

"And when the time comes . . . well, I failed my son once. It won't happen again." He patted me on the shoulder. "Have a good conference. Do us proud." And he left for the elevator.

I finished putting the clinic items away and then went into the prevention team room where Andie was working late. "You're still here?" I asked.

"Yeah. Finishing up the materials for you to take to the conference."

I picked up the color overhead transparencies she'd made of our epidemiological data from the testing program. "These are beautiful, Andie, thank you."

"And here are the handouts for your presentation."

I took them. "What would we do without you?"

"*You* would do just fine," she said. "But Chad and Lionel would be hopelessly lost." She handed me another stack of papers. "They were so excited to go to the conference they forgot to take their handouts. Would you get these to them?"

"Of course."

She shook her head like the mother of eight-year-old boys. "Those two, they'd forget their heads and their dicks if they weren't screwed on."

"Well, maybe their heads anyway," I said, placing the additional handouts into my briefcase. "Can I bring you anything from DC?"

"A boyfriend?"

"I'll see what I can do."

Then she said, "Hey, I know you're going through a rough time. There're no secrets around this place. I wanted to cheer you up, so I got you a room by yourself at the conference. I know you like your privacy."

"How'd you manage that? I thought we were required to double up to save money."

"I made reservations for you and Chad to share a room. After the first night, you'll never see him the rest of the conference and have the room to yourself."

I chuckled and hugged her. "Thanks, Andie."

She sighed. "I wish I could get even a tenth of the action he does."

In spite of Andie's thoughtfulness, I arrived home weary, still feeling sick. I hadn't eaten that day but had no appetite. The house was cold. I turned on the heat and kept my coat on as I waited for the chill to ease. The house felt warmer when Jonno stayed here. Even when he was in LA, it had felt warmer. Now it was as cold as a tomb, as empty as an abandoned warehouse. Yes, I was projecting myself onto my house. *I was as cold as a tomb, I was as empty as an abandoned warehouse.* I hadn't studied Gestalt therapy for nothing.

I wanted to call him. Had wanted to call him Sunday night, just to make sure he was all right when he returned to LA. Wanted to call him Monday night but conveniently fell asleep. John was right. I didn't want to go through again what I'd gone through with Gray. I still hadn't recovered. Why put myself through this all over again?

Because you love him.

I'm not sure that's enough.

Because you feel alive when you're with him.

I felt alive with Gray, too. That can change. Everything can change.

Well, I think we've chewed this over enough for the past two days. What's most important to you right now?

I threw my coat over a chair. I needed to know how Jonno was.

"Hello?" His voice sounded tentative.

"Hey. It's me."

"Hey."

"Look, I'm sorry I didn't handle the news better this weekend."

"It's kind of tough news to handle." He didn't sound angry, didn't sound hurt or defensive. John had been right about his youngest son. Jonno had a solid inner core.

"I was in shock, and . . . well . . . it's just that . . ."

"I know," he said.

Which was good to hear since I didn't have a clue what I was going to say.

"How are you doing?" I asked.

"It's been a rough couple of days."

"Yeah. Here, too."

"I should have told you before it got this far. I know what the future holds for me. I may have another three or four years, and they won't be very good years. I can't ask you—I can't ask anyone—to share such a life." He paused. "Just so you know, if the situation was reversed, I'm not sure I could go ahead with our relationship. I *will* understand."

He thinks I've already decided. *Have I? Could be.* I'm usually the last to know in these matters.

"I just need some time to think about all this," I said. *I've been lost in a blizzard a long time, you see. And a bigger storm is heading toward me. And I don't think I'll survive it.*

"So, here's the deal," he said. "I won't call or write until I hear from you. I won't come up until you say to come. And if that never happens, then I'll remember these past two months as something . . . miraculous. And I'll always be grateful for this time we had together."

I felt a wave of relief. Didn't know what to say. No, that's not true. I wanted to say, *I love you,* but couldn't. Didn't want to mislead him, or give him false hope, or send mixed messages. And since I was so mixed up, what other messages could I send? So instead I said, "I really like you, Jonno. I mean, *really*. I haven't felt like this toward anyone in a very long time."

"That's good to hear," he said. "And you know how I feel about you."

"I know." It was time to end the call, though I didn't want to. "Your father was right. You have a solid inner core."

"Huh. He said that?"

"Yeah. He said that."

"Nice to hear."

"Well, I better go. I've got an early flight and still need to pack."

"Right. Thanks for the call."

"Sure." I held the receiver a moment longer, then blurted out, "Jonno, I—"

The phone clicked off.

We were a hit at the national HIV/AIDS conference in Washington, DC. On Thursday morning, Arthur and I presented on our pilot testing project and were asked to repeat our presentation the next morning for those who had missed it. Then, following lunch, we participated in a panel discussion on taking HIV testing to target populations. Chad and Lionel conducted a workshop on their innovative outreach methods that was also well attended. As Andie had foretold almost a year ago, our Oregon team were pioneers. We regretted Steve couldn't be there with us. As manager of our HIV prevention programs, he deserved much of the credit. But after coming out of the hospital, he'd continued to lose weight and was unable to overcome his deep bronchial cough, finally deciding he didn't have the energy for a three-day conference.

It was Friday afternoon that I was paged and directed to a house phone in the lobby. It was Sandy. She was calling from Providence Hospital. My heart sank at the news. In her best calm, let's-not-get-hysterical voice, she said, "You should know, it's not looking good." Then her voice broke with a sob.

I changed my reservation for the next flight out.

I've been here before: walking down the corridor of some hospital, bracing myself for what I know is coming, pacing myself for what I know will be required. I find Sandy in the waiting room and ask, "How is he?" This sense of déjà vu, that I've been here before, felt this before, known all this before, and am living it again. I keep living it over and over. But why? What is it I'm not getting?

There are others in the room this time. A blind woman sits in the chair across from me, rosary beads passing through her fingers, lips moving in silent prayer; a folded white cane protrudes from the woven bag next to her. A young policeman sits against one of the walls, holding a paper cup of coffee and staring at the floor. He seems to be waiting for something to happen. A skinny youth in a hooded sweatshirt slouches in a chair, watching the television overhead, while a hospital employee wipes down the plastic chairs. Somali, maybe Sudanese, wearing a hijab with her light-blue scrubs.

Finishing her prayers, the blind woman slips the rosary beads into her pocket and reaches for the cane. It clatters to the floor, and she bends, hands outstretched.

"Here, let me get it for you." I pick up the cane, placing it in her hand.

She smiles, staring past me. "Gracias."

"May I ask how your son is doing?"

Her smile turns grateful. *"The doctors, they say he will live, thanks be to God."* She looks as tired as I feel, but her smile is radiant.

"I'm happy for you and your son."

"Thank you. I am finally at peace. I can leave now."

"Vaya con Dios," I tell her.

She asks, *"And your friend?"*

"No word yet."

She removes the beads from her pocket, holding them out to me.

"Please, take these. They will help."

My own exhaustion and sadness come washing over me, like a final wave. I shake my head, forgetting she can't see. *"No, you keep them. I have no one to pray to."*

Her face mirrors my sadness. *"Then I will pray for your friend."*

"Yes, please pray for him."

"What is his name?"

His name? I start to answer and, with alarm, find that I don't remember. My words stumble, my thoughts a jumble. "I . . . I can't remember his name." Not only that, I can't remember what hospital I'm in, or even which city. There've been so many, and I've gone without sleep for so long. I want to tell her there were thirty-one—no, thirty-three. He's number thirty-four, and I can't remember his name. I begin to panic. I can't remember any of their names!

"I can't remember!"

The police officer looks up from his coffee. The youth twists and cranes his neck around to see who's shouting. The cleaning woman stands silent, rag in her rubber-gloved hand, watching. I'm hyperventilating. What's happening to me? Am I having some kind of stroke, or becoming demented like Jake? I know Bill Clinton is president, but that's not really helpful right now. I jump to my feet, look crazily around the room, and shout again, "I can't remember!"

The police officer sets down his cup, and slowly stands, keeping his eyes on me.

The blind woman reaches out her hand. *"It's all right,"* she says. *"It's all right."*

I'm yammering. I know I'm incoherent even to myself. "No, no, you don't understand," I tell her. "There were thirty-one, and then thirty-three, and now there're three hundred thousand. It's a sea of blood. And one of them was my partner. Ten years my partner. He was Australian, you see, and I can't . . . I can't remember his name." I cover my face and begin crying. "I can't remember any of their names."

"Sh-sh." She reaches her hand, finds my wrist, and pulls me down into the chair as she sits in hers. I continue weeping. "Can't remember.

385

I can't remember any of their names . . ."

"Sh-sh," she says tenderly, as if quieting a small child, "*You don't need to remember their names to pray for them. God knows their names. They are written there on your heart. We will pray together, yes?*"

"*I haven't prayed for many years. I don't remember how.*"

"*I will pray for both of us.*"

She closes her eyes and once again caresses the rosary beads. One bead. Then another. And another. Bead after bead after bead, slowly moving through her fingers, and as I watch, my breathing begins to relax. Another bead . . .

Wystan.

Yes! I remember Wystan! He helped found the Victorian AIDS Council, one of several who—

Another bead.

Trevor.

Poor little Trevor, forsaken by his parents, forgotten by his god, dying alone in that hospital without their love, without anybody's love.

Silently weeping, I watch the beads continue passing through her fingers.

Barry. Barry of Barongarook, beautiful boy. So much like Tyler.

Bead by bead, their names come back to me, like memories from childhood, or from another life: *David . . . Giles . . . Nicholas . . . Gray*—

My partner's name was Grayson! He was a barrister. We lived together in Melbourne, in the suburb of St. Kilda, and he loved the Bogong High Plains; they were sacred to him, you see . . .

The beads keep moving through her fingers.

Cal. A saint of this epidemic. His ashes were sent back to Tulsa.

I'm growing sleepy.

Jerald. An incorrigible sinner. And saint, in spite of himself.

My eyelids becoming heavy. So long since I slept . . . so long . . . and still miles to go before I sleep.

Robert Frost, says Gray. "*Stopping by Woods on a Snowy Evening.*"

Yes. Frost. But he offers no poem back. Of course not. How could he? He died over a year ago. I feel myself drifting away . . .

Miles to go before I sleep.

I so want to sleep. Finally, just to sleep, only to sleep. Perchance to dream . . . .

When I next raise my head, I find a man sitting across from me, in the same chair the blind woman had occupied. The waiting room is otherwise empty. The police officer is gone; the young man in the dark sweatshirt and hood is gone, the television turned off; the cleaning lady is gone, *Bon Appetit!* magazines neatly stacked again on the table. The man sits watching me as if he's been waiting for me to wake up. Is he from the hospital? Is he security? Did I make a scene when I freaked out? He's dressed in a dark suit with white shirt, collar unbuttoned, no tie, suggesting an informal formality. Maybe a doctor? A psychiatrist? Tall and thin with a pale white face, he looks neither old nor young. And vaguely familiar.

I pull myself up in the chair, offering a polite smile. "I must have fallen asleep."

"It happens," he says. "Especially on these long vigils."

"You're waiting for someone, too?"

"Yes."

Though in a hospital waiting room, and waiting for someone, he doesn't appear very anxious or concerned. Actually, he looks unflappable, as if nothing ever flapped him. Maybe he's a hospital administrator. Have I spent too much time here? I don't know; are there time limits for waiting rooms in Oregon? He sits there, legs casually crossed, like he has all the time in the world. He hasn't stopped gazing at me, which I find a little unsettling.

"There was a kind woman here," I say, "sitting where you're sitting now."

"She's no longer here," he says.

"No. No, it appears she isn't." He offers no further comment, so I add, "Her son was shot, but he's going to live."

"For now."

387

"Yes, of course," I mumble. "For now."

He continues to look at me as if we know each other and he expects me to remember him. If so, I don't.

"I'm sorry. Do I know you?"

"Oh, yes."

Okay, now it's getting a little creepy. I'm feeling confused, disoriented. "Sorry. I'm normally pretty good with remembering names and faces. Where have we met?"

"Many places. Many times."

And suddenly I know who he is, and I shudder. I first saw him in the hospital room, standing in the shadows as he watched my father weep over his son, sleeping off his drug overdose. He was in Gray's hospital room, too, that last night we were together. I realize he's been with me in every waiting room, at every vigil.

I remember whose vigil I'm keeping and suddenly feel fear. "What are you doing here?" I ask.

"Like you. Waiting. We are in a waiting room."

"Is it his time?"

"I don't know. I'm waiting to see myself."

"*You* don't know?"

"I actually have very little to say in these matters. I come when I'm summoned."

"When you're summoned? I thought it was *you* who summoned."

"A common error."

I'm finding it difficult to organize my thoughts. "Then who summons you? God? Fate? Um, Dr. Kevorkian?"

"You wouldn't believe me if I told you."

"Try me."

"*He* summoned me."

"He? You mean . . ."

"I never come uninvited. Each person determines his or her own time. I only come when I'm called."

"What about me? There was a time I summoned. I would have paid!"

"Yes, you've always been a little in love with death. I suppose I should be flattered."

Always a little in love with death?

I recognize it from Eugene O'Neill's *Long Day's Journey into Night.* "I was eighteen and I 'summoned' you—desperately."

"Part of you did. The ego in pain. But that's not who I listen to."

"Then who?"

"Within each of you there is an essential core of your being."

"You mean the soul?"

"What is *soul?*"

"I was hoping you might know."

He sighs. "Words, words, words. There is a higher identity, or a deeper knowing—the spatial dimension doesn't really apply here, does it?—that part that transcends the self, that is eternal and unbounded. Call it *soul* if you wish."

"You're telling me that all the people who die every day are actually calling you to take them?"

"Yes."

"Then why do they fight to live and fear death so?"

"That lesser part—the ego, the time-based self-consciousness—doesn't understand. It thinks it's all there is. So, of course, it fears its annihilation."

"But some people die pretty horrible deaths."

"Each chooses how he or she wishes to live, and how to die."

"Cancer, gas ovens, torture? AIDS?"

"Yes."

"But . . . why?"

"As Keats wrote, 'The world is a vale of soul-making.'"

Keats? Who'd have thought Death was so well read? I add, "It's also a vale of tears, as the Psalmist wrote."

"The two are frequently found together."

I'm growing exasperated, perplexed by his statements. "I don't understand."

"Doesn't matter."

"But it does. To some of us, it's all that matters."

"Oh, dear. You're one of the philosophical ones."

"Why 'Oh, dear'?"

"Your type never comes along peacefully. The Christian is all excited to finally meet Jesus in person and get his autograph; the Muslim just wants the seventy virgins promised him; the atheist is busy rethinking his position. But the philosophical ones, they want to *understand*. They need to *know*. I suppose it's to be expected. Life was a perplexing puzzle for them. Why should death be any different?"

"I think it's only human to want to know the truth."

"For some maybe, but I doubt most. This age in particular is more concerned with glittering trinkets than truth, with gadgets and gizmos, the next big thing to dazzle, delight and distract."

I also wouldn't have expected Death to be so alliterative. "Distract? From what?"

He smiles. "Why, from me, of course. It's something you learn as a child. How to avoid thinking of your mortality."

From out of nowhere, an image bubbles up from my childhood. "Darby O'Gill," I murmur.

For the first time, he appears quizzical. "Sorry?"

"The movie. *Darby O'Gill and the Little People*. It was the first time I ever thought about death."

"Ah, yes, Disney fluff. I myself prefer the films of Ingmar Bergman."

"No, actually, it was very profound for an eight-year-old. When old Darby is standing in the rain, watching Death's coach descend from the night sky for his daughter, it gave me chills. But it wasn't fear. I wasn't really scared. Something else was happening."

He sits quietly, studying me.

"Death's coach arrives drawn by its fiery steeds, and Darby asks that he be taken instead of his daughter. And his wish is granted. He's allowed to enter the coach in her place."

"I think I see where this conversation is heading, and it's not an option."

"You could take me instead. I'm ready. As you say, I think I've always been ready."

He shakes his head. "Sorry. I'm afraid there are no substitutions in my line of work."

"What, Hollywood could manage it and you can't? I'm disappointed."

"Well, it was a Disney film, so it had to have a happy ending. Unlike life."

"Not necessarily. Ever see *Old Yeller?* I was six and cried for weeks after watching it. Never wanted a dog after that. Not sure I could handle the loss of something I loved so much."

O'Shaughnessy sits in his wheelchair, repeating slowly as he looks at me, "You feared you couldn't handle the loss of something you loved so much."

Embarrassed, I mumble, "Okay, okay, so I can connect the dots, too."

"Is that why it took me so long to battle through your emotional defenses?" asks Gray. "Because you'd feared losing a dog?" We're staring into the campfire, lost in the vast silence of the high plains.

I whisper to the flames, "You were so much more to me than a dog."

The night carries a chill as we sit next to each other, seeking the fire's flickering warmth and light, just the two of us, surrounded by an infinite darkness.

"Would you rather we'd never have met, so you wouldn't be feeling the pain of your loss now?" he asks.

I turn to him. "What is that, a trick question?"

"Just wondering."

I turn back to the fire, fighting the words coming up from within. "You left me."

"I didn't *leave* you. I died. There's a difference."

"Semantics."

The flames leap, lap the night air, reach for their moment of brilliance, and extinction.

"I know why you wouldn't dance with me that night," he says. "And it had nothing to do with a lack of rhythm."

"You left me. And I don't mean died."

"No," he says. "It was a slip, a mistake on my part, a momentary lapse in judgment when I went with that guy in Sydney. There was no love involved. Not what I felt . . . not what I *feel* for you."

I'm fighting back tears as I continue staring into the fire. "No, I don't wish we'd never met. But it does hurt. Each day it hurts all over again. It never stops hurting."

Then comes a sudden realization. I turn to the man sitting in the chair across from me. "This is all a dream, isn't it? I'm dreaming."

He smiles sympathetically— "You have no idea." Then glances at the clock. "It's time."

I feel a sudden panic as he stands. "Wait! I don't want him to die," I say. "Not yet. We've got unfinished business."

"It's not your call."

"I know. I just thought you might be interested in my opinion."

He says with a sudden and surprising tenderness, "You have your own destiny to follow. Try not to meddle in the destinies of others. They know why they've come this way. You don't."

He looks at the nurse entering the waiting room, and says, "You have one last vigil to keep."

I open my eyes and see the nurse in the doorway.

"I was told you can see him now," she says.

Glancing around the empty waiting room, I turn back to her. "Oh, thank you," then I quickly get up and follow her down the hallway. It's strangely quiet, as if we're caught in a vacuum. We meet the cleaning woman, pushing her cart in the opposite direction. Rail-thin, midnight skin, chiseled cheekbones protruding from her face, she smiles shyly at me, bobbing her head. I want to tell the nurse: *See, the cleaning woman is here!* But I'm no longer sure where "here" is.

The nurse stops before a door. "You won't have much time, I'm afraid."

"I understand. Thank you again for your help." I enter the dimly lit room. There's no light coming through the window; it must still be night. A sole bed lamp over the pillow highlights Gray's pale, emaciated face. By this time his handsome features had turned gaunt, a skeletal mask. He's hardly recognizable as he sleeps, cadaverous white, mouth open, breathing ragged. And sitting next to his bed is . . .

Me.

I, too, am asleep, chin on my chest, arms crossed, softly breathing. It was a Thursday night, I remember—his last Thursday night. Not yet the end, but close. In those final days he was in and out of consciousness, mostly out, due to the meds they administered for the pain. His family still visited then. I always stepped out of the room so they could be with him in private, but for these last days I alone was keeping the vigil. There comes a point when family and friends no longer see the reason for being here. For them, their loved one has already departed. Near the end, he was at times delusional, other times surprisingly clear and awake. I wanted to be there for every last minute we could share his clarity.

He's mumbling and staring straight ahead when I open my eyes. I take his hand. "Here. I'm right here, Gray."

His lips are moving silently as he keeps looking across the room. "What do you need? Tell me."

His head lolls over, but he has a far-off look, even as he stares directly at me.

"Do you want some water?"

I bring the plastic cup to his face and bend the straw to his lips, but he doesn't respond, so I return it to the bedside table and take his hand again. "I'm here, Gray," I say softly. His hand is ice cold. I try warming it with both of mine, blow my breath on it. His eyes appear luminous, shining large in the emaciated face. He keeps staring at the opposite wall. I sense another's presence in the room with us. I know who it is, but I've no time for him now. I can focus only on Gray. He whispers my name.

"I'm here," I say. "I'm right here."

"I see him," he whispers.

"Who? Who do you see?"

"It's so beautiful out here."

I can't suppress a shiver. I know where he is. And I know what it means, and I'm suddenly scared. Tears come to my eyes. I grip his hand more tightly. "Yes. Yes, it is," I say. "It's . . . so beautiful out here."

"He's come to take me home," Gray whispers, smiling, like a small boy lost on the plains who's spotted his rescuer and knows he will now be safe.

I get up, close the door, and return to the bed, taking his hand again.

"It's okay, Gray. Go to him." He's appearing blurry through my tears. "You're free. Don't look back. Let him take you home. You're taking my heart with you." A peace seems to be shining from him, as from some inner light. "I love you, Gray."

I whisper it, over and over, gripping his hand as he slips back into unconsciousness, wanting to say something more, to reassure him, to tell him I'll always love him. His breathing slows, less ragged now, coming more easily. No longer struggling.

"I love you," I say one last time, grateful that I'd told him before while he was still conscious. Now, I was saying it for myself.

He never regained consciousness. Ten hours later it was over. I remained with him through those final hours, but sensed he had departed and that I was now keeping vigil over a body abandoned. Whatever was Gray was no longer with me. He was somewhere on the high plains, happy again, returning to his aboriginal roots where the sacred was there waiting for him.

"He just stopped breathing," I tell O'Shaughnessy. "When it happened, there was this numbness in me. No tears. Not even sadness really. Just . . . numb. As if my spirit had departed with him and there were now *two* lifeless bodies in that hospital room." I glance at the clock in O'Shaughnessy's office. "Time's up," I say.

"Let's finish this."

I sigh. "It's finished."

It was maybe our seventh session together, so probably August.

O'Shaughnessy listened as I recounted those final hours in a voice flat and monotone.

"I collected the few things of his we'd brought to the hospital and returned to our house in St. Kilda. I was so tired when I got there but couldn't sleep. And there was so much to do. I'd made lists for when this moment came. *Contact his brother. Notify the mortuary. Alert the phone tree to get the word out to our network of friends.* But I could only stare at the lists. They all seemed impossible tasks. They'd have to wait until the next day. I went into his study and took a card from his desk to write to my mother and father, but could manage only two sentences:

My 'friend' is dead.
I am coming home.

"And so, after making final arrangements—selling our house, wrapping up my work, finalizing his will—I came home. But I felt something was missing."

"Something was," says O'Shaughnessy. "You'd just lost your life partner."

"No. I mean, it felt like something was missing *in me.*"

"Which is a common grief reaction. As you know."

"I know. But I'm not speaking metaphorically. It felt like something *literally* was missing in me. People noticed. They commented. At first, they thought it was because I was HIV-positive like Gray. I wanted to tell them, 'I'm not dying. I'm already dead.'"

We're in Charles's obsessively neat cubicle, where I've come to sign on for another tour of duty. He says brightly, "We have just the position for you."

"I'm not interested in a position. I just came to volunteer—"

Despite my protests, he takes me to another room. It's bare, except for an empty coffin.

"We've been trying to fill it for months," he says. "Go ahead, give it a try."

Admittedly, the coffin is surprisingly comfortable, even cozy as I

395

settle into it. Personally, I favor cremation, but this will be okay, too. Very snug, not claustrophobic as one might expect. More like a cradle. Or a womb. I lie very still as a steady stream of mourners pass by the coffin, hear them talking above me as they stop, gaze down, some appearing sad, some puzzled: "I didn't know it was this serious," some appearing bored. Who invited them to my funeral service anyway? Jerald and Steve are speaking softly. "I always knew he'd die alone," says Jerald. "It's how he lived. Even back in high school."

"Well, you ran in different circles," says Steve.

Jerald turns to him. "I didn't know he had a circle."

"It was a very small circle, I hear."

They move on. More people come, stop, sniffle, gaze, leave. Some look familiar but I can't place them, whether from here, or maybe from my life in Melbourne. I hope they signed the guest book. The line goes on and on. After a time, it gets tedious. I want to scratch my nose but that could be awkward and upset a few people since I'm dead. I should have requested a closed casket. Then I smell the acrid stench of cigarette smoke. How dare someone smoke at my memorial service! Crinkling my nose, I open my eyes to find Christine looking down at me while puffing on her cigarette.

"Is that really how you want to spend your life," she says, "lying there in a coffin?"

"Go away, Christine. Can't you see I'm dead?"

"I'm just wondering how they were able to tell."

Was this woman intentionally placed on earth to torment me?

"Like with my husband Maurice . . ." *Oh, God, here we go again with Maurice.* "He was dead three days before we noticed. It was a terrible shock to everyone."

"Please, just let me rest in peace, okay?"

"If that's what you want. But like I tell my son Martin—"

"Would someone please remove this woman from my memorial service!" I shout. "And don't let her hoodwink you with that bogus story about her grandparents dying in the Holocaust. They both lived into their nineties in Hoboken." She leaves; the air clears again; I relax.

Only one person now remaining in the room. An old aboriginal woman, hair like a Cabbage Patch doll's, all gray-black and frizzy, puffing on a pipe.

"I remember you," I say. "Aren't you Black Mary? Arnold told me the story."

She continues studying me, shaking her head, and not exactly in a sympathetic way.

"But this can't be right. I left Australia over a year ago and returned to the States. What are you doing here?"

She removes her pipe, her voice ancient as the hills. "You brought back only your body."

"Who's she?" asks O'Shaughnessy.

I'm distracted by his question and hurriedly explain, "She was an old aboriginal woman who lived in the early part of the twentieth century. She . . . saw things in her pipe smoke."

"Why did she say you brought back only your body?"

"No, she was talking about someone else. A skier named Cleve Cole. He became lost in a blizzard and died on the Bogong High Plains in 1936. Supposedly, she said the search party brought back only his body. Local lore says his spirit is still wandering—" I stop, stunned by the sudden realization. "Oh, my God."

"What?" asks O'Shaughnessy.

I sit up in the coffin. It's in the middle of the hospital waiting room, the room still empty except for the man lounging in the chair. He notes the coffin. "A bit premature, isn't it?"

Still dazed, I turn to him. "When I returned from Australia, I brought back only my body."

He looks pleased. "Good. Then I think you're ready."

"Ready?"

He stands. "Come, I will show you who you've been searching for in your dreams this past year."

It's dark outside the hospital. Black as night. Blacker. The blackness of infinite space. I can't make out anything, but smell a whiff of smoke on the wind, not the sweet scent of pine or fir as in the Pacific

Northwest—a more astringent smell, and I ask, "Is this Hades or Hell?"

"Neither. But it is Down Under."

Australia? "I can't see anything."

"Let your eyes adjust to the light."

"What light?"

"Look up."

Stars. Billions of stars around us. We're suspended in space. As my eyes adjust to the astral light, I discern a vast, flat landscape with stars arcing over it.

I feel disoriented. "Is this the present? Or the past?"

"Guess again," he says.

I breathe out. "The Dreamtime."

We're standing on some ridge, an immense empty expanse stretching before us. A chilly breeze blows across the high plains. I can now identify the scent: the caustic, alkaline smell of sage and smoke, pungent yet welcome in its fragrant familiarity. Then I see it: in the distance, a bright light—small, alone, like a single sun amid the infinite blackness of space. A campfire. No, larger. A bonfire. There's a car parked nearby. Someone is moving around the fire.

"I know this place," I whisper.

"You remember?"

"Yes. Three weeks after Gray died. I came back here by myself with his ashes."

We watch the figure's movement around the fire, circling and circling, a naked writhing silhouette against the flames, leaping, jumping, turning and twirling around and around the fire. I can hear music, faint from this distance, its pounding, strident beat as I watch the figure dance.

"He was right," I murmur. "He has absolutely no sense of rhythm." It was me and, strangely, not me. Like someone I once knew, but not well.

"You know what the old aborigine woman meant."

"I know what she meant."

"Then you know why you wanted to return here."

I turn to him. "Me? I thought I was just tagging along with you."

"It's your dream," he says. "It's always been your dream."

I had no response to that. Heck, for all I knew, I could be a butterfly.

"And now you know who you have been searching for in your dreams."

"Yes."

The two of us continue watching the figure dancing to Gondwanaland's loud, percussive beat, around and around the fire, the music wafting across the plains toward us in waves—

It suddenly stops.

Yet the figure continues circling the fire, now a heap of glowing embers, oblivious to the fact that the music has ended. Until he notices. We see him collapse to the ground, lying in the dirt, hear him howling like an animal in pain. I feel my heart breaking all over again. I'm feeling sympathy, as for any sentient being in pain, yet also strangely detached. Not indifferent, but . . . detached, the sympathy not just for this one lying next to the fire, but for all suffering humanity. How unnecessary, I think. The pain, the sorrow, it's real, yet . . . unnecessary. Like a young child crying because her favorite doll is broken. Her pain is genuine. You want to hold and comfort her, want her to understand it's really not that important, this broken toy, while also knowing she can't understand that. Not yet. Maybe years from now she'll remember and laugh about it, about being so distraught over, what? A broken doll? But for now, it means everything to her. So, you comfort and console her, for her tears and sorrow are real.

"They don't understand, do they?" I say.

The man watches with the same detached compassion. "No, not really. They're too caught up in their joys and their sadness, in their longings and their losses, and so, they suffer because they don't understand."

"That sounds very Buddhist."

"Oh, sorry. I didn't mean it to be. I try to remain nonpartisan in these matters."

The crying continues drifting toward us on the night's breeze. I want to help him. Want to help all humanity from their suffering, want to save all little children from the sorrow of their broken toys and all adults from the sadness of their broken lives. And wonder: Is this true compassion, or am I just being seriously codependent?

The man says, "It's time for me to go. You no longer need me."

I turn back to him. "You're not as I expected."

"Oh? What did you expect? Something horrific? Ghoulish? Maybe wearing a black robe and carrying a scythe?" He chuckles.

"No. I guess I expected something . . . well, heartless. Without feelings."

His smile turns gentle. "No, that is not me."

I feel strangely warm toward him, as if we've always known each other, as if we've been companions on numerous journeys before. "Will I see you again?"

His smile broadens. "Oh, you can count on that."

"Then I will greet you as a friend."

A fresh wind blows across the desolate night country as I look back to the campsite. The naked figure is now lying quiet next to the glowing embers, staring up at the stars. When I returned to the States, I brought back only my body. It was now time to reclaim what I had left in Australia.

There comes a hesitant voice. "Sir?"

Someone is gently nudging me on the shoulder. "Excuse me, sir?"

I rouse myself to find a little candy striper, a teenage girl dressed in her crisp pink uniform, bending over me, her hand still on my shoulder. Seeing my eyes open, she removes it.

"Oh, hello, yes?"

"Sorry to wake you, but the nurse asked me to come and get you."

I turn to the plate-glass windows. It's light outside. Not really sunlight, this being the Pacific Northwest in winter. But the grayness is brighter.

"If you'll come with me?"

"Thanks." I grab my jacket from the chair next to me and begin following her out of the room. Several people are sitting in there. It looks different with people and with daylight coming through the windows. I gaze around the space one last time with an odd and surprising feeling of, what? Sadness? Maybe regret, mixed with gratitude. Maybe like what a prisoner feels leaving his cell that's been his home for many years, or astronauts leaving the space station that's supported them over the past year. Or perhaps as the butterfly takes leave of its cocoon.

Chapter Fifty

All Things Mortal

[Portland, Oregon, February 25, 1995]

I stopped at the newspaper stand as I came out of the hospital to read the morning headline: PRIMARY WITNESS IN FBI INVESTI-GATION SHOT, IN CRITICAL CONDITION, and thought, *Update: Shot, but no longer in critical condition.*

At least no more critical than any of the rest of us.

The candy striper had escorted me to a doctor at the nurses' station, a young man in his late twenties writing in a chart who appeared to be working on fewer hours of sleep than I was. He looked up as we approached. "Good morning. I'm happy to report your friend has regained consciousness and is recovering from surgery."

"That's wonderful news. Thank you. May I see him?"

"Yes, but, please, only for five minutes. He's very weak and needs to sleep."

"I understand. Five minutes will be fine. I just need for him to know I'm here. Thanks again."

The girl walked me down another hallway to a room where a police officer stood guard outside the door. He requested my ID and checked for my name on his clipboard, then asked me to raise my arms and patted me down. "Sorry, but it's a requirement."

"Of course. No problem."

"The doctor said you could see the patient for five minutes."

"Thank you. I understand."

He opened the door to the dimly lit room. Leo lay in its one bed, IV drips on either side of him. He turned his head and smiled sleepily when he saw me, his voice dry and raspy. "They said a friend spent all night in the waiting room. I knew it had to be you."

The police officer closed the door and I went to his bedside. "Sandy was here in the afternoon and evening. I sent her home around ten."

"Sorry you had to spend the night alone."

I sat next to his bed, thinking of this long night's strange passage. "I was never alone."

He looked wan and exhausted, and I smiled.

"I'm so glad you made it. I didn't want you to die with how things were left between us."

"Me, too."

"We'll talk later."

"I was hoping we might."

But in that moment, I realized that I had already made peace with Leo, that I'd made peace with a lot during the night. As Father Paul warned, it would be an uncomfortable peace, but a peace I could live with.

He asked for some water, and I got the cup and put the straw to his mouth. After he drank, he told me how he'd been shot: Sandy had picked him up from jail Friday morning and driven him to his apartment. He'd gone out early in the afternoon to purchase groceries. It had been a drive-by shooting. Everyone suspected bad apples.

As he recounted the experience, he looked remarkably serene, even for Leo. He looked . . . at peace.

When he finished, I said, "You're different. I've never seen you this way before. What, are you channeling Krishnamurti?"

He smiled. "No. I had a dream. I had the most wonderful dream. So wonderful I never wanted to wake up."

I set the plastic cup aside and leaned forward in the chair. "Like to tell me about it?"

"I dreamt that I woke up, and my mother was here. Sitting where you're sitting, saying the rosary for me like she did when I was a young child . . ."

I felt a chill slide down my back—by now I was rather used to it—as if the mundane tapestry of life had been peeled back to reveal the intricate stitching and patterns of fate on its underside. Leo's face was glowing. "I remembered the sound of her voice. Remembered the feeling of her lips kissing my hair, how it calmed me." He turned to me. "My mother used to hold me as she said the rosary, when I was very young and before she went away. And in the dream . . ." he swallowed, "in the dream she said she'd never wanted to leave me." His eyes began to fill with tears. "And that she's been looking for me all these years." He covered his face with his hands and silently wept.

I laid my hand on his shoulder until he recovered, then gave him the box of tissues from the bed stand. He took several, wiping his eyes and nose. "I know it was just a dream. But it reminded me that I did have a mother, once, and that she once must have loved me."

He wiped his eyes. After a moment, I said, "You know, I've become a believer in dreams. Remind me sometime to tell you a fable about a Chinese philosopher who dreamt he was a butterfly."

The door opened and the police officer stuck his head in. I nodded to him and turned back to Leo, taking his hand in mine. "I've got to go now so you can get some sleep."

He clung to my hand, refusing to let go. I placed my other hand on his. "Get some rest. I'll call Sandy and tell her you're out of danger. And she can tell Fernando. You know how cats worry."

He sniffed, smiling.

Glancing back at the police officer, I added, "Then I'll call Danny and let him know you're going to be fine."

He released my hand and lay back on the pillow, closing his eyes.

After leaving his room, I found a pay phone in the lobby and called Sandy. This was a nice change. The calls I'd made at the end of most vigils were not to deliver good news. She picked up on the first ring.

"The doctor says he's stable," I said. "He's going to live." *For now*, I thought. But that's true of all of us. No guarantees beyond this moment.

"Oh, thank God!" She said she was on her way to the hospital.

"Leo'll be happy to see you when he wakes," I said. "I'm heading home. I'm beat."

"You must've had quite a night."

I chuckled wearily. "You have no idea."

"Go home. Get some sleep. I'll let Steve and Father Paul know." Then she remembered. "Oh, Steve called. Jonno's father—John?—he told Jonno what happened to Leo. Steve says Jonno's very worried."

I was surprised. "But Jonno doesn't even know Leo."

I heard Sandy sigh, could almost hear her rolling her eyes. "No, dummy. He's not very worried *for Leo*."

"Oh, um, of course."

After she hung up, I remained at the pay phone. I'd been struggling with this all week—wanting to call Jonno from DC, checking to see how he was, wanting to hear the sound of his voice. But I continued to wrestle within myself. Didn't want to lead him on. Didn't want to give him false hope that we could have a relationship. Because we couldn't . . . I thought.

You sound indecisive. O'Shaughnessy's voice in my head.

No, I'm not indecisive. I just can't make up my mind.

You know you love him.

I can't do this again. Can't go through this again. Not with Jonno. It would hurt too much.

So, you choose to live without love because it would hurt if you lost it?

You know, it sounded like a perfectly reasonable position until you said it.

To distract me from this no-win argument going on in my head, I dropped in another quarter and dialed to check my phone messages at home. There was a call from my mother: "*Dad said you have a new friend. We're so happy to hear that. Everyone needs a friend. Why don't you bring him by for dinner sometime? We'd like to meet him.*"

I'd mentioned Jonno to Dad recently when helping him prune his Asian pear trees. That was before ... before everything changed.

"Does he like gardening?" Dad had asked.

"He's a landscape architect. He *loves* gardening."

"Well, I'd like to meet him." Dad was like Steve. Whatever he said you knew was sincere. But was Mom making an obligatory invitation, like I made an obligatory appearance on the holidays?

No other messages. I hung up the phone.

"*Everyone needs a friend.*"

The words echoed within me. I'd heard them before. That last time we went into the high plains together. "*I worry about you. I don't want you to be alone. Let someone else into your life. Please. Everyone needs a friend.*"

Tears had blurred my vision that time, the flames bright and dancing and kind of watery, and I'd said, "Tell me again how this isn't sad."

"This isn't sad," said Gray. "This is life."

"Hello?"

What's strange is, I don't recall dialing Jonno's number, don't remember making the decision to phone him. And now, didn't know what to say.

"Hello?" he said again.

On top of that I couldn't speak. *How embarrassing is this?* Due to the fatigue from the long night, or from the last ten years, I found myself suddenly overcome with emotion. Eyes and throat thick with tears, I turned my back to the lobby, gripping the phone, and could only choke out, "Come," my voice hoarse, threatening to break into a sob. I bit my knuckles, stifling my sobs as I wept silently, then whispered, "Please ... come."

There was a pause. "I'll be on the next flight up."

The sound of his voice calmed me, and I slowly exhaled, regaining some control of myself, at least the minimal amount required to function in a public setting.

"Are you okay?" he asked.

"I will be. When you're here."

"How's your friend?"

"He's . . . he's going to live."

"Good. I'm glad to hear it."

I cleared my throat, saying in a firmer voice, "Call my house when you know your flight information and I'll meet you at the airport. I should be easy to spot. I'll be the emotional basket case at the arrival gate."

He said softly, "Then I'll look for an emotional basket case. Bye."

I blurted out, "I love you."

I heard a quick intake of breath, then, "I know. I'll see you in a couple of hours."

I replaced the phone in its receiver, taking several deep breaths, steadying myself.

"Everyone needs a friend."

I dialed my parents' number. They'd probably be out grocery shopping for the week as they did first thing every Saturday morning.

But they were home.

"Hello?"

"Hi, Mom."

"Well, hello, stranger. Dad and I just got back from shopping. We're making breakfast, omelets with ham and hash browns and orange juice. Want to stop by and join us?"

Again, another part of my brain seemed to be taking over, overriding the usual part that would have made an excuse, politely declining the invitation. "Sure," I said.

Mom sounded as surprised as I was. "Well . . . that's wonderful," she said in her chirpy voice. "I'll set another plate." Clearly, neither of us had expected me to accept the invitation.

"I'll be there in about ten minutes."

"I'll tell Dad. It'll be so nice to see you."

"Something else." I took a deep breath. "Over breakfast, I would like to tell you about my life with Gray, and what he meant to me . . . and also tell you about Jonathan, and what he means to me."

There was silence on the other end. I could hear tears in my mother's throat when she next spoke. "I've been waiting a long time to hear about your life with Gray . . . and what he meant to you."

Really? She's been waiting a long time?

"But I didn't want to, you know, pry. And we'd *love* to meet Jonathan."

"Well . . . well, fine. He's coming up this weekend. I'll bring him over."

After I'd hung up, I stood there a moment longer. *She's been waiting all these years to hear about my life with Gray?* I didn't doubt her sincerity on this, but how could I have read my mother so wrong for so long?

I emerged from the hospital. The grayness had burned off, unveiling one of those glorious winter mornings in the Pacific Northwest, crisp, brisk, sunshine bright and blinding. In the distance, Mount St. Helens shone white against an azure sky. *"You should be around mountains,"* I heard Gray whisper, and I went down the steps, thinking: Strange, this little life. Strange, these little deaths that compose it. To those of us for whom life is a daily mystery, a vast puzzle forever beyond our solving, it's very difficult to make peace with such an imperfect world, where there's AIDS and natural catastrophes, periodic genocides and unspeakable atrocities, an imperfect world where we're acutely aware of our own imperfection in it. Yet on such mornings as this, we can gain a momentary respite from the ache of not-knowing, and, if not exactly make peace with the mystery, at least declare a temporary truce for the day. We'll have to see about tomorrow.

I headed for my car, breathing in the chilled wintry air and thinking of the last ten years. It now seemed like a lifetime, and a life coming to a close. I had this sense that the war had ended for me, even though the epidemic had not, and even though I'd continue to be part of it.

What had changed?

I recalled my first conversation with Cal, almost one year ago, and his odd statement, how *fortunate* we were to have been part of this. Part of an epidemic? No, he meant fortunate to have been part of humanity rising up to its noblest and best in meeting a modern plague, fortunate to have witnessed so much courage and compassion, so much grace and dignity, so much self-sacrifice and love. And humor! Undying humor in the face of death. "I wouldn't have missed it for the world," he said.

And in that moment, I realized, neither would I.

Postscript

In 1995, everything changed. With the advent of protease inhibitors, AIDS went from being a death sentence to a manageable chronic condition. New antiviral drugs with names like Saquinavir, Ritonavir and Indinavir soon became available to the general population. When combined with other treatment drugs, the so-called "cocktail," they were effective in preventing viral replication. Within two years, deaths from AIDS in the United States fell from more than 50,000 per year to 18,000. Up until then, the death rate had been increasing by 20 percent annually.

It wasn't "The Cure." But it was enough. Suddenly, after fourteen years of epidemic and the deaths of countless friends and colleagues, people were experiencing an unfamiliar outbreak of hope. The cocktail gave many who were living on death row a new chance at life. And not just in the United States. In 2004, with the active sponsorship of President George W. Bush, the President's Emergency Plan for AIDS Relief (PEPFAR) was launched as a US government initiative to address the global HIV/AIDS epidemic. By 2014, the program had provided antiretroviral treatment to more than 7.7 million people in countries most impacted by the epidemic. It was arguably President Bush's finest moment—and, you have to admit, he didn't have that many.

In the years since, people have moved on with their lives, lives many never expected to live:

Steve operates a large multi-acre nursery and landscaping business with his partner Mark in Silver Falls, Oregon.

Jonathan ("Jonno") has had his own landscape architecture firm in Portland since 1999, working closely with Steve and Mark's nursery business.

Sandy directs the Oregon Department of Human Services' Child Foster Care Program.

Tyler works as a congressional aide to a US senator from Oregon and was instrumental in the 2014 legalization of same-sex marriage in the state.

Lukas has his own hair salon on Broadway Avenue in Portland and still performs regularly at Darcelle's, now billed as "Lady Bianca's Older Sister."

Leo teaches political science and social change theory at The Evergreen State College in Olympia, Washington. His partner of twenty years, Daniel, is a social worker in charge of outreach programs to homeless youth in the Tacoma metropolitan area.

Some lives came to an end:

Jake Caulfield died of AIDS complications in 1998.

President Ronald Reagan, diagnosed with Alzheimer's disease in 1994, died ten years later.

Mickey O'Shaughnessy died of what is believed to have been an intentional drug overdose in 2005.

And me?

I am no longer haunted by dreams of the Bogong High Plains.

Acknowledgments

Although a book may start in the solitude of the writer's soul, its final realization is always a group effort. I am grateful to all those who played a part in this book's completion.

To friends and fellow writers: Hannah Dennison (*Honeychurch Hall* mystery series) for believing in this story before I did and urging that it be told, Dan Berne (*The Gods of Second Chances*), short story writer and WordFest co-conspirator Charolette Conklin, and former *Daily News* features editor Cathy Zimmerman, all of whom provided extensive and thoughtful suggestions.

To those who read different parts of the manuscript at its different stages: Steve Anderson, April Benedetti, David Bennett, Gleenobly Butterworth, Elaine Cockrell, Mark Dykstra, LaVonne Griffin-Valade, Debbie Guyol, Karen Karbo, Michelle Madison, Don Messerschmidt, Gay Monteverde, Stella Mortenson, Darlene Pagan, Dan Painter, Ned Piper, Mayanna Pogson, David Rorden, Gary Rose, Penny Russell, Charlotte Samples, Joy Sieminski, David Skilton, Leslie Slape, Deb Stone, Jeff Stookey, Colleen Strohm, Jaimee Walls, and Laura Wood.

To Chris Skaugset of the Longview Public Library for his help in researching primary sources about the Mount Bogong tragedy, Cleve Cole, and the account of his death, all of which is factual (though the reports of his wandering spirit are not).

To Ann Mottet, former Deputy Prosecutor for Cowlitz County, for help with legal questions concerning Leo's case and sentencing, and to David Grant for expertise on landscape architecture and Jonathan's business, most of which, alas, never made it into the final version. Still, thanks!

Thanks to the phenomenal team at Bywater Books and their new Amble Press imprint: Fay Jacobs, outstanding editor, who believed in the book as much I did; Ann McMan for her haunting cover design, which conveyed both the terrestrial and the ethereal layers of the story; and Michael Nava, managing editor of Amble Press, for his sensitivity to the multicultural issues and perspectives represented in the book. Any cultural stumbles or tone-deaf notes are my responsibility alone.

My deepest and most heartfelt thanks to Bywater Books publisher Salem West, who began championing this book from the first time she read the manuscript and made it happen. I'll always be grateful for her unwavering belief in this project, for her sensitivity, diplomacy, wisdom, and faith in me and my story. Her patience alone will get her into heaven.

Finally, this book is built on the foundation provided by many other writers: Paul Monette (*Becoming a Man, Last Watch of the Night*), Randy Shilts (*And the Band Played On*), David France (*How to Survive a Plague*), AIDS Quilt author Cleve Jones (*When We Rise*), Armistead Maupin *(Tales of the City series)* and Rebecca Makkai, whose powerful recent novel *The Great Believers* appeared while I was working on my story and gave me heart and inspiration. Together, they and numerous others provided me a more expansive view of the time we lived through, placing the epidemic in a wider historical and personal context. They are giants in telling the story of the AIDS epidemic. I stand not on their shoulders but sit humbly at their feet with admiration and gratitude.

About the Author

Alan E. Rose worked with Cascade AIDS Project in Portland, Oregon, from 1993 to 1999, and prior to that was a volunteer with the Victorian AIDS Council (now Thorne Harbour Health) in Melbourne, Australia. He is the author of *The Legacy of Emily Hargraves* (2007), a paranormal mystery; *Tales of Tokyo* (2010), a modern quest novel set in Japan; and *The Unforgiven* (2012), a psychological mystery exploring the relationship between memory and guilt. Living in rural southwest Washington state, he coordinates the monthly WordFest events, hosts the KLTV program *Book Chat*, and reviews books for *The Columbia River Reader*. He can be contacted at www.alan-rose.com.

DISCUSSION GUIDE

1. Grief is universal (everyone goes through it) yet uniquely personal (nobody can know what it feels like for you but yourself). Reflecting on your own experience of loss and grief, what helped you through it? What didn't help?

2. *As If Death Summoned* tells stories from the AIDS epidemic of the 1980s and '90s. There were many. Were you personally affected by the epidemic? If so, what is your story?

3. The author often inserts bleak humor into serious, very non-humorous experiences of grief and loss. What was your reaction to this use of "gallows humor" in the face of such sorrow and suffering?

4. The Narrator experiences a catharsis when his therapist O'Shaughnessy has him write the names of the people he's lost to AIDS. He's carried those names with him for years. Why do you think the act of writing them down causes the emotional breakthrough? What emotional breakthroughs have you experienced? What prompted your catharsis?

5. Mickey O'Shaughnessy has a distinctive approach to therapy—direct, blunt and confrontational. ("He doesn't coddle," warns Sandy.) What do you think of O'Shaughnessy's counseling style? If you were in counseling with him, would it help or hinder your therapy?

6. With Leo's confession, the Narrator feels like an accomplice to a crime and struggles with his moral obligations. Father Paul warns him, "Whatever you decide—to turn Leo in or not to turn him in—you should expect that you will not feel good about the decision." If you were in the Narrator's position, what would you have done?

7. Discovering that Jonno is HIV-positive creates a new crisis for the Narrator, and he retreats from their relationship, unable to face the prospect of experiencing with Jonno what he went through with Gray. Not knowing that protease inhibitors would change AIDS from being a death sentence to a chronic manageable condition, what would you have done in the Narrator's place?

8. The Narrator thought his mother didn't want to face the fact that he's gay, and he is surprised when she says, "I've been waiting a long time to hear about your life with Gray and what he meant to you." What instances have there been in your life where you "totally misread" another person?

9. Amid his increasing dementia, Jake Caulfield tells the Narrator, "Gray understands why you wouldn't dance with him." Such "uncanny experiences" can shake us to our core and make reality seem unreliable. What experiences have you had that you couldn't ignore or "explain away"?

10. The novel affirms that some people change (John's attitude toward gay people, Brandon's attitude that "those people deserved it") and that some people don't (Trevor's parents' refusal to see him as he was dying, Gray's mother's attitude). What dramatic changes in beliefs or attitudes have you witnessed in other people? What changes in yourself? What prompted those changes?

11. "There was once a Chinese philosopher . . ." Dreams figure prominently throughout the novel. ("All that we see and seem is a dream within a dream.") How do you understand the "nature of reality" in a multidimensional universe that includes dreams, alternate states of consciousness, mystical states, and those states induced (or perhaps revealed) by psychotropic substances?

12. Blindness is used as a metaphor in the story (the blind woman searching for her son, being blind in the blizzard) and has been understood differently in different cultures and in different times. In Judeo-Christian tradition, it is usually associated with handicap, even punishment by God. But in some indigenous,

non-Western cultures, it is understood as a sign of deeper (in) sight, and can have a shamanistic significance. What role does blindness play in the Narrator's story?

13. Different attitudes toward death (and life) are presented through different characters. How would you characterize the attitudes of Cal (Ch. 3), Jerald (Ch. 6), Arnold (Ch. 19), Christine (Ch. 23), and the character of Death himself? With whose attitude do you most identify? How would you express your own attitude toward death?

14. Cal Stern, the executive director dying of AIDS at the beginning of the novel, tells the Narrator they were "fortunate" to experience the epidemic, adding, "I wouldn't have missed it for the world." At the end of the book, the Narrator realizes, "Neither would I." What do you think this says about the challenges, suffering, and sorrows that are part of life? Do you agree or disagree?